SPLINTERED TIME

Lillian I. Wolfe

This print edition is published in 2022 by:
Pynhavyn Press ™

www.pynhavynpress.com

First Edition: November 2021
Copyright © 2021 Lillian I. Wolfe
All rights reserved.
ISBN: 978-1-942622-24-6

Cover Design: Barb Hoeter Coverinked.com

DEDICATION

This book is dedicated to everyone who has supported and encouraged me over the past few years. It's your belief in my writing that keeps me going. Thank you from the bottom of my heart.

ACKNOWLEDGMENTS

Many thanks to my High Sierra Writers critique group for their insight, suggestions, and help with this book. I owe a great deal to their comments and thoughts. Thank you, Nicole, Brian, Kathy, Mark, Kitty, and Russell.

Gratitude to my housemate, Patricia, who enables my writing sprees by taking care of the little details, like food and no distractions. Without her contributions, I would go off the rails, so to speak.

I can't overlook my terrific cover artist, Barb Hoeter at Coverinked, who turned my concept into a gorgeous cover. Much love to you, Barb.

TABLE OF CONTENTS

Table of Contents..1

Chapter 1 3

Chapter 2 16

Chapter 3 30

Chapter 4 45

Chapter 5 58

Chapter 6 71

Chapter 7 82

Chapter 8 93

Chapter 9 113

Chapter 10 126

Chapter 11 142

Chapter 12 158

Chapter 13 167

Chapter 14 182

Chapter 15 192

Chapter 16 202

Chapter 17 211

Chapter 18 219

Chapter 19 231

Chapter 20 239

Chapter 21 245

Chapter 22 258

Chapter 23 268

Chapter 24 275

Chapter 25 286

Chapter 26 297

Chapter 27 305

Chapter 28 318

About the Author 330

FUNERAL SINGER SERIES 331

CHAPTER 1

London 1898

MALI'S TIME JUMP HAD CLEARLY MISSED its mark, leaving her mentally scrambling to discern the year. Wide-eyed, Mali turned in a slow circle, trying not to gawk at the various groups of people filling the clearing. In 1798, it was deserted when the time travel unit, or TU, as they called it, had materialized here. Now, it was a fair, with booths of all sorts, pavilions, and skill games, spread across, filling all the space. Overhead, hot air balloons floated in the calm afternoon sky, bright splashes of color against the clear blue.

She and her time travel team, Brayden Coleman and Ross Bonde, had embarked from here less than three weeks earlier in her actual days to stop a time change. They had failed, but when she and Doyle left her grandfather in 1763, she hadn't expected the place to be so different. She could only conclude they weren't in 1798. So what year was it?

"What the blazes, Mali?" Doyle's sharp voice reflected his anxiety and confusion.

She turned to look at him, seeing the wide-eyes and slack jaw of a man stunned at the sight. She waggled her head uneasily, lacking a concrete answer. None of this was what she'd expected.

Several heads turned their way when people noticed their odd garments. If she looked out of place, Doyle's attire was even more so. Knee-length breeches and white stockings had gone out of style completely. Some folks chuckled out loud, not even bothering to hide their amusement, while others merely frowned. A few continued to stare, perhaps curious, as if they expected them to perform, maybe thinking she and Doyle might be entertainers.

"It looks like we've arrived at a country fair," she said, gripping Doyle's arm and tugging him away. She recalled a dirt path ran through the trees a short distance away.

Where she'd once followed Ross and Coleman's haphazard trail through the trees and bushes, she now found a cleared and well-worn walkway leading to an open area alongside the road where more automobiles sat in two neat rows. Newer, better vehicles than she'd seen in 1798. Sleeker and spacious-looking, even. Her mind whirled through the images she'd seen in research books, trying to match the models with something in the early 1800s, but these looked too advanced, like the designs of the mid-1940s. Were these combustion engines then? Cars that ran on gasoline?

Beside her, she heard Doyle's sharp gasp. "Look at those. Are they steamers? I've never seen—"

"I don't think so," Mali interrupted. "We are way out of your time. I don't have any idea what year this is, but the automobile industry has advanced a long way." She cast her eyes to the skies, looking for the hot air balloons and dirigibles, which had been developing in Doyle's era. Apart from the ones they'd seen back at the fair in the clearing, only one or two colorful flyers floated in the atmosphere. Those, at least, didn't look like they'd advanced much, although they appeared larger and sturdier than the ones in Doyle's time. They had been ahead of their time also. As a native of the late eighteenth century, Doyle had not known anything was amiss. She'd accidentally dragged him into this time-hopping.

She ran a hand through her hair, thinking. Now what? They were not in the time where she'd meant to send them, so what happened, and when exactly were they? Judging by the way people dressed, they were some time in the next century or farther. If Varsik, a member of her grandfather's time team with ambitions to change history, had pushed inventions forward, then the styles of clothing, along with the evidence of technological advancements, were not an indication of the date.

They needed to get to London and find out when they'd arrived. Then they would go through the familiar routine of getting money and current clothing for both of them. Afterward, they would find lodging for the night while she tried to figure out what went wrong and why they'd ended up here.

Mali pointed toward the road, and they resumed walking. Doyle's eyes kept darting toward the line of autos in a dirt lot. His jaw dropped, his eyes grew even bigger, and his footsteps slowed. He lowered his eyebrows and his mouth snapped shut, his expression sober. She could almost hear his thoughts in her mind. How would he get back to his time? He didn't need to voice it. She didn't have an answer at the moment.

Even the London Road was updated—made wider, and better paved than the one in Doyle's time. They both stared at it with mixed reactions. Hers more of consternation as she contemplated what the improvement indicated, while his morphed to disbelief.

Voice raspy, he asked, "Mali, do you have any notion what year this is?"

She shook her head, reluctant to look at him, to see the worry in his eyes. "No, not yet. Too much has changed." She took a deep breath, stepped closer to the road to look up and down for any autos coming their way. She glanced at Doyle. "How much money do you have?"

He frowned, but as she reached into her own little purse to count the coins and bills she still carried, he dug his hands into his pockets to do likewise. Their combined wealth amounted to less than thirty pounds.

"It's enough to get us to London, is it not?" Doyle asked, dropping the coins back into his pants and folded the few bills, putting them in his coat pocket.

"Maybe. If we can find a cab or get anyone to give us a ride. Dressed like we are, it could be a problem."

She saw his gaze focus on her billowy dress. It had looked charming in 1728 but was far too clumsy-looking compared to the ones women were wearing now. Then he glanced down at his knee-length breeches and hose, and his mouth twisted into a rueful grimace. "Perhaps we could say we are in fancy dress."

Mali raised an eyebrow. "Fancy dress? Is that what you would call this?"

"An older style of clothing, I suppose. Would it not fit?" Despite the calmness of his words, he tugged at his left sleeve like it might make his pants longer.

"I guess it will have to do." She gazed back at the road and spotted a vehicle heading their way. "We'll get this sorted once we get to London, and I can think it through. Something went awry when we jumped, but I can probably fix it."

He nodded, his eyes darting toward the approaching automobile. She couldn't blame him. She'd pulled him from his own time to the past, and now they'd gone forward, so of course, he was concerned. So was she. But she didn't want him to think she wasn't in control. She could use the threads to move them through time, so she could correct this. All she had to do was figure out what went wrong.

She waved her arm at the oncoming vehicle, and the driver slowed and pulled to the side of the road. She sashayed up to the window and smiled at him, putting her charm forward. "Hello. Thank you for stopping. My friend and I came out for a fancy-dress party. But now we don't have a way back to London. Could you possibly give us a ride?"

The driver, an older man with muttonchop sideburns, looked her over, then lifted his eyebrows when his gaze shifted to Doyle. He looked out of place with the short pants and an oddly cut coat. "Costumes, is it? Well, you look harmless enough. I can take the two of you as far as south London."

"Thank you so much," she said, grinning and motioning to Doyle to come over. "I'm Mali, and this is Doyle. You've saved us a long walk."

He motioned for Mali to take the front seat and Doyle to go in back. Eagerly, she hurried around the auto, climbing in while Doyle slid into the back. She settled down, and the driver engaged the forward control, a hand-high lever jutting from the floor on the driver's right. Mali watched closely, intrigued by the operation. The car moved smoothly and silently ahead, gaining speed quickly. It didn't sound like a steam engine; neither did it have the added roar a combustion engine was reputed to have. Quiet, only the sound coming from air passing made any noise.

Sorting through the options in her mind, she settled on electric. The vehicle was electric. As she recalled, they had enjoyed a short period of popularity just after the steamers, before the gas-powered engine dominated the twentieth and first part of the twenty-first century. Then the electric car had returned along with the compressed air and ethanol hybrid models.

She gazed around the car, looking for any clue to the year, but nothing gave her a hint. Overall, she and Doyle remained quiet during the ride, as did the driver, only asking what part of London they were from.

Doyle answered, "Kensington. Just off St. Anne's near Market Street."

"Good. I know the area a bit. I can drop you at the corner of St. James Square."

"Perfect," Mali interjected. "We do so appreciate your kindness."

He flashed a hint of a smile at her before he turned his attention back to the road.

Within another fifteen minutes, they came into the outskirts of London where newer buildings had grown around old structures, making Kensington more closed in than it had been. Where an open field was when they were last there, a new block of buildings filled the space. At St. James Square, they waved goodbye to the auto and began making their way toward the market area.

"At least the Rusty Plough is still there," Mali remarked while they walked toward the open market. "We can get a room for a night or two. First, let's go trade a trinket for more money."

§ § §

Three hours later, they pushed open the door to a much nicer room than the one Mali had stayed in nearly a century earlier. They tossed two wrapped bundles onto the floor, and Mali threw herself down on the bed. Thus far, they'd learned they had arrived in 1898, Queen Victoria was on the throne, and the majority of the automobiles were electric. Almost everyone had electricity, and life was bustling along in high gear. The water closet down the hall offered indoor plumbing with flush toilets, running water, and bathtubs. Electricity even warmed the water.

The room, however, bore one double bed. Doyle stared at it, then turned his eyes to Mali. "I can sleep on the floor."

"Nonsense. We can share. After all, you told the proprietor I'm your wife."

"To save your reputation. I couldn't very well tell him I was bringing an unmarried lady to a room, could I?"

"My reputation or yours?" she countered with a teasing smile.

"Both of us," he admitted, running a hand through his hair. "But we cannot sleep together."

"Why not? The bed is big enough, and we can stay separated by a sheet or a blanket. Or not... It wouldn't be the first time, Doyle." They had already slept together more than once while in Scotland.

"Are you sure you want to, Mali?"

She picked up a pillow and punched it to gauge its softness, then looked at him. "Yes. I feel the same way about you. A different time hasn't changed anything. In our own reckoning, we slept together last night. Even though it's nearly a hundred and fifty years later, this is still the next night. Unless you've changed your mind?"

"Not at all. I still feel the same, but our connection has changed, hasn't it? I feel like I'm in a dream, and none of it is real."

She tossed the pillow at him, hitting him squarely in the chest. He barely caught the projectile before it bounced to the floor.

"Did that feel real?"

"Yes, very much so." He flung it back to her with a short laugh, and she tossed it back on the bed.

She sat back, bouncing a little, and pulled off her shoes. They were the only things left of the original wardrobe she'd arrived in London with twenty-one days earlier by her time. It was surreal, so she understood Doyle's sense of incongruity. She hadn't gotten used to it either, even though she had a clearer understanding of the time-travel process than he did.

He kept his distance, sitting in the chair by a small table; one very much like the one where Ross Bonde had sat on their first night in London. Her mouth tightened into a grim line. Bonde was dead now, killed in an accident in York. He tried to destroy a workshop owned by an inventor who turned out to be her time-traveling grandfather.

Once again, she pondered what went awry with the time jump. It should have taken them back to Doyle's time. How had they ended up at nearly the end of the 19th century? She'd clearly screwed it up, but she didn't understand how. She'd done what her grandfather had instructed—found the right thread, pictured her destination, and touched it. Her deep sigh caught Doyle's attention and his eyes shifted toward her.

"Can you get us back?" Doyle asked, correctly reading her misgivings.

"I believe so, but I need to think about it more. Try to figure out what I did wrong. Let's change clothes and get dinner." She pointed at the bundles and headed to pick up hers. Once they obtained more money, they'd purchased clothing more suited to the era. She'd borne enough gawking stares for one day and wanted to change before dinner.

The inn's downstairs area hadn't changed much in the past century, still dimly lit, albeit with electric lights now, and crowded with people getting food and drink. Doyle guided her to a table near the front where a little outside light made its way through the amber-colored window. The dinner selection remained the same, offering the featured meal of cottage pie with chicken, carrots, and potatoes. They settled for choice rather than the greasy alternate selection of oxtail stew. The server brought their drinks, apple cider for Mali and stout for Doyle, while they waited.

As she gazed around, Mali noticed a short stack of newspapers at the end of the bar and nudged Doyle. "Can you get a copy of the newspaper?"

He glanced to where her head tilted and nodded. Rising, he worked his way to the bar, spoke to the bartender, and at the man's nod, handed him a coin, taking one of papers. He returned to the table and sat down, then passed it to Mali. "They get a few papers every evening for their guests. Half-pence to purchase. What are you looking for?"

"Anything kind of clue to what's happened in this decade. The automobiles are much farther advanced than they should have been at the turn of this century, and I haven't seen any gas-powered ones. Which means Varsick or Varsi, whichever name he uses, has made more changes. Electric cars came into common use not long after the steam engine. For a while, they were popular, then the combustion engine was invented, and gas-powered vehicles dominated the next era."

"Why?" he asked, his forehead wrinkling with his confusion.

Mali wasn't sure he even followed what she said. Did he even know what a combustion engine was? "For one thing, the engine was more powerful and weighed less than the steam one. The cost of production and sheer weight of the vehicle's boilers made it too expensive for many people to afford. Your friend's steamer cost him quite a lot of money, I imagine. With the new, lighter weight gas engine, the manufacturing costs dropped drastically so more people could afford to buy one."

"That doesn't sound so bad," Doyle answered and swallowed a gulp of his stout. "Why did Varsick want to change it?"

"Long-range consequences. While it seemed like a great plan at first, the population of the world increased. More and more people bought bigger and better cars, factories used more and more fossil fuels, and air pollution became a problem in the late 20th century." She could tell by the squint of his eyes she'd lost him. "I'm sorry, fossil fuels are oil, coal, and the refined products made from them. A finite resource on the planet. And the pollution is—"

"I know what it is," he said, his tone a little sharp. "We've seen enough from coal."

She nodded, then continued. "In theory, the steam and electric engines provided the cleaner power source, but the world didn't revert to them until nearly the 22nd century. By then, the damage was done." She paused to sip her cider. Then their pies arrived, and they didn't resume the discussion until the server left.

"So, you're saying the gas engine caused bad air quality, and the people just allowed this to go on," Doyle recapped.

"Something like that. Bottom line is it began changing the Earth, causing the climate to shift, and making it difficult to live. This city, and this era, was cleaner than it ended up after the change. And now, Varsick has moved the whole development forward. To be honest, I don't even know which timeline we're on right now or why we came here instead of your time. I had chosen the original line and 1798, but something skewed our jump."

"How could it happen?" Doyle's voice carried his deep concern and his amber-flecked eyes grew wider.

She shrugged. "I don't know exactly, but I'm forming a theory. I'll tell you later. For now, I'm going to eat, then go upstairs and read the paper."

Sitting at the table in their room, Mali flipped through the eight pages of the newspaper, scanning every story having to do with business and government. While they'd established they were in 1898, the newspaper gave her the exact date of June 23rd. Starting there, she would review any inventions occurring in the interval spanning the years since Doyle's time to figure out what Varsick might have influenced other than automobiles. What other industries needed to change to bring this much advancement to the world? How had he circumvented the oil and gas revolution, which fossil fuels had dominated for almost two centuries?

As her thoughts went this way, she began to develop a theory on why they'd jumped here instead of her intended target. She didn't like it, but it made some sense. At least more than anything else she considered. She looked up to gaze at Doyle, who sat on the bed reading the pages she'd discarded.

She cleared her throat, and Doyle looked up, his eyes meeting hers, sending a jolt of desire racing down her middle. She didn't want to say goodbye to him. Her breath caught, and she cleared her throat. "I think I know why we ended up here. While I consciously focused on going to your time, I think I subconsciously worried about what changes Varsick might make to the future and the reason I'd time traveled in the first place. So, although I intended to go to one place, my subconscious directed me to a different location. I don't know why this particular time, though."

He set the paper aside and turned to face her, long legs sliding onto the floor, and he leaned forward, elbows on his knees. "You're saying your subconscious diverted us here? That sounds peculiar, Mali. Will you be able to get me to my time? I didn't sign on for this." He frowned and is entire posture seemed to tighten.

"Yes, I'm sure I can. I need to focus enough to override my subconscious if I feel I have to deal with Varsick. Maybe I need you with me to confront whatever the situation is." She spoke hesitantly, unwilling to admit she might need help.

A whoosh of a half-laugh, half-blown air sound started Doyle's reply. "So, I am stuck here or wherever with you until you feel you've done whatever you need to do. My life is in the past. My job is there. I am lost in this time. Without my credentials, I can't work at the job I want. We need money to live if your project takes a long time, and the five hundred pounds you got for your emerald won't last us more than a few months. Did you even consider staying with me in 1798, Mali? Or, was it always going to be a brief visit?" His voice sounded bitter to her ears while anger boiled into his voice.

"I wanted to stay," she replied, determined to keep calm and setting her folded together hands on the table, she gazed at him. "I planned to be there while I figured out what I needed to do. While I want to be with you, I know what the future looks like. It's a difficult thing to carry in your mind when you realize it may all be changed by Varsick's actions."

Doyle stared at her for a few long moments, then stood, grabbed his suit coat, and strode to the door.

"Where are you going?"

"For a walk. I need to think," he said curtly.

"I'll come with you." She started to rise.

"No. I want to go alone." He stepped through the door, gone before Mali could say anything else.

She hesitated, staring at the door, then dropped back into the chair. Her stomach fluttered while she replayed the scene in her mind. *Let him go burn off the steam.*

At least, it was light until late, and Doyle knew this area of London well. While she would have enjoyed the walk, she doubted the conversation would have been pleasant. She'd not phrased her remarks well. Of course, she wanted to be with him, but she had to consider her own task.

Now that he'd brought it up. If they became stranded here, what would she do? What job was she suited for in this life?

CHAPTER 2

Space Station Alpha, 2238

PUSHING HER BLONDE HAIR BACK behind her ears, Anna Brix gazed around the faces at her birthday party, mostly co-workers from her office and a couple of friends from school. Her mother had sent a greeting but not come in person. She taken a holiday on Phobos–only a crazed billionaire would choose to put a health resort on a tiny, airless rock. And only thrill-seekers like her mom would choose to take a holiday there.

But one face she'd hoped to see remained missing. Mali hadn't returned from her so-called think-tank thing, although she'd assured Anna she would be back in time for this shindig. That worried her. Even though she and Mali often seemed at odds, the other girl was her closest friend on the station, as well as her roommate.

They'd met at university and got along well enough that the idea of sharing space with her wasn't revolting to Brix. Never mind, she hadn't had a lot of choice in the deal. The setup had been arranged without Mali having any idea. Everyone assumed the computer matched singles with compatible people, but it wasn't always true.

In this case, they had assigned her to be with the whiz-brain, as most of their classmates had called Mali in school. With her phenomenal memory, Mali had aced every test and had her pick of assignments after graduation. So, all their classmates and educators wondered why she went to work for the Station Advisory Center when she could have gotten a highly sought tech job.

Then again, not everyone knew what Brix knew about Mali and her job. When she'd left this last time, Brix had felt uneasy about the assignment, knowing full well Mali had lied to her. And now she wasn't back when she should have been, no matter how long the job had taken.

She turned her attention back to her party guests, her long ash-blonde hair flipping around her face when she spun toward the huge cake the party chef had just rolled out.

"Make a wish, Anna," someone shouted out.

She smiled, then leaned in to blow out the candles. They all fluttered out except one, but a second puff took care of the stubborn flame. One year to wait for her wish. It's what the little ceremony meant, didn't it? Or had her family gotten it wrong all along. Didn't matter. Her wishes never came true anyway, but maybe this one would.

Putting on her party face, she cut the cake and passed out slices to her guests. Then the dancing started. She drifted onto the dance floor with a gauche-looking guy from her office who'd been trying to date her for months. What the hell? Give him a thrill for one evening and let him have a dance with her.

After the celebration, Brix packed up the remains of the cake, her stash of gifts, and sent them on an auto-dolly back to her apartment. She followed behind it, feeling worn and worried. Mali would have been there if she could have. The fact she wasn't meant something had gone wrong.

She followed the cart into their place, then went through to Mali's private side where her bedroom and powder room... oops, more like office... matched the space of her own area. She'd forgotten Mali didn't mess with girly things like a make-up table and vanity. Empty spots in the bookcase told her she'd taken a couple with her. Everything else appeared to be in place. Then her eyes rose to the shelf above the bed where Mali kept a photo of her family and three antique watches. Only the picture was gone, along with one of the timepieces.

Brix closed her eyes to visualize the room in her mind. The pocket watch. Mali had taken the pocket watch with her. Why? She thought it odd, especially if she had done what Brix suspected. She checked Mali's closet and found nothing out of order there. She hadn't taken many clothes. Brix sat on the bed and studied the room again, looking for other clues to what Mali had been doing. She blinked, feeling a tear of loss at the corner of her eye, and decided to take this to a higher level.

§ § §

On the day after her birthday, Brix marched to her supervisor's office when she arrived at work.

A middle-aged but still robust-looking lady, Margaret Chambers glanced up as Brix strode in, following a thumped single knock on her door. Blinking, she brought her head up, and Brix met her eyes squarely.

"I have a request," she announced with no other greeting. Then she slid the door to the office closed so no one else could hear. "Mali Harper is missing. She should have been back yesterday at the latest."

"That's a strong assumption," Margaret said calmly. "Why do you believe this to be true?"

"Because she said she would be back in time for my birthday party," Brix stepped closer to lean her hands on the front of Margaret's desk.

"Perhaps something delayed her."

"You and I both know it isn't likely." Brix narrowed her cerulean-blue eyes. "Maggie, I'm positive she went on a time mission, and if something hadn't happened, she would have been back, no matter how long the job took."

"You're speculating, Brix. She doesn't work in the travel team group. She's a monitor. Tell me why you think differently."

Brix straightened, pulled over one of the cushioned chairs near the desk, and sat. "Ok. Here's what I know. She left the apartment six days ago to go to a confined think-tank thing, which was supposed to last three days. She took a couple of books, her personal pad, a photo of her family, and an old watch. That was all. She didn't plan to be gone long and promised me she would be back in time for my party. She hasn't returned. Maybe I'm worried for nothing, and the think-tank had a major breakthrough keeping them all for days, but my gut says no."

Margaret pursed her lips. "Your gut has a high accuracy rate, but this makes little sense. Why would they put her on a travel team? What has happened to require it?"

Shaking her head, Brix replied, "I don't know. Mali doesn't talk about her work. She lets me think it's some boring office job, just as I let her think I'm a secretary and frivolous airhead. I've been keeping an eye on her ever since your people contacted me at university. She's tight with information most of the time, but we've become reasonably good friends."

"Does she know anything about your background?"

"No, not really. We talked about more current things when we were in school and since we've been sharing the flat. I talk about boys and dating and what the latest fashion trend is on Mars. But we haven't talked about our families other than I confided I'd lost my dad after she'd told me about losing her parents and grandfather."

Margaret twisted a stylus through her fingers while she thought. "So, she has no idea who your father was or the connection the two of you have?"

"No. I've not told her anything or given her any clues." Brix studied her fingernails and mentally rehearsed her real request, something that might be out of bounds for her to ask.

"What do you want me to do?" Margaret prompted.

Looking up and forcing herself to remain calm, she said, "Can you find out if she went on a time mission and what the status might be?"

Margaret choked out a short laugh. "Is that all? Do you think I have access to confidential TIM information?"

Brix lifted a quizzical eyebrow. "I know you know people who do have access and could probably easily answer the question. I just want to know if there's a valid reason for her not being back when she said she would be. If travel's involved, you and I both know she could have easily been back in time for my party, even if resolving the problem took years."

Sighing, Margaret made a note on her pad and squeezed her lips together, seeming reluctant to speak. Then, finally. "All right. I'll see what I can find out through my channels. No promises, though. It may take a couple of days to get any answers."

"Thanks, Maggie." Brix stood and exited quietly.

She returned to her desk and sat down at the

computer, entering her own search for information. TIM kept tight secrets, but now and then, something leaked. Her own company, Time Excursions, wasn't as squeaky clean as it seemed either. Most of the recreational companies could only take travelers up to two hundred years in the past and couldn't go to Earth. Strictly off-limits, no one could travel to the blue planet except Mali's company.

A government-owned company, TIM could send agents as far back as their time stream could take them. But her company had one covert unit tied into the more extended stream and could go back almost as far. Her company had hired Brix to spy on Mali, but she'd come to care about her friend. Besides, if Mali didn't return, she'd lose her position and the perks of her job.

Turning to her network of contacts, she requested information on any think tank group rumors. Getting nothing over the next couple of hours, she asked about any time anomalies that might require adjusting. The request reached a bit for her network, but sometimes one of them would hear about a secret project, although they rarely had any details. Still, she waited over another hour for any quick responses, but no one reported anything. Her shoulders slumped. She felt helpless to do anything more to find out what had happened to Mali.

"Something wrong?" T-Bone asked from his desk a few feet away. Her somewhat awkward dance partner from her party, Tibideau, who they all called T-Bone, was a nice enough guy. Socially a mess and definitely not her type.

With a toss of her head, she tapped some information into her computer and said, "Just trying to set up a tour group to Minerva." Her lips curved at the name given to Moon Colony 2.

"Who in their right mind wants to go there for

recreation?"

"Don't be such a snob, T. They like to bounce around on the surface and go prospecting for titanium."

"Yeah, like they're gonna get rich on those Podunk tour excursions." He chuckled.

Brix turned back to her computer, checking her messages and the ones on her tablet, but still no response to her query. In her mind, she kept considering if Mali went on a time mission, and they completed it, there would be no reason not to return as she'd expected. Unless something happened to her while she adventured in the past.

She feared Mali had been killed or injured or unable to return for some reason. Lord knows, Brix's father had been in the same situation. Lost in the past, maybe killed, but now long dead to her.

Only her employers, from Maggie through the trio of directors who managed the company, knew her father had been a time adjuster. Brix didn't even use his last name anymore to keep the knowledge quiet. She went by Anna Brixton, taking her mother's last name to avoid any association with the ill-fated team.

Feeling discouraged by mid-afternoon, she pulled her purse out of her desk drawer and headed out of the office toward the nearest bar. She could use a shot or two of the real stuff to soothe her anxiety.

As she settled in on one of the comfortable bar chairs in the sleek-looking Level Two Bar, a woman slipped next to her and ordered a scotch on the rocks. More hard stuff than Brix liked. She had ordered a vodka gimlet, something cut a little. The woman leaned an arm on the chrome bar top and gulped half of her drink down in one shot while she cast an appraising look at Brix.

"Do I know you?" she asked. "You look familiar."

"I don't think so," Brix answered, mentally debating if she should take her drink and go.

"You're with Time Excursions, aren't you?" The woman turned toward her and slid onto the seat next to Brix. "I'm Dianna, by the way."

"Uh, yeah, I work at TE, but I don't believe I've ever met you."

"No, maybe not, but we might have a mutual acquaintance." She paused long enough for Brix to turn her full attention to her. "Mali Harper."

Shocked, Brix leaned closer and whispered. "Keep your voice down. What do you know?"

"Not much. She was part of a TA team sent to the 18th century. I helped her assemble the clothing for it. But I haven't seen them come back yet. As I understand it, they may be overdue. No one is saying much around the office."

"You work for TIM? Why are you telling me this?" Brix's voice dropped even lower, yet carried a tone of alarm.

"Because I know you're concerned about Mali. I have a mutual contact. Watch yourself." Dianna threw down the rest of her drink, then rose to leave.

"Wait!" Brix grabbed for Dianna's arm. "Can you tell me anything else?"

Shaking her head, the other woman pulled her arm away. "No. I've said all I can." She spun on her heel and strode out the door without hesitation.

Open-mouthed, Brix watched her go and wondered who their mutual contact might be. The information only confirmed Mali was on a TA team, but gave her little else to go on. Puzzled, she turned back to her drink and considered her next step. Who else could she find who might know what happened?

Maggie was her best contact, but the one least likely

to delve into anything. Even though she ranked almost at the top of her company's management, she was reluctant to rock the boat. Brix couldn't blame her; she had two almost-teens to think about. Her husband traveled a lot, so Maggie raised the kids. Nonetheless, Brix hoped she'd come through with some information on this.

Finishing her drink, she left the bar and headed down to the third level where TIM's agency resided. While it wasn't common knowledge, the innocent-looking station information office provided the front for the Temporal Integrity Monitoring unit. Brix and her employers knew. She was as sworn to secrecy as Mali when it came to information about her job. Even though Time Excursions' business approval limited them to only the past five centuries of travel, TIM indirectly regulated them. Their management often had meetings with the agency. Just not within their offices. Brix knew only employees got past the front offices.

Brix stood outside the sliding steel door and gazed at it with uncertainty. Setting her nerves, she stepped forward, and the door whooshed aside for her. Inside, an open waiting room with a reception desk greeted her. On one side of the desk, a rack of digital brochures showed information about the space station and the various excursion trips people could take. They could travel to the Moon, Mars, Titan, or any of the other colony destinations. Everywhere except Earth.

Behind the counter, a perky redhead about her age looked up at her expectantly. "How can I help you?"

Brix stepped forward, putting a friendly smile on her face. "I'm looking for a friend who works here. Maybe you can tell me if she's in today and let her know I'd like to talk to her?"

The girl bobbed her head, making the curls around her cheeks bounce as she tapped her computer pad.

"Certainly. What is the name?"

"Mali Harper. I'm afraid I don't know what department she's in."

The girl looked at her screen, and her brow wrinkled a bit. "I'm sorry, but I show she's not in today. I think she might be on holiday. It doesn't look like she'd been in for several days. Would you like to leave a message?"

Brix's stomach dipped a little with the confirmation Mali hadn't been in. On holiday? Would that be what they called a working assignment? "No. I'll check back in a week or so. Thanks for your help." She pivoted back toward the entrance, her eyes noting the security cameras above the door, behind, and to the right of the desk.

Would her appearance here alarm anyone who might monitor the camera? She knew they would know she and Mali were roommates, so it had been risky to come here. Worse, she had learned nothing she didn't already know, but she might have alerted them she was looking for Mali.

As she stepped toward the entry door, a young man came out of the controlled entry and strode toward her, pausing to let her go out. "Pretty ladies first," he said, flashing a grin at her.

Returning the smile, Brix stepped into the hall outside and waited until he stepped through and the door closed before she approached him. "Hi. I noticed you work there. I wonder if you know a friend of mine. I haven't seen her for several days, and I'm worried about her."

The gangly-looking guy stopped and eyed her curiously. "Maybe. Lots of folks work there, though. What's her name?"

"Mali Harper. I don't know—"

"Yeah, I know her," he answered.

"You do? Is she all right?"

He hesitated, glanced over his shoulder at the door, then looked a little nervous. He lowered his voice. "Not here. Meet me at the atrium fountain in an hour." He gave his head a shake and said, "Sorry, I can't help you." Without another word, he stepped away and headed down the curved hallway to the left.

Brix shrugged her shoulders and took the path to the right, certain whatever the guy had to say, he couldn't tell her anywhere near this office.

An hour later, she entered the atrium on the top level of the space station and made her way to the fountain at the central core. This sprawling domed garden offered a haven for anyone on the station who craved a place to get away from the endless gray walls and lack of anything organic. While a significant section of it grew food, using hydroponics, the rest flourished as a garden with trees, bushes, and flowers to give humans a sense of home. While Brix and Mali had a few small plants in the apartment, they didn't compare with the beauty and majesty of this incredible garden. The pleasing scent of lavender, along with the moistness in the air, wafted past as she made her way to the core.

He waited for her already, standing awkwardly with his hands stuffed in his pockets and glancing nervously around. She walked up casually, not going directly to him. She'd changed clothes to something more casual than her work clothes and added a cap she'd tucked her long hair underneath. She faced the fountain, resting her hands on the railing surrounding it.

She glimpsed his movement, sensed him edging his way toward her. He stepped into view and his eyes swept the area one more time, before he stopped a couple of feet away. "Who are you?"

"I'm Brix. Mali's roommate. Thanks for talking to me."

"I don't know if I can tell you much, but you know I shouldn't be talking to you at all. I'm Jax. I work with Mali... Or did. They pulled her off the job about five days ago. We had a big deal come up, and the higher-ups decided they needed her skills. I haven't seen her since." He continued to glance around while he spoke.

What he said stayed vague. Brix wondered if he actually knew more. A big deal... It wouldn't be a business deal, but something more urgent. What was Mali's job exactly, and what did Jax do? She took a chance. "I don't suppose this had anything to do with something requiring an adjustment, did it?"

The sharp glance he shot her way confirmed she'd hit the mark. She followed up. "Did they send Mali some other place or time?"

Alarm hit his eyes. He took a step back and cast a look around again, then subtly motioned for her to follow him. He circled around her and walked toward the rose garden, a more secluded area of the atrium where people often sought a little privacy for more romantic moments.

Brix lingered a little longer, letting him get several yards ahead of her before strolling the same way. To her surprise, he walked past the garden, turning onto a barely noticeable trail through a forest of miniature willows and dwarf ash trees. She hesitated a few moments, wondering why he remained so cautious. No cameras covered the interior of the dome, although they covered the entrances. But if they came and exited separately, no one would suspect anything. Did he think either of them had been followed?

She took the path slowly, not rushing in case anyone watched. Keep it casual. Keep it innocent. When she got to a branching trail, she heard a whistle from the right and turned toward it. She came to a small alcove hidden in the bushes where Jax watched for her. He motioned her to a two-person bench set toward the back, nicely concealed by the bushy willow in front.

Once she settled, he sat down beside her and said in a low voice, "I don't know if anyone is watching, and I can't afford the risk. How do you know about adjustments? Did Mali tell you?"

She shook her head. "I work for Time Excursions, and we hear things there. You know how it is with rumors, founded or otherwise. But to most of us, the possibility of a time anomaly is obvious, and we know one entity controls all time travel. I know where Mali works, even if the sign on the door doesn't say it. But Mali is missing, isn't she?"

He shrugged. "I wouldn't say it yet. There may be some reason why she's not back. All I know is they sent her somewhere to help repair a situation."

Brix took the plunge. "Don't time adjusters usually return to a day or two after they left? It's been five days, so it's not the norm, is it?"

A hint of panic, possibly at the information she seemed to know, hit his eyes and they popped wider. "No. But maybe they can't return to a closer date, and they'll be back at any moment. In fact, they could already be here and are being debriefed."

"Wouldn't you know?" she persisted.

"Me? Hardly. I'm just a low-level time monitor. Same as Mali was. They just needed her era expertise—that's what she told me. I don't think she expected to be sent."

"I see," Brix said softly. Mali was a time monitor... So, yeah, why did the manager send her instead of a trained adjuster? "Where and when did the team go?"

Jax looked more nervous. "I can't tell you."

"Can't or won't?"

"Both. Look, I've told you more than I should have. Just this could cost my job." He dropped his voice even lower as he started to rise. "Keep everything I've said to yourself."

Brix laid a hand on his arm. "Sure, Jax. I won't tell anyone, but maybe you could keep in touch. Aren't you allowed to date anyone on the station?"

"D... date?" He looked bewildered by the suggestion.

"Sure. If anyone asks, just tell them we're seeing each other. You can say you met me at a party with Mali a couple of months ago. Are they really watching you so closely?" She offered reassurance, then slipped a card with her communicator number into his hand. "Call me. We can have dinner or go to a show."

Nodding, he pocketed the card. "Sure. Like anyone would believe it. But we'll see." He left then, pausing to look both directions on the path, then he left with long hurried strides.

Brix leaned back against the bench, giving him plenty of time to clear the area. Why did Jax seem so worried about losing his job? What was so damn secretive behind those doors at TIM?

She needed to find out.

CHAPTER 3

London 1898

MALI STARED OUT THE ROOM'S only window, watching the last light fade. Doyle hadn't returned. Even though she'd expected him back by dark, maybe his anger hadn't cooled enough yet. She knew he would return. He had no other hope of getting back to his own time except for her.

She focused on her inner threads for the fourth time in the last two hours, searching the lines for the one to lead back to London in 1798. But the golden threads weren't as defined as she'd seen them earlier. Three appeared to be the same length, ending within days of each other, maybe. One would be the original timeline, the second would be the new one which was just created, and what was the third? Had this jump initiated yet another alternate dimension? The really long line would take her back to the space station on the original timeline. That would be the one they should be on.

According to her grandfather, she could only jump to a few days beyond the end of the shorter threads, but she could come in anywhere on the long line. Even though she hadn't lived any of those days, they connected when she made the jump to the past in the TU. So Doyle's original time should be on the long one. All she had to do was pick out the right date, touch the thread, and focus on when and where they were going. But it hadn't worked the last time. By her grandfather's reckoning, they couldn't be on an alternate line since they were a full century in the future from 1798. She had to find a reason it went wrong.

She closed her eyes, focusing on her recollection of the jump from Scotland to here. With her eidetic memory, she could review every moment, even slowing the seconds down. She could even recall her thoughts during the transfer. Had anything gone awry? She could feel Doyle's arm around her waist as the golden glow of the process began while the scent of the nutmeg and musk cologne he favored teased her nose. The movement from one place to another played out like a long whoosh of air surging past, rendering a sense of vertigo. She gasped, put out her hand for support against the window frame to offset the vividly recalled seconds of travel. A momentary jerk broke the flow, giving her a slight jolt before the movement resumed. Then came the wobbly landing in the clearing as her vision cleared.

Her eyes popped open. What was *that* break? It felt like a hiccup in the middle. Had she redirected the jump at that point with a thought she couldn't recall? Impossible. She could remember everything, every detail. Her thoughts were focused on London in 1798. She was sure. Yet, here they were.

She growled at herself. Obviously, she'd screwed up the jump with a subconscious thought, like she'd told Doyle, even though she didn't recall thinking about Varsick at all. But how did she choose this time? She didn't know where or when the rogue traveler had gone, so why this year? What had he changed in one hundred years to bring the automobiles to the present state? Clearly, the electric engine had advanced more quickly and combined with the steam engine to power more things cleanly. The combustion engine appeared to have fallen from the energy equation. What else had he changed?

Lights outside the window glowed along the London streets and down by the riverside. The city used a lot of wattage, so it must have a tremendous power source. Rising to her feet, she grabbed the light-weight shawl she'd bought earlier. She needed to walk, get a look at this updated London.

Slipping downstairs, she headed out, distantly aware no one even glanced at her, let alone gave her disapproving looks for going out alone at night. The original Victorian Londoners might have been more concerned.

Outside, a cool breeze off the river encouraged her to pull her shawl tighter around her shoulders as she set off down the street. The same one she'd walked only a week earlier, only many more years in the future. Where sidewalks hadn't existed before, they now ran under her feet, smooth surfaces that wouldn't trip her. At the corner, new street lights glowed, an addition she and Doyle noticed earlier when they'd gone to Market Street.

So many changes—brightly lit window displays, red telephone booths on various corners, power lines running overhead in secure casings. Mali noticed the tires on the vehicles were rubber, and dozens of other things caught her eyes as she walked along.

Goodyear had developed the process, she recalled, in the early part of the century, but had it been adapted to so many uses so quickly? She noticed little evidence of oil in use except as tar to cover the roads. At this point, more things should have been belching dark smoke out chimneys as fossil fuels provided more energy with less expense. That had been part of why it had gained so much dominance in the next century.

Without thinking, she'd wandered down the road toward the river and came to St. Anne's Street, where the library Doyle managed had been mid-way up the block. Was it still there? She turned, walking toward it, eyes scanning the buildings. They looked much like they had when she'd been here a century earlier. The little restaurant where Doyle had taken her to lunch remained, serving drinks and late meals now. Just a couple of doors beyond it stood the library, the same brass plate on the door. Closed for the night, but apparently still in business.

On the street, a pair of bicycles, headlamps lighting the way, went past as a man and a woman pedaled toward the river walk. How were those lights powered? She'd seen the use of bikes earlier, pegging them as cheap, reliable transportation for in-town activities. But she hadn't noticed the lights on them.

"So, you came down to look as well. Or do you need to research something?" The tenor voice called out, sounding flat and tired.

She turned to face Doyle, who leaned against the wall across the narrow street. She nodded. "It's closed. No research tonight. So much has changed, yet so much remains the same."

He straightened, dug his hands in his pants pockets, and sauntered across the road after an auto went past. Mali could see the down-turned mouth, not a pout, but unhappiness shaping it. His eyes looked as weary as he sounded. He stopped a couple of feet from her and gazed at the door up the steps. "I was inside earlier. They remodeled it. Rearranged. No evidence of my ever having been a part of it. Does this mean I never get back, Mali?"

"No, of course not," she answered quickly, although the question made her uneasy. Did she know for sure? "I'll get you back to your time, just a day or so after we left it. I promise you."

"You'll forgive me if I show a little doubt. I am not confident that you can." He sighed and gazed at her, eyes drilling into hers, until she looked away.

"I just need to practice a little." She dipped her head and looked back toward the restaurant. "Why don't we get a drink and talk about it?"

He shook his head. "Not when we can get them for less at the inn. We need to be more conservative with our money. Who knows how long we might be here?"

She nodded, stepping alongside him as he started ambling back to the Rusty Plough. "I'm really sorry, Doyle. I thought this would work. I didn't consciously bring us here. Even if I had been thinking about Varsick, I shouldn't have been able to bring us to this time—if this is where he went, when I didn't know."

"Not helping," he mumbled. "That means you have no control, and we just drifted in the time stream."

"No, that's not it. I had a clear destination in—"

"That didn't work, did it? Look at us. Two people so out of our place we are drifting in time." Doyle halted, turning to face her. He jammed his hands into his pockets. "I had a good job, a plan for my life, and I ended up swept along when you took us to Glasgow. Did you not think this change created some mental upset for me? I honestly hoped it was a dream, and I would wake from it back in my bed, a mere few blocks from here, but now it is in a different time. I loved you, still do. But this is so removed from my life I can barely comprehend it."

"I know that," she snapped back. "And I want to fix it. Honestly, I do. I just need time to work it out."

"Well, apparently, we have a great deal of that."

"Yes, we do," she murmured. "And the beauty of it is we can enjoy it, explore, maybe figure out why we're here, and I can still return you to your life in 1798."

"Even if we've aged ten years in the process?" he asked bitterly.

"We won't. I will get us both back to where we belong. Have a little faith in me, please."

"I don't have any alternatives." He sighed, offered his arm for her to lace hers through as they resumed walking.

Although she still worried, Mali kept her concerns to herself, smiling and displaying confidence to Doyle. She would figure it out. If all else failed, she still had the pocket watch her grandfather had reset for her. It would take them back to Glasgow in 1835. With his help, she could fulfill her promise.

Sitting at the bedroom table, Mali pulled out her tablet while Doyle washed up before bed. She noted the power bar dipped almost to the empty mark. Time to recharge. She'd take it out in the morning and hope for a sunny day.

In the meantime, she reviewed the dates for some inventions with the potential of changing the development to this time. She tried to make a guess ahead to what Varsick might be planning. That is, if she was actually pursuing him, and this whole jump hadn't been a fluke of some sort. She ticked off the ones she'd already noted—rubber, bicycles, advanced electricity—and speculated on others, such as an electrical generator attached to a water source or windmills. Technology destined to develop about fifty years later than this date.

While armies used submarines in the American Civil War, were more of them being built now? How advanced were they when compared to those earlier models? Had anyone started developing airplanes? Those would surely need a combustion engine to work, wouldn't they? One thing was obvious; she needed to do more research the next day to narrow down where to look for Varsick.

§ § §

Come mid-morning, Mali and Doyle stood outside the London Library at St. James Square, the nearest library to them other than the small one where Doyle had worked on St. Anne's. It had also come into being ahead of its time. Mali doubted Varsi tampered with its founding and assumed it was a product of all the other changes. This was part of the domino effect when altering time. Moving some inventions forward enabled other discoveries and related services to change sooner. The travelers' efforts had thrust entire century forward, so far as technology and social benefits went.

"Shall we?" Doyle asked, sweeping an arm to usher her inside. In a better mood today, he seemed more like the charming man she'd fallen in love with than the angry, depressed soul from the previous day.

A privately owned library, the imposing three-story building, built of white marble blocks, stood facing the square. On the second level, Mali noted an arched window flanked by two large rectangular ones. Plenty of light would enter there, she thought. So probably offices or a reading room. If the latter, she might charge her tablet there if sunlight filled the room. On the left, a wooden door beckoned them. They stepped into the musty smell of print books in a stuffy room on the warm day. Book stacks stood in long rows all around them, inviting them to browse.

Tempting though it was, Mali needed to find specific

information and do it quickly. She turned to Doyle, pausing as she glimpsed the look of wonder on his face. His little library held a lot of books, but it didn't compare to the vast number shelved here. A small smile played on her lips to see him so amazed, then she touched his arm. "All right, ace librarian, let's see how good you are at locating books about electric automobiles, combustion engines, and recent inventions."

"All right. I'll look for a card catalog to see how they've arranged these stacks. It should be like the setup I used." He looked around until he spotted the large wooden cabinet with dozens of drawers filled with cards for each volume in the library.

Going to it, he pulled out the first drawer to look at the cards listed. Mali peered over his shoulder, seeing the number on the top started with 100, then a decimal and other numbers followed along with the title of the book. She noticed Doyle's eyebrows pulled closer together as he studied the card for a few moments.

"Ah, this differs slightly from the method I used. I am not sure what the numbers after the decimal point mean."

"I believe that's something they called the Dewey Decimal System of filing. The first number is the major category of the book, and the other numbers break it down farther with the last set providing the exact location in the library. At least, that's the definition I read once." Mali pulled out a card farther back and held it up to show Doyle. "See? Different number on the end."

He blinked. "Well, it certainly makes sense. So, all I have to do is figure out what category the books about inventions are under and narrow it down to those covering automobiles and electricity. Give me a bit of time.."

"Or you could ask the librarian." She glimpsed a

suited gentleman heading their way.

Doyle turned his head, uncertainty flattening his lips. But the look passed when the man stopped a couple of feet from them, displayed a pleasant smile, and asked if he might help.

Doyle hesitated, then nodded. "Yes. I am not familiar with the numbering system on these books, so perhaps you could help me narrow down my search."

"Of course, sir," the man replied and stepped past Mali, who backed up a few paces, stood next to Doyle, and began explaining the system.

Mali cleared her throat. "I'm sorry to interrupt. Could you tell me if you have a newspaper archive?"

The librarian looked surprised at the interruption, then glanced at Doyle, who nodded his head in approval.

Well, that attitude hadn't changed.

"Of course, Ma'am. You will find them downstairs. If you wait a few minutes, I can show you."

Giving him a sweet smile, she said, "Thank you. I think I can find them myself, so take your time with my companion."

Without another word, she whirled away and started toward the stairs to the lower level. Most libraries were situated the same way, she thought, as she recalled what she'd read about the subject. The papers and magazines were always in the basement, if the building had one, it seemed.

Once downstairs, she found rows and rows of newspapers in cabinets, not hanging on wooden dowels as she'd seen at the St. Anne's library, but better protected in drawers. She quickly located the ones from 1850 and pulled out the first. She took it to a table and began reading, looking for any hint when the electric automobiles became so prominent. Even an advertisement might help, so she went through the whole paper, page by page. Then she exchanged it for another and another.

She passed an hour while she accumulated a short list of things to investigate, but no clue in all of this to what Varsick might be doing on this month and date. She found few references to gasoline-powered engines, although some experimentation had been done on it. Sighing, she returned the most recent paper to its rack and climbed upstairs to find Doyle.

As she sought him on the first floor in the stacks, the librarian noticed her and marched up to offer help. When she asked about Doyle, he pointed upstairs. "He's in the reading room, ma'am. Is there anything else I can help you find?"

"Not at this time," she answered politely. Then she followed the stairs to the brightly lit room where Doyle sat in a comfortable-looking chair engrossed in a book. Several more formed a pile on the small table by him.

"Looks like you found a few things," Mali commented as she came beside him.

He waved a hand at the table. "I did indeed. Help yourself to a book and begin reading. It's quite fascinating, actually."

Picking up the top book, she approached a chair near a sunbeam coming through the window and pulled out her tablet. She set it on the windowsill in the direct light with the solar charger facing the sun. Then she sat, opened the book, and began flipping through the pages. With her enhanced memory and training, she could speed read through the entire book in minutes, but she looked for specific information. Who invented the electric engine, and when? How had it become the dominant automobile? What had delayed the combustion engine? Did Varsick have anything to do with the changes?

She made mental notes as she extracted information,

then moved on to another book. By the time she was into her fifth one, Doyle was staring at her in puzzlement. "Are you actually reading any of those?"

"I read quickly, and I have an excellent memory. You know that." She closed the volume she'd just scanned. "I'm hungry. Are you?"

"Yes, I could eat," he answered and snapped his book closed. He rose as she did, gathering up the pile of books. While he did that, Mali picked up her tablet, checked to see indicator register as charged, then stuffed it into her handbag, before she followed Doyle back downstairs to the librarian.

"You probably could have left them up there for the man to gather later," Mali said as they left the library.

"I could have, but why create extra work for him?" Doyle flashed a grin at her. "I know how heavy these volumes get after a day of lifting them."

Just a short distance from the library, they found a busy-looking pub to grab food and drink. They barely made it inside before the pub's proprietor hung out a closed sign. This much about England hadn't changed.

Over cider and a ploughman's lunch, consisting of bread and cheese, egg, and pickles, Mali and Doyle exchanged information. "It looks like some inventors were the same, just doing their work earlier than they originally did," Mali said. "But it seems they had financial backing they might not have had originally. And Calliope Steam is still around, only now it's Calliope Steam *and* Electric. I would say my grandfather's company branched out, but I can't see any indication he is still alive and part of it."

"Still alive? Mali, he would be over one-hundred-and-eighty years unless he was time jumping throughout the developments."

"We know Varsick is time hopping. My grandfather

could be, as well." Even though he'd told Mali he planned to stay in his Glasgow home in that era, she didn't trust him not to do more traveling.

"Here's what I think," she continued. "Varsick isn't actually getting the patents anymore. He's helping the original inventors to get them done sooner whenever he can. Usually, more than one person worked on the inventions at various times and locations, so Varsick located the one most likely to succeed and assisted with the design, pushing it to success ahead of the original plan. With the changes earlier, the inventions were likely accelerating on their own. No surprise there. But for them to overtake and stifle the gasoline-powered industry was beyond expectation. Given it was Varsick's intent to prevent the pollution from fossil fuels from choking the twenty-first century, I would say he's well on his way to succeeding."

Doyle took a sip of his ale, his eyes focusing on the bits of foam in it as he thought. "What about coal mining? Is it still a big industry? We have known all along that it produces an unhealthy black smoke, but no one has been overly concerned about it."

"Not too much in your era, but now people are aware of it. It appears they've cut back a lot on using it as fuel. The new trains are electric, running on several high-power batteries, something they didn't accomplish until 2094. Which means Varsick is leading someone to technology way beyond the original development."

"I don't see how, though. The power plants still need fuel to create electrical energy, don't they?"

She shook her head as she took a bite of the bread with sharp cheese. "Alternate power sources have been around forever with the wind and running water. Varsick just led them to a more efficient way to use them to get all the power they need."

Shaking his head, Doyle sipped his ale as his forehead wrinkled. "It seems somewhat far-fetched to me. That's allotting a lot of changes to Varsick's influence. How could he do it?"

She sat back, pushing her hair back from her face as she tried to piece it together to make sense. "The thing is he knows who is working on what, how to encourage them in the direction he wants, then provides the funding and designs. If we were to jump_forward another fifty or sixty years, we'd probably find many of the inventions of the next two centuries have already been developed."

"Is that a bad thing?" Doyle asked as he turned his pint glass in his hands. "If it is improving people's lives and making the world a cleaner, healthier place, is Varsick doing something terrible? It doesn't seem it to me."

"In theory, no. It's not a bad thing. I understand Varsick's objectives, but how he's going about it is disrupting history and creating alternative paths. If what my grandfather said is true, he'll end up with one alternate path benefitting from all the changes, while the rest only have partial changes. I don't even know if my future exists any more on the original line, let alone the other ones."

Doyle leaned forward, elbows on the edge of the table. "Since you are still sitting here talking to me, I can assume that in this timeline, you have not been nullified. So, you have clearly been born and have returned to the past. Isn't it a validation of a sort?"

"I guess it is," she said after a long pause while she considered the truth of the statement. If she had been erased from the future, she couldn't be here now. Or could she? Since she was an anomaly in this time, could she still exist? Her head hurt.

She shoved back from the table. "Let's go see what else we can learn today."

"The water looks much cleaner, and it doesn't stink as much," Mali remarked as they walked along the Thames River. In 1798, pollution filled it with garbage and human waste. It still looked muddy, but the stench and human pollution that had nearly gagged her were gone, leaving a healthier-looking waterway.

Ambling beside her, Doyle nodded and sniffed the air. "You are right. It is much improved from my time. That's another positive aspect of this era. Is this Varsick's doing also?"

She shrugged. "Maybe. Or possibly it's a by-product of his other changes."

Just below the bridge, they spotted an unfamiliar structure crossing the river with several gates to route the water through. A new, imposing building squatted on the far side with access to the flat top of the structure. "It's a water gate or dam across the river," Mali said, recognizing the design as one used to control flooding. But this one had generators connected to it. "It's generating power for the city." She pointed to the thick lines running from it to poles and transformers. "This is one of the electrical sources for this end of London. I'll bet there are several more along the river in just the London area."

"Exactly how does it work?" Doyle asked.

She paused and began drawing a sketch of the basic design of a water-powered generator using a stick on a small square of dirt surrounding a stanchion along the river. While she explained, her eyes kept darting toward the structure, and she pointed out various parts out to Doyle. She blinked as a tall, thin man came out onto the edge of the dam. Something about the way he moved looked familiar, like the arrogance in his stride and the upward tilt of his head. Could it be?

She nudged Doyle's shoulder with hers and pointed. "Do you see the man there? I think it could be Varsick."

Doyle turned his head and squinted to where she gestured. "It could be, but he's fairly far from us. It could be someone with the same build."

"Come on." She began running toward the bridge. She heard Doyle's footsteps behind her as she sprinted onto the span over the water. When she drew closer, the man noticed her and spun around to hurry back into the building. Definitely Varsick.

Drat! But she could catch him before he left the area. What she would do when she did was only an embryonic thought, but she would figure it out when the time came.

Leaping off the bridge, she headed for the generator plant just as she spotted Varsick coming out of the building. He headed for the alleyway behind it as Mali poured on more speed. She flung her body around the corner just as Varsick turned back to face the end of the deserted alley. He gazed at her for a moment, dipping his head in an acknowledging nod with a smug smirk. Then he closed his eyes and reached his hand out as if to grasp something. In the next instant, he vanished in a glow of golden light just as she almost reached him.

"No! Wait!" Mali stumbled to a halt where Varsick has been only moments before. Her shoulders slumped. She'd almost caught up to him, but could she have stopped him from making the jump if she had? She narrowed her eyes, gazing at the spot. Was there a hint of the threads' glow left behind? She reached out to it, feeling the energy and getting a sense of where the thread went.

"Mali, what happened?" Doyle gasped for air as he came up, stopping a few feet back from her.

She turned to look at him. He'd bent over, resting his

hands on his knees as he took several deep breaths. His eyes squeezed shut with each inhale. Still feeling some pain from his wound of a few days earlier, she thought. Her own injuries almost healed, and she barely noticed them.

She glanced back at the thin golden line of light, and her eyes glittered with her excitement. "Varsick jumped. I've detected the path. We can follow him."

"Follow him?" Doyle echoed, his mouth dropping, as Mali motioned him forward and reached her other hand back into the fading afterglow of Varsick's time jump.

CHAPTER 4

Space Station Alpha—2238

"I HAVE SOME NEWS." MARGARET raised her eyes from her desk to look at Brix. "Sit down. I'll tell you what I've learned."

Brix pulled up the chair and lowered herself into it, her stomach tightening with the expectation of bad news. Almost a week had passed since she'd asked Maggie to check into Mali's disappearance. Her roommate had still not returned, so it didn't look promising.

"A contact inside TIM told me a TA team ran into some problems on their assignment. When the TA unit returned eight days ago, only one member came back... the pilot." Margaret dropped her eyes to the papers on her desk

"Did Mali die, or is she stuck in the past?" Brix asked when Margaret didn't elaborate.

Her boss shrugged. "I've told you all I know. My contact didn't provide more information about what happened. Most of the details are secret; only the higher-ups have any more information."

"Who was the pilot? He'd know more, wouldn't he?"

"Yes, of course. He has the entire story, but I don't

have any information on his status either. Apparently, he's being kept under wraps. I don't know his name." Margaret leaned back in her chair, flipping a stylus in her fingers while she waited for Brix to speak.

"Do you have any guesses who it might be? Who else was on the team?"

Margaret shook her head. "No, not really. My contact didn't give me any names and didn't even confirm Ms. Harper was on the team."

Brix remained silent, her expression neutral while she processed everything she'd learned, looking for anything to help her. Had she missed any clues in anything Dianna or Jax had said?

As the seconds ticked by, Margaret shifted forward and asked, "Are you all right, Brix?"

She drew in a deep breath, exhaled, then said, "I need to know if Mali was alive when the pilot left her. Hellfire, she was more than my assignment. I lived with the girl for over a year, and we were friends. I want to go find her if she didn't die there."

"Brix, it's not possible—"

"Don't tell me that. I know our company has done some distant research. I know we have a unit capable of going back almost as far as the TIM units go. At least two-hundred-and-fifty years ago. Is it far enough to find Mali?"

"I don't know," she answered. "But I can't allow you to use the unit. The directors wouldn't approve of using it for this purpose. While you're a valuable asset to us, Mali Harper isn't our concern."

Brix shot to her feet and placed both hands on Margaret's desk. "She should be. She's Adelle Morrison's great-granddaughter, for heaven's sake. Don't you think she might have some of her ancestor's gifts?"

Margaret jerked back and scooted her chair a couple

of feet away. "That means nothing right now. The unit is off-limits to anyone except for the validated missions. I can't just ask them to allow you to take it. You're not trained and not part of the travel program. Your assignment was to watch Harper, not form a bond with her."

"Well, I can't watch her now, can I? Unless I get back to wherever she went and find her."

"You bring up another problem. We don't know where or when Harper went, so there's no starting point."

Brix spun away from the desk, her shoulders hunched in frustration. She took three deep breaths before she turned back to Maggie. "I may have a way to find out. Will you, at least, put in a request to allow me to use the unit if I can pinpoint a place and time?"

Margaret stared at her for a minute before she spoke. "I can put in the request, but I doubt the directors will approve it even if you know the exact minute. It's hopeless, Brix. The odds of finding Harper are miniscule."

Of course, she was probably correct, but it didn't stop Brix from wanting to try. No one went after her father or his team, but maybe she could find Mali and the other guy who went with them.

"File the request," she told Maggie. "Get it started through the process while I try to narrow down the details." Brix started out the sliding door.

"You're wasting your time."

Brix paused and glanced back. "My time to waste."

She marched out, headed to the main exit, and passed by everyone else at their desks. A co-worker asked if she was okay, but she ignored him.

She had a bad feeling the day Mali left the apartment for her "think-tank" meeting. She'd sensed then she might not see her again. However, Brix also felt she had the skills and training to change the outcome if she could just get the information she needed.

Returning to her apartment, Brix changed from her office work clothes into more comfortable jeans and a light sweater before she strolled into Mali's room again. Maybe her roomie had left a clue somewhere, a hint to where she was going. Earth was the obvious place. Since there had been an anomaly, it had to be on Earth and big enough to affect their timeline. Had something else changed in the past two weeks? Would she know if it had? But the fact she knew Mali was missing meant, at least, her friend had been born in the present time. Whatever had happened didn't change that.

She sat down at the computer and turned it on, waiting while it booted up. Password protected, but Brix knew where Mali hid her codes. She opened the drawer, reached upward until her fingers pressed against a flat code stick tacked there, and pulled it out. Her lips twitched into a wry smile and she entered it into the computer, then she heard Mali's voice read the code aloud, "f-one-r-e-five-nine-f-exclamation-y."

"Welcome, Mali Harper," the computer voice said. "How can I help you?"

She was in. "Show the last ten files I accessed." In a few moments, a list of files and dates displayed on the screen. Only two of them occurred just before Mali had left. She touched the most recent one. Clothing styles of the 18th century. Could she figure out which pages Mali had looked at? Narrowing down the decade would help, but it seemed Mali hadn't bookmarked or noted them. She could only make guesses.

The other file gave her even less information; it was an essay on slang terms in Great Britain for the same century. From this, she could deduce Mali went to Britain in the 18th century.

Her stomach dipped a little when she realized how far Mali had gone. Could Time Excursion's extended time unit even reach the era? Did it have access to those earlier time threads? Even if it did, she still would have an extensive area to cover.

She needed insider information, and the only person she knew who could help her was Jax. She'd spoken to him twice since their initial meeting. He hadn't given her any more information. Still, he made an effort to establish they were friends, so they wouldn't look unusual if anyone noticed their meetings.

Clicking her message button on her tablet, she said, "Hey, Jax. How about meeting for a drink after work today? We can go to the Earthview Lounge on level 4. Let me hear from you." She clicked the message off and turned her attention back to Mali's room.

Staring at the bookshelf, she wondered which books her roommate had taken with her. Judging from the space, they had been thin volumes, probably guides of some sort, but she couldn't recall which books had been on the shelf. She'd only seen Mali's room a few times since they'd moved in together, and she had paid little attention to the titles, just found it amusing she had so many printed books.

She gazed at the shelf with the watches again. Mali had taken the pocket watch. Why did she choose the particular one? Was it from the era? Or did she just want to have something from home with her? Questions, questions. And she had no answers.

Her communicator beeped. Jax would meet her.

§ § §

The Earthview Lounge was precisely what the name indicated. When the rotation aligned, guests could see a breathtaking view of the planet. Brix sat at a window-side table, sipping a moon breath cocktail—a combination of vodka, mint, and dry ice to give it a fresh air impression—it tickled her nose as she drank. The Earth was full this evening and still bathed in enough sunlight to allow the blue, green, and brown colors to gleam vibrantly.

From here, the world looked serene, plentiful, and an ideal habitat. Only when you were on the surface did you see how lean the vegetation was, how the rivers looked muddy, and the wildlife was minimal. A few hundred people still lived there, but it was a tough life, always scrabbling for what you needed to survive. The experts said the world was slowly returning to its tropical state. Yet, it would be another century or two before it could sustain an increased population again. The last war had nearly decimated the entire planet.

"It's pretty, isn't it?" Jax slid into the seat across from her.

"From a distance, yes." She turned to face him.

Jax wasn't a handsome guy, but his wide, gray eyes radiated kindness and intelligence. His face had character—a slightly crooked nose and thin lips with high cheekbones pulling the flesh upward. She liked him.

"I hear it's pretty ugly on the ground," he commented. He'd grabbed a Titan Ale on the way and put it to his lips now.

"I wouldn't say ugly," Brix answered. "Just not so fine as it looks from here. How can you drink such crap?"

"Look who's talking? Your smoking drek will choke you—and the flavor? Ugh."

"I like mint. It clears my head and makes me happy," she answered. "What's your excuse?"

"It has bite and just enough alcohol to give me a light buzz. Titan barley is an acquired taste." He smirked, then took another swig.

With a shake of her head, she leaned forward, lowering her voice. "I need some information, Jax, and I think you have it. I swear on my life I will never tell anyone if you confide in me."

He looked wary. "I don't know, Brix. I've signed a security—"

"I know, but this won't actually violate anything. Not really, if you think about it. You'd like to help Mali, wouldn't you?"

"Of course, but—"

"I've learned only one person came back from the adjustment. Do you have any idea who it is?"

He dropped his eyes to study his drink. "I can't... It's uncertain... Look, I'm not sure. I only hear rumors about this stuff. No one tells my group anything."

Her voice dropped lower than usual when she leaned closer. "I'm desperate, Jax. What have you heard?"

He lifted his head to face her, then his lips moved close to her left ear, and he whispered, "The hot team for these missions is Bonde and Coleman, or so they say. But—" He stopped himself and cast a nervous glance around the lounge.

"But what?" Her voice purred with the suggestion of a lover's whispering.

"But... that's it. That's the story. It's all I—" His words cut off the moment Brix's mouth covered his while her hands pulled his face closer to hers. If anyone watched, they would only see two people flirting, not an intense conversation.

Surprised but not acting it, Jax pulled her into his arms, urging her closer. A pair of kisses more, then Brix pulled back and reached for her drink, a sultry smile on her lips although her attention remained on Jax. She sipped, then said, "I think there's a possibility Mali is alive and trapped in the past. I might get help to her. But I need to know when and where. You know about the anomaly, don't you?"

He pressed his lips together and turned his eyes to the view out the window. He lowered his voice even more. "I can't tell you. It would violate my oath to TIM. I could lose my job and never work for any secure agency again after I got out of jail."

"I just need a location and a date, Jax. It's to help Mali. My contacts aren't good enough to get the information. I don't need to know any more about it than just this one piece. Please. Help me."

He brought his eyes to meet hers. She hoped he saw the sincerity in them.

"You promise?"

She nodded.

"Swear on your life and those of your future children?"

Pursing her lips, she nodded again.

"Don't make me hunt you down and rip out your tongue if you betray me," he growled.

Taken aback, she jerked her head back. Jax wasn't even capable of doing it. "What?"

He shrugged and leaned toward the middle of the small table, urging her to do the same. Mouths almost touching again, he whispered, "Against my survival instincts, I'm trusting you. London, July twenty-third, 1798."

Brix pressed forward until her lips met his in a heartfelt kiss. "Thank you," she murmured, pressing a hand against his cheek. "I won't breathe a word about how I got the date."

He pulled back a little. "I don't see how it will help

you or Mali, but I hope it does." His hand caressed the back of her neck for a moment before he leaned back into the chair again.

"Do you know Coleman or Bonde?" she asked, her voice still soft.

"No, not personally. I know the names and might have seen them in the hallway... But, no. I haven't seen or heard anything about it other than what I told you. All of it is way above my pay grade."

She nodded. "I get it."

The conversation shifted to safer topics, and they talked for another few minutes, then Jax finished his drink. "Good to see you again. Maybe later." He flashed a smile, then took the long way toward the exit.

Brix watched him go while she nursed the rest of her drink. Maybe it tasted a little too minty, but it was still better than the Titan concoction. Since she had the date and place now, she had to hope Margaret could get the time unit's use approved and it could make the jump. She wished she had more to go on.

Thirty minutes later, she rose and sauntered out of the bar, casting a smile at some men whose eyes followed her. She'd grown used to being watched. She had the figure and the looks men liked, but most would be disappointed if they knew she had a brain as well.

She'd barely stepped through the door and turned to go back toward the central hub when she literally ran into the woman from the Level Two Bar a little over a week earlier. Brix hadn't been looking forward, her eyes on the other corridor, and had turned right into her.

"Oh, I'm sorry," she blurted out. "I—My fault. I wasn't looking." She reached a hand to steady the other woman who'd nearly fallen.

"It's all right. I'm fine. Just pay attention in the... Oh, it's you. I've actually been looking for you. Can we talk somewhere?"

Looking for her? Brix's eyebrows tightened in puzzlement, but she nodded. "Dianna, isn't it? Let's go to the squash court. It should be quiet there at this hour."

Dianna dipped her head in agreement, and Brix led the way to the stairs rather than the lift down. Part-way down, Brix pushed open a door on the second floor and motioned to Dianna to follow her.

"The court is down another lever," the older woman objected.

"I know. There's a room here more private than there. Follow me." Brix led her to the core, then to the left, ending up in a large room with six enclosed cubes. While not large, the space provided enough room for them to speak with no one overhearing.

Brix sat on the padded bench on one side while Dianna took the opposite one. "Study rooms... I'd forgotten we had these on the station."

"I used to take advantage of them a lot," Brix said. "Totally quiet. You can't hear anyone else through the soundproof walls. I used to practice my piccolo in here, and no one had a clue."

"You play piccolo?" Dianna asked, doubt in her voice.

"Yep. I was pretty good at it also, but I haven't touched it in the last year. Now, what's this about?"

"You wanted word on Mali Harper, didn't you? Well, I have a little, but I need to be circumspect about sharing it."

"I understand, but why are you telling me?" This part Brix didn't get. She didn't know Dianna and vice versa, so why was the woman going out of the way to give her information.

"I may have screwed up and caused a problem for the adjustment team Mali went with. My orders were to slow them down, not to endanger them." She laced her fingers together and twisted them. "I don't know if I'm responsible for an accident or not, but Harper may be stranded. One of the team made it back a few days ago. I understand he was injured and needed care, so he's been on administrative leave. But the team leader was killed, and Harper left behind."

Brix caught her breath. At least she was alive. Although the reality of Mali being stranded in another era alone worried her. She thought she was strong and intelligent, but Brix wasn't so sure. Mali didn't have a lot of practical experience. "Where? Do you know where?"

Dianna shook her head. "London area, 1798 or Glasgow in 1735. She needed clothes for both those eras."

"Did she have money? A way to survive."

"Some. Not as much as she could have. But she had some jewelry she could sell for more cash. All the team had some." Dianna dropped her eyes to her hands, not wanting to look at Brix.

"Why were you to slow them down, and who ordered it?" This whole story sounded peculiar to Brix.

"My boss didn't want the team to resolve the anomaly too soon, but I don't think he realized Harper would be with them. I don't think he would have wanted anything to happen to her."

"You're not making sense. Why would this person be concerned about Mali?"

She shook her head.

"Who is your boss?" Brix persisted.

"I can't tell you," Dianna whispered like he might be listening to her. "But he wouldn't want to see her hurt. That much I can say."

Springing to her feet, Brix glared at Dianna. She caught her breath and fought the urge to shake the information out of her. Who was this woman, and how did she fit into the events? She spun around and slammed her fist into the padded wall cover above the bench. Taking a deep breath, she turned back to Dianna. "You mentioned someone returned. Who? Where is he now?"

"Uh, I don't think I can tell—"

"I think you can. I need to know. If you've come to me out of guilt and want me to do something about it, then you need to give me more to go on. Now, who is it?"

"Coleman. Brayden Coleman. He was the engineer and pilot for the TU."

"Good. Now, where is he?"

"He's... Well, I think he's still recuperating. He might be in his own quarters or in the infirmary."

"Station infirmary?"

She shook her head. "No, the one at TIM. They have private facilities within their section."

Brix digested the information for a few moments. "One last question. Do you know his apartment number?"

"'Fraid not. I just know he has one on the station."

"Anything else you wish to confess?"

"That's all," Dianna took a deep breath like she'd held something in a long time. "I didn't expect the mission to go this wrong."

Staring at the floor and feeling numb, Brix collected her thoughts while fighting the urge to take her fury out on the other woman. Not her fault, she told herself. Dianna did what she was told to do. It wasn't supposed to cause any harm. She coughed at the dryness in her throat, then muttered, "You can go now. Message delivered and accepted."

"This... uh, this is just between us, right?" Dianna asked, her skirt rustling as she stood.

Brix looked up and blinked. "Sure. Just us."

In another moment, Dianna had skittered out the door, closing it behind her. Brix dropped onto the bench, pulled her legs up, tucking them close to her chest, and then wrapped her arms around them. She'd been right to be worried, but she hadn't expected this result. Dianna had slowed the team's progress but didn't tell her why. She wouldn't tell her who ordered it, but Brix assumed it was someone with a high level of authority in TIM. Why would they want to screw up a time-adjustment mission unless they wanted it to go wrong? Did they want the future to change?

She pressed her finger to her forehead between her eyes, where she felt a headache building. Tired and stressed, she figured. She dropped her head onto her knees and closed her eyes. Now she wanted to talk to Coleman. So, who did she know, who could discover where his apartment was located?

She stood up, stretched, and left the cube, her thoughts more on getting food and turning in early than on solving another puzzle. But she would figure this out and find a way to locate Mali.

As she came around the curve leading to her apartment, she noticed a person dressed in dark clothing hurrying down the corridor about ten yards from her door. Maybe someone late to work. She turned the lock on her door, pushed it open, and came to a dead standstill without setting a foot inside.

CHAPTER 5

London, 1898

"HURRY, DOYLE!" MALI GAZED at the wisp of golden thread still hanging in her vision. Pivoting to look back, she reached out to grab his hand as he got closer, her fingers beckoning him on.

Instead, he planted his feet as he frowned, his eyebrows pulling together as they reflected his consternation. "What are you doing?"

She pointed to where she'd been looking. "There's a trace of a thread here. I think I can follow it to where Varsick jumped. Hurry."

"No."

"What? We have an opportunity. We have to take it." She whipped her head toward him, her eyes wide, startled by his reluctance.

"No, we don't," he answered firmly, stepping back a step. "If you go, then I'm stranded here. You promised you would get me back to my time. If I go with you, I have no idea where I'll end up, and I'll be stuck there."

Frustrated, Mali stalked toward him. "You won't be stuck. I can get you back from wherever we're headed just as easily as from here. Now, let's go. There's still time to catch up with him."

"You really want to deal with Varsick, don't you? That's why we ended up here. Because you willed it, even if you didn't consciously think about it. I will not continue to follow you through time, Mali. I need to go back to my time. " His jaw locked in a firm line, and a muscle twitched at the edge.

She'd halted a few feet from him as he began to talk. She could hear the air he pulled in through his nose as he glowered at her. Her shoulders slumped, and she blew out a silent curse. "Oh, Gaia's spit, Doyle. You're not going to lose any time in the past. I can take us back to the day after we left, and you'll pick right up with your life no matter how long we spend moving through time. Think of it as a holiday and a fun adventure."

His eyebrows shot up as his mouth fell open. "Fun adventure? I was shot in Scotland a few days ago and tumbled out of a hot-air balloon! I don't think I can endure much more of that kind of fun."

"Are you serious? We have the opportunity to observe the future. Look at what we're seeing now. Think what another fifty or sixty years might look like." She moved closer now, her eyes pleading with him to seize the moment.

His lips trembled as his jaw clenched and relaxed a couple of times. He ran a hand through his hair and turned away from her for a moment. "I must be insane." His words sounded like they'd been dragged from his insides and his shoulders slumped in defeat. "But you're not leaving me much choice. If I don't follow you, then I lose everything from my past and have to attempt to live in a world for which I have no skills or preparation."

"I promise I will take you back to your time after I figure out where Varsick is and what he's planning." She held out her hand again. This time, Doyle took it, albeit with hesitation, and followed her the short distance back to where Varsick had disappeared.

Mali squinted at the spot, strained to see the lingering thread, and reached her hand out to pull it in. "It's in your mind," her grandfather had said, but he was talking about her life threads, not someone else's. Those threads floated freely, like the ones she'd seen as a child. The one from Varsick's jump wasn't hers.

She groaned and dropped her hand. "It's gone. We wasted too much time. It's vanished."

"I don't understand."

"The remnant of the jump was to the location where Varsick went, but it wasn't one of my threads. I could have used it, but it's faded away. Now, we've lost him again."

She continued to stare at the spot as if a thread might materialize again. "Wait a minute," she whispered. "I have total recall. I can visualize that thread exactly as it was." She closed her eyes, took a deep breath, and focused on her memory of it. After a few moments, it formed in her inner vision. She grasped for Doyle's hand, catching his wrist and locking her fingers around it. *If this works, I need to make sure he goes with me.*

She felt the tension in his arm, the uncertainty of what she was doing. She picked the thread and visualized Varsick, destination unknown. She sensed the waver at the start of a jump, and opened her eyes to a haze of golden light.

It's working! She gripped Doyle tighter.

The sensation of movement started, the sense of vertigo. Doyle caught his breath and they jumped. For a moment, she felt weightless, then the solid ground formed under her feet. She heard a grunt from Doyle, letting her know he was still with her. She looked around and her jaw dropped. The power plant remained in front of them, the perspective just a little different.

"Did he jump farther into the future?" Doyle asked.

Mali looked around. "I don't know. We could be a few years down the road, although I don't see anything different. The trees look the same. I'd say we went a few minutes ahead at the most."

"I don't understand." Doyle pulled his hand away and walked back toward the bridge, stopping after a dozen or so steps.

"I tried to conjure the same thread I saw and apparently got enough of it to initiate a jump, but since I didn't know the destination, it simply deposited us in the same place."

Dejected, she caught up with him and resumed walking.

"I still don't understand how you found him here."

"Neither do I. That's the biggest puzzle of this whole situation. I had no idea where he would be going, but somehow, we came to this time."

As they strolled back to the Rusty Plough, Mali figured she might as well take Doyle back to his time. Then she'd need to say goodbye and either try to find Varsick on her own or return to her grandfather's time to get help. Maybe Andover could explain what happened.

"Let's extend our room another night, enjoy our last night here, and we'll make another attempt to return to your time in the morning."

"Why not do it today?"

She felt the bounce return to his step. "I want to focus on the target before I do it again. It's easier for me to meditate at night."

"That sounds like an excuse to me. What else do you have in mind, Mali?"

"I just want to take my time and clear my head of any other thoughts."

Over dinner, Mali noted the far-away look on Doyle's handsome face. Usually, he remained upbeat, but this excursion to his future seemed to depress him. Perhaps going to the past hadn't been as jarring as visiting the future. She wasn't sure how she'd feel if she moved forward in time.

"I'm truly sorry I pulled you into this time-hopping." She laid her hand on his to reassure him. "I will fix this, although I love having you with me. Without your help, I would have been alone and maybe dead. I do care deeply about you, Doyle."

He turned his gaze to her. "Being honest, I have mixed emotions about you. I love you, Mali. But this life of yours is... abnormal. Unnatural. I thought possibly I could adapt to it and be with you. But I feel so out of place, so lost outside my own time. Can you understand that?"

"I can. I had the benefit of knowing what I was going back to and my purpose. While I wasn't trained for field work, I knew what to expect. Although I hadn't anticipated everything blowing up, literally. I also didn't know about my grandfather's pocket watch being able to transport me to him." She sighed and pulled it from her pocket, gazing at it.

In the low light of the pub, she could glimpse the slight glow of a thread woven into the watch. Her grandfather had reset it to bring her back to him in case they had problems. How had she not noticed in all the times that she'd picked up the watch since she'd inherited it? Maybe her grandfather had tucked the first thread into it tighter. Or maybe she just wasn't seeing as clearly since she'd been denying the time threads since she was nine-years-old.

"What are you thinking, Mali?" Doyle asked, his hand touching hers as she cradled the watch.

"Sorry. I drifted off a bit there. I'm still trying to sort out how the threads actually work, and how my family ended up so involved in time travel. I gather many of my ancestors were time walkers, as my grandfather called them. So, I wonder how many other people can do it. Obviously, Rashid and my grandfather do. I don't know if my dad did, but grandfather said he had the talent. But if he did, why...?" Her voice trailed off as she thought about her parents and how they died.

"Why what?" Doyle prompted, curiosity showing in his eyes.

"If my dad could time travel, why didn't he and my mother come back home? They could have jumped to another day and been safe instead of perishing in the fire. What if they didn't? I warned them."

"You what? How could you do that?" Doyle pulled his hand back and swallowed a big swig of his ale. His eyes darted to the stairs to their room. "Perhaps we should go upstairs to talk about this."

She glanced around, noting a couple of people watched them, their faces grave and intent. Had she been talking loud enough to be overheard? Were any of these people working for Varsi? His recruits had waylaid her more than once. "Maybe you're right." She shoved her chair back, sprang to her feet, and wove her way to the stairs with Doyle following.

Once they were safely behind the door, Mali dropped onto the bed, urging Doyle to sit beside her. She kept her voice low in case someone might be listening as she explained her parents had been killed in a club fire on the space station. "Fires like that are almost unheard of on the station. Most things aren't flammable, but the club used real wood, real tablecloths, and real candles on the tables. As the curtains were not fireproof, they went up in flames in minutes once the blaze touched them. Investigators never figured out what started it. The club was cited with multiple violations of safety codes. Fifty-three people died that night, and dozens more injured. It was the worst disaster on the station since we built it."

"That is horrible, but how could your parents have escaped if it spread so quickly? And what do you mean by fireproof?"

"It means they treated items to prevent them from burning easily." The second question was easier to answer, and she'd forgotten he'd not heard the word. "That's the thing, though. If my grandfather told me the truth, my dad knew how to use the threads. He just didn't do it. He could have taken the two of them a day or two ahead and been out of the flames. After they'd died, a little over a year later, I wished so hard that they hadn't that I called the threads out, and I returned to one of my birthdays with them. Once I realized I could do it, I went to the club on the night they died and told them what would happen. My mother told me to go home and never tell anyone about the threads or that I'd been there. I thought they would escape and come home, but they didn't. Why didn't they do it?"

"My Lord, it is creepy listening to you talk about this so matter-of-factly. I can barely grasp the enormity of it while you are taking it for granted. Maybe your father was not as adept at it as you thought? Maybe he tried and failed." He caught both her hands in his, squeezing them gently. "Sometimes, in a panicked situation, people don't think clearly. That could have happened to them."

Tears burned at her eyes as she wanted to deny that could have been the case. Not her dad. Even that night when she told them, he seemed level-headed, reacting to the emergency but not panicked. Doyle could be right, and Dad just didn't have the skills to save them by jumping. But that didn't seem right to her. She shook her head as if it would clear it. It was over now. They'd been gone for many years.

"You're probably right, but it's one of those questions that will bug me for a long time."

"Bug you?" he asked, his mouth twitching with a denied smile.

"Bother. Keep coming back to my mind. It's a twentieth-century term. You know, like a bug pesters you while you're eating."

He laughed. "I like it." Then his expression sobered. "Mali, would it be so bad to come back and live in my world? To marry me and have a normal life with kids and a couple of pets? I have excellent prospects, you know, and I expect to afford a house soon. You could write books, you said."

"It's not you, Doyle. I adore you. It's my ambition and this crazy time-walking thing that interferes. I don't know how long I could be happy without some of the luxuries I have in the future, like my tablet. It's completely out of place here, and even though I can charge it from the sun, it will fail one day. Then I would be devastated."

"Couldn't you go get a new one?" His lips parted into an amused smile.

"Oh, sure. I'll just take a walk to get what I need. Given my success at doing it, you could lose me within a year." Her self-depreciating laugh caught Doyle's sense of humor and they chuckled over it together.

She'd almost convinced herself that she could live in the same time with him, but now she doubted that assumption. She loved Doyle, but she didn't belong in his time any more than he belonged in this time or her time. Sure, she could go do her job, then hop back to his time to cook dinner and go to bed, but how would that work out? Would they age together? What if she got stuck in an era for a few years and returned to the day after she'd left, then she'd be those many years older than him.

Besides, if she were to have a time to return to, she needed to stop Varsick from making any changes on her original timeline, or he could wipe out her future. She'd joined TIM to do exactly this kind of thing, even if she hadn't realized how dangerous the job could be.

Doyle excused himself and went out the door. Maybe to the water closet, or perhaps he was going for another walk. Mali let him go. He needed to work it out for himself. She still wished he would travel with her until all of this was settled, then maybe they could revisit the decisions again. She might not want to keep time-hopping, or he might enjoy it more than he thought once he got used to it. But for now, she had to sort out the right thread on the correct timeline to get them back to London in 1798.

She sat in the chair by the window and gazed out it, letting her vision go unfocused as she called out to the threads within her. Gradually, they emerged before her eyes, twisted strands, some looping from one to another of the three main strands that represented her lines. The longest was the original one she'd come back on, while the shortest was this jaunt to 1898.

Mentally pulling the original line apart at the top, she found the longest thread in that bundle, which would be the day she jumped from Scotland to here. Yes, she saw that thin line that connected to the short, thin grouping. Digging down further, she found the next longest thread, and that one should be the one when she pulled Doyle with her to Glasgow. Within that thread were more thinner strands that represented the days. She could find the one where she left and add a pinch of a line to it to take her back to a day or two after she'd jumped. That meant she would be back in a time she had not yet visited. It would work. It had to.

By the time Doyle returned, Mali had crawled under the blanket, ready to sleep. "We'll get an early start," she told him. "I want to go someplace secluded so our departure won't be noticed. Is there a small park with lots of bushes near?"

Doyle nodded as he slipped off his coat and began unbuttoning his shirt. "Yes. I know one. It's about six streets from here. With all the new buildings in the area, there are a couple of newer private gardens."

"Sounds perfect. This will work, Doyle. I know it will."

He took off his shirts and pants, hanging them over a chair, then slid into the bed beside her. Mali snuggled a little closer, not sure of her reception, but he slid an arm around her shoulders and squeezed her a little. This was awkward. She'd basically ended their potential relationship with her declaration that she couldn't stay in his time, yet she still loved him and wanted it to be more.

Doyle must have felt it also as he made no move to do more than hold her. No kisses, no teasing words even. She watched as he turned off the light and closed his eyes. Tears gathered at the edges of her eyes for the loss she was already feeling. She pressed her face against the pillow and slept.

§ § §

A shake on her shoulders brought Mali awake, blinking into Doyle's face as weak sunlight slipped through the window. "Morning already?"

"It's daybreak, and we should get going as soon as

we can."

Doyle had already dressed and made a bundle of his previous century's clothing. None of the garments would be appropriate in 1798. Neither would Mali's, but they'd deal with that once they got there.

She slid out of bed, taking the blanket with her, and retrieved her clothes. She carried them down the hall to the water closet. The inn had running water and flush toilets this time around, but nothing in the sleeping rooms yet. Maybe in another century. She sighed and washed up, then dressed quickly.

Within another few minutes, she and Doyle had gathered up all their belongings and headed downstairs, leaving their key at the bar. A server saw them as she set up platters behind the bar.

"Leavin' wit'out breakfast?" she called to them.

"Yes. We have an appointment this morning. Key is on the bar," Doyle replied.

The woman bobbed her head once and resumed her task as they went out the front.

"Two less to feed." Mali grinned at him as he looped his arm through her elbow to escort her properly.

"I would have liked to eat, but maybe we'll arrive home in time to get tea and biscuits there." Doyle winked, in a much better mood with the prospect of returning to his time.

They hurried across the road and down the streets toward a residential area where Mali spotted the greenery ahead behind a low stone fence. "Is that the place?"

He nodded, urging her ahead. "Yes. We'll have to climb over the fence, but no one is around at this hour."

"Might someone see us from their windows?" Mali asked, concerned about breaking into a private garden.

"I doubt it, and I know a spot where we can enter with no one on the square being able to see us. Once we are in, we can stay within the bushes."

"Clever boy."

He flashed a grin at her and led her to the far end of the garden. Here the bushes grew close to the wall, but there was a spot with just enough room for them to slip in unseen. Nervously, Mali scanned the street for anyone coming their way or any cars heading down the road, but as Doyle had said, it was quiet and deserted.

With one last glance, Doyle planted his hands on her waist and lifted her to the top of the wall. Mali perched for a moment before twisting and sliding off and down onto the other side. She stepped into the narrow opening in the bushes, and in another few seconds, Doyle dropped down to where she'd been standing. He urged her on as she shoved branches back to give them room to pass between them.

The sweet scent of the fuchsia-colored blossoms welcomed them, adding a comforting layer to their security. Mali plucked a cluster and shoved them into her hair, a way to take the fragrance with her. "What kind of flowers are these?" she asked.

"It looks like rhododendrons, I think. I'm not a botanist, so I could be wrong." Doyle pressed ahead of her and led the way to a small open spot, not even worthy of being called a clearing. He stepped in and turned to face her. "How's this? Private enough?"

"Cramped," she said as she looked around and above them to be sure no one could see from an upstairs window. The tall bushes provided adequate cover, and she didn't see anyone peering out. "It will work."

She caught his hand, focused her mind, and squinted her eyes. *The threads are within you,* she reminded herself, but she usually saw them as a vision in front of her. She heard Doyle's steady breathing as she pulled the image into focus. There. The trio of strands appeared, then she narrowed it to the longest one, the main timeline. Peeling strands away, she found the one she needed.

"Here we go," she whispered, her hand gripping Doyle's tighter. She imagined pulling on the string, finding the spot just beyond the end to move them a day ahead of when they left 1798. A golden haze surrounded them, and the sensation of time travel started, a touch of unbalance, and movement hit her. Doyle's fingers squeezed hers until moments later, they felt a jar as their feet touched the ground.

Mali's vision cleared, and she looked around. Dismayed, her stomach dropped like a rock as she realized the awful reality.

CHAPTER 6

Space Station 2238

FURNITURE SAT ASKEW, SOFA CUSHIONS scattered to the floor, drawers and cabinets opened, a favorite vase smashed. Someone had invaded Brix's apartment. Was it the person she'd seen scurrying away? How had they broken the code to the door?

Alarmed, she hurried past the disarray in the living room to her bedroom. Things had been moved in her vanity, and a couple of drawers sat part-way opened and messier than she'd left them. But it didn't look like anything was missing. Her bedroom seemed intact, the bed still made, but another slightly open drawer beneath the bed caught her attention.

Brix didn't keep any work or personal documents at home. Her room held her clothing, shoes, and a case of accessories in the closet. She hurried to check the jewelry box, the only thing with anything of actual value in the room. The lock on it remained secure. Nothing seemed to be gone, so she suspected whoever had broken in had hurried through it, giving most things a cursory glance.

Satisfied her possessions were safe, she directed her

attention to Mali's room. Here, too, the drawers in the desk had been searched. She didn't know if the intruder had found anything. The books had been moved, but none appeared to be missing, other than the few Brix had noticed before.

Worried, her eyes shot to the shelf across from Mali's bed. The two watches remained in place, apparently untouched. The intruder had moved a couple of knickknacks. She could see the disturbance in the dust around them, but nothing else appeared touched. Her nose twitched as she detected a musty scent in the room, something like a man's cologne, familiar but not connecting it to a specific person.

More mussed up than hers, Mali's bedspread and pillows were askew. She knelt to pull out a drawer. Various papers, notes, and two pairs of archery gloves were stuffed into it, not neatly. She didn't know if someone had rifled through them or if Mali was just messy.

The next drawer held folded clothing. Even those looked as if someone had moved them around. Whoever it was had been searching for something specific. Did the person find it? Brix had no idea.

Feeling numb, she went back to the watches, peering at them to see the details. They looked the same. If the intruder had touched them, she couldn't detect it. She squinted at them, catching a faint golden haze around them. *Odd.*

She left the rooms, closed Mali's door off, and pulled out her tablet. Time to report the intrusion and change the exterior door code. All the while, she contemplated who it was and what he'd been seeking.

§ § §

Brix stood outside a residential door, number 3-28C, on the third floor of the space station but hesitated to press the buzzer. She hadn't known any apartments were on this level, thinking it was primarily businesses and a couple of restaurants. But her contact told her this was Coleman's place. Mustering her courage—after all, what could he do but refuse to see her?—she pressed the buzzer and waited.

"Who are you?" the house computer's precise voice asked.

"My name is Anna Brixton. I would like to see Mr. Coleman."

Dead silence as Brix waited to see if anyone would open the door. The seconds dragged until she felt like she'd stood there for way longer than it should take to answer. *Had the computer shut down? Evidently, it wasn't programmed for politeness.*

At last, she heard the door slide open, and she straightened her shoulders. But it stopped, leaving a narrow opening, enough for a partial face to peer out at her.

"Do I know you?" His voice was a pleasing but slightly rough tenor, and she noted a red rim around the light blue eye.

"No, you don't. But could we please talk? It's important." She flashed a small, friendly smile, hoping it would disarm him. Coleman was not what she'd expected. *This was a bold time adjuster?*

He hesitated, ran his tongue across his lower lip, and asked, "About what?"

"Can I please come inside?" she asked. As he still paused, she added, "I don't want to talk about it while standing in the corridor."

Reluctantly, he slid the door open and stepped back

for her to enter, then closed and secured it. He turned to her, his eyes roving over her tall frame as she gazed at him with equal scrutiny. Above-average height, slim, and well-muscled, Brayden Coleman was a handsome man, although the tightness of his jaw and mouth suggested he wasn't pleased with her company.

"What's this about, Ms. Brixton?"

Brix swallowed her nerves. "I'm Mali Harper's roommate." She watched his eyes narrow and his body tense at the mention of Mali's name. "I'm asking you to please talk to me. Help me understand what happened to her. She is missing and long overdue from when she should have returned."

He shifted from wary to alarmed, his eyebrows lifting as his eyes grew stone cold. Brix rarely saw a visible shift in the color and intensity of a person's eyes, but his turned positively icy. He crossed his arms over his chest and took a step back as if she might blow up on him. "I can't help you."

"I believe you can," she answered, not moving or altering her voice. She tried to remain calm since she needed to convince this man. "I'm probably asking you to divulge something your employers would prefer to remain secret, but I'm not doing it to cause them or you any trouble. My need is purely personal. Mali is a good friend, and if there's a chance I can get her back, I will take it."

To her surprise, Coleman chortled, although the laugh sounded hollow. "So, I should just ignore my employment agreement and tell you what you want to know. Do I have that right?"

"Yep, that about covers it." She glanced around the apartment, noting the spacious living room with a large sofa and two comfortable-looking armchairs. They faced a wall with a pair of windows looking toward Earth. She estimated it was at least twice the size of her space. "Can we at least talk about it? Let me try to convince you."

After a moment of staring her down, he motioned to the chair on the left. "Sure, why not? I have nothing else to do. Would you like a cold drink? I can offer Lunacola or pure water."

"Water is fine," she answered, hopeful the courtesy meant she had a chance to break through his barriers.

As he walked to the kitchen, she noticed he limped and favored his left leg. He injured it on the mission, she recalled. Enough to put him on medical leave. What had happened? Was Mali involved?

In a minute, he was back with a glass for her and the plum-colored cola drink for himself. "Hit me with your best shot, Ms. Brixton."

"For starters, please call me Brix. Everyone does, and I prefer it. As I mentioned, I am Mali's friend, and we room together. The last thing she said to me was she'd be back for my birthday party, which was three days away. She didn't make it. It's been three weeks since she left."

"Sorry to hear that. But this concerns me how?"

"Because I know she was with you and another man on a time adjustment."

He stared at her, jaw muscles flexing as his mouth compressed to a tight line as his eyes narrowed. Her stomach lurched, and she expected him to throw her out bodily. Finally, he growled out, "Did she tell you that?"

A brief laugh escaped her. "Hell, no, she didn't. She made up some far-flung story about a think-tank thing for a few days. But I'm not dumb. I knew she worked for TIM, and through various means, I've learned she traveled on a mission. You were on the same trip, so I want to know what happened when you left her there. Why you did it? Was she hurt?" She paused, then hastened to add, "You don't need to give me any details, but give me at least something."

He sat silently for a minute, gulped down the contents of his drink, and slammed the glass on the side table. "That's a hell of a request. Answering is definitely a violation of my contract. I should turn you in for spying. You already know confidential information, and if anyone in TIM provided it, then they're guilty as well."

Brix bit her lower lip and dropped her eyes to hide her anger at the threat. She took a few moments to calm herself before asking, "What about decency, Mr. Coleman? Wouldn't it be the right thing to tell someone what happened if it meant they could rescue Mali?"

He sprang to his feet and paced, his fury radiating like an angry star about to explode. Then he swung to face her. "Rescue her? Dammit, if she hadn't been so freiling stubborn, I wouldn't have left her. I tried to get her to board the TU, but no, she had to fiddle around with a local fellow she'd met, then—" He stopped cold, realizing he'd said too much.

"So, you just left her?" Brix could barely believe what he'd said. Mali stayed with a man in the past. *What was he suggesting? Mali went—what was the term?—oh, yeah, native.*

He glared at her, turned away, and stared out toward the Earth. "Stupid girl never listened to reason. She didn't follow the rules or her orders. Granted, she wasn't trained for the mission, but all the more reason to pay attention to Bonde's orders. Maybe things wouldn't have..." His voice trailed off.

"Wouldn't have what?"

He growled, back still turned to her, then he swung around. "Wouldn't have gone off the rails, and Bonde wouldn't have been killed."

Anger gave way to anguish as his face crumpled, and his eyes grew misty.

"Is that why you left her? Because she screwed up the mission?" Brix tried to keep her voice steady, although she wanted to scream at him. Did he intentionally leave Mali behind?

"Hell, no. I didn't leave her. She left me!"

"What?" How could Mali have left him if he was in the TU? He brought it back, not Mali, so he didn't make sense.

Coleman ran his hands through his hair, lifting it between his fingers as if he extracted the memory. "She was standing there, arguing with me when her boyfriend came up and grabbed her shoulder. Then, in a flash of yellowish light, they were both gone. Vanished..."

His voice cracked. He took a deep breath, and his voice sounded shaky, torn with emotion. "I hobbled down to where she'd been, and she was gone. Just disappeared. Nothing to indicate she'd ever been there. No sign of either of them." He wiped his hand across his face as if it could erase the events.

Stunned, Brix sat stiffly as she replayed his words over and over, trying to find a rational explanation. Coleman had a breakdown; someone had said it, and he was unfit for duty at present. Medical leave meant more than his injury. He was mentally screwed up. *That had to be it. What he said just didn't make sense.*

Or did it?

Brix remembered she and Mali had talked about the timelines once and how the travel units used them to go through time. They'd both professed curiosity about it, neither one telling the other they each worked for companies using the units. Mali had said something then about time threads and how some people saw them. What if Mali did? Brix didn't tell her about her own experience. Once, just after her father disappeared and was presumed dead, she recalled seeing golden threads but thought it was part of her grief, a hallucination. To her knowledge, Mali had never used them. At least, she never admitted as much.

Going with the theory Mali had time walked, Brix said, "It's okay, Mr. Coleman. You didn't abandon her. She traveled somewhere else."

He dropped his hands, his eyes looking watery and redder than before. "What do you mean?"

"I believe she time jumped," she answered, throwing out a lifesaver for him to grab.

"How?"

"I've heard some people are capable of it. Mali may possess a latent talent. Do you have any idea where or when she might have gone?"

He shook his head. "No. I was trying to get her in the TU so we could return home. None of this would have happened if she'd just..." His voice broke, and anger returned to his face in a dark scowl.

"Look, do you have pills or anything for your nerves?" He gave her a barely-there nod. "Perhaps you should take one and wash your face. Get calmed down."

He tasted his lower lip again. "Maybe you're right." He slipped off through the door on the right.

Brix took his glass to the kitchen, peered into the fridge, found a bottle with the same-color liquid in it, and refilled his glass. She took it back to the living room and set it down, then resettled in the chair and waited.

About five minutes later, Coleman came back out, calmer, and face looking more relaxed. He glanced at the refilled glass and murmured, "Thanks," as he sank into the chair. "I apologize for that. It's an image I can't forget."

"Why was she arguing with you?"

"She wanted to make one more jump to follow up on our mission. We didn't have the power to do it and get home. I was senior; she should have obeyed me."

"Mmm, obedience isn't a strength of hers," Brix commiserated.

"Understatement."

Brix shifted her position, leaning forward with one arm on her knee. "Thank you for telling me what happened. I'm sure this is difficult for you. However, I'll keep this entire conversation between the two of us. No one needs to learn you talked to me."

He looked at her, swallowing hard. "Thanks. It feels better to say it to someone who doesn't assume I'm crazy. Honest to Juno, I wouldn't have left Mali behind if she hadn't disappeared. I even waited another couple of hours, hoping she would come back."

"You said she wanted to make one more jump. Did she say anything about where?"

He closed his eyes for a moment as if seeking the information in his memory. "One inventor we were investigating was a man named Andover Morrison. Mali had a theory about him and believed she would find him in 1763 in Glasgow."

"Did she pick a particular day?" She needed something to home in on a little more than a full year. Hard enough locating her in a city like Glasgow, but it would be nearly impossible without at least a range of days.

"Our discussion never got that far. I was dead set against it. Sorry I can't give you any more than that." Coleman slumped down in his chair.

"What is your travel status now?" Brix asked.

Taken aback by the question, he blinked. "I'm on medical leave. They say I'm not mentally fit to go back to the unit yet. I lost a good friend on this trip, as well as Mali. She shouldn't have been on the team. She wasn't right for it."

"I understand. Thanks for talking to me."

"Out of curiosity, Brix, what do you think you can do to help a girl who vanished several centuries in the past? If she hasn't come back by now, she's not going to."

"Maybe she just needs a little help. I'm not counting her out yet." Brix got to her feet, gave Coleman a last nod, and headed for the sliding door. From his chair, he keyed the open command, and it slid aside to let her out.

She mulled over the conversation as she returned to her apartment, trying to read in what wasn't said. Coleman appeared to care enough about Mali to hang around, but he didn't attempt to take the damaged unit to Scotland to find her. It meant he either believed she'd vanished and was likely dead, or his own return was more important to him than finding her. She wasn't sure which it was, but if he was injured, she put her credits on the second option.

Now she had a place and a date, albeit a general one at that, but it was a place to start. She'd see what she might find out about Andover Morrison and possibly narrow it down a little.

She stopped to grab a quick meal to take back to her place, then she checked the messages on her tablet. One came from Jax; she listened to it first, hoping he had news. Turned out, he only wanted to check in and asked if she would like to get a drink and tacos after work the next day at the Gringo Pub, a popular place on the second floor. "Sure, why not?" she replied and sent the message back. The following one came from Margaret. She wanted to see her first thing in the morning.

Her heart skipped. Possibly her boss had news about her request to use their time unit. With hope for approval, Brix hurried home to eat and do some research. If they accepted it, she'd needed a firmer date to shoot for than 1735.

Three hours later, she'd read through several journals chronicling the life of Morrison, beginning when he was in his mid-fifties. Before that, she found no mention of him. His alleged birth date and place were on record, but no follow-up about his education or training. Then one day, he showed up at a patent office in Scotland and filed a design for a steam engine. Once it was granted, he founded a company to produce steam automobiles and literally became the father of the industry.

What bothered her was the lack of any previous information about him. He rarely gave interviews and only talked about the present, nothing about the past. In so many ways, it read like the bio of a man who suddenly appeared, a time traveler perhaps. Was this the man Mali and Coleman were sent to stop? She shut off her computer after she scribbled down the founding date for the Calliope Steam Company. She'd look for more information after work the next day.

CHAPTER 7

Space Station 2238

SEEING MARGARET TALKING TO THE AIR and typing at her tablet keyboard, Brix paused at the doorway to wait. When her boss motioned for her to enter, she stepped inside and stood along the wall.

"Right. I'll get the information compiled and to you by lunch," Margaret concluded and tapped behind her ear to end the connection. "Thanks for waiting, Brix. I don't have good news. Sorry. The directors will not approve your request to use the special time unit no matter how critical the matter seems to you."

Brix's face fell, her neutral expression shifting to disappointment with the downward curve of her lips.

Maggie hurried to add, "If you were asking to go back to the limit of one of the standard ones, they would do it. But to go back as far you're asking for a questionable rescue mission, they feel they can't stretch their covert operations that much."

"I see. So, for the things they want to examine, it's okay, but to save a life, it's against their ethics." A touch of bitterness came through, even though she tried to hold it back.

"I know it's disappointing," Maggie agreed. "But if

TIM believes they can find her, then they will probably send someone back."

"You know what bothers me?" Brix asked. "If they did, and they found her, we wouldn't be having this conversation. The only way would be if someone like me goes back, finds her, and brings her back to a day or two in the future from when I left. Otherwise, she would have returned, and all of this wouldn't have happened. Think about it. The paradox of time travel has many facets."

Conversation over, Brix turned to leave when Maggie spoke again. "I am sorry, Brix. If anything changes, I'll let you know. In the meantime, you can work on the Helios file. There's a group of eight wanting to go to Phobos."

"Of course. Thanks." Back to doing travel planning for her. How long would she have before the authorities declared Mali dead?

While she worked, Brix pondered how she could get access to one of the TIM machines. She doubted they would consider working with her for a mission to the past if they hadn't already sent one. She kept thinking about Mali and her friend just vanishing in a golden cloud before Coleman's eyes. He wouldn't make up a story like that, so it must be true. How could it happen? What did Mali do to jump? She had a wisp of a theory, but it was a long shot.

Her mother had once said Brix's father was a time walker, someone who used threads to step to a different time and place. Dad never talked about it, and Mom only mentioned it the one time when Brix was about nine. Then Dad disappeared and never came home. Mom spoke to someone from his office who said there had been an accident, and he wasn't coming back. Not that he was dead. *Just he wasn't coming back.*

Since she had seen thin golden threads once, she thought those might be threads like her father had seen, but she didn't know how to use them and didn't try. If Dad had vanished, she didn't want to go the same route. Now, she wondered if Mali had done the same thing.

When she accepted the job to spy on Mali, she knew the girl was Andover Harper's granddaughter. Harper led an adjuster team that went back and never returned, presumed lost. Later, she learned her father, Aldus Stigler, had been on the team as well. She and Mali had that in common. But if it tied anything together remained to be determined.

After work, she met Jax at the taco bar and had ordered a margarita and two veg-chick tacos while they caught up. She told him she'd been trying to figure a way to use one of the long-range TU's but wasn't having any luck.

"Aren't they all used by TIM?" Jax asked, biting into his taco.

"Mostly, yeah," Brix answered. "A couple of other companies each have one. But they have limitations on how far they're allowed to go. Do you know why TIM hasn't sent a team back to look for Mali?"

He shrugged. "Maybe they have. I don't hear about everything going on in the travel section. I just monitor the line, looking for anomalies."

"Have you noticed any lately?"

"No, actually. Once the big one settled down, there's been nothing of significance."

"Of significance? Don't you report all of them?"

"We just note them if they're little burps on the line, within a defined range, and it settles back to normal. If they continue to expand or exceed the range, then it becomes an action event. The one Mali found was huge, but it either self-corrected or something the TA team did got it back on course. It settled down shortly after they went back."

"Got it. I just thought every bump would be a potential problem."

"Nope. Those action events don't occur often." Jax finished his taco and ordered a second margarita. "Another for you?"

She shook her head. "I have some research to do tonight, and I'd better get to it. Thanks for the company and the invite. Let's do it again soon." She slid out of the chair, kissed her hand, and blew it in his direction, watching his warm smile light up his face. Feeling a little guilty about flirting with him, she sauntered away. Actually, she liked Jax, just not in the way he fantasized.

Brix spent the rest of the evening on the computer. She finally connected Mali's family tree enough to know Adele Morrison was her great-grandmother and previous ancestors had born the moniker of Andover. Yet the coincidence of Andover Morrison being in Glasgow in the 18th century and Andover Harper disappearing at about the same age suggested something entirely different. If Mali could time walk, then the jump to Glasgow was to find her grandfather.

She'd drawn lines all over a blank page as she attempted to correlate the dates with what little she knew, but none of it helped her. She needed to find a way to pin down the date. Maybe Mali decided to stay, and she didn't need rescuing at all. She tossed her stylus down and rose to fetch a cup of tea.

Cup in hand, she went into Mali's room again and strode to the shelf where the two watches rested in a thin layer of dust. *Ha! Who said a space station wouldn't get dusty? Wherever people are, you find dust.*

Picking up the dangly-looking timepiece, she squinted to see if the little gold thread looked real or just a blur of the metal. It still looked like a thin cord and glowed with a pulse. Not a blur, a distinct strand.

What if the timepiece held a way to jump people through time? Maybe Mali had triggered a similar one in the pocket watch. Turning it in her palm, she studied the back and looked for anything to activate it. She didn't see much. A little engraving on it in a language she didn't recognize and a few fancy designs around the edge. The gadget to wind the timepiece sat at the top, a rounded knob. She flipped it over again and studied the front. The thread emerged from the case near the top knob, but she couldn't tell if it wrapped around it. If it did, would just turning it trigger the jump?

A tingle of excitement warmed her at the possibility. Still, Brix set the watch back on the shelf, not eager at this moment to discover if the knob activated it, but she tucked the details in her mind. She reached for the other timepiece, a twentieth-century design, although still a mechanical one. Half-closing her eyes, she peered at it until her vision blurred. Although she detected a goldish glow surrounding it, she didn't notice any threads attached to it. While the light could have been an illusion, she had a hunch it might have a strand concealed in it. She set it down, rubbed her eyes, and picked up her tea, ready for bed. She'd let her subconscious work on the information she'd discovered.

She checked the door lock, something she'd done several times since the previous night. She'd reported the break-in, of course, but nothing seemed to be missing. Station security had advised her to change the lock codes on the door and use a verification key to prevent any further incursions. While she'd done those things immediately, she remained nervous. They didn't provide any other information about the intruder or even tell her if they'd caught the culprit on video. She had no clues as to why anyone went through the apartment. Did it tie in with Mali somehow?

§ § §

Brix hunched over her desk, focused on getting the tour Margaret assigned to her set up. She studied the time unit designated for the Phobos excursion in the 2125 trip, wondering how far back it could actually go. If she volunteered to host the trip, it would give her a bonus at work but also give her access to a TU. Would Margaret go for it? She'd been to Phobos twice before, so she was familiar with Mars' most friendly moon. Comprised of researchers, the travelers wanted a look at the first colony established there. The next group attempted Mars. Her lips quirked into a smile as she thought about Coleman growing up on the latter. No doubt he'd been to Phobos numerous times as he was growing up.

As if summoned by the thought, her tablet beeped, indicating a new message. Once she saw the name, she answered at once. Coleman's face appeared, eyes darting back and forth between his screen and something off to his right.

Barely waiting for her greeting, he said, "I'm sorry to bother you, but I need to talk to you again. When can we meet? I suggest the atrium in the greenhouse. Hardly anyone goes there after hours."

"Um, yeah, I can meet you, but I know a better place." She quickly told him about the second-level study pods and how to get there. They agreed on a meet time, and he broke the connection.

Surprised, she leaned back and wondered what had prompted Coleman to call her. She hadn't expected to hear from him.

As she made her way down to the lower levels, Brix

noticed a girl trailing behind her. A coincidence? Maybe. She looked like a university student, with tights and a loose sweater, bopping along to music in her head. Brix had been like her when she'd gone to school, but something seemed off. The girl had a tablet in her hand, presumably schoolwork work, although she paid little attention to it.

Following her uneasy feeling, Brix walked past the study cubes and continued on to the spa. She turned in and approached one of the automated displays where customers could select whatever services they might like. A whirlpool, a hot sauna, a massage. *Oh, that sounded good.* She paused to read what the service offered, but she kept an eye on her tail's reflection as the girl stopped outside the sliding glass door and glanced her way three times.

Brix pressed a button to buy a mini-massage, a quick session guaranteed to leave her feeling relaxed. As the ticket popped out, the girl moved on down the corridor. Going into the private room, Brix pulled out her tablet and messaged Coleman, warning him not to go to the study rooms and saying she thought someone was tailing her.

He acknowledged, then suggested they go back to his original suggestion. "I think it could be suspicious if anyone is watching our movements," Brix replied. "Do you know the Last Chute?"

"Bar? Of course. Yeah, it should work. Crowded and dark. In about an hour?"

"Deal."

Removing her blouse, Brix stretched out while the automated masseuse performed magic on her back and neck muscles. She relaxed into it and thought about the possible tail. Given what she was doing, it didn't surprise her someone might be following her. She hadn't been secretive about much, but seeing Jax, even under the guise of a social relationship, probably rang warning bells in TIM. The girl tonight likely worked for them and was waiting to see if she met up with someone.

Thirty minutes later, a refreshed-feeling Brix headed out of the spa. She turned toward the lifts, paused, and pulled out a compact to check her hair and make-up. She also used it to look behind for any sign of someone following her. Nothing suspicious she could see, so she stepped into the lift and hit the third-floor button. No one joined her, and she went up alone. She stepped out, looked around, then walked to the right until she came to another bank of lifts. After another glance, she took one of those back down to the bottom floor.

The door opened onto a darkened corridor with small arrow-shaped lights pointing the direction to the Last Chute, a dark, somewhat rowdy bar where spacers liked to hang out. Inside, her eyes flicked from area to area, noting who was there. A couple of rough-looking guys talked to a petite, dark-haired, slant-eyed girl who seemed to enjoy the attention. In another place, four dock-doggers played a game using multiple dice, each slapping the other on the back with every roll. Dozens of space jocks swapped stories and drank more than they should. A typical crowd for this place.

Most importantly, no one paid any attention to her. She slipped up to the bar and ordered a nebula, a drink with dark rum, pineapple, and tonic water that practically glowed in the dark.

While Brix had come down here a few times, she avoided it mainly because it wasn't actually a station bar so much as a haunt for the spacers, who came in on cargo ships and heavy transports. Being a beautiful woman, she took a risk whenever she wandered into the area. Proving the point, a roguish man edged his way beside her and put his hand on her backside. She dropped her nearest hand on his and squeezed his wrist. "Move it off, spaceman."

He backed off a little, squinted at her. "Din'cha come down fer that, little tart?"

"No. I came for this drink. It only looks good in a dive this dark. So, find yourself another treat." She picked up the glass of swirling luminescence and wandered toward the outer rim, where she expected to find a different kind of spacer.

"Over here," a voice called as she started to pass. She slowed to gaze into the dark corner where a man hunched at a small table, his coat collar pulled up, and a cap tipped down, concealing his eyes.

"You talking to me?"

"Yeah, brick house, I am."

He used the code word, but damn... he didn't look like Coleman. She eased into the bench seat next to him, close enough that she nearly sat on him. With so much noise and music around them, the only way they could talk was if they were almost mouth to ear.

"Do you have a plan yet?" he asked.

She shook her head. "Not quite, but I have options. Why?"

"I might be interested." His mouth was so close to her ear she felt his breath against it. A hint of ginger teased her nose, suggesting he was drinking a Martian Mule.

"In what?" She leaned her head against his shoulder, getting closer so they could keep their voices low.

"Going back for her."

She almost bumped his nose as she raised her head in surprise, but he jerked back just in time. "Why would you want to do it?"

"Because it's my fault. It's on my conscience. I can't

Page 91

sleep without nightmares and guilt tugging at me."

Brix studied his face for a few moments, seeing the dark circles under his eyes, the puffiness of the lids. He had the look of a haunted man. Was leaving Mali really the reason, or was there more to it? Would he be useful or a burden? It didn't matter. She didn't have a way yet. "Right now, I don't know how I'll get there, let alone take someone with me."

"If you figure it out, I want in. I don't think my company is doing anything to find her. Besides, there's unfinished business there."

Brix tucked her head again, a shy smile on her lips. "What do you mean?"

He nuzzled his head against hers. "I'll tell you when, or if, we get there. For now, it's my business."

"I'll think on it," Brix said, then slid away from him. She leaned back, letting her obvious attributes drop toward him. A show for anyone watching. "Don't call me. I'll contact you."

Then she sashayed away, her hips rolling with the bluesy music oozing through the bar. She put on a good show and anyone who noticed locked eyes on her as she made a solo exit.

Coleman's interest puts a weird twist in the plan, Brix thought as she mulled over the brief conversation. She hadn't expected he'd want to return to the past, but if the situation ate at his soul, then maybe returning would be a solution. She asked herself if she wanted him along with her or not. He seemed somewhat fragile right now as if his nerves were stretched to the breaking point. He could be either an asset or a real liability if she got a TU. If she resorted to trying the watch, she didn't know if she could take him with her.

As Brix approached her apartment, she heard the familiar whoosh as a door behind her slid open. A neighbor going out late, she assumed, but the hairs rose on the back of her neck. She began a turn to check when an arm hooked around her throat and someone—a man, she was sure—pulled her into his body just as something pricked her neck. Adrenaline shooting through her, she flailed her arms and tried to fight him off. She twisted and kicked with her foot, attempting to escape his grip. Her brain spun as dizziness almost dropped her into a puddle in her assailant's arms. Uncoordinated, she couldn't make her arms and legs move as she directed them. She was losing both her control and her thoughts. She cursed as everything seemed fuzzy and unreal. Then her world blacked out.

CHAPTER 8

Austria 1889

MALI BLINKED INTO THE SUNLIGHT as she stepped onto a green, lush-looking lawn in a village next to a river. The quaint houses and buildings appeared to be about the same vintage as the London they'd just left, but this certainly wasn't that city or the Thames River.

"Well, Gaia's Spit," Mali muttered. "Is this even England?"

Behind her, Doyle answered. "I don't believe so. I can't read the signs."

She turned to look where he stared, and her eyes froze on the white sign with black lettering that looked like it might be German. "I think we're in Germany. I don't know what went wrong this time, Doyle. This was not remotely in my mind."

"How did it happen then?" He did a slow turn to look in all directions, a scowl twisting his face.

She couldn't blame him. Closing her eyes, she focused on the images in her mind that matched the words on the sign to what they meant in English. She hadn't actually studied the language, but she'd looked at the books for the courses, so her perfect memory could call them up. She even had pronunciations, although without hearing them, she couldn't get them exactly right. "I'm sure it's German. The notice says the bridge crossing the Inn River is just ahead."

As they walked toward the heart of the town, Mali tried to translate the business names on the shops they passed—bakery, grocery, hardware–all the various stores that provided for the population's needs. She noticed several had a common word within them, which she surmised was the town's name, *Braunau*. When she realized it, a chill snaked up her spine as flashes of history popped into her mind. Hitler—Adolphus Hitler, the nightmare who started World War II, had been born in *Braunau am Inn*. Not Germany, but Austria. She'd seen Varsi's termination list. In his ideal plan, he wanted to eliminate anyone who created the horrors that unleashed Hell on Earth.

She grabbed Doyle's arm as her head spun with the shock of the implications. "Doyle, I suspect Varsi is somehow hijacking my time jumps."

"What? How on Earth, assuming we are still there, did you come to that conclusion?"

"Because this town is where one of the tyrants he's pursuing was born. I need to find out what year this is." She fell back to the usual routine for functioning in a new location.

Before they'd left her grandfather, he'd given her a few items she could sell or barter for money. She figured they wouldn't need much while they were here, so she pulled out a simple gold ring and looked for a jewelry or pawn shop.

Twenty minutes later, they'd exchanged the ring for cash, more than Mali had expected, and found a small cafe to get rolls and chocolate for breakfast. She picked up a newspaper to read while they ate and located the date, March 23rd, 1889. *Too early for Hitler.* He was born on April 1st of this year. So, why had they come here to this particular time?'

She scanned through the paper more slowly than usual since she had to translate but saw nothing significant in it, not in the world news and not even in this area. "I don't know why we're here. If Varsi brought us, I can't figure out his reason."

Her gaze shifted to the streets, where automobiles crawled along the quaint streets of the town. All ahead of their time, more advanced than they should be, readily available to the common man, and still electric.

"My heavens. I would love to own one of those."

She glanced at Doyle; his eyes trained on the vehicles with wonder lighting his face as his mouth hung open. For him, they represented a promise of the future, not an anomaly. His mouth twitched with a tentative smile.

Leaving the cafe, they strolled along the streets, looking for any reason to be there. Beyond the town limits, lush fields burst with various colors proclaiming spring in the Bavarian region. The breeze from the hills carried the fresh scent of the winter-fed streams. For Mali, the entire world looked enchanting. Life on a planet was amazing compared to being on a dull, steel-gray space station, although she missed the view of the stars from her window.

She looked across the narrow road and noticed a very pregnant woman preparing to cross. The lady glanced both ways, then stepped into the street, just as a roadster spun around the corner on a path to hit her.

"Oh, no!" Mali cried out and dashed toward the woman. Arms extended, she knocked her out of the path moments before the auto almost ran her down.

But Mali wasn't fast enough. The vehicle clipped her hip, spinning her around and tossing her onto the crude road. She rolled away and clambered to her knees in time to see the vehicle speed away.

Doyle arrived moments later, worry lines etched on his face. "Are you all right, Mali?" He bent his knees to get an arm around her to help her up.

"I think so," she gasped. Then felt a shooting pain in her hip and winced. "It bumped me, but it doesn't seem too bad. Help the lady up."

By now, several people, having witnessed the accident, raced toward them. Doyle reached the woman at the same time as another man did.

The newcomer kneeled by her. "Are you hurt, Frau Hitler? I will call for a doctor." He looked at another man and said, "Hermann, bring the doctor. Hurry!"

While Doyle might not have understood the German, Mali did.

She could read the confusion in the woman's face as the shock from the sudden accident left her stunned. She gazed toward the thoroughfare and then at Mali and Doyle as she tried to piece together what had happened. Mali hobbled over as each step on her right leg shot a little pain into her hip. Doyle bent to help lift her to her feet.

"Wait, Doyle. Are you hurt, madam?" Mali asked, afraid the baby might have been damaged in the fall. She hoped her German was adequate.

In hesitant German, the woman replied, her voice shaky and her hands cradling her belly as if to check on her unborn. "No, I think not. Maybe I have bruises, but I am alive, thanks to you."

"And your baby?"

"It seems safe also, but I will go to the doctor, to be certain. How can I thank you?"

Doyle and the other man helped her to her feet, not letting go until they were sure she was steady on her feet.

"Your life and a healthy baby will be thanks enough," Mali answered, rubbing her hip. Bruised, she guessed, but she nothing worse. "Are you certain you're all right, Frau—?"

She waited to see if the woman gave her name. At least she knew why the auto driver wanted to harm her.

"I am Frau Klara Hitler. My thanks again. I will go to my doctor now."

And there it was. Hitler's mother.

Mali kept her composure, and she expressed her hopes the baby would be fine. She watched the woman limp away, her left leg clearly bothering her a little but mostly unharmed from the fall.

Mali took a step down on her right leg, and it nearly folded on her as pain shot into her hip. Doyle grabbed her, sliding an arm around her, then pulling her close to him to support her weight.

"You're hurt. How bad is it?" he asked.

"I don't think it's broken, but my hip feels like a knife is stabbing it."

Mali leaned on his arm and hobbled to a bench in a small park where she could sit and let the pain ease. She called it dumb luck that she hadn't been hurt worse. Although the automobile moved quickly, it wasn't at full speed.

Doyle sat beside her, his brow wrinkling in concern. "Should we try to locate a physician to look at that injury? You could have been killed."

"It doesn't seem to be. Let me rest for a few minutes to see if the pain eases up, and I can put pressure on my leg without my hip hurting too badly. I doubt I'd be able to stand at all if I'd broken it." She hoped that was true. Most likely, a bone bruise or a slight crack, neither of which was treatable here, and only allowing healing time would ease the injury. He was right that she had done something a little rash in trying to push Frau Hitler out of the way, but she wouldn't let whoever drove that vehicle—and she had a good idea—hit a pregnant woman. That wasn't an option.

To Doyle, she explained why the woman she'd saved from possible injury or death was significant. "So, if I'd let that car kill or injure her enough to miscarry her baby, then the result would alter the future again, splitting it off another direction and changing my original timeline once more. Serious consequences might occur before the new line splits off if all the people that Hitler's War affected aren't killed."

Doyle rubbed the back of his neck as he leaned forward. His eyes squinted while he sat in quiet thought. She wasn't sure if he understood her concerns and worries about how the future might change and what it meant to her personally.

After a long silence, he said, "Considering all the evil this Hitler fellow did, I might agree with Varsi's approach to the problem. If he is that evil, then maybe eliminating the threat is better. Let the people live who should have, and possibly the future will improve. Is that not a possibility?"

"Yes, and no," she said. How could she explain the impact additional people might have on the Earth if the science continued as it did, and the atom bomb still got invented and used in a later war? If they stopped one tyrant, it didn't mean another might not rise to fill the gap. No matter how much they might try to prevent it, history had shown that power-hungry people stepped forward too often to guarantee the outcome Varsi was attempting to reverse. "I've heard it said that if one evil person is thwarted, another will rise to take his place."

"Really? Is the world so twisted as all that?"

"You've read the history books, haven't you? Look at all the people who wielded power throughout the centuries. Who tried to expand their holdings at a cost to those who would defend their territories. The list goes on and on."

"One would hope that we would learn from the past and not yield to that kind of weak desire," Doyle answered.

"Maybe. In the 22nd century, after almost destroying the planet we lived on, people finally realized that war and conquest were detrimental to the health of their world. That was World War III. It spurred humanity into space to set up colonies on other planets, none of them so well-suited to humans as Earth."

He dropped his head and sighed. "Sounds like a dismal future for our world. Yet you advocate this man should continue to commit horrible crimes for fear that even more terrible things will happen? You're saying these events have to happen in order for space exploration to occur so that you will be born on a space station. Are you fearful that you will be born on Earth instead?"

She stared at him, swallowing hard. "I'm afraid I won't be born at all. Changes are unpredictable, Doyle. People alive right now in my time might not be after a timeline change."

"But you will be alive in the past, won't you?"

"I don't know. It's an unknown about time change. No one really knows if someone from the future who is in the past when a significant change occurs is eliminated only from the future but will still live in the past. Most experts say no."

Doyle got to his feet and paced around the bench a few times, no doubt trying to wrap his head around a theoretical concept that sounded impossible. "If that were the case, and you were not born in the future, then you might vanish before my eyes, never having existed. Do I understand that correctly?"

She nodded. "Actually, you would never meet me, and all this would not happen."

"I do not see how that could be. You said there are alternate timelines, so isn't there a possibility that you and I might still exist in one of those?"

"I don't know. None of my teachers or experts took alternate timelines into consideration."

He frowned, shook his head, then offered her his hand. "Shall we see if you can walk yet?"

As she rose, Mali put a little weight on her right leg, felt a slight twinge, but nothing like it had been. "I think so. We just can't rush anywhere. But I want to go looking for that vehicle. If Varsi is controlling my time jumps, I want to know how and why."

Doyle continued to support her as they started a slow stroll down the sidewalk, heading in the direction the auto had gone. The more she walked, the better Mali's hip felt. Sore, but not as painful, although she suspected it would be stiff and aching after a night's rest.

Over thirty minutes later, they had covered the entire town center and began branching out into the streets beyond the main road. As they passed a multi-story building on *Salzburger Vorstadt*, Mali nudged Doyle. "That's the house where Hitler will be born."

"Are you positive? It looks like a brewery," he remarked.

"It's actually an apartment building with several places to rent. The brewery is just one tenant. Not much different from London, is it?"

"No, I suppose not. I guess I had expected something more upscale for a future tyrant."

"Many tyrants come from humble beginnings." She

urged him onward. "Lack of wealth tends to spur them on, it seems. I don't know which is worse, those born poor or those born into wealth. The world has seen its share of each."

As they'd strolled, Mali kept an eye out for the vehicle that had struck her. Many of the autos they saw resembled the one which had careened around the corner. They might see a dent or something in the left fender. Had it hit her hard enough to leave a depression?

Then, as they turned a corner, they located not only the auto but Rashid leaning against the side, arms crossed, and watching them approach as if he had been waiting for them. Mali halted, pulling back on Doyle's arm. She expected Rashid to jump before they got to him, but he made no move to do anything of the sort. She resumed walking, approaching him cautiously.

"Killing an innocent woman? Really, Mr. Varsi, that is pretty despicable."

"Ah, Ms. Harper, almost as judgmental as your grandfather, I see. What is the life of one woman whose only achievement was to produce the monster that nearly wiped out an entire race? How can you say it isn't worthwhile to save the lives of all those people he executed?"

"You don't have the right to decide that," she answered. "It was tragic and terrible, but who knows what killing him might alter in the future?"

He shrugged. "Perhaps we can speculate; try to project, but you know that's impossible. Come with me and let me explain my grand plan to you. A plan to ensure that the Earth will not suffer the terrible fate our ancestors created for it. Your grandfather is not a disbeliever, you know. He just doesn't like my method of achieving it."

Mali glared at him, not wanting to hear any of what

he had to say, yet dismayed that her grandfather might have thought it was a good idea. She opened her mouth to tell him no and where he could take his plan when Doyle spoke up.

"I would like to hear your plan. Try to convince us it's a good idea and will work."

"Ah, so. There is a level-headed man," Varsi crowed. "Someone who wants to learn more before he judges. Are you any less than the same kind of person, Ms. Harper?"

She cast an annoyed glare at Doyle, who paid no attention, then motioned to Varsi to lead the way. She would hear him out, but she doubted anything he might say could change her mind.

Varsi led them to a small building a block away, where he opened the door and motioned them inside. They stepped into a den-sized office. Clearly, Varsi had been there longer than they had as he'd pinned up a rough layout of the town onto the wall. On it, he'd noted the apartment building they'd passed where the Hitler family lived. Next to it, another paper showed a timetable where he'd studied Frau Hitler's activities for several days, looking for a repeated pattern in her routine. This much Mali could see with just a brief scan of the place. Varsi knew the lady would cross the street at nearly noon since she did it every day.

"You stalked Frau Hitler," Mali stated, her mouth twisting into a down-turned line as her fingers unconsciously curled into a fist.

"I did reconnaissance, my dear. This is a battle, and I approached it as such. Listen to what I have to say before you reproach my tactics."

"I know enough from my grandfather," she shot back.

"Do you? Don't be so haughty, young woman. You know nothing except what history books tell you. They don't tell the complete story. Sit down and learn." Varsi pointed to a pair of chairs that faced the desk as he turned to address Doyle. "And you as well, young sir. Although you are not familiar with much of what I will say, you may still give me your thoughts on the matter."

Varsi stepped in front of his desk, sat on the edge, and crossed his ankles confidently. "When your grandfather and I conceived this plan, we envisioned a world where the great wars that killed millions of people and created the weapons that ultimately decimated the planet did not occur. We studied the inventions and discoveries that led to pollution, exhaustion of resources, and more war. Then, we narrowed it down to which power sources were cleaner and more sustainable until humanity progressed to the tri-fusion engine that now powers the future. While we realized we couldn't advance technology to that level with the resources available in this era, we chose to advance steam and electricity."

Despite her dislike of Varsi, Mali listened to him with interest, her forehead wrinkling into a frown. Her grandfather hadn't told her much about the plan, glossing over part of it. But so far, it was as he'd stated. "You've accomplished that already. Electric cars are outpacing the introduction of gasoline-powered ones, so why would people trade their clean-running and fairly inexpensive models for a combustion engine?"

"Most people wouldn't," Varsi answered. "But companies that create the power would want to take advantage of the combustion engine. That is why I have been working to guide them to water-driven generators. The more we can achieve with water and wind, the better for the environment."

"So, how does this tie in with attempting to kill a woman and her unborn child?" Mali crossed her arms across her chest, accusation showing in her narrowed eyes.

"Ah, yes, the unforgivable sin you see me intent on doing. Your grandfather and I have argued about this ever since the plan formed. While he is against it in theory, he also sees the reason behind my thinking. In your eyes, it is unnecessary to kill someone before they create a situation that leads to the loss of thousands of people. If the Hitler child is born, he will lead Germany on a path that will do just that. His regime will exterminate men, women, and children because they are not the vision he is selling to the Aryan German population. In our history, he persuaded the people to believe the Jewish people did not deserve to live. He set the country on a quest for world domination of that ideal, thus starting the Second World War.

"Over seventy million people died in that war. Seventy million. Think about it. Those people did not deserve to die. Not one of them. The soldiers, the civilians, the innocent. So, do you still argue that killing a woman carrying the baby who will cause this is unjust?"

Mali gulped down her first objection as she considered his words a little closer. Her eyes rolled to the map at her right, then back toward Doyle. He looked dumbfounded, with his mouth hanging open in disbelief as he leaned forward with his hands between his knees, eyes half-closed.

"I understand the reason for your thoughts, but killing the woman to kill the child is not right. If your solution is to end the life of the Führer, then let him grow up before you do it. Don't take the mother's life; she isn't the guilty party."

Varsi chuckled. "You sound like your grandfather. He didn't like the plan either. But it is quick and efficient, and the mother will not suffer the loss of her child."

"It's barbaric," Mali snapped back. "Why not try to re-educate the boy as he is growing up? Show him it is wrong."

"I am a time traveler, not an immortal. I don't have time to spend trying to insert myself into a future monster's life to convince him not to do something terrible. Even if I could, do you seriously think I could make him believe differently?"

"I don't know, but my grandfather was right when he said you couldn't kill every leader who caused a war. While I regret so many people were lost in the confrontations that plagued the world, I know if all of them had survived, it would significantly alter the future."

"Indeed, it would. They would have more descendants, more people to populate a clean Earth, and travel to the stars in due time. I see a vibrant future where you see disaster. You can't know what that future might look like, but soon, I will take a look to see what happens."

Mali bristled. "You're insane. You could wipe out all of us with this plan. Our future might not even develop to the stars if you screw up too many things in the past. Every single temporal ethics professor stressed that."

He waved a dismissive hand. "Of course, they did, but they don't know. It's only speculation. So far, as you've seen, the changes create an alternate line before any significant change to the original timeline is made. This is a test line, Ms. Harper. Not the main one. I will try the changes here first, monitor them, and then apply them to the main one if they are successful."

Mali couldn't quite believe how Varsi made it sound so reasonable and sane. Experts had debated how specific alterations to the activities along a timeline could have a devastating effect on the future. One key person, who doesn't survive if a time traveler alters his life, could cause a domino effect with unpredictable results. Here Varsi was proposing not one but a multitude of changes that could do it. "You don't know that the result will be the same on the mainline if you apply it to one of the alternate ones. That line is already creating a different future. Events may change on it that will have nothing to do with the original line. Who knows how many changes you've already wrought on the timeline?"

"You could jump ahead to see, Ms. Harper. Isn't that what you're doing now? Why did you come to this particular era? Was it because I said something about it when we met in the past?" Varsi's unnerving gaze held hers without blinking.

He was challenging her? She fumed. "*I* didn't direct us here. You must have done it. How are you doing it?"

"Me? No, I think not. I have nothing to do with your time jumps. I may manipulate time a little, but not to that extent."

"You must be," she stated firmly, her hand sliding to her sore hip. "How else would we end up where you are?"

"Are you telling us you didn't direct the jump here?" Doyle blurted out. He'd listened while they argued, but he hadn't commented until now.

"I did not. I have no way to know when and where you might connect with the time stream."

Mali felt off-balance, at a loss to explain how they'd gotten onto Varsi's trail if he wasn't leaving a path for them to follow. On the one hand, she believed him to a point, but she had no other explanation. She certainly didn't do it on purpose. She'd had no idea where he was.

Varsi straightened and stepped behind his desk. "But back to the point, which is am I doing the horrible act of murder that you seem to think it is, Ms. Harper?"

"Yes, I still believe that because you're taking an innocent life. It's like you're blaming Hitler's mother for giving birth to him." She had a hard time getting past that, despite knowing that Hitler would be responsible for so many deaths. "If you feel you have to stop him, then wait until later when you can take only Hitler."

"Humph, so, you think it would be okay to kill two-year-old Adolph rather than the unborn baby?"

"Not okay, but at least more reasonable."

"And you, Mr. Martin—is it? Do you agree with Ms. Harper?"

Doyle shifted his shoulders uncomfortably and cast his gaze to the floor. "I do not know, to be honest. I can see your point of view, Mr. Varsi, but it seems to be a rather brutal and cowardly way to kill a potential future problem. There must be other alternatives."

"Indeed. I would be open to hearing them," Varsi answered, his words precise. "I doubt that trying to change the child's basic nature would be a viable solution, and I see no scenario where someone could do it alone. Those who wish to be dictators, conquerors, and power-mad rulers have a basic drive to do just that."

"What is it you want?" Mali asked. "You want to control history and rewrite it, but to what end? Aren't you similar to those people you describe?"

"You misunderstand what your grandfather and I set out to do here. We had two goals in mind at the start. One was to prove that the timeline is not destroyed by any incident that alters the flow but adapts by creating a branch off the original one. The other was to change the way the world arrived at our time without creating an almost uninhabitable Earth. Now that you've seen what the planet was like before the twentieth century, can you not understand the desire to have it remain beautiful?"

"Is that your sole purpose?" Mali asked. "Is that

worth bouncing through time and changing the progress to suit your agenda?"

"It is." He paused as his eyes shifted to the right for a moment while his right-hand fingers drummed lightly on the desktop. "The last war on Earth nearly eradicated my family. Those who survived, including my grandparents, barely made it to the Moon colonies. They had nothing left of their lives here. The world's weather had already grown erratic, unpredictable, and devastating. Then the all-out destruction of the war reduced it to rubble, billions of dead, illnesses, and no hope for a life for the few remaining. This is the destruction we wanted to stop. Our people will still move into space and onto other planets, but not as a last desperate act."

"That doesn't sound like an auspicious future," Doyle said in a shaky voice. "All of this happened because of the fuel source?'

"Not just one thing," Mali answered. "Many factors contributed to it. Greed being a big one."

Varsi arched an eyebrow and nodded. "She has that one for truth. People are greedy. Even when they have great wealth, they want more, and they become ruthless. When someone is in a position of power and control, they become a threat to the entire world. In the twenty-first century, one percent of the population held the world's wealth while some were barely getting by, and others were starving. In a world that should have been able to support everyone."

"Don't dismiss over-population either," Mali interrupted. "Too many people on the plant; people breeding recklessly, unable to support their children with food, clothing, and a home, yet they still had more. If you add all those soldiers, who died in the wars, Mr. Varsi, then the numbers will grow even more, and the poverty will increase. The land won't be able to sustain that many people."

"Yes, those are serious concerns, Ms. Harper." He paused, cocked his head. "May I call you Mali?"

She nodded. Why not? He probably would, anyway.

"Many matters will need to be addressed over time," he continued. "I believe China put in population controls in the mid-twentieth century. Limited the number of children a couple could have to one. At one point, someone in the United States suggested a zero-population growth option, only produce replacements. Roughly seventy-five percent of the population in America had no children, but that still amounted to over seven million who had three or more children. You see, I am not ignorant of the statistics. The problem is that some countries did not cut back as much, culture and religion playing a part in the family growth."

"That sounds terrible," Doyle said. "People want to have families, raise children to carry on their bloodlines. I want a family, not just a wife. Children running around the house."

"As do many." Varsi shrugged, looking back at Mali. "You were an only child on the station. Such is the case with the ten percent of couples who live there. Your parents applied to have a child. It's how it's done where people live in limited spaces. You may not know, Mr. Martin, but in the future, people can live a normal lifespan that exceeds one hundred fifty years. Science has slowed the aging process, so you can be quite healthy and youthful for a very long time. So, the government limits children to replacements for those who die. More than that, the process is quite selective. Only those who qualify may reproduce."

Doyle's mouth hung open in shock. "What? How can a society do that?"

"Doyle, you need to understand humanity on the

space stations and colonies are living in confined areas. We must provide oxygen and gardens for their survival," Mali explained.

"This is your future?" he asked. "No wonder you're skittish in this world. You don't know what it is like."

"You heard his words," Varsi said. "He gets it. Our world is unnatural, and even though we are gradually transforming Titan into a world that can be a second Earth, it takes a long time. More years than you or I have. Can I assume you see my point of view, Mr. Martin?"

"I see it to a point, but can you really stop what will happen to the planet in another four hundred years?"

"Not stop it, but slow the destruction caused by humans. Yes, to a degree. We can extend the time we have before it becomes uninhabitable. It can give us the chance to build the colonies before we need them and not have to rush."

Mali rose, pacing the room as she thought. Torn with indecision, she shifted her gaze from Varsi to Doyle. She understood what Varsi and her grandfather were trying to do, but it clashed with everything her professors had taught her. She just didn't see how it could possibly work without creating other problems. It disturbed her that Doyle was getting a glimpse of a bleak future, knowledge that would now color the rest of his life, even though it wouldn't directly affect him unless he chose to change time periods. Her eyes went to the chart where Varsi tracked Frau Hitler, and her stomach roiled with unease. No. No matter what, killing her to kill the monster was not an option she could condone.

"You figure out another way, but don't kill the mother," she stated.

"May I assume, from this, that you will not interfere with my plans again, Mali Harper? If you do, then I will need to neutralize you by whatever means necessary. I do not wish to alienate your grandfather, but I can't let anyone stand in the way of my plan."

Her lips tightened as annoyance built within her. She resented the underlying threat of Varsi's declaration and what he meant by neutralize. It could be anything from locking her up to murdering her. She didn't doubt he was capable of it. He'd already tried once.

She spoke calmly, without anger showing. "For now, I won't intervene. I think I need to speak with Grandfather more before I make any other promises."

His eyes narrowed into a hard look that sent a shiver down Mali's spine. "I will accept that for now. Do not cross me, woman." He waved a hand toward the door, dismissing them.

Mali nodded at Doyle, who had half risen from his chair already, and walked briskly, albeit painfully, to the exit. Doyle trailed a couple of feet behind her, his steps as swift as hers. Once outside, she turned to him, caught his arm, and leaned against him as her hip objected to the pace she'd set out of that shed. His arm shot around her waist to give her more support as he shook his head.

"We need to have a doctor check you out, Mali. That injury might be more serious than you think."

"It might," she agreed, feeling the deep pain in the bone. "But we need to get away from here as quickly as possible."

She led him away from the building, looking for a more secluded spot to attempt another time jump. She needed to get back to Andover to get help. To the right, she noticed a grove of trees that offered a bit of cover and motioned to Doyle. "Over there. They should hide us from any stray eyes in the neighborhood."

With Doyle's help, she hobbled into the thicket, noting that they looked like fruit bushes with some kind of berry growing on them. The foliage went down low enough to offer sufficient cover to hide them for the short time it would take to do the jump.

She pulled out her pocket watch and squinted her eyes, detecting the faint glow of the thread. Andover told her it would bring her back to his home about a month after she'd left. "Hold on to me," she told Doyle, waiting for him to do it before she pulled the screw knob on the top, ready to twist it.

"You there? Hold. What are you doing?" she heard someone yell in German, her mind barely translating it before she heard thrashing through the trees toward them. "You are trespassing. You are intruding..."

Doyle whispered, "Who's that? Are we—"

"About to be in trouble? Yes," she said as Doyle's arm clenched around her waist.

CHAPTER 9

Space Station 2238

BRIX'S HEAD ACHED. EVEN HER eyes throbbed with each heartbeat. She forced them open, confused, as she tried to stare into the inky darkness surrounding her. Where was she? She reached a hand out and felt nothing in front of her. Turning slightly to the side, her hand touched a metal wall, and she ran her fingers along it a little way, exploring the curve. It might be an outer wall of the space station.

She recalled the brief struggle, then the grogginess before she blacked out. Someone had drugged her outside her own apartment and brought her here. Why? She eased back against the wall for support as she sat up. Had she stumbled onto something more important than her missing roommate? Something those in charge didn't want anyone to know about?

So, she'd made a few inquiries, but had she learned something to warrant this treatment? She had every right to be concerned about Mali. Suppose someone wanted her friend removed from the station and *lost* in the past, then any attention directed toward her disappearance might be viewed as a threat. Was contacting Coleman a mistake? Had he told someone about her?

Slowly, she pushed herself up the side and found she could almost stand without her head bumping the ceiling. She edged her way around, estimating the dimensions on each side. Roughly three meters in length by two meters wide and a little over one and a half meters in height.

Movement made her dizzy, a remaining symptom of the drug, she guessed, and her mouth felt dry. No water anywhere in the room. Nothing else. She would definitely see someone soon if they intended to keep her alive. She strained to recall the storage bays configuration and if they had an internal release to the hallway.

She shifted around, reaching for the corridor wall, a straighter line than the curved exterior, and using her fingers, searched along the bottom edge for a release button or emergency lever. When she hit the opposite side, she raised her hands six inches higher and repeated the search. Still finding nothing, she repeated the action. Over and over. By the time she'd reached above her head and found no indication of an internal mechanism, she accepted she had no options and sank back to the floor. She leaned against the wall, head pressed against it in a vain attempt to hear any sounds, and waited for anyone to come.

Most concerning was what they intended to do with her? If they had locked her into a storage vault along the station's outer curve, it meant they must have a use for her. Otherwise, they would have simply spaced her, tossing her out an airlock with the garbage. The only things she knew for certain were she was locked in a finite space with only limited oxygen, no food, and no water. Someone would either be back soon, or she would die. Not a good prospect.

Then what? Where on a space station would give her safety? She needed to get off without being grabbed again. Her options were limited.

Her best chance for escape was surprise. To be right on the opening when it started to move and spring out at whoever came. She braced herself for a confrontation, hoping she might overwhelm them and break free.

The wait seemed like hours while she took shallow breaths and tried to remain calm to stretch out the available air. She dropped her chin forward and closed her eyes, weariness creeping into her with each breath.

I'm going to die here. Why? What did I stumble into?

A movement of the metal jarred her head, catching her by surprise. Her eyes popped open, and she pulled herself into a crouched position to spring out as soon as she had enough clearance. Light seeped into the darkness as the cover started to shift upward. Eye adjusting, she made out the legs and lower torso of someone. Once she had enough room, she made a move, diving into the person who prepared to step under the auto-lift door, not expecting his target to be on top of him. She collided with a solid body and knocked the person down, ready to stomp on him and bolt down the corridor.

As she raised her leg to kick, his hands shot up, grabbed her foot, and twisted her ankle sideways. She fell into the corridor on her side and flipped onto her back. For only a moment, she saw the overhead lights before a man launched himself on top of her, fighting to grab her arms and hold her down.

"Quit struggling," a deep, unfamiliar voice said. "I'm not going to hurt you. My boss wants to talk to you. Says she has a deal for you."

"And you expect me to believe you?" she spat back, not slowing her struggle to get free one bit.

"Look, we're trying to help you. But if you want to be difficult, I can knock you out again."

He leaned down on her body, straddling her to hold her still with his weight. She was unable to wriggle enough under him to break her hands free. Letting her muscles relax, she hoped she would get another opportunity to escape.

When she'd calmed down, he slid back, pulling her arms up with him, which brought her to a kneeling position. As he rose, he shifted her arms over her head. With both wrists locked in a one-handed grip, he slipped a security band out, snapped it over her wrists, and yanked it tight enough to cause her to gasp at the pain.

Guess no one told him to be gentle.

Well, if that wasn't a damn uncomfortable position, Brix didn't know a worse one. Hauling her to her feet, he pointed her down the corridor and shuffled her toward the core before turning her onto a different path, away from the storage bays. She didn't know which level she was on or where they were headed. Nothing was marked here, no indicators of any kind to tell her where she was, and no other people in the passage. They continued down another hundred or so meters, where he opened a security-controlled sliding door and pushed her through it.

Once inside, she halted, planting her feet as she gaped at the electronics within the room. She stood in a control center with a dozen holo-monitors displaying various things from gravity, temperature, velocity, and the Earth. One of them was a tube with a stream of golden threads running through it—not solid cords, but the time stream's transparent carriers. She'd never seen them like this, all gathered together into a clear tube connected to the top and bottom of the floor and, she suspected, through the entire station.

"What is this?" she asked in a raspy voice.

"This is the alternate control center for TIM," someone answered, a familiar woman's voice coming from off to her right. Brix twisted her head, squinting to see who had spoken. The lights came up in the room, and Dianna stepped forward to greet her. "Will you cooperate with us now, or do we need to leave you restrained? I'm sure Gene won't mind strapping you to a chair, but it would be much more pleasant to just behave and listen to what I have to say."

Surprised and curious, she nodded. "You could have sent an invitation."

"Not really. Please sit down." She pointed to a chair at a small conference table and took the one opposite it. "Who are you working for, Ms. Brixton?"

Brix's eyes widened. "You mean my employment? I'm with Time Excursions, but you already know that."

"I mean, for whom are you snooping with this Harper business?"

"No one. I'm doing it for me." She shifted her gaze around to see the other people in the room. Two paid no attention to the scene, keeping their attention on their jobs. At the same time, the other three hovered around with mixed expressions of interest. What the frack was going on here? This woman had contacted her, not the other way around.

"Why are you concerned with Mali Harper's disappearance?"

"She's my roommate and my friend. I'm freeling worried about her! Why shouldn't I be?"

"Oh, for Cavender's sake! You're telling me you actually care about the girl? Wasn't she just an assignment for you?" Diana slapped her hand against the table in annoyance as her eyes narrowed.

"How did you know I was assigned to observe her?"

Brix blurted out, then bit her lip, realizing she'd just admitted it.

"I have many contacts. So, your story is you're concerned about Mali and want to find out what happened to her?"

Brix nodded.

Silence followed.

Brix shifted uneasily in the chair, cleared her throat. "Are you TIM security? Is it such a secret a friend can't wonder what happened to her?"

Dianna flicked her fingers at the other people, a signal. They moved back to their jobs as if they hadn't been part of the interrogation at all. The head lady sat back and studied Brix for several moments.

"Anna Brixton, you have been quite resourceful in learning about what happened, but your contacts aren't enough to give you the entire story. But I will tell you now, and I want you to forget all about Harper. Do you understand?"

Brix wanted to say no; she didn't understand, but she didn't think the woman would appreciate the answer. She nodded her head once.

"Here's all you need to know. They orchestrated this last time jump from the past, not the present. The person doing it wanted Mali Harper to be on the adjustment team, so we ensured it happened.

"Because she needed to be there. She's a catalyst for what is about to come. That is why she was sent back and, ultimately, why she stayed there. Your queries have become awkward, to say the least, but you must stop. Believe me. She is fine in the past and will not be returning here."

"And if I don't believe you?"

"Oh, please, don't go there," Dianna said, exasperation in her voice. "She was only your assignment to observe, Anna Brixton, not to befriend. Your assignment is now terminated."

"I don't understand." Since university, she'd been watching Mali and speculated she was someone significant, but this new information shocked her. They needed her for the past, not the future? It made no sense.

"What's to understand? You did your job, and it's over. Forget about Ms. Harper and get on with your life. Is that clear?"

"Translucent."

"Wonderful. Now, keep out of TIM's business, and you will have a good job with excellent opportunities."

Brix hesitated, thinking about what they were saying and the hidden threat. She ran her tongue over her lower lip. "I understand."

"Good. Gene will escort you back to your apartment. You will report to work as normal tomorrow and go about your business. But know this, we will keep an eye on you." Dianna rose and left through a door behind her. Who *was* this woman? She didn't appear to be the person she'd presented herself to be previously, but was she part of TIM's management?

Gene tapped her shoulder, raised a hand with a pair of dark wraparound glasses. When he put them on her face, she realized they were blackout shades. She wouldn't see the path from this room to her apartment. She rose awkwardly, hands still secured behind her back, and allowed him to grab her right elbow to lead her.

§ § §

Brix stared in the mirror, noting a few new bruises and her bedraggled-looking hair. Discarding her clothing, she stepped into the shower and scrubbed herself clean, washing and rinsing her hair. She rubbed her wrists, where red marks were giving way to light blue bruises from the wrist restraints. After she dried off and dressed in comfortable pajamas, Brix strolled to the kitchen, requested a peanut butter and jelly sandwich, and sat down to eat it. Only then did she realize her hands were trembling. Something seemed totally off about this whole scenario. It didn't make sense to her.

Dianna had passed herself off as the head of the fabrication department when she'd first talked to Brix in the bar. Now she was in charge of TIM? Or was it a shadow TIM, another company working within the main one? She recalled rumors saying someone might be bucking the board of the company. Was this what they meant? Was Dianna secretly working against TIM?

Was Mali really vital to something in the past? Or was this whole scenario a ruse to get her to quit making inquiries into what happened? Who set it up? Who was giving Dianna instructions?

First, Dianna gave her information, then she staged this. Why did she tell her anything at all? Brix would play along for now, but she had many questions and an uneasy feeling about it.

A message light blinked on her tablet. From Coleman, sent almost five hours earlier. That would have been around the time she'd been abducted. She opened it and listened to the voice message. "Brix, please take adequate caution in your endeavors. I am pulling for you, and I mean what I said. Contact me only at this number. I think we are both being tailed."

She sat on the sofa in the small living room and played the message a second time, listening for any signs of distress in his voice. What if he'd set them on her? Did she dare take the chance to get in touch with him again?

She didn't doubt Dianna would take action if she failed to follow instructions. She cleared the message, wiping it from the computer storage, but memorized the number. If anyone checked her tablet, she didn't want any evidence of a call from Brayden Coleman to be found.

Again, she entered Mali's room and picked up the dangly timepiece, fingering the various charms. *Why did it have the thread?* If her hunch was correct, this watch was unique and might carry her away from the space station. Or she could forget all about her friend and just have a good life. Hell of a choice.

Lurking at the back of her mind was another unanswered question, which pursuit of Mali's disappearance might resolve. What actually happened to her father? Another link she shared with Mali; both of them had lost someone in the past.

She took the watch with her when she returned to her own bedroom, tucked it into her work slacks pocket, and crawled into bed.

§ § §

Throwing herself into her job with gusto the following day, Brix worked to set up the tour of Titan for the research team. Decision made; she approached her boss about guiding the group.

Margaret looked up from her tablet, where she studied a report of some sort. "Fieldwork, Brix? You really want to do that?"

"I do. I don't mind getting off the station now and then. It's been a couple of years since I've gone anywhere. I'd like to have a change of scenery." Brix played it off lightly, not wanting to seem too eager but giving the impression she just needed a break.

"Well, I'll see what I can do. You're certainly qualified

to be a guide even though you haven't done it. Maybe we can send you along with one of our experienced ones."

"That would be great if it works out." Brix flashed a cheerful smile and returned to her desk. She popped a pain pill to address the headache and other aches she experienced this morning. Even though she hadn't been seriously injured in the altercation the night before, she'd certainly sustained a few bruises and pulled a couple of muscles. She needed to work out more if she was going to take on trouble.

Still trying to figure out what it had really been about, she did a little research to try to determine which part of the TIM unit she, been in. As the computer displayed the station layout and the level for the agency, she studied the space they had on the floor. If there were any secret corridors, they didn't show, so she looked for a spot where one might exist and still have enough space for a hidden room. While the area TIM occupied was quite large, it didn't hint at how much room the actual time units used. Then a thought occurred to her. The hidden storage she'd been in might not be on the same level.

She pulled up the next level and studied it. Unassigned space sat right above the TIM unit, and a short distance down the corridor, she spotted a bank of storage bays. Bingo! She'd love to sneak in and really look around, but the chances of making it were slim to none. With a full staff and secured entries, access wouldn't be easy. She'd have to think about it. She closed her tablet and resumed working on arrangements for the tour.

After lunch, she got another message from Coleman. He wanted to meet, but her inner voice told her it wouldn't be a wise thing to do unless it turned out to be urgent. Eyes were on her and likely on him as well. She declined, telling him she had something to do and a meeting might be risky. A terse note back said, "twenty-hundred hours, your place."

Well, her apartment wouldn't work. Brix told him no, but got no other response. So, she went to a film after work and get home later, like an hour after Coleman might show up there.

Brix checked her tablet for the time as she came out of the theater after seeing a holo-film of "War of the Worlds," the thirteenth remake of the H.G. Wells book classic. Arguably, not the best version, but not the worst either. At least the effects were high quality, and the holo-projection put her right in the middle of the action. For two hours, she'd forgotten all about her current worries.

Hungry, she stopped at a vegan burger joint on the same level and had a loaded burger with a side of *sank-ji* chips. The roasted vegetable chip tasted similar to potatoes but more manageable and less expensive to grow in the hydroponics lab. Her tablet buzzed as she ate, the third time since she'd missed the meeting with Coleman. She ignored it. What was he doing? Standing outside her door?

Finally heading to her apartment, Brix noted she was over forty minutes late as she approached the door. She let out a held breath upon seeing the passage empty. No sign of Coleman lurking in the corridor. While she hadn't detected anyone following her, she sensed someone had been keeping tabs most of the evening. She unlocked the door, slid it aside, and stepped into the darkened living room. "Lights on," she called, setting her things down. As the space lightened, it revealed a person sitting in the shadowed part of the room. She slid the door shut, locked it, and whirled to face him. "How did you get in here?"

"I know people. A friend helped me out."

"So much for security. What do you want?" She crossed her arms and glared at him.

"I told you, I need to talk with you," Coleman answered, rising to his feet.

"And I told you it wasn't a good idea. I'm being watched."

"So am I."

She took a good look and realized he'd dressed down, wearing old worn jeans, a loose-fitting shirt, and a ball cap on his head. "What's with those clothes?"

"My disguise. With a little prosthetic make-up and a quick stop into a public restroom, I changed my appearance and walked out right under the watcher's nose. If they think you don't know they're there, they get careless. I'm sure by now he's figured out I gave him the slip."

"One problem. My tail is keeping an eye on this room. If you leave, they'll put it together, and we'll both be in trouble. What the hell is going on, Coleman?"

"Call me Bray, please. No need to be so formal. As to what's going on, your guess is as good as mine." He moved to the open dining area and sprawled out in a chair. "I'm still classified as on medical leave. My leg has healed, although my brain may still be suspect. I've recovered enough to go back to work. However, I don't think they want me to do it. I went by the offices today, and I wasn't permitted to enter. My codes, badges, and retina scan are locked out, or so I was told."

"Why would they do that?" Despite her annoyance, Brix wanted to know more.

"Like I said. They don't want me to go back to the past again. Or they suspect I broke their travel rules, and I'm on suspension indefinitely. They haven't terminated my employment yet. I'm still on leave, but I expect it to happen. I'm sure there's an investigation into what happened to Bonde and Harper, but I told them all I know. If anyone can find out any more, it won't be on this station."

Brix pulled a cold Luna Cola from her fridge, handed it to him, and then poured herself a white wine spritzer. She sat across from him at the table. "Something weird is going on. Let me tell you about last night." She began with her abduction, then filled him in on everything.

"That's crazy! Somehow, you and I have to go back and—"

He choked off the words as a double set of knocks on the door sounded. Brix shot a glance at it, then at him, alarm showing in her eyes. "Damn! They can't find you here."

"Where am I supposed to go? We're on a space station," he murmured.

She shook her head. They didn't have any hiding places in the apartment. If it was who she thought and they searched, they would access everything, even Mali's room and closets.

"Who is it?" she called out, flipping on her audio feed to the door.

"I think you know, Ms. Harper. Please open the door." The voice was male and sounded like Gene.

"Hold on. I just showered. I need to put on clothes. Give me a couple of minutes." She could only buy so much time. Bray retreated to a corner of the living room, where he ducked behind the sofa. Did he think it might hide him?

Desperate, she grabbed Mali's watch from her pocket. What the hell? She'd been thinking about doing this anyway. She hurried to Bray's corner and caught his arm looping hers through it. "No time like the present. I hope this works."

"What?" he asked, stepping a little closer to see as she twisted the winding nob on the timepiece. Her indigo eyes narrowed to better view the strand wrapped around it. With another three twists, it glowed, and a hazy light enveloped them, tugging as if invisible hands grabbed their arms and legs.

"What the hell?" Bray sputtered as they started to shift.

CHAPTER 10

Scotland 1738

DISORIENTED, BRIX FELT LIKE SHE was falling, then her feet touched a surface, and her knees folded, pitching her face down to a softer texture than a floor. The scent of chlorophyll filled her nose, and she lifted her head a little to see the fuzziness of green vegetation around her. Grass? Not exactly like the lawns in the biodome, but the same feel. Where was she? She took a minute to regain her composure and began to push up to a half-sitting position. She looked up, then turned her head away from the sun overhead. "Jaysus, that thing is bright."

To her right, she saw Bray climb to his knees, then he pushed up to his feet and looked around. "What the hell?" He turned to her, mouth hanging open. "How did you do this?"

Brix shook her head, her stomach queasy at the unfamiliar environment. *We're on Earth. The watch brought us here. But where exactly?* She pushed to her knees, finding it harder than it should have been. Why did she feel so heavy?

Bray walked to her, slid his arms under hers, and

lifted her up. He still held on as her knees almost folded again. When she felt steadier, she pushed his hands away.

"You'll be all right in a few minutes," he assured her.

Brix gazed around them, her eyes growing wider as she stared into the distance, seeing hills and mountain tops rising to the sky and the blazing light from the sun. Then her eyes dropped to the more immediate surroundings, a dirt-packed lane lined with tall trees and a large—

Her mouth fell open. "My gawd, is that an actual house or a what?"

At the end of the lane, not more than three hundred yards away, sprawled a huge country house.

"Quite a sight for a first-timer, isn't it? I take it you've not been to Earth before?" Bray stepped beside her. "Now, the real question is how did we get here?"

Still staring ahead, Brix held up her left hand with the watch dangling from her fingers. "I believe this is a time teleporter, and a similar one is how Mali disappeared on you. A time thread was wound into it. When I twisted the winder, it activated the thread. Whoever set it up wanted Mali, presumably, to arrive at this location and time."

"As odd as it sounds, and given we're here, it just might be feasible." Bray held out his hand. "May I look at it?"

She handed the timepiece to him and turned her attention back to the house while he studied it. When she glanced back, he was peering at it closely, eyes squinted.

"I don't see it," he said. "Either it goes away after the jump, or I just don't have the eyes for it."

She took it back and gazed through her slitted-eyelids again to see the remnant of the thread hanging loose. "Both, I think. I only see a little bit of it left in the watch, but enough you could have seen it if your eyes were attuned to the threads."

"Well, I could see them in the TU," he said defensively.

"No need to get excited." She slipped the watch between her breasts and dipped her head toward the end of the lane. "Any idea whose house it might be?"

Bray stared at it a few moments. "Actually, I might know. Mali had the idea her grandfather might be alive in Scotland. In fact, she obsessed with the idea Porveerah, the new inventor of the steam automobile, might be this guy. Let's go find out if there's a connection."

"If we're in the eighteenth century, our clothes are going to be tragically out of period," Brix said, brushing a hand down her dark green sheath dress and stacked heels.

"Yes, we are," he replied and put his arm around her waist to steady her as they walked up the long driveway toward the house. Earth's gravity pressing on her body caught her at the door, and his grip tightened.

She hesitated, taking a deep breath and trying to think what to say, but Bray stepped in front and knocked. Brix heard footsteps on the other side, their sharp tap sounding on the floor as someone approached the door. She smoothed a hand through her hair and put on a friendly smile when a man dressed in black clothes, who looked like he came straight out of a history hologram, opened the door.

"May I help you?" he asked in a proper English voice, his eyes sliding from one of them to the other with unspoken disapproval.

"Perhaps," Brix said. "I am looking for a friend of mine, and I believe she may have come here. Her name is

Mali Harper. Have you seen her?"

He lifted an eyebrow at the mention of her name, but otherwise, his expression didn't change. "Who might I say is calling?"

"Brayden Coleman and..." Bray's voice trailed off to let Brix supply her own name.

"Anna Brixton. Is she here?"

"Come this way. I will show you to the library. Please wait there." He opened the door and gestured for them to follow him.

Not much of a talker, Brix thought. After a quick glance at Bray, she followed the man into the house. She gawked at the highly polished wooden floor, woven rugs, and heavy curtains on the thick glass windows. She'd only seen one like it before, and it was on exhibit at the university museum. More wood of a deep brown hue gleamed as a few feet ahead, a staircase rose from the main entrance to the second level. They turned to the right, which led to the library, a comfortable-looking spot with a dozen bookcases, mostly filled with leather-bound books.

The servant motioned to the chairs, then left them. Brix lowered herself slowly into one of the sturdy armchairs, then gazed around and soaked in the sheer luxury of the room. She'd read about country houses like this one, but her imagination hadn't pictured anything quite so magnificent. Out of the window, she could see a slightly distorted but lovely view of the countryside with purple-toned hills marching toward the distant mountains. So, this was ancient Earth. She quite liked it and was eager to see more.

"You've been here before, right?" she asked Bray.

"This house? No."

"Not that, silly. This country, wherever we are."

Bray nodded. "Yeah, I believe we're in Scotland. I've

been in Great Britain a few times on assignments, but to Scotland only once."

"It's so beautiful," Brix said with a sigh. "If Mali chose to stay here, I can understand why."

"It has its attractions," Bray agreed as he turned his eyes to where she stared out the window. "Nothing on our colonial planets resembles this in any way. But Mars has its own beauty, and little by little, we're adding green to the red landscape. Gardens on the moon remind us of this place, just like the garden on the station does. People seem to respond—"

"I believe all humans need to connect with the natural beauty of their homeworld, no matter how long they've been detached from it."

Both of them turned their heads to see the man who'd spoken. He'd entered the room so quietly, they hadn't noticed. Brix recognized him at once from the picture in Mali's room.

A handsome middle-aged man, he offered them a warm smile. "Welcome. I am Andover Harper. My man tells me you are looking for my granddaughter, Mali."

Brix popped to her feet, offering a hand along with her own smile. "I'm Anna Brixton. Most people call me Brix. And this is Brayden Coleman. He was with Mali when she came to Earth." As soon as she said it, she questioned if she should have volunteered the information.

Harper took her hand in a firm shake, then turned to Bray, who had climbed to his feet with less enthusiasm. "Brayden, Mali talked about you and what happened in York. I am sorry for the loss of Ross Bonde. He was a good man and a good adjuster. Welcome to my home. You are in a small village near Glasgow in 1740, in case you're wondering. Since you arrived here, at this precise spot, I presume you used one of the watches Mali owned."

"We did," Brix confirmed, turned away from the men's eyes, and pulled the timepiece out of her bosom. Blushing, she handed it to Harper, who inspected it with interest.

"Which one of your activated it?" he asked.

"I did," Brix admitted raising her hand a little like a school girl answering a quiz.

He looked at her for a few moments with keen interest, those vibrant green eyes digging into hers. "You have an unsuspected talent, I would imagine, Ms. Brixton. Not everyone can activate the time threads. It takes someone with the gift. Did you get it from your father?"

"I guess," she answered. "I didn't know him very well and didn't know he could do it, but I know it wasn't from my mother."

Harper regarded her again for a few moments. "You don't use your father's last name, do you? If I'm not mistaken, your Aldus Stigler's daughter."

A thrill of surprise ran through Brix as she nodded. "I am. I found it best not to use his name."

"Please sit again." He rang a bell, and the butler appeared so quickly Brix thought he must be waiting near the door.

"Robson, bring refreshments. I believe our guests could use a little sustenance."

"Of course, sir." Robson executed a short bow and left to see to the request.

As they settled, Harper took another seat at an angle to them and said, "My condolences to you also. I'm sure you're wondering about your father's fate. If you know who I am, you know he was part of my time adjustment team dispatched to this era and we didn't return. Your father was a good friend. As a team, we had agreed to attempt to change some detrimental events in the past that affected the planet's future. Unfortunately, Aldus took ill after we'd been working on the project for three years and never recovered."

Brix stared at him, silent for a few moments. She'd lost her father the day he'd left the station when she was nine. She and her mother had come to terms with his death long ago, so it took a bit to realize he'd been alive here in the past. "We'd assumed he had died in an accident. We thought the whole team had. But you're telling me all three of you intentionally chose to stay here to try to save the Earth. Do I understand that correctly?"

"For cripes' sake, Harper. Didn't it seem a little arrogant of you to think you could do it? That you had the right to do it?" Bray spoke up, leaning forward and anger blazing in his eyes. "You and Varsick or Varsi—or whatever his name is—brought future technology with you and applied here. Didn't you think it might be hazardous for our future?"

"Of course, we did. But we ran the scenarios and planned the changes carefully," Harper answered calmly. "We have no desire to wipe out space exploration, but we wanted to save our mother planet from the terrible destruction the last war did."

"You're not God," Bray said. "Maybe it took destruction to reduce humanity to manageable levels and to make them realize how easy it is to destroy what is good. Man has always been capable of decimating what keeps them alive, but they never seemed to learn the lesson."

Harper turned a smirk of a smile on him and said, "Perhaps you speak the truth, Mr. Coleman. But did we need to let the Earth suffer so much for the teaching?"

Not wanting this to turn into an argument, Brix spoke up. "Okay, we all agree humanity created a huge disaster, but we came here to find Mali. I'm her roommate on the station. I've been worried she was lost here and needed rescuing."

Harper held up his hand to halt the discussion as Robson brought in a tray of sandwiches and the tea service. They paused as he poured for each of them, then retreated.

"Please help yourselves," Harper said as he sipped his tea. "So far as my granddaughter goes, she is fine. She was with me for a few days a couple of years ago and planned to return to 1798 to take her young man back to his proper time. I believe she was still deciding whether she wanted to stay with him or not."

"She hasn't returned," Brix said flatly. "Even if she came back after fifty years here, I would have known. She would have come to our apartment."

Andover shrugged. "Then she probably stayed with her young man. I haven't seen her since, although I had hoped she would return here to assist me. If you wish to find her, I suggest 1798. I believe you were there before, Bray."

"I was. The last time I saw Mali, she vanished with Doyle Martin. I had no idea what had happened to her. Not until Brix figured it out and we made the jump to here. But there's something more puzzling us."

"And that is?" Harper prompted when Bray didn't elaborate.

Bray turned his eyes toward Brix with the unasked question in them.

Swallowing a sip of tea to wash down a bit of an egg sandwich, Brix wiped her lips and started to recap what had happened. "Information on the problems with Mali's mission was really scarce on the station. In fact, nothing was even reported, not even within TIM. She just didn't come back. I've learned enough about the time missions to know most adjusters return within a day or two of their departure dates. When Mali hadn't returned after several days, I got concerned and tried to find out what happened. I made inquiries with some of my contacts and got some news, but nothing was helpful. Within a couple of days, a woman named Dianna caught up with me. She told me a story about how Mali had been assigned to a time adjuster team because her boss wanted her there."

"Really?" Harper's opened more as he set his teacup down.

"Truth. Then I found Bray, and we talked about what happened on the mission and the last time he'd seen Mali. I'd already begun to suspect the watches were time travel objects; I could detect the thin thread when I looked at one of them. I knew Mali had taken the pocket watch with her. Then, I was abducted on the way back to my apartment last evening and taken to a storage bay. After a bit, a man named Gene took me to another room where I learned my abductor was Dianna, who seemed to have a whole crew working for her in a secret area of TIM. You wouldn't have any idea about that, would you?"

Harper rose and strolled over to a bookcase, pulling out a red leather-bound book. "I do have some insight. Dianna actually works for me. She's the twenty-third-century contact for my team. I did want Mali to be brought to this era, although she slipped up a bit and the team went to the date the anomaly registered."

"You knew the bubble would bring an adjuster team," Bray stated with an undertone of accusation. "Why did you want her to come here? Your actions created a dangerous mission for the team. She could have been killed."

"That was not our intent. As to why, because she is family. I left her to her uncle's care only to learn later he put her in a protective care agency as a homeless waif. I wanted her to come back to be with me."

"But she didn't want to stay," Bray noted.

"No, she had other plans, although she hinted that she might return. Nothing is restricting when you can time walk."

"Time walk?" Bray repeated before Brix could voice it.

"Uh-hmm, it's someone who has the ability to use those time threads to travel independently. No time unit needed. It runs in my family and, I believe, in yours as well, Brix."

"Mine?" she questioned. "But I can't do it."

"You can see the threads; you can do it," Andover stated. "Had you noticed them prior to using the timepiece?"

"Maybe. On a couple of occasions, I saw something. They looked like little golden lines floating in front of my face. I thought they were illusions or light refracting off an object."

"Fair assessment. In some ways, they are. They originate within you, and the image is generated from your mind. It helps you to focus on a destination."

"Wait a minute," Bray interrupted. "How does this correlate with the lines in the TU?"

"The ones in the units and the control center are also manifestations of a sort. Since they were originally linked to it by a computer using Adele Morrison's brainwaves, they were transferred into the computer, which is now the receiver for the activities of the entire timeline. Well, it's way more complex than my simple explanation, but it's the general idea."

He set the journal on the coffee table. "Some of the information is in this. Exactly how the designers made the computer is a mystery only the original team knew. Based on what they did, additional travel units were manufactured, but others are not as robust as the ones made for TIM."

Both Brix and Bray looked confused at the explanation, but they'd seen enough of the timelines to know they existed. Whatever way the geniuses on the team created the original project did it, they had harnessed time.

"So, since I can see the time threads, I can use them. Is that what you're saying?" Brix asked.

"Precisely," Andover replied. "Just as Mali can use them. She didn't start using them until she came here, although I believe she had a few experiences as a child. Did you never touch them when you saw them, Brix?"

"No, I didn't know what they were." She squinted at the dangly watch again. "The thread is almost gone from this one now."

"That's normal. I made fashioned it, linked the thread, and it's good for one use. I can set another one with a different destination. But as you know, with time travel you cannot occupy a space you were in previously. So, each time device is a one-shot trip to a specific location." He poured another cup of tea and reached for a chicken sandwich. "Now, let's talk about you two and what you plan to do here."

"We came to find Mali and make sure she's okay. If she chooses to stay here, I don't blame her," Brix said.

"After the last time I saw her, I wanted to see if she and the guy she literally dragged into this survived," Bray added.

Andover looked them over again and chuckled. "You do realize you broke every rule set by TIM in traveling to the past the way you did and dressed as you are. Luckily, the chatelaine's watch brought you almost to my doorstep and not to the middle of downtown Glasgow as Mali's did. I suspect you don't have any currency for the period or anything much to barter for it. Am I correct?"

"We left in a hurry," Brix said. "Some of Dianna's crew were about to break down my door, and they'd threatened me."

"I'm sure they misunderstood my instructions to try to keep this whole project quiet. Since you were looking for Mali, they must have thought you knew more than you do."

"You mean to tell me everyone in Dianna's group knows you're alive and what you're doing here?" Brix asked. She couldn't believe the whole subterfuge was occurring to hide Harper's actions in the past.

"Of course. They were part of the plan, as was the alternate monitoring center. They covered up earlier time anomalies, but none made as big a splash as the one triggering the adjustment team. It was part of the plan. We're not trying to wreck the future, but to repair it."

He sounded so reasonable Brix could almost buy it. "Isn't it risky?"

"A little, but we won't do anything to the main timeline to cause a disaster. Little changes, see the impact, then try another. That's been our approach. Now about—"

"Wait," Brix interrupted. "You said the main timeline. What do you mean? Isn't there only one?"

Harper's mouth twitched in a brief smile before he suppressed it. "There is one main timeline for our universe. However, a significant change in the past can cause a new timeline to branch off, beginning an alternate universe. Correcting the damage caused by the event will prevent the offshoot, which is what TIM has done with time adjusters. Repair the event and keep the main timeline on course. The switch-up is the team at TIM doesn't understand that the timeline branches.

'You're making this up," Bray said. "If this is true,

TIM has no reason to be doing anything."

Harper arched an eyebrow and nodded his head. "Pretty much the case, Coleman. Unless they want to ensure the timeline remains exactly as it was. But they don't accept this theory of mine. Actually, my grandmother first proposed the alternate universe to the university's board as she did time research. No one believed it. It's not an easy theory to prove, but my team is doing a major experiment here to show it works."

"How?" Bray asked. Brix frowned, as confused as he was.

"Ah, that's a discussion for another time. Now about your money situation?" Andover asked.

"No, we don't have any valid currency," Bray answered. "Any I had left when I returned was turned back in during the debriefing. And I only have a Martian gold ring for bartering."

Brix shook her head. "Nothing here, except for this fake pearl pendant." She fingered the trio of black pearls on a chain around her neck.

"Not worth much at all," Andover agreed. "I will give you cash from this century to carry you through about two weeks. You can try to find Mali during, assure yourselves she is fine, and return, with or without her, to your future. However, if you decide to stay in the past, you'll be on your own unless you choose to return here and assist me. I'll set up two time devices for you. One, the chatelaine watch I used before, will bring you back to me at a different date in my future. The other, a pendant watch, will take you back to the station. Or you can try time walking yourself, Brix."

"I'm not certain about that. How do I manage it?"

"You need to practice by visualizing the threads. You won't have many as you've only deviated once. Each of them represents a specific line you're on and each bump on it is a significant event in your life. Using these, you can estimate the time you wish to return to, then call it in to your mind and touch the line mentally. Sometimes, using a finger gives it a more solid feeling, although it is the same. If you're successful, you move through time as you did to come here. The longest line–it will be easy to spot—is the one that brought you here" He paused and directed his attention to Brayden. "By maintaining contact with her, holding her hand, or gripping her shoulder, you'll move with her also, Bray."

"I'd try a short jump if I were you," Andover added. "Maybe try to go to London on August 30th, 1798, to try to find Mali. You know where she might be, don't you, Bray?"

"Yeah, I have a few ideas where we might find her."

"Good, let's see if we can get you some suitable clothing for the latter part of this century. Judging from what Doyle arrived here wearing, it had changed a bit from history. I may not be able to get you the long trousers, Bray, but we'll see what we can do."

As the morning drifted to afternoon, Brix practiced trying to see the time threads and tried on dresses Andover had delivered from a shop in Glasgow. Readymade wasn't common, so all the items were used and repaired garments. A green gown caught her fancy as she tried it on. Maybe it would suffice if she didn't wear the wired undergarment making it stick out to the sides. Left to just hang, it was a little uneven but more natural-looking. With hair long enough to curl or pin into a bun, she looked like she could be from the era. Shoes were another issue, but those came from the town, and she found a pair of flats to her liking.

By the time she made her way downstairs in the period clothing, she looked like a lady of the era. Bray wore pants reaching slightly below the knee and leggings under those, along with buckled shoes and a sea-blue waistcoat. Long hair or a powdered wig was appropriate for the present, but for their travel era, his hair would be fine, or so Harper assured them.

Andover waited for them in the library, promised goods on the coffee table—the travel objects, a bundle of notes, and a small pouch of coins. Enough to give them leeway to find Mali. "Are you ready to go?" he asked as he gave Brix an approving look.

"Yes. But I don't think I can make the jump. The lines are too muddled for me to pick out a specific date or place." Brix shrugged her shoulders. "Is there any way you can send us there?"

"I suppose it makes sense when you haven't been there even once," he agreed. "Let's see what I can do. Where, exactly, did you arrive in London when you came in the TU, Coleman?"

"A clearing in some woods south of Kensington. We got a lift into town from a farmer and stayed at an inn called the Rusty Plough. Market Street was near, a couple of streets over." Bray closed his eyes, trying to picture exactly where they'd been.

"Okay. I have a pretty good idea. I've traveled to London a few times, so I think I can get you close. Give me a few minutes, and I can set up another one-use artifact."

He went to his office while Brix and Coleman waited. She studied the pair of time objects. Her original chatelaine watch looked precisely the same as it had in Mali's room, with the thread barely visible in the mechanism. The other, a simple key lock, looked more straightforward with the line connected to the key. A simple turn would activate it.

Harper returned about twenty minutes later with a

perpetual mechanical calendar in his hand. Brix could see the thread woven through the year, month, and date wheels, which were set to their target date. Harper held it up to show them. "My invention. But it will do the trick. Now, hold on to it, Brix. Don't let go until you feel solid ground under your feet. You just pull the end of the thread to activate."

"But, isn't it an illusion?" she asked.

"The thread is and isn't an illusion. It's a manifestation. I can grab the thread I need and use it as if it is a solid one. It twists and bends as I require it to do and links to trigger. When you tug it, even if you don't feel it, the thread will activate."

The explanation sounded more like magic or sorcery to Brix, but then time travel as a whole did. Holding the calendar in her left hand, she nodded to Coleman, who locked his arm through her elbow. She felt nervous even though they'd done this once before, but it was all so strange.

Brix focused on the thread, reached to pull it as her lips twitched, and an off-balance sensation hit her again. She felt Bray pull her arm tighter and the world around her shifted.

CHAPTER 11

Glasgow Scotland - 1738

WHEN THE VERTIGO OF TIME TRAVEL dissipated, Mali gazed around her. They stood in the garden at Andover Harper's residence in Glasgow while a light rain fell. The plants looked mostly dead, although she could see little nubs on the roses and a hint of green peeking through the dirt. She couldn't tell if the twilight haze came from the cloud cover or if the sun was setting.

"Is this right, Doyle? The garden looks like it's already died."

Doyle pulled his coat closer around him, raising the collar against the rain. "I'd say at least three to four months have passed from when we were last here. Was it only supposed to be a month?"

"That's what Grandfather said. Let's get inside." With a brief glance at the watch, Mali stuck it in her bag. Had Andover set it incorrectly? She turned and hobbled the distance to the back entrance, pulling herself up on the steps and knocking. As she leaned against the door frame to ease the pain, Mali rubbed at her arms and waited for someone to respond. She glanced up at the overcast sky. It suggested more wet weather soon. She knocked again. *Where was Robson?*

"I'm not getting an answer," she said as Doyle came up.

He took a peek through the back windows. "I don't see any sign of activity in the kitchen. Perhaps no one is home. Should we search for a key?"

"Well, we can't just stand out here. The rain is going to get more intense. Where should we begin?" She gazed around, wondering where the object might be.

"I suppose you had no need to hide keys on the station, did you?" He stepped into the side garden where a few shrubs hid the base of the house and looked for anything that could hide one inconspicuously. Nothing there at first, then he noticed a broken teapot. The spout had snapped off, but the pot was fine. He picked it up, shook it, and smirked at the sound of something rattling from side to side. Opening it, he dumped the key into his hand. "I found it."

He returned to the back stoop and opened the door, shoving it aside for Mali, then followed her and called out, "Hello. Is anyone home? Mr. Harper?"

No answer. Mali frowned as her eyes darted around. She'd expected to find Robson here, at least. "Maybe they're shopping in Glasgow," she murmured.

"That is a possibility. I'll put the water on for tea, then I'll see if there is anything to eat. You settle on the sofa and get the weight off your hip."

"I expected someone to be here." Her grandfather had two servants who took care of the cleaning and cooking while his butler handled serving the food and running the household. So, where were they?

She sank into the sofa, then pressed her fingers against her sore hip. A little hiss of pain slipped out of her lips, but it didn't feel like anything more than a bruise. A hot bath would help if they could manage the water. That's where the servants would come in handy. She noticed a newspaper on the end table and reached for it. Her heart skipped a beat. March 3rd, 1738. This was way more than a month after they'd leftover, over three years. Had her grandfather made a mistake when he'd placed the thread in the pocket watch? *Oh Spit! Now I have to tell Doyle another jump went wrong.*

He brought tea a short time later, along with a few biscuits. "Not a lot of food in the larder," he informed her, "but we do have some bread, cheese, and jam besides two jars of biscuits. They are a bit stale."

She sipped a little of the tea before she told him the bad news. "I don't know when Andover might be back," she added.

"He might have moved forward in time," Doyle said, taking it more calmly than she expected. "Or he may return in the next few days. It's clear this time travel thing is not exact."

"I'm sorry, Doyle. I honestly want to get you back home soon. As I said, the good news is when we do, you won't have missed more than a day or two."

She leaned back, shifting her hip to relieve the pressure on it, and sighed. "Can we talk about what happened in Austria?"

"Of course," he answered. "It was eye opening for me, I must say. How is your hip?"

"Just bruised, I'm sure. I'm not in much pain unless I press against it, so it should be fine in a couple of days, although I may limp a bit. What I'm concerned about is your impression of what Varsi was talking about. Do you think it's wise to attempt to reverse everything, leading to the disaster of the final war?"

"To be honest, I don't know what to make of it. It sounds unreasonable for people to kill so many for any reason. Wars are terrible, but unless you're defending your country from invaders, I see no reason to fight. It has always been about protection or a king or emperor, who wants more land. What was the last war about?"

"Power, money, control. Megalomaniacs trying to seize as much as they could from others. It was ugly. People counted for nothing in the war. In the end, the fallout from the weapons destroyed most of the land. Humanity had already set the world on a path of desolation. Too many things affected the climate and created erratic weather, big storms, and lack of rain in key growing regions."

"It sounds terrible. Given what you've said, I might side with Varsi. Prevent as much of the war as you can. But I also believe you need to control the population so you do not overtax the Earth. Why is it so hard for people to see?"

"Weren't you the guy who said you want to have children?"

"I did. And I do. But in the era I am in, it's perfectly all right. We need more people now. But having too many when the world is strained to feed them makes no sense." He shrugged and took a bite of a biscuit. He frowned, then dipped it in his tea. "Definitely stale."

"Too bad everyone can't see as clearly as you do," she replied. Mali knew logic and truth didn't always sway people when emotions were involved.

Hadn't she just proven that? She'd stopped Varsi from killing someone because she emotionally didn't accept it was proper. But his logic was sound. Two deaths to prevent thousands. On the other hand, what was to stop someone else from rising in Hitler's place? If a revolution was coming, would it happen with a different leader? Would the next one be even worse? She couldn't say, didn't know. History books helped with clarity in the past sometimes, but not in the present.

"Do you think your grandfather would mind us spending a day or two here for you to heal?"

"No, of course not. I only wish he were here. I need to talk to him."

"Possibly, he will return soon. Let's get some sleep. When you put it all together, we've had quite a long day. I'll clean up the dishes and meet you upstairs, unless you need help to get up there."

She sat up, feeling stiffer than before. "I may. I'll wait until you're done."

In the end, he had to help her up the stairs to the bedroom—the same one she'd used when she was here before. It looked the same, nothing to indicate the place wasn't in regular use, except no one was there. She thought it odd, but not too alarming. Her grandfather was a time walker, after all.

§ § §

The next morning, Mali struggled down the stairs, her whole body aching after it had time to rest. Before her hip demanded all her attention, but now sore muscles and other bruises had shown up.

She'd taken time to examine herself before she dressed and confirmed the injury as just a banged-up hip, as were the other half-dozen bruises on the same side where her shoulder and arms had hit the road with half the weight of Frau Hitler on her as well. For a moment, she wondered if the woman or the baby had been injured in the fall, but their lives were in the future now. Sadly, time travel did nothing for healing.

In the kitchen, she found Doyle up and preparing a tray with tea and biscuits. If nothing else, they had those to fill their hungry stomachs. If they were going to stay a few days here, they would have to get food. Her grandfather had an icebox of sorts to keep food cold for a short time, but nothing for long storage.

Doyle shot a quick smile her way as he poured boiling water into the teapot. "Did you sleep well?"

"Like a log, but I'm quite stiff this morning." She pointed at the small table with two chairs in the kitchen. "Let's eat here. It has a pleasant view out the back." Without waiting for an answer, she settled in the nearest chair.

Doyle set the tray down, then took the other seat. "PerhapsI can get enough water heated for you to have a hot soak. It might help the soreness."

She glanced at the vessel he'd boiled water in. "I suspect it would take many trips with that pot. Somehow, the servants managed enough hot water in the tub to provide a soothing warmth, but they had to have an alternate heating source and much larger containers."

"I am surprised your grandfather hasn't set up an indoor system to fill the bathtubs directly. Even though they are not common in this era, I believe he knew how to do it." Doyle poured the tea and added a bit of sugar. He popped a biscuit into his mouth, then washed it down. "I'm starving this morning."

"Me, too," she said and followed his example, blowing a bit on the hot liquid before pressing her lips to the cup's edge. "We'll need to find more food if we're staying here."

"Do we have much choice? Either we wait for Harper to return or we attempt another jump. Is there any limit on how often you can do one?"

"I don't think so. But it is a little draining each time I do it. And I'm worried each jump is creating another branch on my timeline. I need to figure out why I haven't been able to connect with your time and the jumps seem to follow Varsi, even though he claims he has nothing to do with it. Is something or someone else interfering with my jumps and how?"

Doyle gazed at her for a few moments as he seemed to weight his words. "Is it possible you are connected with him on a subconscious level? I mean, could he be projecting his thoughts or plans to you?"

"No. Not likely," she answered. "Why would I be? I only met the man for the short time we were at his place. If he could send thoughts to me, why would he?"

Shrugging, Doyle answered, "Well, apart from trying to run you over, he seemed to want to talk with you and attempt to convince you to his side."

"I don't know about that. It seems like a long shot. Still, if my grandfather didn't make an error on the thread he looped in my watch, then something changed this jump also, bringing us here at a different time. If that's the case, then possibly there's something here we need to discover." Her eyes grew brighter at the thought, although she was still confused as to how it could be happening. Was this all in her subconscious? Had she picked up enough clues from the exchanges between Varsi and Andover to alter the jumps?

"Where do we begin looking?" Doyle queried. "Do we check the house? Perhaps Harper left some indication of where he was going or when he would return."

"Good idea. Let's go to his office. If he made travel plans, he might have left some notes." With renewed energy, she finished the last biscuit, washed it down, then used the table edge to lever herself to her feet. Maybe her grandfather had running water in his bathroom, and she could use his tub for a therapeutic soak.

Doyle came to her side to offer support as they walked to the office at the house's front left corner. She hadn't been in this room before, but she'd seen Andover come out of it. Now she stepped through the entry and gazed around a plain-looking but tidy space with a single bookcase, a file cabinet, and a large desk positioned to face the window. Behind it, a comfortable padded chair sat slightly askew where he'd last risen from it.

Mali detected a scent of leather, stale flowers from the vase of dead roses on top of the cabinet, and just a hint of something she couldn't identify. She limped to the seat and lowered herself down, relaxing into the cushion.

"It's a pleasant room," Doyle commented. "But there are not many places to search for information, are there?"

"Nope. I'll take the desk and you can start in on the file cabinet."

He took a couple of steps toward the cabinet before he paused. "Mali, what exactly are we looking for?"

"I have no idea. Just look for where he could have gone or who he's had business dealings with. Any clue to where he is now or when he might be back." Mali pulled out a drawer to begin her own search.

A calendar sat on the top of a short stack of papers, and she picked it up. Handmade, it amounted to a clipped together set of fourteen pages with the days marked in boxes. Andover had scribbled notes in the squares. She stared at them, uncertain she could make out his shorthand.

Some of it looked like nothing more than squiggles, while other entries were initials and times, possibly for meetings. He'd penned a note to meet with James Watt on February 13th, followed by the number 39, which seemed to suggest the year. Were these dates he'd made jumps to another time or were they reminders of future events? Could he have scheduled an appointment so far into the future? Maybe he was there now.

The question was, why would he do it? He'd already

patented a much more advanced steam engine design, so what business would he have with Watt unless he had come up with something else her grandfather might want?

Mali pulled out her tablet, noting the power was low again. Frowning, she berated herself for not turning it off to conserve the energy. She glanced out the window and frowned at the dark clouds filling the sky. The mini-computer needed to charge today if the sun was out long enough to do it. She opened a notepad in it and began keying in the entries with dates. Another item showed a note reading LGH-pat, which she puzzled over, but it sounded like Andover had another invention to patent. Wrinkles creased her forehead as she pondered, finally coming up with the London Guild Hall. The date on the entry was May 11, 1778.

In her mind, she recalled the inventions and searched for one around the date. But her grandfather was rewriting history, meaning it might be an invention from later on he moved forward ten or twenty years.

She closed the calendar, then progressed to the papers under it, finding a few drawings of various things, including automobile designs and machine parts. She pulled out an inked drawing of a large building with the name lettered on the side reading Calliope Steam Automobiles, with the word steam crossed out. Was it his original plan for his car production business?

She noticed the planned opening date of March 23rd, 1768. Almost a year after her adjuster team had destroyed the workshop there. Behind it was the design for the initial vehicle to be built, the elegant-looking Road Tamer roadster, similar to the one she and Doyle had driven to Cornwall.

"I think this could be it, Doyle. Grandfather set the grand opening date of his motor company on this calendar, like a planned timeline to production. Maybe he's moved forward to be there at the event."

Doyle turned from the file cabinet where he'd stacked five folders on top. "When?"

"March of Seventeen-sixty-eight."

"Wouldn't he have needed to oversee the building or conversion?" Doyle asked as he peered over her shoulder. "Nice design."

She paused to reason out the possibilities. They'd been here with him for about a week, then left for three days, but they'd returned to a different date. If he had moved to 1768, then he would have been living in the future at the point his company would open. She had no idea when he exited this one.

She realized something else. "What if this calendar isn't just for this year but for the overall plan for the eighteenth century? Does he have others covering the next two or three centuries?"

"Is it possible?" Doyle asked. "My heavens, how much can he impact in one lifetime?"

"When you can time travel, quite a bit. And his body is from the 23rd century, so he, like me and everyone else, has an extended life span, up to a century-and-a-half old."

"Incredible," Doyle murmured, looking her up and down with narrowed eyes, no doubt wondering if she was already a much older woman than he'd surmised.

"Nope," she said.

"No, what?"

"I'm twenty-four."

"Ah, I see." He cleared his throat like something had stuck in it. "So, do you think this is the best possibility of where he is?"

"I do. Can I get us there? That is an entirely different question. I can certainly make the attempt, but let's give it a—"

"Ho, there. What are you doing here?" The male voice was familiar and carried the authority only a major-domo could wield.

She turned to face the butler and smiled. "Hello, Robson. Doyle and I arrived here last night expecting to find my grandfather. We were just—"

"Snooping through his things like common thieves." the butler's mouth crooked down in disgust as he put his hat on a rack outside the office.

"No, we're trying to figure out where he went, so we can go meet him," Mali replied a touch haughtily. She resented being addressed as a thief, although she was being sneaky. "Is he returning soon?"

Robson lifted an eyebrow. "That I don't know. If he is, he will send word for me to get the house ready. I have not received any such missive, but I am making my weekly check of the premises. I spotted you through the window. Now kindly put all the papers back where you found them. I shall inform your grandfather of your actions."

"We meant no harm," Doyle interjected, stepping quickly to the file cabinet to replace the folders while Mali slipped the documents in the top drawer.

"Perhaps not, but it is a violation of trust, don't you agree?"

"I sup—"

Before Doyle got another word out, Mali cut in, "No, I don't. I came here using the watch he'd given me, and I expected to find him. But it appears to have gotten the date wrong. I merely wanted to see if we could figure out where he'd gone and catch up with him there. As his only heir, I might fear something happened to him."

Robson raised both eyebrows at her impertinence, then chuckled, "You're his relative, for certain. Same sharp tongue."

A remark from the butler piqued her curiosity. "You said my grandfather would have sent word if he was returning. How?"

"Why, he sends me a note, of course."

Mali's brow wrinkled. "Again, I ask how? How can he send a note from the future?"

"That is his business. I presume he has a messenger deliver them." He slipped off his coat and stepped into the hall to hang it on the rack, then came back and asked, "Since you are here, is there anything I can fetch for you? Tea, perhaps."

"Well, the kitchen seems a bit short on food," Mali admitted. "And we've been eating biscuits, so we're getting quite hungry."

"Of course. I'll bring you tea and sandwiches for now. But I think I can manage a proper dinner for you later, if you'll permit me."

Mali nodded her approval. She wouldn't say Robson had forgiven her, but he seemed to be bent on making sure nothing like starvation happened.

As he stood at the door, his face a mask of authority, she and Doyle dutifully left Harper's office. She bet with herself Robson would lock it after they left. In retrospect, it surprised her it hadn't been locked when her grandfather had left. Robson noticed her favoring her hip as she walked past him.

"Are you injured, Miss Harper?"

"Just a few bruises. I was hoping to soak in a warm tub later. Is there a way to get hot water into the bath?"

"Yes, of course. I will take care of it after I make your tea. Please make yourselves comfortable."

Settling on the sofa in the main room, she and Doyle waited as Robson went to the kitchen, then Doyle said, "He is an odd one, isn't he?"

"I suppose working for my grandfather has made him more... flexible than your standard butler." She smiled as she considered the man accepted he worked for a time traveler and believed it. Now, he dealt with her bouncing through time with a friend along. "I wonder if he's ever taken Robson on a time hop with him."

"He seems to have adapted well," Doyle said. "Better than I have, at any rate. It still feels like I am in some bizarre fantasy."

"It's how I felt when I first jumped. I thought it was a dream. Even when my team and I arrived here, I couldn't quite believe I was standing on the planet in the past. So much is different for me, but I don't regret being part of the team. Except for Bonde's death. I never anticipated it."

"What about now? If Varsi is willing to kill to change the future, is it something you would consider doing if you thought the act justified?"

As she turned her head to Doyle, she caught the serious expression in his eyes. "I don't know, Doyle. Theory is one thing—convincing yourself it is warranted—but the actual act is another issue altogether. It's one thing if your life is directly threatened, but quite another when it is so abstract as killing someone who appears innocent, but may turn out to be an extremely bad person. Taking a life is against everything I was raised with. Even though I had martial arts training, it wasn't with the intent of ending someone's life but as protection should I need it."

Doyle's look softened. "Is it dangerous on the space station?"

A brief laugh escaped. "Not exactly, but there are always those who attempt to get a bit too friendly or to relieve you of some credits. So, a defensive move or two is a good deterrent."

"In some ways, I would love to see this station in the cosmos where you lived, but I doubt it would be a wise idea. I could never live any place where I couldn't go outside and enjoy the beauty of world."

"Well, having seen what this Earth looks like, I can understand. London is sometimes stinky, smoky, and damp, but the gardens are beautiful, and the countryside is magnificent. I could explore this place forever. It's why I feel such a conflict with my mission of stopping the changes yet wanting to see the Earth's beauty saved."

"Is the future really so bad?"

She nodded. "From the images I have seen of future Earth, I'd have to say yes. The destruction was terrible, but even more was the desolation. Beautiful places now are wastelands in the future. Excessive use of carbon-based resources greatly impacted the planet. It changed too much for most of the Earth to survive the change. People, animals, insects—they were all affected by it. Only small numbers of them survived. It exterminated whole species.

"Some were saved when humanity made a rushed effort to get to colonies in space. The first were the Moon outposts, but people lived under domes. They started small and added a dozen more modules to grow the colony, and they all interconnected. Then they built the second and third ones, growing them the same way. But life on the Moon is harsh."

"And how is life in the space station?" Doyle shifted his position and dropped his hand on top of hers, squeezing it gently.

"Better than the Moon. It's clean, the air is filtered, and the temperature is controlled. We have a good supply of food, and some shipments come from both the Moon and Mars colonies. Like the Moon, Mars is under giant domes, except they are attempting to transform Mars into a habitable planet, which means one with a breathable atmosphere."

"It differs greatly from living on this planet, doesn't it?"

"Uh, yeah, it is. Worlds different."

He lifted his hand to her face, caressing her cheek and turning her head to face him. "Then why don't you want to stay here?"

A hint of moisture touched the edges of her eyelids as she saw the desire in his eyes; the hope she would remain. "Strange as it might sound, I would miss things about the station. The music, the clubs, the lifestyle I've known all my life. It's completely different from this era. At the same time, this world is much more straightforward, I guess you could say. Not as duplicitous."

Doyle laughed. "I wouldn't count on that. We have our fair share of shysters and crooked politicians, not to mention threats of violence now and then. Is there ever a period when the Earth is at peace?"

She breathed a heavy sigh. "Not for long. Sometimes I think humans are not a peaceful race. Someone is always wanting more or what someone else—"

Robson interrupted to call them to the dining room for tea. Doyle rose, offered his hand to assist her, and they followed the butler. A beautiful setting of tea, sandwiches, and cakes awaited them. She didn't know where he found all the ingredients unless he had a secret stash or raided the neighbors, but she was grateful for actual food. "Thank you, Robson," she said with sincerity. "You have truly saved the day."

After she polished off the last of her lunch, Robson showed her to a downstairs bathroom where a claw-footed tub bore hot-and-cold water fixtures. Robson explained they connected to a small wood-heated boiler supplying the downstairs of the house. She almost squealed in delight, but restrained it to a small squeak. She knew her grandfather must have figured out a hot water system.

Alone, she stripped off her clothes and eased her aching body into the soothing heat, sighing as she let her muscles relax. She slid in up to her neck and rubbed gently at the bruises, paying particular attention to her hip. It looked nasty, a large dark purple discoloration, but the heat felt divine on it. She closed her eyes, her mind sorting out the threads issue, and drifted off for a bit until the cooling water woke her.

Dressed and refreshed again with her aches lessened, Mali joined Doyle in the parlor, offering a pleasantly content smile.

"You look better," he said. "Perhaps I should take a bath as well. I could use a lift."

"The water is cooling a bit, but maybe Robson could add enough to warm it. But, I think I can find the right thread to take us to York for the grand opening of Calliope Steam Automobiles."

"You think?"

She bobbed her head. "While I was relaxing, I visualized the location and the thread to take us there."

"May I reserve judgment until we actually arrive on the proper date?" He attempted to sound dubious, but the humor broke through and his blue eyes twinkled.

She didn't think he was taking her seriously. But no matter, she felt sure of it.

CHAPTER 12

York 1768

As Mali stared at the outer wall surrounding York, she almost bounced with joy. "At least, it's the right city, Doyle."

A short distance away, an outside marketplace offered goods and food. She caught Doyle's arm and tugged him forward. "Now, if the year is correct, we should be able to figure out where my grandfather's company is located."

Taking a more direct approach than the last time she'd been there, she walked up to a man selling pies from his market stall and asked for two of the meat pastries. As he wrapped them in paper, she asked, "Would you know where I might find the Calliope Steam Company? I understand it is somewhere close to Monk Gate."

He thought about her question for a bit, scrunching his forehead, before he said, "Methinks 'tis closer to Bar Gate, miss. You can walk around the outside, but faster through the city center and go from there."

She passed payment to the vendor, tucked the goods into the drawstring bag at her waist for later, and returned to Doyle. "He says it's near Bar Gate. So, do we cut through town or walk around?"

"I've been here a few times, so go through."

They crossed the bridge into the city, and Mali recognized the inn where they'd stayed before and knew the streets leading to the center of the town. She hoped the manufacturing plant wasn't near the office they'd blown up. She didn't need to relive that moment. For her, it was only a couple of weeks in the past, not years.

For a moment, she wondered if her grandfather was staying at the house he owned here in town under the name Porveerah. But he'd let it out to renters when she'd been here last, so probably not. Soon, they approached the city center and spotted the turn to take them to Bar Gate. Several entrances crossed over the river as it wound through the medieval city. Bar Gate entered from the northwest, she recalled. A defensive fortification, each entry had one or more stone towers with guard stations and a portcullis to block out enemies.

Within a short time, they arrived at the gate and crossed the river to outside the walls, where more merchants had stalls or tents. More significantly, larger buildings, such as the ironsmiths and welders, filled bigger spaces outside the town walls. Spots to build within the walls were scarce, so she expected to find Calliope in this area.

A few minutes later, she spotted a factory-sized building to the left, away from the walls. Made of stone and mortar, it loomed over the surrounding buildings. She looked for a sign or something to indicate it was her grandfather's business.

As they came to the wooden door of the front entrance, she saw the hand-lettered sign reading Calliope Steam Automobiles and Radiators—Owner: Andover Morrison, Esq. "This is it," she told Doyle. "Let's go in."

He followed her lead, looking somewhat less enthusiastic about it. He kept back, letting her do the talking. Mali sensed a certain reluctance on his part, but she couldn't pinpoint the reason.

Inside, the front of the building looked like any office with a well-dressed young man installed as the receptionist. A ledger book sat on the desk, although he currently wrote on a sheet of parchment. His head popped up as they entered, dark eyes flicking from Mali to Doyle. "Good afternoon. May I help you with something?"

"Is Mr. Morrison in?" Mali asked.

"May I tell him who is calling?" the man asked.

"Yes. Tell him Miss Mali Harper and Mister Doyle Martin are here to see him. He will know who we are."

"Please be seated," the receptionist said as he stood up from the desk and motioned to a bank of four wooden chairs on the right wall.

As they sat, he disappeared through another door on the left. Mali waited, fidgeting with her small handbag, suddenly uncertain if she should have come or not.

"Are you worried, Mali?" Doyle asked.

"Not exactly. Just unsure of the welcome. I'm not sure if we're on the same timeline we were on before and if Grandfather knows I have time traveled. Granted, Robson knew me, so I assumed we were on the main path versus the alternate one."

"This is all very confusing," Doyle stated. "If we keep traveling and things keep changing, we will soon have too many alternate routes to take if your grandfather's theory is correct."

"I know. I've been thinking about it as well. But I can see more than one set of threads when I look at them, and so far, I still have just the two bundles, which means the original and the one deviation we just took. If we're on the original path, my grandfather will only recall us arriving in Glasgow, heading to confront his partner, and us leaving to return to your time. He won't know anything about us deviating to the next century and Austria."

Just then, the door opened, and Harper strode out with the receptionist on his heels. "Mali! What a surprise to see you. And you as well, Mister Martin." He crossed to her and took her hands, pulling her to her feet for a hug. As he released her, he extended his hand to Doyle for a shake. "Come on back, both of you, and you can tell me what brought you here."

The receptionist gave them a flinty look, as if they had disturbed his boss and upset his day, but Mali smiled sweetly and followed her grandfather to the back. Doyle strolled right behind her. As she stepped inside, she halted, and her mouth dropped at the huge production line her grandfather had set up to build his autos.

On the assembly line, several workmen, using more modern-looking tools than she expected the time to possess, worked on an automobile's chassis. Behind the car, another assembly group installed the wheels and tires or tyres, as the sign on the racks holding them stated. Behind that, men placed the engines and steam chambers into other autos.

Off to the right, a smaller line appeared to be making radiators, both for the vehicles and for home use on two separate work stations. On the left, floor-to-ceiling boards formed a room, and behind it, another assembly line revealed more workers building the engines. Parts and supplies in crates and on shelving lined the walls. Her grandfather had a small fortune invested in this company.

"The official opening of the factory is tomorrow," he

told her as she stood, eyes wide and mouth gaping, at all the work going on. "I wanted to have a few models assembled to show the investors and impress any onlookers and bankers. Come into my office where we can talk."

Andover opened the door to the boarded area, which turned out to be a clean, functional office with windows facing the production floor. He sat on the edge of his desk and crossed his arms. "So, what do you think of it?"

Mali hesitated to speak, still flabbergasted by its enormity, but Doyle jumped into the gap. "It is quite impressive, Mr. Harper. I suppose I should say, Mr. Morrison. You have an astonishing set-up here. I have never seen anything like it."

"Why, thank you. Your words are gratifying to hear. This era doesn't have a model for anything along this line, so I took a huge risk here. But I'm confident our new steam cars will be successful."

Still amazed, Mali found her voice. "It is unbelievable what you've done, Grandfather. This will set a standard for the future that will only improve with time. But why radiators?"

"They were my starting product, Mali. I began building the home heating radiators about ten years ago. They've proven quite popular and successful. They also provided an example of what I could accomplish, making it easier to find investors. Now, tell me, what brings you here?"

She chose a chair and sat as Doyle leaned against the window, watching the workers. "I'm not sure which timeline I'm on, so I don't know if you remember sending me off from Edinburgh to return Doyle to his time. Or if you recall asking me to come back and help you stop Rashid Varsi from deviating from the plan."

Andover gazed at her for a few moments before he

spoke. "Last time I saw you, I believe we talked about you coming if you chose to. When you didn't return, I figured you decided to either stay in 1798 with Doyle, or you went back to your own time. I take it that wasn't what happened."

"Not even close. I somehow ended up in London, decades more in the future, at a time when Varsi, now calling himself Varsick, was there and had set up water-driven power plants on the Thames River. Electric cars are now the rage."

He peered at her, lips tight and jaw tensed. "What year was it?"

"Eighteen-fifty-eight. We still saw steamers on the road and even a few combination ones with electricity and steam, but no gas models. Anyway, we encountered Varsick there. I tried to talk to him, but he time-walked before I could get to him. After that, I attempted to take Doyle home again, but we ended up in Austria in 1889, the year Hitler was born, and in his hometown."

Andover's eyes narrowed as he showed concern. "How did you do that? You don't have the threads to walk to a country you've never visited. If you hadn't traveled via the TU, you would have been limited to only the space station and the full years since your father's birth into the past. That part is genetic, passed along from generation to generation."

"I don't know how I did it." She shook her head. "If I did. I thought maybe Varsick intervened somehow, but he denied it."

"You talked to Varsi?"

"I did. After I prevented him from killing Frau Hitler using an automobile. He wanted an opportunity to present his grand plan to Doyle and me. So, we listened."

"And?" Andover prompted, his eyes focusing on her.

"He was very convincing," Doyle said, turning his

attention back to the conversation. "I could see why he felt the way he did and his logic in what he was saying. I understand what you both want to do regarding the Earth. But is it the wisest course?"

Andover had shifted to watch Doyle as he spoke, and he now turned back to his granddaughter. "And your thoughts, Mali?"

"Like Doyle, I get it. But Varsi still thinks stopping the madman and preventing all the deaths is the way to go. I don't agree."

Andover nodded. "Are you sure of that, Mali?"

"Reasonably sure. I haven't done the math, but if the world was struggling in the twenty-second century, it wouldn't be any better with more people." She gave him a sad look, not liking the conclusion she'd drawn any more than Doyle or her grandfather did.

Now he nodded, his lips a thin line, but he straightened up, put on a smile, and changed the subject. "Will both of you come to the grand opening tomorrow? I'd like you there."

"Of course," Mali answered. "But Doyle and I need to find a place to stay and probably a change of clothes for such an auspicious occasion." She flashed her most charming smile at her grandfather.

"You can stay at my house," Andover said. "I expect we can find something suitable for you two to wear. I have several contacts in the town who can provide clothing on short notice."

For a moment, Mali wondered how her grandfather always seemed prepared to accept drop-ins and provide for them.

"Let me write down the address for you, and I'll include a note for my housekeeper, so she knows I sent you."

Thanking her grandfather, Mali turned her head to

look out the window where all the activity continued. She counted at least three dozen workers building the automobiles. It appeared three of them were supervisors or foremen, since they seemed to direct the work. Another man inspected each completed section of the product. "How did you finance all this?" she asked.

"The traditional way, with backers. I convinced them it would be a high-profit business. Once we reveal this autos to the wealthy, they will all want one or more. Even the middle class will be able to afford a lower-priced model, which we'll introduce after the big push. Most of the backers will be here for the unveiling tomorrow, along with a half-dozen bankers who loaned me some of the money. So, it is a big dog-and-pony show, which is what I think they called it in the 20th century."

"Sounds exciting," Mali said, already thinking about what a lady of the era would wear to such an event. But time and fashion had been so thrown off by this point that her knowledge was likely incorrect. She noticed Doyle had returned to staring out the window, seeming to be fascinated by the production flow. She was sure it wasn't a new phenomenon, but the idea of using it for automobile production might be novel. Certainly, people constructed carriages on some kind of assembly line, not by one worker making each one alone.

"Would you like to go on the production floor and see the work going on more closely?" Andover asked.

"Yes, it would be enlightening, wouldn't it, Doyle?"

"Indeed," he answered, pulling his attention away from the window.

He straightened as Mali stood, and they followed Andover out to the floor, where the sounds of hammering, chattering, and steam hissing as units being tested filled their ears. The scent of electricity and the moist odor of steam hung in the air. It excited Mali, although building the vehicles heralded the bigger changes ahead.

Andover took them to the first station, where the men assembled the body of the steamer. The parts were pre-cut, Andover explained. "I made a deal with the metalworker a few shops down to cut each part to my specifications, so when they arrive, they are ready to be pieced together and bolted in. From their completion here, we take the body to another shop where it is painted. When it comes back, we add the engine and the interior, which has leather bench seats and a windscreen. Last, we put on the wheels and lock them down, connecting them to the braking system. It's still a simple form of what will come in about three or four decades, but somewhat advanced for now."

That was an understatement, Mali thought as she watched the men assemble the parts and bolt them together in only minutes. The tools looked advanced but still basic, not as sophisticated as the specialized ones on the station, yet the workers managed them with skill. A few younger men functioned slower than the others or did simple tasks.

"Apprentices," Andover said when she asked about it. "Need to teach the younger ones how to do the job. Trade schools aren't common yet."

Doyle followed along, listening and studying the work being done as Andover explained each step. But he didn't say much and nodded his understanding. To Mali, he seemed moody, not his usual buoyant personality. Concern grew within her.

After the tour, Grandfather sent them off to his home, summoning a carriage to take them. He said he would be a few more hours, but he would be home in time for dinner, and she should tell the housekeeper.

On the way over, Mali gazed toward her companion

and asked, "Is something wrong, Doyle? You've been pretty quiet."

He glanced at her, shrugged his shoulders, then turned back to peering out the window. Her heartbeat stuttered, and lump of dread settled in her chest. What was bothering him?

CHAPTER 13

York 1768

DOYLE STARED INTO THE DISTANCE for a little longer before he turned his attention to Mali. Anxiety swept across his eyes as they kept darting away from hers. Wetting his lower lip with a swipe of his tongue, he leaned close to her and spoke softly. "Mali, the more I see and do with you, the more I realize I do not belong here. You have given me an exciting and unexpected glimpse into the future. However, I belong in my own time. I shouldn't be privileged to see all this and have it influence my thinking. I will change the future if I am not careful."

"No, you won't," she answered quickly. Then she realized he could. If he moved up in prestige in his time, he might have influence, and with even the small amount of knowledge Doyle had of what was to come, he could change the course of some events or policies. "You have gained some insight, but keep in mind the future is mutable, whether you apply the knowledge you've gained or block it out. You will do whatever you feel, in your heart, is best for your family, your country, and the world. I know this."

"I'm glad you're confident of it." He looked away from

her, his shoulders slumping as he slid down the seat. "I think you need to take me back to my time before I see any more."

His words hit her like a blow, and her stomach flexed in dismay. While Mali knew she needed to return him to his time, she kept putting her worries and concerns in front of his needs. Not to mention her inability to actually jump to where she wanted to go. This was her first successful attempt, and she worried if she would be able to repeat it. Besides, Doyle came with her throughout this, and the thought of facing any jumps without him almost paralyzed her.

She took a steadying breath and whispered, "I need you. I was hoping you would stay with me."

His head swiveled back toward her, face half-hidden by the shadows in the carriage. "Don't do this, Mali. I love you, and I probably always will. Yet, you and I are not fated to be together. You know that. I don't belong in your world, and you would not be happy in mine. Please take me home." His voice choked as he said it. Although he held his emotions in check, she could see the need in his pleading eyes.

Holding her own tears back, she managed a strained answer. "I'll talk to my grandfather after dinner. With his help, I'm sure we can do it."

He dipped his head before he looked away again, leaning his head against the door frame. Mali felt the same regret and despair as she shifted a half-turn away from him to look out the window on her side. The carriage jolted into a wealthy-looking area of York where the tall houses sat closely together. Still, they looked elegant with beautiful carved wooden doors painted in rich colors and embellished with brass knobs. Whatever else she might say about Grandfather, he'd left the 23rd century with enough resources to set him up well in the past.

A three-story affair, Andover's house sat on a corner, so it boasted a small lawn to the front and the side. Primarily built of stone with wooden trim, the place looked pretty new or else recently remodeled. Mali let Doyle pay the driver as she stepped to the front entry. She'd barely knocked on the door before a woman, about her height only a little meatier, opened it and scanned her with a look of suspicion hiding behind her half-smile.

"Hello, Mrs. Renfrow," Mali said before the woman could speak. "I'm Andover Morrison's granddaughter, and this is my friend and traveling companion, Doyle Martin. Grandfather said to hand you this." She thrust the introductory letter out to the housekeeper. Mali surmised knowing her name helped the woman consider them a little more favorably as she read the missive, nodding her head.

"Yes, yes. Very well. You are Mr. Morrison's granddaughter, he says. So, I am to welcome you to the house and show you to our guest rooms. You would be needing two, I assume."

"Yes, please," Mali replied with a demure smile as the woman stepped back to invite them into the house. Of course, they would observe the proprieties of the era.

Having seen her grandfather's Glasgow home, Mali expected the elegance and luxury in this residence, although it clearly exceeded the farmhouse's grandeur. Doyle followed with his arms tight against his chest. Mali thought he seemed uncomfortable, perhaps comparing the opulence to his modest flat in London.

Renfrow led them to the stairs and set a quick pace up two flights to the guest rooms on the third floor. She paused along the hallway, opening the door to show them the common bathroom, which looked far more modern than the era supported. Indoor plumbing and hot water for the spacious tub.

Mali breathed a sigh of gratitude, and her heart leaped with joy to find a large bed in the room. Her hip bothered her after climbing the stairs, and she sat, testing the firm mattress. She thanked Renfrow, expressing her wish to take a rest before dinner. She spared a brief nod toward Doyle as the housekeeper urged him to come to his room.

Alone now, she welcomed the solitude to process Doyle's request. She pulled her legs up, tucked her face against a pillow, and allowed her emotions to overwhelm her.

An insistent knock on the door woke Mali from the sleep she'd fallen into after her tears abated. Sitting up, she slipped to the door to see Mrs. Renfrow about to pound again. She halted her fist mid-air, saying, "Your grandfather is in the study and wishes you to join him before dinner."

Mali nodded. "Please tell him I will be down shortly. I want to freshen up a bit."

Renfrow nodded and turned away without another word. Mali wasn't sure if it was simply her nature or if she didn't care much for the two travelers who had dropped in unexpectedly. With a shrug, Mali headed for the washbasin in the room and cleaned her face, washing any trace of the tears away before she combed her hair and straightened her dress. She wondered if he had summoned Doyle also. With her emotions still raw, she hoped he hadn't.

Downstairs, she went into the room Renfrow indicated, where Andover sat at his desk, a glass of whiskey sitting to one side of the journal dominating the desktop. He wrote furiously in it, no doubt making notes of the day's work and progress.

His head came up as she came in. "There you are. I want to talk to you for a bit before dinner. You seemed anxious and troubled this afternoon. I assume it had to do with your encounter with Rashid in Austria."

"Part of it. I'm disturbed by the whole plan in different ways. On the one hand, I see what you are trying to accomplish. On the other, I see the pitfalls and failures are much more likely to occur than Varsi is willing to admit." She sank into the comfortable, velvet-covered armchair in the room. A pair of beautiful day dresses draped across a settee on the other side of the room drew Mali's eyes to them.

Andover noticed. "Either one would be splendid on you tomorrow."

With a smile, she thanked him. "I'll try them on after dinner. I think the green is stunning, although the rose color is translucent. Now, back to Varsi, he wants me to join him in his endeavors. You know I can't condone killing anyone, but he says you agreed to the plan when you started."

Andover set his pen down and sipped his whiskey, a stall for time while he framed his words. She'd seen it before. Her grandfather rarely spoke without considering how his statements might be interpreted. "I would not say I agreed to his plan. Although, I did conditionally accept it. As I said before, killing people was never part of the agreement. If he could stop the wars in another way, I would support him. As you might guess, I never imagined he would be able to do it. If there is unrest in a country, any number of factors could trigger a war."

He sipped again then leaned back. "Perhaps killing Hitler would have stopped the near annihilation of the Jewish people. However, those victims were only the cause the man directed the violence toward. If a different man came along, it might be a different demographic.

Perhaps it would have been the Protestants or some other race of people, those who were not pure Germanic. In America, it was a race that turned one American against another—the color of a man's skin. Even then, there was more at stake than that. It had to do with economics. War always has the money factor. Each of the great wars represented huge losses of life and great advancements in technology, leading to improved economies. Nonetheless, the expense of the endeavor lies with the foot soldiers who died."

"So, what should I do? For one thing, Varsi is intent on making the changes to the original timeline. It's one thing if he corrupts one of the offshoot timelines since they are being written with the new parameters. However, on the primary line, he runs the possibility of wiping us all out."

"On the main timeline," Andover mused as he turned the glass in his hand. "Would you like a whiskey, Mali?"

"No, thanks. I don't drink, although I do seem to be developing a fondness for hard cider," she confessed.

Andover went to the bar he had in the office, pulled out a cider bottle, added ice from a bucket, and put it in a glass for her. "At your command, my dear."

"Where do you get the ice?" She took a quick sip, letting the crisp, fruity taste linger on her tongue.

"You should know by now I have given up little of the true pleasures of my life in the future. I have an icebox and a rudimentary chilling system making ice. I am tempted to patent it; however, it will come along for the rest of the world soon enough."

He returned to his desk, then said, "Now, about changing the main timeline, the truth is it may not be the original either, but it is certainly our main one. Changes to it can affect us or put us on a new offshoot."

"Wait a minute. What do you mean it may not be the

original?" Mali sat forward, setting the glass on the edge of his desk.

"Think about it, Mali. If we can time travel, then people even farther in the future can do it as well. The timeline has likely been altered more than a few times, and corrections probably weren't applied to it once they figured out the changes made alternate universes." Andover stated it so matter-of-factly Mali felt her world tumble within her. Was any of this real?

"So, why are we concerned about it? Why is Varsi intent on changing it, and why is TIM spending money trying to protect it?"

"Many questions, granddaughter. We're concerned about the main one because, as I just said, it does affect each of us unless we have physically chosen to live in an alternate timeline. Why does Rashid want to change it? Personal reasons. Although I thought he was going to do it to create an alternate timeline. The chances are high he could kill Hitler, and no one from TIM would make it back in time to undo his actions, but you already thwarted his first attempt." He raised his glass to her. "Perhaps you should continue to dog him and prevent the worst of his actions if he stays on the main timeline."

"Are you joking?" she asked. "Why in Gaia's name would I do that?"

"Because he's invited you to join him, and you seem to have a connection to him."

"How do you figure that?"

"You're following his time hops somehow, Mali. I can't explain it because you've made some you shouldn't be able to make. Jumps Varsi can do. So somehow, you are picking up on the lines."

She shuddered at the thought. She'd seen the threads of the one Varsi made in London. Maybe she'd also picked up something when she'd pursued him to the

TU in Edinburgh. She hadn't made a clean jump since then except for this one, not even when she'd used her pocket watch.

"We'll discuss this more later. We must get to dinner before Renfrow gets annoyed when we're let the meal get cold." Andover crossed to the door, holding it open for her.

On the other side of the central staircase, they entered the dining room. Although Mali noticed the fine table settings for three and the elegant candleholders, her eyes centered on Doyle. Seated on the left-side chair, leaving the end open for Harper, he gazed at his folded hands on the table's edge.

Mali took the seat on the opposite side, acknowledging Doyle with a nervous smile as she noted his solemn expression. This had to be as uncomfortable for him as it was for her. If he had the option, he would have gone somewhere else for the night, she suspected. While they hadn't fought, their split was the same simple statement she'd made previously. Truly, irreconcilable differences.

Over dinner, a feast of roast pheasant, new potatoes, and savory bread pudding, Andover regaled them with more details about the new automobiles. They had three of them ready for the unveiling on the morrow. While Doyle expressed a little interest, he mostly remained quiet, then excused himself as soon as dinner was finished. He barely acknowledged Mali except for a brief nod as he left the table.

After he'd gone, Andover asked, "What has happened between you and your young man?"

She bit her lower lip and dropped her eyes to the table as she replied, "He's not mine anymore. He wishes to return to his own time as soon as possible."

"I see. Time travel relationships are awkward, Mali. If

you can't come to terms with a time you can both live in, then it's best not to pursue it."

"I think I've known it from the beginning, but Doyle just realized it in the past two jumps. He's overwhelmed by what he's learning, not able to cope with the knowledge of the future, and worried about whether his own choices will be influenced by it." She shifted her eyes to her grandfather, a pleading look in them. "Would you be able to help me return him to 1798? I promised to make it two days after we first jumped out of there to Glasgow. I don't think I can guarantee my time walk will be successful."

Andover finished his glass of wine and wiped his lips. "I can make another time object laced with a thread for the date and place you can use to take him back. And you have your pocket watch for me to reload with a revised date to return here. Does he wish to leave immediately?"

"I believe so. He's been quite melancholy since we left your factory."

"Very well. You go tell Doyle we'll do it in an hour. That will give me time to wind the threads into the objects. I'll set the pocket watch to return you here tomorrow morning, so go pick your dress for the ceremony." He stretched out his right arm, the hand opened toward her.

Mali stared at it a moment before she realized what he wanted. "Oh, my watch. It's upstairs in my room. I'll get it and bring it to your office." She jumped to her feet, turned, then paused to look back. "Thank you, Grandfather. This means a lot to him."

She hurried up the two flights of stairs and picked up her purse, then went to Doyle's door and knocked. "Doyle, I talked to my grandfather. He will help me take you back," she said when he didn't open the door, then waited. Did he hear? Had she spoken loud enough?

Then a footstep creaked on the other side, and the door opened part-way. Doyle peeked out through a narrow opening, his eyes showing worry and unease. Whatever affections they had between them were dying with this decision. "When?" he asked.

"In an hour. Come down to my grandfather's office in an hour."

With a brief nod, he pushed the door shut. Mali's shoulders sank, his depression weighing on her. She thought he'd be happier with the news. Just as she was sad about the circumstances, so was he. She loved him and would always remember him. Knowing she was taking him home simply finalized the decision they'd made. No turning back once it was done.

Back downstairs, Mali handed Andover her watch, then picked up the two dresses and retreated to the downstairs washroom to try them on. A tall mirror in the room showed her the green silk dress fit her perfectly, accenting her figure and looking oh-so-elegant without overdoing it. She twirled around, liking the flow of the dress and the fact it laced up the front, which made it easy for her to put it on alone.

She almost didn't try on the rose-colored dress, a more frothy-looking garment. She pulled it on anyway, struggling a little with the puffy sleeves and the buttons up the front starting at the waistline. Once she had it on, she caught her breath at the beauty of the gown. It, too, had a grace and elegance to it, making her seem avant-garde in this era. Whichever friend had loaned Harper this dress had high-fashion taste and money. The material was fine quality silk with detailed lace touches.

Indecisive, she turned her gaze to the green garment hanging on the hook, then looked at herself in the mirror again. Even though this dress made her look beautiful, it seemed to whisper it needed long, upswept hair to make it perfect. Unless Andover could loan her a wig, she would be more natural in the green. Decision made, she changed back into her own clothing and made her way back to the office.

Andover was working on the pocket watch when she came in, so she quietly set the dresses down and sat to watch him thread the golden strand into it. Illusion, she reminded herself, but she could see it there as clearly as if it were real. He made a little twist with the thread, setting it a certain way, then linking it to the winder on the top.

He looked up then and smiled. "That should do the job. Don't tamper with it in any way, Mali. Just twist the winder once in the counter-clockwise direction to activate the thread. I expect to see you back here tomorrow morning. Of course, you have all the time you need to say goodbye to the fellow."

Expressing her thanks, she took the pocket watch and put it in her purse. Her grandfather held up the other item, a common-looking timepiece with nothing distinguishing it except the slight glow. "This one will take you and Doyle to August the twentieth, seventeen-ninety-eight. All he has to do is hold your arm while you twist the winder. Ah, here he is now."

The door had just opened, and Doyle stepped into the room. Both sets of eyes flew to him, and he stepped back nervously. "Am I early?"

"Not at all," Andover answered. "Come in and relax. Are you quite sure you want to do this?"

"I am, sir," he replied with confidence. "It is what must be, I am sorry to say."

"Yes, I understand. Are you certain you don't want to stay for the ceremony tomorrow then go back?" Andover's tone suggested his disappointment with Doyle not staying.

"As exciting as it sounds, I think I should leave now."

"All right, then. This is ready to go." He handed the plain-looking timepiece to Mali. "Just a little wind and visualize the date, time, and place. Doyle, take her arm, or you won't be along for the ride."

Doyle quickly grasped her elbow and edged a couple of steps closer. He managed to mutter a thank you to Andover, who responded with a little wave and a brief smile just before Mali initiated the jump.

As Mali concentrated on the destination place and date, the room felt as if it tilted slightly as it began to blur. She experienced the time disorientation and sensation of weightlessness as Doyle's hand slid down her arm, gripping her tighter.

Please, get this right, she prayed silently, although her heart ached at saying goodbye to Doyle. In a few seconds, she touched solid ground, bending her knees a little against the unsteadiness of the arrival. Still, she'd improved a little each time.

Doyle managed an upright landing, only having to adjust his feet a bit. Eagerly, he gazed around him, verifying their location. "We're here, but is it the right date?"

Looking up, Mali welcomed the dark night sky with clouds blocking the stars and moon, although a few gas lamps cast some light along the deserted river walk. As she turned around, she realized they were in the London park near the river. The same place where she'd encountered a pair of playful dogs several days earlier when she'd first arrived with Bonde and Coleman. So naïve and inexperienced, she'd jumped at every unfamiliar thing. Back then, Doyle had laughed at her reaction before he knew she was a time traveler. She shook off the memory.

"It must be late," she said. "I don't see anyone in this area, which is good because I wouldn't have wanted to just appear in the grass."

"Me, neither," he replied as he started to walk, going back up a street toward his flat. "Let's see if we can find something with the date."

She followed him along the pathway, not wanting to get separated at this point. She wouldn't go back to her grandfather until she knew they'd come to the right time. As he hurried down the street, he passed the pub where someone had dropped a newspaper outside the entrance. At least, it was part of the paper.

Doyle snatched it up and scanned the top for the date. "If this is current, then we're here. It's Sunday, August 23rd, 1798."

"Wonderful." Her voice lacked enthusiasm. This is where they would part.

"My flat is only a couple of streets away." He turned to her, a sad smile on his lips.

"I know."

"Oh, that's right; you've been there. I am not quite sure what more to say, but... Thank you for getting me back safely. You take care of yourself, Mali. You have a big task ahead. I wish I were the person to protect and help you, but I am not. My path is here, in this place and this time."

He looked more awkward than she'd ever seen him. Worse, her lower lip was trembling as if she would burst out in tears at any moment. She caught her breath, feeling the tightness in her throat as she spoke. "Doyle, I—I will miss you. Can we at least part as friends?" she extended a hand to him, wanting so much to touch him one last time, to kiss him and feel his lips against hers.

He caught her hand, "Of course, we can, even though it hurts to know we won't see each other again." His eyes searched hers for something; she didn't know what. All he would be seeing would be the tears forming at the edges.

She couldn't help herself; she flung herself into his chest, wrapping her arms around him in one last hug. For an awful moment, he didn't react, then his arms closed around her as he lowered his head to the top of hers. "I will dream about you, dearest," he whispered. "I wish we had another solution. I just don't see how."

"I know," she said, fighting the threatening tears. "I wish you a wonderful and amazing life. Maybe I will learn about you in the future because you wrote an astonishing book."

He laughed. "I thought you were going to become the writer."

He alluded to her off-hand remark about becoming a speculative fiction writer when she thought she might stay with him. Before, she had committed herself to seeing the mission through to stop Varsi before he ruined the future.

"I'll remember you for always," she whispered.

"As will I." He caught her face between his hands then brought his lips to hers in a farewell kiss. Not as passionate, nor like a lover's, it still lingered a few seconds before he pulled back. Giving her one last sad look, he turned away and strode briskly down the sidewalk.

Mali watched as he reached the corner then turned toward the river, gone forever. Although she certainly had the means to visit him if she chose to do it, it wouldn't be fair to him. She'd almost mentioned it, telling him she could come back and see him often. However, he needed to get on with his life without her popping in and out of it.

She turned back toward the park, ambled down the

road, then cut across to Market Street, where she walked past the Rusty Plough Inn, her eyes lingering for a few minutes. Backtracking, she pushed the door open, surprising the night clerk. Even though the bar was closed, the clerk still watched the door, although he'd been dozing when she entered.

"Do you have a room available for the night?" she asked.

"Yes, ma'am, but it's two-thirty. I gotta charge you the full night's fee."

"That is fine. I only need a place to sleep before I'll be moving on." She figured the watch would return her to Andover's early, so she might as well get a good night's sleep here before jumping back.

Her room turned out to be the same one she'd had before. As she stepped into it, she gazed around, seeing the same lumpy bed, table, and chair which had been there several days earlier. In detail, she recalled Ross Bonde sitting at the table, making plans, while she did her best to be part of the team.

Could she go back and change what happened? She'd thought about it a couple of times since Bonde's death. If she could jump to a day before he died, she could warn him. Problem was, she was in the same time and place, so she couldn't overlap herself.

Stripping off most of her clothes, she slid under the covers and reflected on her poor decisions during their mission. She'd allowed herself to fall for Doyle, made mistakes leading to Bonde's death. She didn't even know what had happened to Coleman. Was he able to return to the station?

On top of it all, she'd missed Brix's birthday. Even if they weren't super close, she still counted the girl as a good friend, and she'd expected to be there. If she jumped back to her own time, she could, at least, fix one thing. On the other hand, which was more important? Keeping her promise to her roommate or saving their future?

Then, unbidden, her thoughts went back to Doyle, the first man she'd really loved, and tears filled her eyes as she accepted she wouldn't see him again. She buried her face in the lumpy pillow and sobbed.

CHAPTER 14

London England – 1798

"I DON'T THINK I'LL GET used to this," Bray complained, wobbling to regain his balance. Beside him, Brix stumbled and dropped to her knees with a little unwomanly grunt. He offered her a hand to help her up.

"It isn't the most graceful," she admitted. She took the offer and struggled to her feet, trying not to stand on the dress's hem. "I wonder if they get easier when you do it more often. The TU's aren't like that."

"No, they're not," he agreed, turning around in a slow circle. "I think we're in a park, but I'm not sure which one."

Brix could see the shrubs surrounding them hid most of the buildings, with only a few short enough to see over. She took a moment to touch one of the fuchsia-colored flowers covering the bush. Still damp from the morning dew, the petals felt like soft leather. "These are so beautiful. What are they?" She leaned closer to inhale the sweet, slightly nutty fragrance.

Bray glanced at it. "No idea." He continued to gaze at the bushes, then pointed to a barely-there open area. "I think we can get out by going this way. There isn't much of a path."

He led the way, shoving branches aside as he followed the dirt trail while Brix stuck close behind him. Still getting used to the abundant foliage, she drank in the new scents and the warm air of late summer. While she'd been on the Moon and the other colonies for quick visits, she'd never traveled to Earth. For the first time, she enjoyed the beauty and fresh smells surrounding her.

"How could humanity have caused such terrible damage to this world, Bray?" she asked, her voice choking a little. "Didn't they realize a balance needed to be maintained?"

He paused to gaze back at her. "Greed. Arrogance. Denial. Whatever. They wouldn't listen when experts told them it was happening. It was warming faster than it should have, and people couldn't adjust to the changes. Then the war broke out and made a total mess of it."

"You said 'than it should have warmed.' Do you mean it would have done it anyway?"

Bray held a thick cluster of branches back and urged her past him. "Some of our scientists believe it still would have happened. The planet is cyclical. It went from a warm, tropical planet to an ice age when most of it was frozen. Once it warmed out of that, humans began to spread across the landmasses while it continued to warm. At the time of the war, it would have been well into tropical temperatures again. But without the slower adjustment, many animals, fish, and humans hadn't adapted to the change."

"What do you mean 'adapted?'" Had her professors talked about this at University? She didn't recall hearing anything about it except humans had accelerated the warming, bringing erratic weather resulting in a devastating effect.

"If the world had warmed over time naturally, then each new generation of living species would have been able to adapt to the new environment gradually. Some may not have been able to handle it and would have died out to be replaced by a new species which evolved for the temperatures and conditions." He surged ahead of her to continue to sweep the branches aside. "The accelerated warming didn't allow time for the changes to happen. In some areas, crops failed due to lack of water or too much heat, while the opposite was true in others."

"It must have been a terrible time. Look, I see an opening ahead." She pointed past his nose.

"I believe so," he agreed and pushed toward the expanse of green grass, growing more visible with each step.

Once they cleared the bushes, they walked casually toward the gate, hoping no one noticed them suddenly emerging. They looked for any landmarks to help Bray figure out where they were. In the future London, taller buildings would stand out enough to get an idea. At least, he was reasonably sure of the city and Harper's ability to send them there.

"I'm not as familiar with this part of London as I am with a couple of other areas, so I'm not quite sure where we are."

"Can't we ask someone?" Brix suggested when she noticed people walking along a path through the park.

"I guess we could, but it tends to draw suspicion toward us, letting them know we're not locals. And dressed like we are, we'll stand out anyway."

"Exactly." Brix smoothed her skirt, pushed a couple stray leafy twigs off, and set off toward a man who was mid-way on the trail and heading their direction. She remembered she needed to sound more like the locals, but she'd never had any intent to do this kind of time travel, so she'd have to wing it.

Bray hurried behind her, brushing his jacket while he walked and trying to look comfortable in the shorter breeches he wore. "Let me do the talking." He came up even with her.

"He might be more receptive to a woman," she answered.

"You don't sound like a native."

"And you do?"

"I will. Just stand by me and look beautiful."

She grasped his arm the way she saw a couple walking farther down the path do. "Okay. We'll try it your way."

As they approached the stranger, a man about Bray's height with a cluster of hair on his chin, Bray pulled them to a halt to wait until he was close enough, then spoke in an almost proper English accent. "Excuse me, sir. My lady and I are from out of the area, and we appear to have gotten turned around. Could you tell us the way back to St. James Square?"

Brix smiled sweetly when the man's dark eyes rested on her assets. He returned the friendly look, then he peered at Bray's clothing and hid his amusement poorly. "Certainly. If you go to the corner, then turn to the right and go about ten blocks, you'll come to Kensington Road. Follow it south, and it will lead you to the park. Or you might want to consider a cab if you are in a hurry."

Bray dipped his head and offered his thanks, then urged Brix to walk with him as the gentleman resumed his way past them. "All right, we'll find a cab or carriage when we get to the corner. We're farther away than I thought we were. Once we get to the market, I want to buy a pair of long pants."

"Do they have clothing stores in this era?"

"Not really, but they do have used clothing for sale in the market." Another man passed them with an amused smirk on his lips, and Bray gritted his teeth and pressed on. "They have the bonus of being inexpensive, which is good since we don't have a lot of money."

"I'm grateful Mr. Harper gave us as much as he did." Her head swiveled from side to side while she tried to see everything they passed.

At the corner, Bray hailed a cab within minutes, assisted Brix into the back, and they motored down the rough roadway to Kensington. Bray asked to be taken to Market Street. When they passed landmarks along the way, he pointed them out to Brix as if to validate his expertise.

For Brix, the ride was novel and exciting. She'd never been in a motor car, and even though it jostled and bounced, making for a somewhat uncomfortable ride, it still thrilled her. She'd felt worse jolts in some of the ground vehicles on the Moon. Besides, it beat walking in the ill-fitting shoes she wore. How did women tolerate these torturous things on their feet?

When the cab pulled over to the side of the road, Bray hopped out and handed the driver a few precious coins for the ride. Not waiting, Brix exited on her own and now stood facing the shopping street. Her eyes roved from one passing woman to another, studying their clothing. Bray slid his hand under her elbow to urge her to the inside of the walkway. Then they made their way into the market. Staring delightedly at everything, Brix paused at each stand. Her eyes danced over the end of summer produce being offered.

"Let's get apples," she begged, glimpsing a bushel basket of them at one of the stands.

Bray hesitated a moment before bartering for two ripe-looking red ones. He handed one to Brix and whispered, "Wipe it off before you eat it." Setting the example, he rubbed the apple against his jacket to polish it.

Brix followed his actions and wiped hers against the fabric of her chemise, as Harper had called the undergarment. "Why?" she asked as she watched Bray bite into his apple.

"In case there is anything nasty on it." He resumed walking, urging her along. "Washing is the best policy, but these look clean. It's just a precaution."

"I don't think wiping would actually do any good. Except to get any dust off it."

Bray shrugged and walked on. She took a big bite of her apple, pleased with the crisp, fresh taste, and trailed behind him, her eyes darting everywhere. She studied the clothing people wore and compared her dress to the other ladies. Her garment wasn't too far from the fashion, she decided. No need to spend money to try to bring her up to the current trend. But, yes, Bray looked really out of place and drew attention.

He took care of the problem within another half hour, locating a stand selling used clothing where he found a pair of long black pants. Even though they were a little too tight on his muscular thighs, they looked fine and a big improvement over the breeches he'd been wearing.

"Worst part about unplanned time hops," he mumbled as he joined her. "Clothes change fashion too quickly. Usually, it's the women's clothes."

She laughed. "I would have thought getting money

was more difficult."

"Not if you have jewelry to trade at the equivalent of a pawn shop." He pointed to a dealer coming up on the right who offered money for rings, bracelets, and necklaces.

While he took care of trading a ring for some spending money, Brix watched the streets where fancy-looking steam cars flowed past on a reasonably frequent basis. She thought the automobile came into common use a little later, but maybe she'd heard wrong.

"Now where?" she asked when Bray came out of the shop.

"We'll go to the library where Doyle Martin works," he answered. "If Mali made it back here, he will know where she is."

"That's the guy who made the jump with her, right?" She looped her left arm through his right, the way the others did, and walked alongside the shops while he stayed next to the roadway.

Bray guided her across a street and down another block.

"I smell something like mud. You know, it's a musty, moist scent," she said, sniffing the air. "Are we near water?"

"The river is just a few blocks ahead, but we're turning at the next corner on St. Anne's. There's a private library about mid-way down the block where Martin works."

"He's a librarian?" Brix questioned and chuckled. "I might have known Mali would connect with someone like that."

They crossed the street at St. Anne's then turned to the left, working their way down the road. Brix spotted a pub and lifted her face to catch the scents of food and beer coming from it. "Maybe we could get a bite to eat there after we see the librarian," she said, looking toward it wistfully. Everything smelled so good.

"Sure," Bray said without even glancing at the place. "If it's still open."

"Why wouldn't it be?"

"They serve lunch between eleven and one, so if our business takes a little too much time, then we might not make it."

Her eyes popped wide, and she turned her head toward him. "Are you serious?"

He nodded. "That's the norm here."

They hurried up the stairs to the library's entrance. Once they stepped inside, Brix detected an unusual scent and noticed a scrawny guy sitting at a desk, making notes and looking at the books sitting along the side. She guessed he was checking them in, a manual process for the era. Was this Mali's librarian doing this tedious job?

Of course, in her time, all Brix had to do was request it on her tablet, and it would be there digitally in seconds. Or, she could summon it through her link, where it would download directly into her brain if she needed the information quickly.

Bray stepped up to the man, who pushed back his glasses as he raised his eyes. "I am sorry to trouble you, sir. I'm looking for Mr. Doyle Martin. Is he about?"

Ah, not Mali's, then. Brix found a smile for him anyway.

"Yes, sir. I believe you will find him downstairs in the newspaper archives." The small man pointed to the stairwell and turned back to his task.

Thanking the guy, Bray led the way to the stairs, and they started down to the basement. Brix felt the clerk's eyes following her until she descended out of sight. Poor man had probably never seen the likes of a woman like her.

As he reached the lower level, Bray's shoulders relaxed a little. He took the last step, gazed around the vast open area, and strode toward a tall, slender man near the cabinets lining one wall. The fellow leaned over a rack of newspapers, placing a small stack onto the wooden rods which held and separated them. He looked up at the sound of the approaching footsteps, his mouth parted slightly, and his eyebrows lifted in surprise.

"Coleman?" he queried.

His clear blue eyes shifted to scan Brix standing just behind Bray. She caught her breath. Definitely handsome, this guy's sharp cheekbones could cut paper, and those soulful eyes captured hers like a magnet attracted steel shavings. She could see why Mali tumbled for him.

"I'm glad to see you safely here, Mr. Martin. Is Mali around the area?" Bray stepped closer, offering his hand for a shake.

Martin seemed stunned and simply stared at Bray for a few moments. "What are you doing here?"

"Looking for Mali. After you two jumped, I went back to my home to deal with my injured leg, you know. Now I'm back to find her. Is she all right?"

Martin stepped away from the papers and urged Bray to follow him to the back corner farthest from the stairs. Brix trailed behind them, her eyes darting around the room until the librarian started to speak. "Keep your voice down. Sound carries in this building. Yes, she is fine, I guess. She brought me back to this time a couple of days ago, but she didn't stay."

"She's gone, then?" Brix blurted, disappointment evident in her voice.

He nodded. "She brought us to a park near here, then we walked here before we parted ways. Perhaps she'll come back, but I cannot say for sure."

"Where did she go?" Bray asked.

"I don't know. Mali planned to catch up with Mister Varsick and try to either stop him or join him. I am not sure which way she will turn on this."

"Why would she join him?" Bray ran a hand through his hair, his mouth turning down in a frown.

"It is quite complicated, mate. He is persuasive, and he believes what he is doing is for the good of the planet, but he and Mali disagree on some points."

"Can you tell us what you last did before she brought you back here?" Bray's mouth tightened.

Doyle glanced at the clock, noted the time, then said, "I have some business I must finish before I can take a break. Can I meet you at the park by the river in about an hour and a half?"

Bray's jaw tensed as if he wanted to argue it or force the information out of Martin right now, so Brix stepped closer. "That would be fine, Mr. Martin. I'm Anna Brixton, by the way. I'm Mali's roommate."

The librarian looked surprised again but took her offered hand and shook it with a firm grip, eyes widening at her equally strong one. "Delighted, Miss Brixton. From the space station?"

"That's right. So, Mali had told him about the future.

Doyle smiled briefly before he added, "I'm impressed both of you would come looking for her. I'll tell you what I know when I meet up with you."

Bray dropped a short nod. "See you then," he muttered before he spun on his heel and started back to the stairs.

"Don't mind him," Brix piped up. "We'll be waiting for you when you get there. It's a pleasure to meet you."

"Likewise." Martin walked to the staircase with her.

"Perhaps you can talk some sense into Mali."

Brix pondered his statement as she climbed the stairs. What was Mali doing? She had a feeling Bray knew more about the situation than he'd told her. Come to think of it, he really hadn't told her much about their mission. If Mali was still pursuing it, then maybe she needed to come up to speed on it.

Bray waited for her at the top of the stairs. Smiling politely at the assistant, they left the library and stopped at the bottom of the entry stairs. He turned to her and nodded toward the nearby storefront. "Well, you wanted to go to the pub, so let's get something to eat."

CHAPTER 15

London England – 1798

AS PROMISED, DOYLE MARTIN JOINED them in the park alongside the Thames. Brix perched on the bench's back while Bray paced back and forth. Martin stopped a few feet away and shook his head.

"You're as reckless as Mali is," he said, giving Brix a disapproving look. "A proper lady would not do that."

"Did I ever say I was a proper lady?"

Bray hissed at her through his teeth and tilted his head toward the seat.

She reluctantly climbed down and slid beside Bray, tucking her feet beneath her dress.

Bray hunched forward with his arms on his knees. Doyle took the seat on the other side, which pressed them close together to talk.

"So, what can you tell me about what happened?" Bray asked.

Brix caught that he'd said "me," not including her in the equation. "*We* want to catch up with her wherever she is. I've been worried since she didn't return. Is she all right?"

Doyle's eyes softened a bit as she spoke. "She is well

physically. I am not too sure about emotionally. Let me start at the beginning." He started with the jump from the clearing in the current time to Glasgow in 1763 and what happened as they began looking for Andover Harper. Then he related everything that happened as they confronted Varsick at his home near Edinburgh.

"I really don't know why the housekeeper helped us avoid the law, but I was grateful for it. Mali's theory was that since she was aware that both her grandfather and Varsick were time travelers, she didn't want the local constabulary investigating them. So far as the fellow that attacked went, it seemed he had been a problem in the area and had made quite a few enemies."

"Enough to not count his victims as enemies, I presume," Bray said.

"Let's leave it at that," Doyle answered. "After Mali's grandfather healed, Mali tried to bring me back here. However, the jump went awry, and we ended up a century later."

Then he explained that they seemed to be following Varsick's travels rather than getting back to this time. "We ended up in Austria, where Varsick attempted to kill Hitler before he was even born."

"He didn't, did he?" Bray asked, alarm flashing in his eyes.

"No, Mali interfered. Even got bumped by an automobile Varsick was driving. When we tracked him down, he wanted to talk to us."

"About what?"

Taking a long breath, Martin told him about Varsick's plans and the dilemma the man presented. By this point, they'd been talking for close to an hour.

"So, where were you before Mali brought you back here?" Brix inquired. As enlightening as all of this was, she wanted to catch up with her roommate. Not that either of them would have a room after this unless they could somehow fix it.

"York. Her grandfather opened the Calliope Steam Automobile manufacturing company there in 1768, so we went to find him. I think Mali planned to go back to him after she left here, but she didn't tell me where or when. Once she realized I didn't want to keep hopping with her, she decided to not give me any more information."

"Did it end poorly between you two?" Brix's voice gentled with sympathy.

"Poorly. You might say that, but really, it simply ended. Mali didn't see how it could work between us. I don't want to live in a different era, and she said she couldn't live in this one. Too many differences, she said." His mouth turned down, eyes reflecting his regrets. "She was right, I'm sure." He rose, stretching his legs, as Bray got to his feet.

"I'm sorry it didn't work out for you, Doyle. Really, I am." He offered him his hand. "Thank you for all the information. We'll see if we can locate her and help."

"Good fortune, Mr. Coleman. A pleasure to meet you, Miss Brixton."

"Now what?" Brix asked as Doyle walked back toward the library. She sighed. He seemed to really care about Mali, and it must have been hard for him to make the decision he did. Just as it, most likely, was difficult for her to end it.

"Now, we try to figure out where we're going next and hope that you can manage the time-walking thing. Otherwise, we'll be stuck in this era." Bray started trekking back toward Market Street.

"It's getting late. Who knew it would take us so long to get the information we needed? Maybe we should find a place to make our plan while I try to figure out how to use the threads." Brix still had reservations about them, but at least she'd done it once with Andover Harper's help.

"Let's see if we can get a couple of rooms at the Rusty Plough Inn. They might remember me since I was here just a week or so ago at this time. Maybe I can pass you off as my wife. We told them Mali was my sister."

"Well, this is getting interesting. Do you have a wedding ring, mister? 'Cause I'm not going to go in there without a band on my finger." She pointed meaningfully to her left ring finger.

Bray laughed, but he agreed. They stopped by the jeweler's stall and bought an inexpensive bronze ring that he slipped on her hand. As they walked toward the hotel, he said, "It'll probably turn your finger green."

Once they acquired the room, a different one than either Mali or he and Bonde had occupied, they settled in and looked around. "Not bad," Brix noted. "Where's the bathroom?"

"Outside," Bray said.

"You're kidding!"

"No. Indoor plumbing wasn't a thing yet."

"I don't get it. They've advanced the steam autos to this era, but they haven't improved the plumbing? What kind of thinking is that?" Brix threw her hands up in disgust. She hadn't expected it to be this barbaric.

Bray chuckled at her exasperation. "Guess the auto was more of a priority. To be fair, some parts of London may have upgraded by now, but this inn has not."

Shooting him an unamused glare, Brix stormed out the door to check out the facilities.

"Just out the back door by the stair," Bray called out as she left.

She thumped down the stairs and looked around the room where a few people ate their evening meal and considerably more were drinking it. Shaking her head, she peered down the hall that ran beside the stairs and went down it, eyes searching for the privy door. She noticed the unmarked wooden one on the right side but nothing on the left, except a turn leading to a hallway along the back of the building.

A door branched off to the kitchen with possibly an office on the right side. Brix went back and checked the door she'd passed. Finding it unlocked, she pushed it open and stepped outside into a small yard where two wooden structures, each about three feet square, squatted. She didn't need any signs to tell her what they were as the odor made it clear. Disgusted, she opened the door, confirmed her suspicions, and went about her business as hastily as possible.

Returning upstairs, she hurried to the washroom on their level and scrubbed her hands as well as she could with a sliver of soap and cold water from a pitcher. Wiping her wet hands on her dress, she trudged back to her room. Not even towels in the washroom.

Bray sat at the table in the room, staring out the window with a blank look on his face suggesting he was miles away mentally. He didn't even notice her come into the room.

"That was disgusting," she announced. "I hope that wherever we go next, they have decent sanitary facilities."

Bray blinked, turned his eyes toward her. "Yeah, I think even a few more years into the future will be a huge improvement. Oddly, I think I saw even more changes than were here when I last came. More lights, more steamers, and more people. It's like the time ripple is still updating."

"Is that possible?" Brix didn't totally understand what he meant. In theory, she knew that a time alteration could cause a wave to flow out and make changes that people living in the time wouldn't even be aware were different.

"Maybe. Or other shifts have occurred after my team was here."

"I think you should tell me what happened that brought a TA team to this time and how Andover Harper fits into it." She settled on the bed, folded her hands on her lap, and locked her eyes on him.

Bray shifted the chair around to face her, gazed at her briefly, then said, "So, your father was Aldus Stigler, right? The third man in Harper's missing TA team. Is that why you have so much interest in this situation?"

"In a way, I guess. When I met Mali, I had no idea who she was other than a really smart girl who aced her schoolwork. She was subsequently hired for a station's operations job before she even graduated. I was recruited in a similar way, but more along the lines of my connection with her resulted in the job. My employers were... are interested in her, although they never told me exactly why. They selected me—more like rigged the process—to be her roommate when we graduated from university. My task was to befriend her, keep an eye on what she was doing, and report anything I learned. You can imagine that I learned very little from her, not even a hint of where she worked, even though I knew. She never said anything to give me a hint."

"You were spying on her." Bray's eyebrows rose as if defying her to say differently.

"I was. When Mali left on the assignment, she made up a story about going away for a weekend think tank. It tipped me off that something else was going on. Honestly, I had a really bad feeling when she told me about it. I've grown very... *fond* of her over the time we've lived together. She thinks I'm an airhead with a passion for clothes and partying." Brix paused, and a wry smile touched her lips. "Well, maybe the clothes part. I do like to shop."

"You're saying you didn't know she had a connection to your father through Andover Harper?" Bray questioned, his eyes narrowing a little.

"Not a clue, Bray. I didn't connect the Harper name at all, and I didn't know any details about my father's work or his death. I just knew he worked for a government agency, was sometimes away for a day or two. Neither my mom nor I asked any questions. We understood what he did was confidential. Until Andover Harper told me, I didn't know he was a time adjuster."

"That must have come as a surprise. I'm sorry you had to learn about his death this way."

"It was a little startling when he said it, but my mom and I had come to terms with his death a long time ago. Hearing it just brought a sense of closure, no more wondering what had happened. I wonder if I'll ever get back to tell my mother."

She picked at a loose thread on her dress, considering if she should cut it. She'd hate to have a whole seam come unraveled. Maybe she could tie it back in. Pulling her thoughts around to the present, she turned her gaze back to Bray. "Now, your turn to tell me what happened."

Bray cleared his throat with a couple of little coughs, indicative of his anxiety connected to talking about it. Brix knew he was suffering from the loss and angst caused by it.

He started by saying, "You know, Brix. This isn't easy to talk about. Losing Ross on that trip has been a hard blow, not just to TIM but to me personally. He was my trainer, my work partner, and a good friend. He was also one of the most careful men I've known. So, from the start of the mission, Ross was agitated over having Mali on the team. I gathered he'd had a discussion with the director about adding an untrained era expert to the team. From Ross's view, he considered it a risk, but Edmondson told him the decision was made, and she would be going with us. I think it shocked Mali as well. She really wasn't prepared to be a field agent, and she only had a half-understanding of what we did."

"Are you saying that someone higher up insisted that she be on the team?" Brix asked. "Even though she hadn't been trained for it, someone at TIM chose her for the mission?"

"That's what it looked like. So, Bonde resented her being added to the team, and he took his resentment out on Mali. In all honesty, she knew her stuff for the most part. Her era expertise was spot on, but she had no idea what to do in the interactions with the era. Kind of like you."

"Me? What have I done?"

"For one thing, a lady doesn't perch on a park bench. You're more forward than most ladies of the era would have been, but I suspect those who might have talked to you are writing you off as an uncouth American."

"That's rude," Brix objected. "I am an uncouth Stationer."

"Whatever. Anyway, that's where the trouble began. When we got to this time period and discovered all the changes, we began to realize that it wasn't one interference that caused it but a series. We wondered how it hadn't been detected on the timeline earlier."

"I think we have the answer. Dianna's team intercepted any anomalies, making sure they never got to the right eyes."

"I guess. I still don't see how Harper and Varsi made so many changes, but only the big one Mali caught raised the alarm. Anyway, once we figured out the pair had an office in York, we went there."

Bray told Brix what had happened when they tried to destroy the plans and lost Bonde. "Mali insisted on returning to this time to see if we had succeeded, which is when she and Martin disappeared. Just vanished while I was trying to get her to come onto the TU to return home. I had no idea what had happened to her. Not even a guess she could time walk."

"So, you freaked out about it and ended up on medical leave for the leg injury and your obvious mental issues," Brix concluded.

He shrugged.

"Do you know why Harper and Varsi are trying to change the future? Doyle Martin didn't say much about their reasons, but it seems that Varsi is going to great effort to do it. Why try to kill baby Hitler?"

"To stop a war, I would imagine." Bray gave her a sideways look. "Do you even know who Adolph Hitler was?"

She shook her head. "Not really. I think I've heard the name."

"Maybe it's only relevant to those who've studied twentieth-century history, but he was the man who started World War II. A war that nearly exterminated a whole race of people."

Brix's mouth fell open, then slowly closed. "Oh... Then I see why Varsi might want to stop him."

"Except that could mean a huge change to history. Suppose all of the people who died during that war didn't die. In that case, millions of additional variations on the timeline could be created that might affect our future. This is what the TA teams attempt to prevent. So, Mali trying to stop Varsi from killing him means she is still working to prevent a change to our future."

Brix pressed her lips together in a frown as she

thought. "Well, two things I can tell you that will change in the future are you and me. We've made an unauthorized trip to a forbidden era, and we've not hidden the fact that we're time travelers. I doubt we'll get away with a slap on the wrist, even if we save the future."

"Good points. I'll also add if you don't figure out how that time-walking thing works, you and I will be stuck right here. So, you'd better make it work." He stood to stretch. "I'm going out for a walk to give you some time alone."

"Wait, where and when are we going?" she asked as he reached for the door.

"York in 1768. I'll see if I can get a more exact date."

"But I don't know if I can go to somewhere my timeline doesn't go," Brix complained as she jumped to her feet.

He looked back over his shoulder, his face stern-looking, and said, "Figure it out."

As he closed the door, she stared at it for a full minute, daggers shooting from her eyes. "That way-ho," she muttered. "Like I can control it. I don't even know what I'm doing."

On the other hand, she had no intention of spending the rest of her life in this dump of a year. If she had to be exiled in the past, she wanted a more modern period. With an exasperated sigh, she went to the chair he'd vacated and sat down at the table, then stared at the dirty-looking window. She closed her eyes and tried to picture the time threads.

Golden strands. Golden threads. Golden light. Anything?

Nothing. Brix tried several more times without any luck.

She had a headache and decided to lie down with her eyes closed to see if she could relax more. After a while, the sun dropped down low, so she lit a candle and settled back against the pillow, her eyes watching as the flame's flickers made her feel drowsy.

Unexpectedly, she glimpsed a long string of gold rising out of the flame. Tamping down her excitement, she continued to focus, willing the thread to respond to her. Then another appeared beside it, shorter but solid. Why two? She had made the trip back to Harper's home, then the one to this point. So, she must have a separate one for each of the jumps. Which one did she use for the hop to York? How did she determine when and where? Harper hadn't told her enough.

She closed her eyes momentarily, then opened them again. The threads had gone, only the flame flickering now. Her stomach dipped at their disappearance. *Why? Where did they go?* In an epiphany, she realized she'd been trying too hard to see more. She'd tried to force a revelation of the time point in the longer line, the one representing her initial jump. She sighed deeply. *How the hell am I ever going to make this work?*

CHAPTER 16

York England 1768

MALI BARELY WOBBLED WHEN SHE arrived in her grandfather's back garden in York. Smooth as silk. She was finally getting used to this time-hopping and not experiencing vertigo, particularly with short jumps. With the sun sitting low in the eastern sky, she guessed she'd arrived close to seven in the morning. She glanced around, noting the neighbors' houses where upper story rooms might have a view of the backyard, and hoped no one noticed her sudden appearance.

She knocked on the back door, surprising Mrs. Renfrow, who ushered her in. "What are you doing out there, Miss Harper? Your grandfather said you'd gone somewhere last night, but I had expected you to return by the front door."

"I know. I am sorry. I got a bit turned around. Is Grandfather up yet?"

"No, miss. I am just starting on the bread for the day, so he won't be up for another hour yet. Why don't you wait in the parlor, and I'll bring you a cup of tea and biscuits?"

"Tea only, please. I am not hungry at the moment." Mali had eaten a light breakfast at the Inn in London before she'd traveled since it came with the room. She'd become more conscious of money's value since she'd been stranded in the past.

She took a chair in the designated room and thought about what Doyle might be doing this morning in his own time. Probably getting up early, reading the morning paper, and confirming the date was correct. Then he'd go to the library to check on everything while not quite believing he hadn't missed any days in the time he was gone. No doubt his assistant would have questions about what happened to him on Friday afternoon, but Doyle could deal with that. A sad smile tilted her lips down. She missed him already.

The tea arrived, and Mrs. Renfrow fussed over cream and sugar before she returned to her work. It was an odd life well-to-do people in this era lived, waited on, and pampered. She didn't believe she would ever fit into it.

§ § §

A decent crowd gathered in front of Calliope Automotive for the official opening. "Far more than I expected, but that's all to the good," Andover told Mali when he escorted her to the front of the building, and they marched inside. Nervously, she ran a hand down the front of her green dress to smooth it once she realized she would be on display as much as the steamers.

Andover motioned her to a chair in his office. "We have another half hour before the great moment, so relax. I'm going to check on the autos for the demonstration, then we'll start moving them into place. I have hired a couple of men to keep the road clear so they can drive down it."

He hurried through the door to the back while Mali gazed out the front windows at the crush of people trying to get closer to the entrance. A pair of broad-shouldered fellows, who looked like they usually worked the docks, patrolled the front. They kept the crowd back while attempting to maintain an open walkway for the key investors and bankers.

Then, with a bit of fanfare and his own security, the Lord Mayor arrived. Several chairs had been set up behind a rope for the invited guests, where her grandfather's receptionist, finely dressed for the occasion, showed the mayor and his wife to their seats. After that, other invitees began to arrive. One after the other, they were met and led to their places. They started chatting with their neighbors, leaving Mali to conclude it was like a social event. Amused, she watched the onlookers pointing and gaping at the dignitaries.

Finally, her grandfather hurried back out, looking dapper in his good suit and hat. He offered his arm to her, and they stepped out the front entrance to applause as if they were actors making an entrance. Andover smiled and waved, acknowledging the potential buyers on the street before leading her to a reserved seat and turning to greet his special guests. After making the rounds, he motioned for silence, waiting while people settled down before he began his speech.

While he thanked everyone for coming, Mali studied the crowd. Some of these people would never be able to purchase one of the steamers, while others looked ready to hand money over right now. As Andover introduced his guests, the crowd cheered. The mayor spoke for a few minutes, acknowledging the new business and all the factory's work enriching their city. Speeches done,

Andover pivoted to face the head of the street and waved toward the upper end of the road, drawing everyone's eyes in that direction.

A collective gasp of appreciation filled the air when the first steamer began quietly rolling toward the factory. The beautiful red roadster drew approving comments as the crowd first darted into the street to see it head-on, then parted to allow it to drive right in front of the building. Turning the vehicle, the driver backed it into the open lot at the end, climbed out, and stood by it, ready to answer any questions.

Even though Mali had seen the car on the factory floor, she still caught her breath when it rolled in front of her. More advanced than the original first steamers, her grandfather had employed design from the future to make the vehicle more graceful and practical. While he didn't make it completely enclosed, it still sported a generous cover over the passengers to protect them in foul weather.

The next steamer had begun rolling forward once the first had reached the front of the building. A bigger model, painted forest green, caught the crowd's attention, and the whole scene repeated while that one swept past and turned into its parking place next to the first. With a backseat, this model could seat four, making it an excellent family vehicle. Although a bit boxy-looking, it still looked sharp, with white trim outlining the doors and the top edge of the roof.

The last one to arrive followed the same routine, although this one was solid black, sleek-looking, and glistened in the sunlight. After that, people shifted forward to look at the machines more closely while Andover showed them to his guests, explaining the features with fervor.

After thirty minutes, give or take, Andover guided his

guests into the building to tour the manufacturing area. All the while, Mali had remained in the VIP area, smiling at people and watching her grandfather with unexpected admiration. He cut quite the figure of a successful businessman. How had he gone from time traveler to car entrepreneur?

But she still worried about the impact these advancements might have on the future. How much would they change people's lives, and would it alter history too much? While she should have argued with him about these changes, she couldn't help the swell of pride she felt at his accomplishments. Would it be so bad to make life easier for people in this earlier era?

Now, she hung back, returning to the reception area to sit while she turned her gaze to the people still admiring the new vehicles. Even though she knew she was at the beginning of a change in the world and history, she also felt detached from it. This wasn't her world, just as the near future wasn't. She missed the advancements and conveniences of the 23rd century, even if she did love this beautiful planet's openness and the freedom to go to so many places. She hadn't realized how limited her life on the station had been. Once anyone had gone planetside, how could they easily return to the confinement of the station?

She already missed Doyle's company. If he'd been here, they could at least be having a conversation and looking around the city. Not for the first time, her thoughts turned to Brix, surprised to realize she missed her roommate. Sure, they hadn't been close buddies. Still, they'd spent many a pleasant evening chatting, eating, and sometimes going to clubs or movies together. She liked listening to Brix's descriptions of some of her dates and how some guy or the other was such a dirtbag because he couldn't keep his hands off her. Mali hadn't dated much, too busy with her work, and frankly, not eager to get back into a relationship with anyone until she'd met Doyle. Then, she had to fall for a guy in the wrong century.

She still hoped to get back to the station for Brix's party if she could just resolve the issue with Varsick, as he now called himself. She hoped her grandfather could help her figure out a plan so she could see her path clearer. She knew she had to prevent any significant changes to the main timeline, so did it mean killing Varsick? The thought made her uneasy. She'd never killed anything except a plant. When she'd decided to go into the time management company, she'd imagined the time adjuster's job quite a bit differently. She never considered it might lead to killing someone. Yet it was precisely what Bonde had been prepared to do when they'd gone to destroy her grandfather's workshop.

Getting bored, she got up and stepped outside again, her eyes scanning the expressions on the people looking at the autos, trying to read their thoughts. One woman who peered at the green vehicle looked doubtful, suspicious even. Mali figured she didn't trust the new contraption, thinking it would be dangerous to everyone in or near it. Next to her, a man looked at it eagerly, his eyes sparkling with excitement and dreams of driving the beautiful machine down the road.

As she watched, people began to disperse, the show over and having seen enough of the new horseless carriage. They had things to do, jobs, house chores, shopping. Mali glanced toward the end of the street and blinked at what she saw.

A flaxen-haired woman came walking toward her from about fifty yards away. She knew that woman! *Brix! It can't be! Did my thoughts somehow summon her here? No, surely, this must be a look-alike.* But when she came closer, a big smile blossomed on the girl's face, and she picked up her pace, nearly running toward her.

"Mali!" Brix called when she was almost to her. "Thank the stars I found you!"

"Brix?" Mali managed to get the name out, still not believing what she was seeing. "You're here? How?"

Brix reached to pull her into a brief hug. "It's a long story, but maybe we can go inside or something?"

"Of course," Mali answered, recovering her sensibilities when she realized a few people watched as the taller woman had hugged her. Not to mention, Brix was dressed in clothing far adrift from current fashion. Not her space station garb, thankfully, but something from a little farther back in the century.

"Are you all right, Mali?" a male voice asked, and only then did she realize Brayden Coleman was with her.

Things began to click together if Bray had come back with a TU, but why bring Brix? And how did he know she would be here? Did this event create an anomaly?

She caught Brix's hand and pulled her toward the alleyway between Grandfather's building and the next one. Bray followed them. Mali looked around to be sure no one was near and asked, "How did you get here?"

Brix held up the dangly watch Mali had left in her room. "I figured out how to use this, and it took us to your grandfather in 1767. He knew we could find you at the opening celebration for his company and helped us get here."

"I don't understand," Mali said, worry creasing her forehead. "Are you working for TIM?"

Bray laid a hand on her arm. "It's a long story, Mali. We need to go someplace private to talk. As you can see, Brix and I are a little out of fashion for this era."

"My grandfather's house. We can go there. I'll tell him to meet us there, then we can take a carriage to it."

She paused to give Bray a brief hug. "Glad to see you're okay. All healed?"

"Yep. We'll wait here for you." He squeezed her arm, then stepped back against the building with Brix.

Mali hurried to the front of the building, rounded the corner, and stumbled to a stop as another familiar face walked toward the shop's front entrance.

Rashid Varsi, aka Varsick, looked dapper and definitely dressed for the period.

Well, Gaia's spit, what is he doing here, and which version is he? Mali's knees felt weak. She backed up and pressed against the wall, then she peered around the corner to watch Varsick enter the building. No reason to panic, she told herself. If they were on the original timeline, then he probably arrived to congratulate his partner. Unless he came back from the future, in which case, she had no idea what his intentions were. Taking a deep breath, she walked to the entrance and pushed the door open. Varsick wasn't in the reception area, so he must have continued through to the production floor.

"Did a gentleman just come in?" she asked the receptionist.

He glanced up, a pleasant expression on his face, suggesting nothing out of the ordinary. "Yes, Miss Harper. Mr. Varsick just arrived. Were you looking for him?"

"No, not exactly. That is, I just noticed him while I was outside and wasn't sure I'd seen him." She paused, feeling awkward and realizing she didn't need to explain herself. "I'll just go on through." She waved a hand toward the door.

As she scurried through, her eyes darted to the activity on the floor. A cluster of investors, bankers, and the mayor huddled with Andover on the right, where he was now introducing Varsick to them. Her grandfather seemed to be taking it in stride, so she presumed nothing was wrong, but he hadn't mentioned he expected his partner to join them today.

As the handshakes and polite conversation progressed, Mali made her way to Andover's side, glanced toward Varsick, and managed a weak smile. "This is a surprise, Mr. Varsick. Excuse my interruption."

As he started to speak, she shifted her attention to her grandfather. "I need to go back to the house. I wanted you to know I have company and will be taking them with me there. Please come when you can."

A wrinkle of puzzlement touched Andover's forehead as he nodded. "Of course. Is there a problem?"

"I don't think so, but we may need your advice. They're... like us." She wanted to couch the words so anyone who might hear wouldn't know what she meant.

"All right, my dear. I will see you once this is concluded." He patted her hand to reassure her, then he turned back to his party. She noticed Varsick's eyes on her, felt them following her, but ignored him while she strode across the floor. Time to return to her friends waiting in the alley.

CHAPTER 17

York England 1768

AFTER RENFROW USHERED THEM INTO the parlour for tea, Mali waited until the housekeeper left, then sat forward in her chair. "Now, tell me what's happened? How did you get involved, Brix?"

Her roommate pressed her lips together and shifted her weight in the chair. "Well... The truth is... You don't know everything about me, Mali. It isn't a random selection that you and I are roommates. People with... influence... arranged for me to be paired with you. While we shared classes at university, we weren't really close, so it wasn't a logical choice for the computer to match us." Her voice faltered as Mali's face stilled, and her eyes narrowed.

"Why would people with *influence* want us to room together? Are you working for these people?" Mali's voice faltered as she considered the implications. "You were spying on me? Why?"

Brix's answer came out in a rush. "Indirectly, I do—did. You realized I worked for a travel agency, but you never asked for any details. My company has connections to TIM, and your bosses knew all about you and wanted more information. If you think about it, you and I never really talked about our jobs. You couldn't tell me where you worked, but I had been briefed. When you didn't come back for my birthday, and a few more days passed, I went to my boss—"

"Wait! I didn't come back? You mean, I've not returned to the station at all?"

"Well, not within the two weeks since you left. Usually, time travelers return within one to three days, which is why I began to worry something had happened to you." Brix sat straighter, her concern laced into her defensive posture.

Mali's eyes shifted to Bray. "What about you, Brayden? Did you tell TIM what happened? Were they even going to send anyone to find me or make another attempt at the anomaly?"

He met her eyes straight on, his mouth a tight line. "I wasn't in very good shape when I got back. Straight to the med bay, then on medical leave. I I had no idea what happened to you, Mali. Last time I saw you, you and Doyle vanished without a clue. I didn't even know what time walking was or that you did it. Truthfully, I'd begun to think I hallucinated it. So did Edmunds and two doctors. I was still on leave at my place when Brix contacted me."

Stunned, Mali couldn't say anything as she slowly pieced together what they said. First, the shock she didn't return to the date-plus-one from when she'd left the station, then Brix had the resources to begin looking for her. Where was the blonde, fashion-statement airhead she'd lived with? Had it all been an act? Why not? True, she'd been playing a role also, but one which was much closer to who she was.

Conversation halted while Renfrow brought in the

tray of tea and sandwiches for them and retreated as swiftly as she'd come.

"You'd better start at the beginning," Mali said and settled back to listen.

Brix told her everything that had happened, who she'd talked to, and what she'd learned. Mali's eyes grew wider as she spoke about Dianna abducting her and what they were doing. Bray chimed in with his part of the story, leading right up to when he broke into their apartment and the people attempting to get to them.

"That's when I used your watch to take Bray and me to your grandfather's house," Brix added.

"How were you able to use the watch? I thought you had to be a walker to do it," Mali blurted out.

"Apparently, I am," Brix said, then she explained. "Like you, I inherited the ability from my father. He was part of your grandfather's Time Adjustment unit."

"You're not related to Varsi," she whispered, certain the dark-featured man wasn't Brix's father.

"No. My father was Aldus Stiegler. He arrived here with your grandfather and Varsi, but he died about three years later. At least, that's what Mr. Harper told me. He helped us get here to connect with you."

"I'm sorry, Brix." Mali didn't know quite what to say. Brix had mourned her father long ago, just as Mali had mourned the loss of her parents. "Wait a minute. You said my grandfather helped you get here?"

Brix nodded. "He reset the watch to take us to London, where he said you were going with Doyle Martin. So, we looked for him when we got there."

"You found Doyle?" They hadn't mentioned being in London. "And he told you to come here? When?"

Brix blinked, as if the question confused her. But Coleman answered. "We arrived the day after you left."

Mali closed her eyes a moment, taking a deep breath.

"That would have been this morning for me. I only left him this morning. I stayed at the Inn overnight, and jumped here this morning."

"We stayed at the same place last night." Brix's eyes widened. "We missed each other by only hours. It seems impossible."

"Time travel is like that." Mali stood, took a few steps around her chair, processing their words. They'd seen Doyle on the first day after she'd left him. "How was he?"

"Fine," Brix said. Her eyes followed Mali. "Is anything wrong?"

She shook her head. "No. I'm a liitle surprised. So, he was okay?"

"He misses you," Bray said. "We found him at work, and he met us later. He's heartbroken but realistic about the breakup. He'll be fine, Mali."

Mali put her hands on the chair's curved top, an unexpected weight pressing on her heart with sadness. He was moving on, even though it was what she'd wanted. Her throat felt tight, so she took another deep breath. "Now what? Are you going to go now that you've found me alive and well? If I never returned home, I guess you can assume I died in the past. But the good news is there still is a station."

"What do you mean? Of course, there is," Brix stated. She lifted her hand to adjust her hair, patting the rolled bun at her neck.

"It only means nothing Varsi has done has changed the future enough to nullify the base. If he manages to do that, none of us may exist, not there and not here."

"I thought the changes created alternate timelines?" Bray looked confused. "Your grandfather said—"

"It's a theory." Mali paced as she talked. "Although it seems to do it, I don't know if the alternate line is stable or if the change might roll back on the primary one. My own time-hopping confuses me, and I'm not sure which line I'm actually on. You talked to my grandfather on the original timeline, right?"

"If that's what the watch took us to, yes," Bray answered.

"But my grandfather said nothing about you coming here today. He would have known if you talked to him."

To follow up, she filled them in on everything that had happened since she'd last seen Brayden. Two cups of tea each, a tray of sandwiches, and a plate of afternoon cakes later, Mali ended her update by adding, "Now for the wrinkle here—Varsi is in York. I saw him at the grand opening right before we left. My grandfather didn't seem surprised to see him, so I guess he expected him. The thing is, I'm not sure if he's the original one or an alternate."

"That confuses me so much," Brix said. "I'm still trying to understand exactly how the timeline is splitting to create new universes. It sounds like a strange theory."

"Actually, it's been around a long time," Bray interjected. "I don't think there's ever been any evidence of it before. It's hard to explain and present logically. Still, if you can time walk to both universes, then you might manage to gather proof of it." His voice rose a little with enthusiasm.

"Except no one will believe you, even with proof," Mali said. "My grandfather presented the theory on it at TIM, and no one accepted it. Part of what he is doing is to prove it. But they will never actually understand he's done it. If they create an alternate universe, history gets rewritten. All any version of us in the new world knows is what the revised account says."

"That's a bit of a problem," Bray agreed. "Let's hope Harper is right, and it doesn't affect the main timeline."

"Unless Varsi somehow changes the main one with

something that doesn't split." Mali stepped around her chair to grab a napkin to wipe her hands. "If you'll excuse me, I'm going to go upstairs and change my dress. I borrowed this, and I don't want to take any chances with it."

As she hurried to the third floor, Mali thoughts centered on being left forever in the past. But was it what happened? Perhaps she stayed on Earth, setting up a life in the future, possibly even in the same century, if her grandfather and Varsi completed their save-the-Earth plan. That might be a world worth living in.

Without Doyle. Her inner voice had an evil sound in her mind. Yes, without him. She wouldn't try to change his life again. He'd decided to stay in his own time.

She slammed into her room and began stripping off her dress, refusing to speculate any more about him. She changed quickly, stepped into the bathroom to wash her face, and put cold water on her eyes as she felt despair welling up in her. There, niggling at the recesses of her mind, came the notion she was beginning to convert to her grandfather's plan. What of her mission? Was it all negated by the alternate timelines? Except... Except what?

She was trying to sort too much in one day. Enough for now. Giving herself a mental slap, she straightened her shoulders and marched downstairs.

While Brix and Bray still sat in the parlour talking to each other, Renfrow had cleared out the tea service. "I'm back," Mali announced, sweeping into the room like she owned it.

Bray turned his head to peer up at her. "Good. We're discussing our options now."

"What do you mean?" She sat down, her gaze traveling from Bray to Brix.

"Well, I don't feel we can go back to the station," he

answered, his eyes rolling upward as if he saw it there.

"Why not?"

"With Dianna's shadow crew apparently gone rogue, it would appear they consider us a threat to their operation," Brix explained. "There are only so many places you can hide on a space station, and I don't intend to spend my life as a fugitive there."

"I don't understand." Mali shifted her eyes from Brix back to Bray. "Why are they after you?"

"We know too much about what they're doing. I expect their intent is to shut down the time unit completely. No more adjustments to the past; let the flow happen." Bray crossed his healing leg over his knee and leaned an arm on it. "Whether this was part of your grandfather's plan or if Dianna and her crew decided to do it is another question."

"That's crazy," Mali said. "How can they do that?"

Bray glanced at the carpet for a moment before lifting his eyes to hers. "A big reason TIM hasn't sent another team into the past is because our time unit—the one we used—is the last functional one they have, and it needs repairs. The operation itself is in trouble, with less funding available. If your grandfather's theory is valid, no action taken to correct events in the past will be needed. They'll self-correct. No need for adjusters or monitors."

"I can't believe that's happening," Mali whispered. The whole idea alarmed her. What about her? "I need to go back to my life there." But they'd already established she didn't return. Or did they? They only knew she hadn't returned within the two weeks before Brix time-walked. She might return to a later date or a different timeline.

"I don't think any of us can return, Mali," Brix said calmly. "You and I can time walk, but we can't stay there. We all know too much about their operation."

"Let's take this entire issue up with my grandfather. Dianna is his ally, and possibly the others are as well. This may be a misunderstanding, or it's in a different timeline. He should be back soon."

"Mali may be right," Bray conceded, his eyes flicking to Brix, and back to Mali. "Let's talk to Harper to see if he can fill in some blanks. I don't believe if I'd like to spend the rest of my life on Earth, although the early twentieth century might not be a bad time to live in if Varsi eliminates the wars. There were several of them, as I recall."

Mali shot him an annoyed look. How would stopping the major wars help the problems on Earth any? The classes and lectures she'd taken at university told her no. More people would only add to the troubles.

The decision to discuss the whole situation with her grandfather made Mali asked Renfrow if Andover had two more guest rooms her friends might use. As it turned out, the big house had more than enough space to accommodate six guests, so the housekeeper soon led Brix and Bray upstairs to their rooms.

Mali went to the back garden, sitting on the stone bench surrounded by blooming flowers with fragrant scents on the wisps of air touching her cheeks, and contemplated her future. If she had one. She didn't wish to be stuck in the past, but both Bray and Brix were saying it would be dangerous to return home. What were the possibilities of getting to one of the colonies? Would she even be happy in a confining dome on the moon or Mars?

The Titan colony was still developing, and terraforming was in its infancy. Even if she returned fifty years into her future, it wouldn't be advanced enough to give them an actual home planet.

But suppose she joined forces with her grandfather

and Varsi. In the new scenario, they would alter this planet's course, even if it was in an alternate universe, so they might live on this world in the future. Would that be a bad choice?

CHAPTER 18

York England 1768

AS SHE APPROACHED HER GRANDFATHER'S office, Mali heard muffled voices through the door. Recognizing Varsi's deeper tones, she stepped closer and leaned her head against it to listen.

"We must pursue the original plan, Andy. You can't back –"

"I believe we need to reassess the plan, Rashid. We've made many rapid changes, but we need to see the long-term effect before continuing. Let's talk about this tomorrow."

Behind her, Mali heard footsteps from the hallway and straightened and knocked. She didn't need Mrs. Renfrow to catch her snooping.

A chair scraped back, and a few moments later, the door swung open and Andover peered out. "Mali. I wasn't expecting you, was I?"

"I'm sorry. I didn't mean to interrupt. I'll come back."

"No, no. Come in." Andover stepped aside as he

waved his free arm in invitation. "This will interest you, I'm sure."

She stepped into the room, noting the dapper-dressed man who sat in the straight back chair at an angle to the desk. Varsi turned a pleasant face to her, dipping his head in acknowledgment.

"You know Rashid," Andover said. "You remember my granddaughter, don't you?"

"Of course. She tried to kill me the last time we met."

"Well, you shot her friend and me," Andover said in defense as he shut the door and returned to his office chair. "You have to admit you weren't acting rationally at the time."

"I was quite upset," Varsi said. "I believed our plans were being destroyed."

"And you were using a substance you shouldn't have been," Andover stated.

"Quite. But you have to admit you wanted to stop my plan."

Mali clearly recalled the incident at Varsi's home where he tried to murder all of them and escaped to the TU unit while she pursued him. It was only a couple of weeks earlier for her, but years for these two. Clearly, they'd sorted things out since then. At least the bit of conversation told her this Varsi was not the last one she had encountered in Austria but the one from the altercation.

"Rashid dropped in today to be at the opening of our initial endeavor to get the steam automobile going and progressed to an affordable and fuel-efficient option before the combustion engine becomes the primary fuel source. We're doing everything we can to make steam, then electricity, the first choice," Andover told her as he motioned her to a chair near the bookcase.

"If the interest shown in the autos today is any

indication, I think we will have a big hit." Varsi rubbed his hands together, giving him a somewhat greedy appearance.

"I don't doubt it," Mali replied drily. She already knew how successful their plan would be so far as the shut-out of the gas guzzlers. At least, well into the 19th century anyway. She assumed it would continue through the next century and beyond. Why would anyone change from relatively inexpensive power to something costing cost much more and polluting the environment?

"We still have much to do." Andover slid his chair around to get a better view of both her and Varsi. A big smile filled the lower half of his face; he'd clearly had a successful day. "The investors are quite impressed, and the banks are anxious to loan us money to increase our production. The mayor wants the black display model as soon as we can polish it up and deliver it. At least thirty other well-to-do businessmen placed orders to be delivered in the next two months. I think once the steamers are on the road and motoring from town to town, they will become the new status symbol for the wealthy."

"What about the roads?" Mali asked. The ones existing now were not adequate for the vehicles to run smoothly. Horse carts didn't require as good a road.

"We already have cobblestone streets in York, as you might have noticed. The next step will be getting the road from here to London smoothed and widened. It will take time, but even as it is now, the autos can manage. I'm investing quite a bit in getting a company to do the work."

"It sounds like you have it all planned out. My friends, the ones I mentioned earlier, and I need to speak with you later," Mali said. She bounced to her feet. "I hope you don't mind them staying here tonight."

Andover's eyebrows lifted as he considered that. "And Rashid will also be spending a day or two here before moving on. I believe we, including you, will have much to discuss before he leaves."

Her heart beat faster with a sense of unease at the idea of Varsi and her friends all being here at the same time. This could go poorly if the subjects of discussion got out of hand. "I'll see you both later then."

"Dinner will be in about an hour," Andover reminded her. "Please let Renfrow know all our guests will be joining us at the table."

"I will," she acknowledged and slipped out of the office as smoothly as possible.

Well, *that* complicated things. Still, Mali had to admit it would be a prime opportunity to find out if her grandfather supported Varsi's plans or if they could change them. Combining the information with what she'd learned from Bray and Brix could alter her plans for the future.

Dinner turned out to be a reasonably pleasant affair with no one diverting the conversation to the station problems or radical plans for the future. Mainly, it focused on the new automobile and expansion plans which would distribute it to the whole island, and possibly on to Europe, within two decades. Both Coleman and Brix pretty much kept quiet through most of the dinner, only speaking when Andover directly addressed them.

After dinner, Varsick excused himself and retired to the parlour to have an after-dinner drink while Mali and the others remained in the dining room to speak with Andover about what had happened on the station. Mali turned it over to Bray to provide the details.

Bray started with his return to the station and the situation he'd encountered. Then he pretty much went into a condensed version of everything he and Brix had told Mali.

"Wait a minute," Andover interrupted. "You're telling me Dianna had some of her people abduct you on the station, Ms. Brixton?"

At that moment, Mali realized this Andover was not the one Brix had spoken to years earlier since he would have known the whole story already. They were definitely in an alternate universe. So, did she stop Rashid from killing the baby in this version? Did she return Doyle to the correct timeline? She needed to figure this out.

"Yes, I told you this before, but we were in the past, so I guess you wouldn't be aware of it now," Brix said. "I have a little trouble figuring out the time changes."

"No, but Andover should have been aware of it if we were in the same universe," Bray commented, following the reasoning as well as Mali.

"Which timeline are we on?" Mali asked, her mouth feeling dry as anxiety struck her.

"The main one, of course," her grandfather answered without hesitation.

"But you didn't see Bray and me about five years ago in Glasgow?" Brix asked.

"No, I don't recall that."

"Then we must have jumped to an alternate timeline," Coleman concluded before Mali could voice it. "How could it happen?"

"It couldn't," Andover said.

"Then this is an alternate timeline," Mali said. "If you don't remember it, then you are a different version of yourself. Or..." Her words died as she considered another possibility.

"Or what?" Coleman asked. "We either jumped to an alternate timeline, or we were already in one. But the watch was set for the main line, wasn't it?"

"Let me think about that," Harper said as he scribbled on a notepad he'd pulled out. "But let's get back to what happened on the station.

"It disturbs me to learn Dianna's people attacked you and tried to break into your apartment just before you used the watch to jump to the place I programmed into it." Andover got to his feet, paced across the room, turned, and strode back, a frown etched in his face. "I will need to investigate this. If something has changed on the station, then we may need to adjust our plan. We never intended to destroy TIM or even end the TA teams."

"I think there are only three time units left," Bray commented. "One was in the field when our team took the second unit to London. The third one is wherever you have it here in the past, assuming it survived."

"It did. Varsi took it somewhere from the farm near Edinburgh. I watched it go." Mali joined her grandfather in pacing. "What happened to the others, Bray?"

"Damaged, unable to lock onto the time threads. Management hoped to get some expertise to replace the bad parts, but it didn't happen. No money for it."

Andover shook his head. "This makes no sense. Money shouldn't have been an issue. I think this may be a change to the timeline occurring after the last jump you did. Since Mali wasn't able to stop us, the line didn't get corrected, and a new alternate universe was created going forward from there. But the earlier time bumps remained, and somewhere, something must have changed the status at TIM."

"How will you investigate?" Mali asked.

Her grandfather stopped pacing and cast a startled look at her. "By going there, obviously. I'll time walk back and talk to Dianna."

"Sounds risky," Bray said. "If she's turned to a new agenda, then she may not be too receptive to you back on the station."

"That is a possibility," Andover admitted. "Maybe someone needs to come with me. Are you game, Bray?"

"It's too dangerous for Brix or me," he answered after a moment's hesitation. "The rebel group has already demonstrated its stance against us. If I get caught, they'll find a way to secure me there or kill me."

"Kill?" Andover mused as he rubbed at the stubble on his chin. "Yes, maybe they would resort to murder if they think the prize is worth it."

Mali considered everything they'd said and her own position in the mix. She turned to her grandfather. "I'll go with you. As far as they know, I have been in the past and not a part of any investigating Brix and Brayden have done. They won't know I have the ability to time walk. I could always spin a story about the pocket watch allowing me to go both ways. Would they know any different?"

Andover looked thoughtful before he replied, "No, they wouldn't. They knew I could time walk and might have suspected you could as well, but they don't know how much I can use the time threads. But you gave me another thought. Even if they capture us, we can still walk out of there at any time. Nonetheless, I'll rig your watch to bring you back here twenty-four hours after we leave, and I'll take a different object for me in case they somehow prevent me from walking. We won't let them know you're capable of time walking, Mali."

She agreed, although she felt a little nervous about the plan. Going back to the station would be a risk for both of them. If it all went wrong, it would leave Brix and Bray stranded here, with Rashid being the only other time walker who could help them. Brix might be able to walk, but she wasn't skilled at it. Not that she was much better, Mali conceded.

"I don't like it," Brix said. "It puts Mali in jeopardy there. At this point, TIM and the rebels have written her off. Finding her back would mean another potential problem. If you're together, they would figure you told her everything, Mr. Harper."

"Another fair point. Who knows? But I'll work on the issue." Andover rubbed his hands together. "Let's get Rashid in here, so we can talk about some of the issues in our plan."

Although she nodded, Mali wasn't looking forward to confronting Varsi again. She'd heard enough in Austria and still didn't see how killing the warmongers would change the world.

As Andover left the room, Brix and Bray tried to talk her out of the plan. She remained adamant about doing it. "He's my grandfather, and someone has to have his back. I'm the only choice for this. As of now, Dianna and her team don't know we're aware of their duplicity. We'll try to stay separated, but in touch, so the other can initiate a rescue if something happens to either of us. Worst case, we can both time walk so we can get off the station."

"They could shove you into a storage bin like they did me," Brix objected.

"And I can hop out of it," Mali answered.

"What about us?" Bray asked. "What do we do if you two don't come back?"

"I've thought about it. What do you plan to do even if we do?"

"We thought we might join you in whatever you decide to do," Brix answered. "If it's to change the future, then your grandfather has two more helpers. If you think we should try to stop them, then we'll side with you. No matter what, we can't go back to the station and expect to live a happy life."

"You and Brayden could go to the Mars colony. He grew up there, so he has contacts on the planet who could probably help you both get settled." Mali shifted her gaze from Brix to Bray to see if he agreed.

He frowned. "Not too keen on returning there," he answered. "And they know where my apartment is at Aldrin City on the moon colony. It wouldn't be safe there. I'd rather pick a time here on Earth and live the best life I can. I think Brix agrees."

The blonde nodded her head to confirm.

"If we don't change what is happening on the station, I guess exile may be the solution for all of us," Mali answered.

Just then, Andover returned with Varsi and introduced him as Rashid Varsi, former Time Adjuster, to Bray and Brix. They turned their attention to him as he began to explain the plan again. It hadn't changed since the last presentation Mali had heard. The man was consistent. Andover interjected a few objections by saying, "We haven't completely agreed on that," or "This is a point we need to discuss more."

When he'd finished, Varsi put on a confident smile, his dark eyes sparkling with enthusiasm. In Mali's mind, she saw the definition of a fanatic. "My concerns are about over-population of the Earth if the people who died in wars don't die and add more than their own numbers to the future population. Can the Earth support so many people and not suffer from pollution which will ultimately make it uninhabitable? Is that what happened on Mars, Bray?"

"It's a theory, but so far, not proven," he answered. "But I think it's a valid concern."

"Also, will killing the people who instigated the wars actually prevent them?" Brix asked. "If people are riled up enough to back the war, isn't it likely someone else will do the same thing?"

"That is a possibility, but with the alternate universes, we might have the chance the test out the theory before committing it to the main timeline," Varsi replied.

"That's another thing I'm opposed to," Mali said, disapproval clear on her face. "I don't think we should tamper with the original timeline at all. You, personally, have at least two alternate lines you can experiment with. However, the main one has already been changed enough."

"Well, you are full of negative remarks, Ms. Harper, but do you have any solutions? We are trying to save the planet, but apparently, you don't believe it will work. Is the loss of a few bad people so disturbing you value them higher than everyone they killed with the wars, even without the damage to the planet?" Varsi's words came with a bite, and Mali involuntarily took a step back.

Bray spoke up in the slow drawl he sometimes used. "I could point out those wars spurred a great deal of the technology making our future possible. The nuclear reactor, advanced metals, the fusion engine, improved communications, and computers are all by-products of war."

"You are correct, but we are from the future, and we already know how they work. By releasing the technology in a controlled fashion over time, we can have the advances without the bloodshed and damage." Varsi moved closer to Brayden, talking with his hands while his eyes blazed with his visions.

"Unless you screw it up," Brix tossed in. "You think you have a plan worked out, but it doesn't mean people will cooperate with it. They may advance differently."

"It appears we all have a great deal to think about in regards to our plan, Rashid. But it grows late, and we'll think better after a good night's sleep. So, let's have a nightcap, and you all can turn in for the night. Mali and I have more to do." Andover picked up a bottle of brandy from the sideboard and half-filled the glasses on the table.

After they drank with no toast other than to a good night's rest, they filed out of the dining room. The others went up to bed, but Mali and her grandfather headed to his office. Andover showed Mali in and said, "Wait here a few minutes while I go change into my travel clothing. I assume you don't have any from the station with you."

Shaking her head, she said, "I left rather abruptly when I transported to Glasgow."

As he slipped out of the room, Mali fidgeted. Nervous energy, she realized as she picked up a gadget on the desk. A piece of metal looked like a little skinny pot and she suspected was an automobile part. She was just flipping it back and forth in her hand when the door pushed open, drawing her attention. Brix slipped into the room.

"Mali, are you sure you want to do this?" she asked in a low voice.

"While I'm not crazy about the idea, I need to do it. Among other things, I want to see what's happening on the station for myself. I promise we'll come back at the first sign of trouble."

Brix's eyes and the straight line of her mouth showed her worry. Mali was surprised at how much concern her friend showed for her. Their relationship had been friendly but not overly close over the past year. Still, she felt they had grown closer in the past couple of months. Despite that, she didn't expect the concern Brix displayed now. "See that you do. Don't take any foolish action. If you suspect danger, stay away from it. Listen to your instincts."

"Did you?"

"No, I ignored them—more than once—and trouble found me. Steer clear of it." Without warning, Brix grabbed Mali into a hug. "Stay safe and come back." Then she turned and scurried back out the door before Andover returned.

About ten minutes later, Harper opened the door and stepped inside. He had dressed in black jeans, a long-sleeved black nylon shirt, and sneakers, perfect for the station. Clearly, he had a secret wardrobe stashed in the house.

Mali looked him over, seeing the future apparel through more educated eyes now. If you considered fashion changes through the years, men's clothing hadn't changed much from the twentieth century to the twenty-third. Just the fabrics and durability had upgraded, but the style remained essentially the same. But they were drastically different from the current era.

Taking a moment, her grandfather locked the office door, then turned and handed her the pocket watch. "I've reset the thread in it. It will bring you back here at midnight. If I've got it programmed right, then you'll arrive in your bedroom or at least in the house. So that's your get-out-of-jail card."

Mali smiled a little at the antiquated term he used as she took the watch and slipped it into the hidden pocket in her dress. She thought the phrase related to a game people used to play. How had he been able to prepare both his timepiece and hers in such a short time? "Will you show me how to link a time thread to an object?"

"Sure. When you're more experienced with the threads. It's not something everyone can do, though. Rashid can't do it, but I learned the trick from my mother – your great-grandmother." Andover moved to the center of the room and held a hand out to Mali to join him. "Are you ready to do this?"

Taking a deep breath, she caught his hand, "As ready as I'll ever be." Despite the words, she worried about what they might find on the station.

CHAPTER 19

York England 1768

BRIX LINGERED OUTSIDE, HIDDEN BEHIND the stairwell, long enough to see Andover return to his office and to glimpse a hint of the golden glow from under the door for only a few seconds. Certain the light indicated their departure, she still tiptoed back to the office door and reached to turn the handle. It wouldn't turn.

Locked. Why would Harper lock it? Brix frowned and contemplated trying to pick the lock. However, she didn't have any idea how to go about it. Locks on the station were all electronic, not ones using a physical key like these. She bit her lower lip and stepped back. Not that she didn't trust Andover, but she'd hoped to find a little more information about his plans while he was gone. She couldn't help feeling both men were not leveling with Mali, Bray, and her.

That was it then. Mali was back on the station, and she could only hope her friend would return safely. After her experiences the few days before she and Bray jumped out, she didn't expect Mali to have a warm reception there.

A creak from the wooden floor above drew her attention, and she remained still as she listened. In the quiet of the house, she heard water running, then switched off. Someone using the accommodation, she deduced, but remained still for a minute or so longer. She hadn't done anything wrong, but she didn't want to be seen downstairs by either the housekeeper or Varsi. Satisfied the way was clear, she stealthily climbed the stairs to the third level and lightly knocked on Bray's door. In the quiet, she heard his footsteps on the wooden floor come closer, then his low voice asked, "Who is it?"

"Brix. I want to talk."

Bray opened the door and stepped back to let her in. He hadn't changed for bed yet but had put on the slim-cut pants he'd worn when they left the station. She didn't blame him. She should have gotten more comfortable also. The borrowed clothing from Andover felt strange on her body, and the stiff undergarments pressed uncomfortably against her chest.

"They've gone," she said. She looked around his bedroom, noting the similarity to hers except it sat under the eaves of the house, so the bed was tucked under the slant. Room enough for the occupant to sit up in bed, but not much clearance for anything more. A dresser sat on the door wall, and a wardrobe stuck out on the north side. Like her room, it included a wash basin with running water but not a bathroom. They shared the common one at the end of the hall. Smart to put the major plumbing on the same side as the kitchen.

Bray nodded and motioned for her to sit on the blue velvet-covered bench at the end of the bed. "Yeah. Not too happy about that, but it's her decision."

"What do you think of Varsi?" Brix sat, crossed her legs at the ankles, and leaned back against the bed.

"He's a rocket, just shoving his way forward without any regard for what might be in the way. He may crash, but he'll do it his way," Bray replied as he sat on the edge of the bed close to her.

"Is he a real visionary, though? Do you get the feeling it's his plan more than Harper's?"

"To some extent, I do," Bray leaned back on his elbows and closed his eyes. "He envisions a huge change. One that could impact the future in too many ways. The devil is in the details, as the old saying goes. While it's one thing to have big plans capable of changing history, the unconsidered smaller events might overturn something and threaten the survival of humanity in a different way."

"What do you mean?"

"Well, ending the wars is the big issue. On the surface, it's a great idea. People won't die. But there will be more humans occupying the planet. If the Earth is managed properly and people limit their growth by not having large families, the world can support them. If not, then the problem is increased, and failure to provide could occur earlier than it did for a different reason." He rolled on his hip to face her, bracing his head with his left arm.

"So, you're saying the same situation could happen, but with different circumstances." She twisted to gaze back at Bray.

"Exactly. You heard the conversation down there. Mali's quoting the official line from TIM. Make no changes; only correct what went wrong. Basically, let everything happen as it did originally. It includes technology."

Brix's forehead wrinkled in thought. "But Varsi and Harper have the patents and construction details to move technology forward, don't they? Wouldn't that ensure the same inventions could happen in a peaceful environment?"

"Maybe. Maybe not. While the technology is delivered

via Varsi with patents, the money might not be available to finance the actual development. He and Harper brought the details of how to make the tech, but without the money to purchase and refine the materials needed, they won't be successful at getting a space station and colonies in place for any failure on Earth."

"Or they may not need them if the planet is able to provide for all the inhabitants," Brix added.

He arched an eyebrow. "You got it. Now, so far as Harper's part of the plan, I think he'd like to save the Earth. God knows, it's a noble desire. Look at the beauty of this planet. It's difficult to think that in five hundred years, it will be failing, unable to provide for the inhabitants. But I think the bigger picture for Harper is he wants to prove the alternate universe theory. He claims, and he could be right, if the timeline isn't corrected within a set number of days from a change rippling down it, then the line splits with the new line veering off from the original one. So, the bigger changes don't happen in the current timeline."

"That's confusing," Brix said. "Since he's introduced the steam automobile today, does it create a new timeline?"

"In theory. But even Harper isn't positive which timeline he's on. If it's an alternate one, it may not work the same as the original. When our team came back, we worked on an anomaly that didn't trigger a response in time. Things get dangerous trying to correct a big change, and that's how we lost Ross Bonde."

"He was your friend as well as the team leader, wasn't he?" Brix's voice softened as she glanced down.

"Yep, he was my initial trainer and partner, but we were good friends as well. I miss him. We always knew there was a chance we could die. So, we tried to be careful. We slipped up, and he paid the price." Bray looked down at the floor, his lips a tight line.

"It's okay to mourn," Brix said, her heart sympathizing with him. She thought she'd mourned the loss of her dad until Andover told her he'd died later here on Earth in the past. Somehow the knowledge changed her grief, and she needed to process it all again.

"I thought I had," he mumbled. "I had plenty of time while I was on leave to recall every moment of the event, every detail, and then feel like, somehow, I was also responsible for losing Mali."

"Why?" Brix asked. Bray hadn't actually talked much about what had happened.

"I was so angry at her for wanting to go back to 1798, but she said she wanted to see if Ross's death had made a difference. I accused her of coming back just to see Doyle Martin. Maybe it was an accident he ran into her, but it could have been her subconscious desire. Either way, I was furious when he showed up in the clearing, following her back to the time unit. We were arguing, Martin grasped her shoulder, and they both disappeared. I had no idea what had happened. I didn't know she could time walk."

"It wasn't your fault, so you can let it go now. Just as it wasn't your fault Ross was killed. You can't blame Mali either," she cautioned.

"I don't. She tried to warn us before the building blew up. She got caught in it as well, getting tossed into the woods by the explosion. Yet, she managed to get me back to the TU. I'm not sure I ever told her how grateful I was." Bray shifted and rubbed his hand down his left thigh.

"Your leg bothers you," Brix said, noticing the move.

"It's still a little sore and tingles if I don't move it enough," he admitted. "Slow healing wound."

"And now, Mali's gone back into a dangerous

situation," Brix said. "It's weird knowing if everything goes well or at least according to their escape plan, she will be back here tomorrow. Yet, in reality, she and her grandfather could spend unlimited time on the station before coming back."

"True. But it was the fact Mali didn't return within the time she'd told you which alerted you to a problem in the past," Bray said. "It works both ways. If she's not back tomorrow, then something happened to them in the future."

She nodded. "Right. All we can do now is wait to see. After that, what are we going to do here?"

"As I see it, the best way to keep track of what Varsi does is to work with him. It would be easier to prevent a disaster if we're on top of whatever he does. So, we can agree to support his plan and become part of the team."

Brix thought about his words for a minute or two before she spoke. "Are you sure you want to?"

"Reasonably." He slid off the bed and came around to face her, stretching his leg as he did. "I see the opportunity to prevent a disaster in the future by working with him, but the other opportunity would be to kill him before he goes any further. Stop the plan right now."

"I can't quite see murder as a good option. I don't think Varsi's a bad man or an insane one, but he's a visionary who believes he has a solution." Brix shifted her position to turn toward Bray. "If I don't go along with it, would you blame me?"

"Naw. I don't think so. Although you could be the only way I could get out of a tight spot." He flashed a quick grin. "Seriously, if it comes down to just the two of us and Varsi, then I think we're better with him than trying to find our own place in time."

"You're probably right. It's just...." She pushed

herself up and gave Bray a hug.

"Just what?" he prompted, putting his arms around her.

She pressed against him, and sighed against his shoulder. "I never thought I wouldn't be going back to the station. I didn't say anything to my mother. She'll be devastated if I don't return."

He squeezed her to him. "Are you close to her?"

"Not so much anymore," Brix said, her voice catching. "When my dad died, we clung to each other for the emotional support to get through it. Then I went to University and began working. We drifted apart, but I still kept in touch, calling at least once every few days, seeing her a couple of times in a cycle."

"Hey, you can still do that," Bray said as he rubbed his hands across her back. "You can time walk, Brix. If you are careful and can go directly to her apartment, there's no reason you can't go see her whenever you want. Just don't get caught on the station."

Brix pulled back, gazing at him in surprise. "Well, hellfire, I didn't think of that. I am so stupid."

He pulled her back into the hug, his arms enveloping her as he chuckled. She leaned into him and released the breath she'd been holding, feeling as if a heavy burden had been lifted from her shoulders. Thank heavens she had Bray with her. She wouldn't have wanted to have to do this alone. At the same time, she felt more than just camaraderie with Brayden Coleman. She felt warmth flood through her as she pressed her hand against his cheek. "Thank you," she whispered.

"For what?" He pressed his hand over hers.

"For insisting on coming with me when we used the watch."

A strangled chortle punctuated his reply. "I didn't have any other choice. But I'm not sorry." He lifted her hand and pressed his lips to her palm.

Her breath caught. This situation was bringing them closer together, but was it false affection she was feeling? Did Mali experience this with Doyle? Still, her sentiment was sincere when she replied, "For what it's worth, I'm glad we're in this together. Now, I am ready for a good night's sleep."

She yawned, pressing her hand over her mouth as she started for the door.

"Sleep sounds good," Bray agreed. "Try not to worry about Mali."

With a slight smile on her lips, Brix stepped into the hallway and strolled the two doors down, then continued to the bathroom at the end of the hall. As she passed Mali's room, she paused, wondering if her friend had left a note or anything behind in case she didn't return in the morning. She almost opened the door, then continued on. By her reckoning, it must be close to midnight.

On her way back, she hesitated again, then she heard a thud in the room as if something big had hit the floor. Alarmed, she grabbed the handle on the door and pushed, but it wouldn't budge. Something heavy pressed against it.

CHAPTER 20

Space Station September 2238

THE ROOM LIGHTS IN MALI'S APARTMENT flicked on as soon as the sensors detected movement. Blinking against the brightness, Mali darted looks in all directions to ensure she and her grandfather were alone in the main room.

Beside her, Andover inhaled deeply as he did his own examination of the surroundings. He'd impressed her with the smooth and precise jump, not something she could manage with her fledgling skills. Following his lead, Mali drew in air through her nose and frowned, surprised at the air's sterile odor. Not a foul smell, just lacking the fresh scents she'd come to enjoy on Earth.

Silently, she padded to the entry door and leaned against it, listening for any sounds beyond. Did anyone watch the place, or had Brix vanished long enough for them to have given up the search?

At first, it seemed unwatched, but then she heard the muffled sound of someone speaking and adjusted her hearing to make out the words. It sounded like a shift watch as one man gave what sounded like a report. Backing away from the door, she motioned her grandfather toward her room bedroom. Once they passed the inner door, Mali eased it shut and pushed her grandfather farther back.

"Nice place," he whispered as he gazed around.

"It is. But we've got a guard at the door. I'm going to change clothes to something more suitable for sneaking around the station. Don't do anything to attract their attention."

She slid her closet open, grabbed a pair of dark blue leggings and a same-colored jersey, then slipped into the bathroom to change. She grabbed a long pageboy wig and settled it on her head. If she wanted to move around the station, she needed a disguise. She grabbed her opaque moonglasses and put them on. A glance in the mirror assured her it would work.

By the time she came back out, Andover had the computer up, eyes scanning the screen as he checked the latest station report. "You shouldn't have done that," she hissed, tossing the dress on the bed.

"Why?"

"Because someone may be tracking my computer. We're liable to have security at the door any minute."

"No matter. I have what I need. We're on the right date, by the way. Are you taking your eighteenth-century dress with you?" He pointed to the garment.

"Of course," she murmured and reached in the closet for a small backpack. She tossed a few more things in, then zipped it closed and strapped it on her back. "Now what?"

"We hop to another area of the station where we won't be noticed. Take my–"

They heard a commotion outside the apartment door–brash voices demanding entrance and a voice arguing back, pointing out he worked for TIM security. Andover grabbed her hand and initiated the hop a few moments before the sliding door opened and feet thudded into the living room.

Within a heartbeat, they'd arrived at their new destination, and Mali detected the scent of oranges as her eyes adjusted to the moonlight pouring in the domed ceiling of the station's greenhouse. Trees surrounded them as they'd come into a small plaza situated in the middle. Mali shook her head in disbelief. "I'm amazed at your accuracy. How can you control the landing zone so precisely?"

Andover grinned. "You'll learn to do it, Mali. I'm very familiar with this little plaza, so I just envisioned it in my mind as I directed the jump."

"But you used the time thread for it, didn't you?"

"As I told you, our personal threads are within us. We can control them however we wish. I selected the mental thread to the time and the place, but the fine-tuning is up to me. Once you've done a few dozen jumps, you'll get the hang of it."

"A few dozen? I've messed up just about all of the few I've done."

"Well, there's something else at work in those misfires," he said as he motioned for her to follow him. "Let's see if we can find out what's going on here. I want to set up a meeting with Dianna."

§ § §

From a room within the Travel Center Hotel, Mali and her grandfather planned their next step. Mali gazed around the room, noting it looked like any hotel room anywhere. A comfortable place to wait while your ship was being serviced or to rest between space hops. Andover pulled out a tablet from inside his suit and sent a message to Dianna asking for a meet-up.

"I didn't know you still had one of those," she said as

she sat on the other bed.

"Of course. I keep it charged so I can use it when I jump to the station. Fortunately, the solar source is easy to find on Earth. You've charged yours, haven't you?"

She nodded. "A few times. How often have you come back to the station?"

He pressed his lips together, eyes rolling to the left as he thought. "I'd say about ten times since I disappeared. Usually, they're quick visits to talk to my associates here."

"More people than Dianna are involved in this plan for the future?" she questioned, surprised people who were still on the station would go along with the idea.

"I do. Three, to be precise."

"I see. What is your relationship with Dianna, Grandfather? She helped me assemble the clothing and other necessities for the TA mission." Mali recalled Dianna had met her in the fabricator room, ready to assist, even though Mali found out later she didn't actually work in the area.

"We're good friends. She believes in what we're doing and has supported me from here."

"Friends? That's all?"

He met her eyes, his brow wrinkling with a questioning look. "Yes. I haven't had an interpersonal connection with her, if that's what you're thinking. But we have worked closely together for a long time. The personal connection you're looking for? Ross Bonde. They were a hot item for at least a decade."

Mali's eyes grew wider as something clicked into place. "Oh. I'd heard the little prank she pulled on my team might have been to tick off Bonde, but it came back on me."

She took out her own tablet, thinking she might get some information from within the station. She'd like to download every history book of the centuries after the eighteenth. If she had to live in the past, she wanted to know what to expect. Her expertise only went through the last decade of the twentieth century. Now it appeared to be changing.

"How so?" Andover asked.

"She changed my money fabrication order to bills which were not viable in the period where we were. Bonde blamed me, but I knew what I put in the computer." She still felt angry about the incident, and she'd like to confront Dianna about it.

"Okay, I've pulled up the station layout," he said and pressed the control button for the screen on the e-center. With another press, the station schematics displayed on the large console. Most areas were clearly labeled for public consumption. TIM's section simply noted Visitor Information in the front office area. However, the rest of the station behind it and to the left and right along the ring had no indication of occupation or use. Anyone who knew what TIM really did could figure out it belonged to the time travel agency.

But the intriguing part centered on the space just above TIM on the fourth floor, where another relatively large area bore no labels. This would be the location of the second monitoring area. Positioned right above where Mali had worked, they could easily tap into TIM's setup feed.

"There," she rose and pointed to it. "This has to be the duplicate setup. Back this way," she dragged her finger to the left and into the hallway, "would be the entrance Brix talked about with the storage bins beyond that."

Agreeing, her grandfather made a note of it on his tablet. "I don't know anything about the setup. I had no idea the team here did it."

"Do you really think I'd be in danger if I contacted friends at TIM? I'd like to find out what they know."

"I absolutely think it's too risky," he answered. "They'd want to know how you got back without a TU. You don't want to let anyone know you can time walk. And if there are people within who are involved in this alleged conspiracy, they might want to capture you as they did Brix."

She slumped down a little. She wanted to see Jax, talk to him. Brix said he'd helped her. So maybe he could tell her more about the situation. Disguised, she could hang outside the TIM unit until he came out, then make subtle contact with him. No one else would need to know.

"Ah, there she is," Andover said as he got a response to his message. "Surprised, she says." He read the rest, keyed something into the tablet, then grinned at her. "She says the Mad Mud Coffee Shop on the second level. It's just a small place and pretty open to anyone passing by, but if we get there early—"

"I know the place. I've been there a few times myself," Mali interrupted.

CHAPTER 21

Space Station 2238

MALI SAT AT A BACK TABLE while Andover took his mello-caff to one at the front. As she watched him take out his communicator, tap it, and place it on the table, she pressed a fingertip to her receiving device embedded behind her ear.

"Can you hear me?" he asked in a low voice.

"Very clear," she answered, taking a bite of a sweet roll she'd bought with her beverage. She took a sip and frowned at the taste of the artificial coffee. Now that she'd tasted the real thing, the drink paled in comparison.

Right on time, Dianna arrived, marching in like she owned the place. She paused to look around, spotted Andover, and nodded, holding up her right hand with her index finger raised. An acknowledgment before she hurried to get a drink before she joined him. Mali dipped her head, her eyes dropping to her tablet to hide her face behind the wig's curtain of hair falling forward.

Dianna sat across from Andover and spoke first, her voice coming through to Mali as if she was seated next to her.

"Well, you are a sight for long-neglected eyes."

"Neglected? Has it been that long?" Andover replied. Mali could see his white teeth as he grinned. "I thought I kept in touch rather well."

"Really? It's been a few years since I've heard from you, Andy. I was beginning to think you really had perished." She didn't sound light-hearted or amused. Her tone carried a touch of bitterness.

"No, that can't be right. I talked to you about six months ago." Mali glanced up to see Andover drop his hand on top of Dianna's.

"Maybe in your dreams, but not from anywhere on this station," she complained, her voice dropping off so much at the end that Mali barely heard her.

"Something's happened," he stated. "Something has changed on the station since the last time I saw you. What is going on, Di?"

Dianna lifted her head to look around the shop as if she expected someone to be watching. She leaned closer. "We've had to act on our own more, Andy. I expected you to come for us once the changes rolled down the line, but week after week, then month after month went by, and it became obvious you weren't coming for us."

"The job isn't finished yet," Andover answered in a quiet voice. "Rashid and I are still making changes to ensure the plan works. We've made great progress, but there's still much to do. I told you that not long ago. Don't you recall?"

She shook her head. "No. I told you, it's been years. You said you would come for me, but the changes have happened. You didn't come back... until now."

"What do you mean? 'The changes have happened?'"

"The Earth is still livable. The climate has changed a lot, but it hasn't been reduced to the rubble people expected. There were some tense moments last century when it looked like a huge war might happen. Then President Asleson managed to negotiate with General Kwok to avoid a war. So, your plan to reduce the carbon emissions on Earth worked. It's overcrowded still, but new colonies are being formed to handle the overflow."

"New colonies, you say," Andover asked, his voice sounding a little dry to Mali's ear. "Where are those?"

"Two more on the moon. OPEN has a colony on Titan going well and is planning a new one on Mars, even though the 22nd-century one failed to survive. They have better technology now to do it."

OPEN? Mali quickly looked up the name on her tablet.

Off Planet Expansion Nodes, a company that arranges for migration to the Moon, Titan, and soon to Mars, it stated. *We specialize in creating self-contained living modules to allow life to grow in a new environment. Several modules can be combined to create a community.*

She stared at the images of the modules, some set up on the moon in a cluster. They looked like dozens of giant bubbles on the surface.

"I am amazed," Andover said, a genuine sense of awe in his voice as he lifted his hand and leaned back. "But I'm also a little confused since we didn't advance our project that far yet. Something must have altered a key point earlier in the timeline to create this change."

"Does it matter?" Dianna asked. "You've achieved your goal. While the colonies and the space station are nice, I still want to live on Earth like you promised. Are you going to keep your word?"

After a pause, he answered, "I will. Just not right now. I need to check a few things before I can feel it's safe to transfer you to a planet."

"You still have the time unit, don't you?" Dianna's

voice sounded worried. "I mean, you'll need it to move us to the planet. TIM's computers aren't working now."

Mali's head rose as her eyebrows shot up. *What is Dianna talking about? TIM's computers are down?*

"Yes, of course, we have it. How many do we need to move?"

"Six. I've had to add one more since Rawlin got married a year ago. We're not all looking at the same place or time, though. Three of us want to go to San Antonio, Texas, in 1985– my first choice, while Rawlin and his wife dream of living in Tennessee in the same year. Gene chooses to go to Boulder, Colorado, in 1935. He heard it was lovely then."

"All right. We can do that. I'll need to prepare the TU for the three hops. That will take some programming work since the unit here isn't operational. What happened to the computers? Did your group have anything to do with the failure?"

Mali lifted her head to get a look at Dianna's face as she answered. Her eyes widened before she narrowed them.

"Goodness, no. We just keep track of the timeline and the changes in the shadow monitoring room. We didn't have access to the secure computers, so we had nothing to do with it. Just one day, the folks came into work, and they'd been wiped clean of the time data along with all details of how to build and maintain the time units. Even backup copies were gone. Everyone was shocked. Our group was just as flabbergasted as the TIM team was." Dianna paused to look around again, making sure no one was watching her. "We thought maybe you and Rashid did it."

Dianna glanced around the shop again, and Mali ducked her head.

"I can't stay any longer. Just tell me when you'll be

back to transport us off, so I can let the others know."

"Six weeks," Andover answered quickly. "I'll contact you when I return. I'll need to set the TU down where no one can see it, so I'll have to work out those details. My regards to everyone and tell Rawlin I send my congratulations."

Dianna nodded, reached across to clasp Andover's hand in a friendly shake, then rose. Mali watched as Dianna's eyes darted around, sliding over her briefly as she left. Mali sprang up and followed her out of the shop while staying several paces behind her. She sped up as Dianna pressed the button for a lift. She just managed to slip into it with her. Once the door slid shut and the unit started to rise, Mali reached over and pressed the stop button on it.

Alarmed, Dianna whirled toward her. "Why did you do that? Who are you?"

Mali removed the glasses and aimed an intense stare at her for five full seconds before she spoke. "I thought you might recognize me, although the hair may have thrown you off. You screwed me over, Dianna."

The other woman gaped at her, studying her face. "Oh, my heavens. If it isn't the granddaughter. Mali, isn't it? It wasn't personal. When they set the mission to try to correct the time anomaly you caught before we did, our standing instructions from Andover were to attempt to interfere with its success as much as possible. I thought throwing in some unusable money would take you a while to rectify."

Mali glared. "My grandfather's instructions?"

"Well, he didn't know you'd be sent back, did he?" She put one hand on her hip and leaned back against the metal wall. "Although I think that one of our people may have made some adjustments to your TU's solar collectors before your mission."

"What?!" Mali was livid. Her fingers balled into a tight fist, itching to pound into Dianna's smug face. "You could have stranded all of us in the past. As it was, you got Bonde killed."

"I did? From what I heard, you were responsible."

Mali gritted her teeth and took a step toward her. "No. If you hadn't started eroding my competency with him, he might have trusted me more and told me his plan before it got out of hand. I could have been more of a partner in the team. Instead, I was left out of the loop until the last minute. I blame you for it."

Dianna slid sideways, working her way toward the resume button to restart the elevator. "So, what do you want to do about it? Get into a bitch-slapping contest in the lift?"

"Yeah. I would like to beat the haughtiness out of you, but it wouldn't do any good. Maybe I can just talk my grandfather out of helping you. He just won't come back for you. How's that?"

"You wouldn't dare." Dianna's face turned to rage.

"Wouldn't I? You stranded me in the past with your antics. I'm pretty sure I won't be able to return permanently to the station." Mali moved another two steps closer. "Aren't you even wondering how I got here?"

"I assumed Andover brought you."

"He did. But I'm like my grandfather. I can do what he does. I can always find you, Dianna." She closed the rest of the gap to stand almost nose to nose with her. She reached around her and pressed the resume button. As the lift began to move again, Mali leaned back, shifting her right arm as she did, then slapped Dianna hard enough to shove her two feet away from the door.

As Mali put her shades back on, Dianna cowered back, her hand pressed to the side of her face. The lift stopped, and Mali stepped out, leaving a stunned person behind her.

Not looking back, Mali went down the hall to the next bank of lifts and took one back down to the Travel Center level.

Andover waited for her inside their room. He'd gotten himself a glass of something that resembled Scotch without the kick. He frowned at it. "This stuff is terrible."

"Fake," Mali answered as she slid the wig off her head.

"Where did you go?"

"To confront Dianna."

"Did you hurt her?"

"Not really. Just a little disciplinary slap." Mali settled on her bed.

Andover turned on the entertainment unit and requested an update on the Mars Colony. "What the heck is OPEN?" he muttered as he saw the name on the screen.

Mali filled him in on what she'd found, then turned her attention to the screen where the history of the Mars Colony was being shown in a video format. Everything Dianna had told Andover was true. Mali rechecked the date to confirm they really were only six weeks from the time she'd left the space station for London.

"How could so much change without it being a major event? The timeline should have exploded with an anomaly."

"You would think," Andover replied. "But this could be an instance where a simple change continued to grow and turned into a major event later on."

"I read the European president brokered a treaty," Mali said, then entered the name into her tablet, pulling up the references related to the time of the war. "Petrine Asleson, born in Denmark in 2201, became President in 2230. She was well-educated, a student of political science, and a Rhodes scholar. It says she spoke Chinopan and negotiated directly with Ching Kwok. But the original general who started the war in our history was Pang Tau, not Kwok. Let me look that up."

She quickly keyed in the Tau's name and read the details of his attempts to begin the war. He raised his army by forcing more young men and women to join as he prepared to launch a nuclear attack against Europe. The American block was neutral at this point, following the economy's collapse, which Mali confirmed in her remembered history. But, Fai Shiau, Tau's second-in-command and a trusted aide, attacked and killed Tau during a dispute over the plan. His death opened the way for Kwok to rise to power in the Asian coalition.

"It says Shiau had the people of the three major countries of the coalition so riled up that Kwok nearly went through with the war until Asleson opened up communications with him. Much of the war was related to trade sanctions, which hurt the economies of China and Japan. The other factor was the lack of respect the rest of the world showed them. Honor is significant to them. Also, China was bursting at the seams with excess population and unable to offload any to other countries due to restricted immigration. Asleson made many concessions to avert a war, but in the long run, they paid off for both sides."

"In what ways?" Her grandfather asked.

"For one," she said as she read a little farther, "they established OPEN as a mutual space expansion program that gained world financing. As the population was increasing all over, it became harder and harder to provide for the people. Space expansion was a necessity. At this point, the space station was only partially built, and no colonies were on the moon."

"That's true," Andover agreed. "The space program

was making slow progress. But the Mars colony should have been established before the advent of the war, which means the program hadn't come along as much as it had before the change."

"Let's order dinner brought to the room here," he added as he turned off the entertainment unit. "We need to try to figure out what actually caused Tau's aide to turn against him and if that was precipitated by something we did."

"Could it have just been random?" Mali asked as she pulled up the delivery menu from one of the station restaurants.

"Possible." Andover opened the desk drawer and removed a pencil and a sheet of paper. While just about everyone used their tablets for recording information and contacting people, most hotels still placed a few pieces of paper, pen, and pencils in the rooms in case someone wanted to send a written note or draw something out they wanted to keep more private. He drew a straight line, then began making bars across it and wrote decade numbers by each one.

"Would you like Italian?" Mali asked. "The rigatoni with vegan sausage looks good."

He scowled a bit. "I've forgotten how the vegetarian meats taste since I've been away. But I suppose it's as good as anything we'll get on the station."

"I could order macaroni and cheese," she offered. They used to joke about it when she was a kid because she loved it so much. "They even make with adult additions like bell peppers and onions."

"That actually sounds good. Get that and a standard salad for me."

She entered the order, added a dessert choice, and pomegranate water for her, hot tea for Andover. Then she turned her attention to what he was doing.

"Let's start with the anomaly that happened to bring you to London in 1798, then check each decade for anything that might have changed regarding people of the era rather than inventions and events. We're looking for a person that gained prominence who hadn't before or one who was well-known but isn't anymore."

"That could be a wide field, Grandfather. Let's see if we can get the computer to do it. If I can make the parameters specific enough, I think it can." She began inputting the search details into her tablet's comparison program and gave it the first decade of 1800 to 1809 to search. She wasn't sure if it could manage the match, but since she had the original history for the 18th to 21st centuries, she could at least do those.

The food arrived, delivered by an automaton cart, so they didn't have to deal with the possibility of being recognized by a human. They paid in physical credits rather than electronic ones since neither of them was recognized on the station's computer accounts anymore.

"How do you still have credits?" Mali asked, amused that he had money.

"I had a stash when I left on my last mission. I knew I would be coming back periodically. When I needed more, Dianna would get them for me," he told her, a sly grin on his face as he picked up his food and took it to the small table in the room.

"So, you say you didn't have interpersonal relations but were you and Dianna a thing before you left?" she asked with a bit of hesitation. Did she really want to know?

"No, nothing like that. She was a friend at the office. But we had some ideas in common that grew into the plan Rashid, Aldus, and I put together. She agreed to be our eyes and ears on the station. She knew it would take several years before I could return to take her to the planet at the time of her choosing."

Relieved, Mali sat and took a bite of her food, relishing the taste of the pasta. "So, that was the deal for the rest of the team on the station also, I guess. Are you still going to do it?"

He looked up and swallowed a mouthful before answering. "Of course. Just not as soon as Dianna is expecting it. If we can undo the anomaly that changed this, life on the station will go back to what it was before."

Mali frowned. "Isn't it risky to keep changing things? Trying to correct an alteration that went wrong could make it worse instead of better."

"That is true, which is why we have to be very careful doing it."

"Forgive me, Grandfather, but I don't believe Varsi is careful about what he does. He takes risks, figuring the payoff will be worth it."

"He may be right, Mali. There are big stakes in what we're doing, but I think the last war shouldn't have happened for other reasons, and he and I didn't get to the point of changing it. That means that other things we plan to do before we get to 2230 haven't happened yet. This Earth may have been saved from the war and even reduced pollution, but it's still in need of rescue."

She remained skeptical but said nothing. She finished her meal while she checked the results from her search and started the next decade. Nothing so far, but she had her doubts that this method would turn up anything. Too many variables. She didn't feel inclined to try to look for a needle in the haystack. Now that she'd actually seen one, she knew how impossible a task that would be.

After she put the empty dishes back on the automaton and sent it scuttling to the restaurant, she ran the next decade, then the one after that without finding anything leading to a problem. When she hit 1860 to 1869, she got a hit of a well-known man who died earlier than he should have in her history. Following the last name, she had the program search both accounts for any matches that might indicate a different outcome for any offspring, but that didn't pan out. Disappointed, she went on to the next ten years.

Two hours later, she'd run every decade she could and had two additional hits, neither of which panned out. "That's it. The search doesn't help us. The change may be so subtle that the computer can't pinpoint it."

"Well, you tried your best, Mals," he answered, standing and stretching. "I'm ready to get some sleep. How 'bout you?"

"I'm still keyed up, but go ahead. I'm going to watch the moon for a while and think while I wind down. I can do that in the dark." She moved to the seat next to the porthole window showing a clear view of the moon's surface, not more than twenty-five kilometers away from the station's locked orbit with it. From here, they never saw the dark side of the moon.

Looking out, she could see the little bumps of the colony domes that spread out like bubbles in bathwater. Aldrin City was the largest and the one nearest to the edge of the Plato crater. That was the first one built, then Lunar City grew after that. That one wasn't too far from the first one. A little farther away toward Mare Serenitatis, she could make out the smaller towns of the two new installations, much smaller than Aldrin City but visible, nonetheless.

All this was done by a new coalition that came together because of the war negotiations. It amazed and surprised Mali. Most of Earth's problems had resulted from people not working together and greedy people looking for ways to profit. So, what had changed in the equation? The man from Chikorpan or the woman in the European Coalition? They'd been assuming that Kwok was the wild card, but what if it was Asleson? What if she was the new player in the picture? Did her information about the war even mention the European leader?

She glanced back to where her grandfather slept soundly. They'd been on the run since they arrived on the station, then researching for hours. Now, the timestamp showed nearly six in the morning. Still, she had one more thing she needed to do.

CHAPTER 22

Space Station 2238

THE BEST PLACE TO TOUCH BASES with Jax was a little coffee bar tucked in the curve near the lifts. The sparse seating discouraged most patrons from enjoying their purchases there. Mali bought a lite mello-caff and a maple-flavored doughnut while she waited at a petite table in a dark corner. Disguised again, she relaxed as people passed by without paying attention to her. She tensed when a pair of her former colleagues ambled by, but they didn't even glance her way.

Fifteen minutes before his usual start time, she spotted Jax as he turned into the shop and marched straight to the counter to order his morning mud, as he called it. He preferred a stronger beverage than the TIM unit provided. As long as she'd known him, Jax never failed to come to the office without stopping to pick up a drink and a sweet roll.

As he shifted away, she slipped up beside him and whispered, "Don't react, Jax. It's Mali. I need to talk to you."

"Huh?" he responded, swiveling his head to peer at her. "Mali? You don't... Oh, never mind."

She'd lifted her sunglasses enough for him to see her eyes, then lowered them again. "Let's sit at that table where I left my drink, okay?"

He glanced that way, picked up his order, then followed her over. "I thought you were lost in the past or dead," he said as he sat down. He stared at her, eyes wide and mouth open like he saw a ghost.

"I got stranded, but I managed to return," she replied, not willing to give him more details. "Tell me what's happening at TIM? Is Edmundson still there?"

Jax nodded, his eyes continuing to dart toward her. "For now. He's been downgraded so far as the decisions go. With the TUs not operative anymore, he doesn't have much to do. How'd you get back?"

"I can't tell you." She stalled then switched back to her questions. "You're still monitoring the timeline. Right?"

"Yeah, but we don't see much. Just lots of thick lines flowing through the system, nothing changing day after day. I honestly don't know what we're doing."

"So, you're not seeing any anomalies?"

He shook his head. "You guys must have corrected the big one even though the word was Coleman said the team the mission went sideways."

"Really? Of course, we fixed it," she lied. If they thought her team did it, she wasn't going to tell them any different. She wrapped her fingers around her cup and smiled at him. "I heard the computers crashed, but I guess it didn't affect the timeline monitoring. Nothing happened at all for you?"

"Oh, yeah, it did. About a month ago, I came to work, and everything was down." Jax paused, taking a bite of his roll, followed by a gulp of coffee. He wiped his mouth with the back of his hand.

Two station security guards walked up to a few feet from the coffee bar and gazed around, obviously looking for someone.

Jax hunched down some and went on. "All the office computers were dead. Took them hours to get 'em back up. When they finally restarted, the time-holo popped right up. It's been steady ever since, a nice smooth feed. But the other machines in the engineering offices, nada. As far as I know, they haven't been able to restore the programs."

"Yet the holo is working? Are you sure it isn't a static display?" This made no sense to Mali. If the data was wiped, then why would the holo timeline display remain? "Are you getting readouts on the screens as well?"

"Yes, Mali. They still come through, and they've been steady, nothing wavering at all."

"Have you run diagnostics to be sure you're not getting old data?"

"Absolutely. The engineers came down to check, but they appear to be the only computers working properly in the entire office. And it's not just us. Other companies who employ the timelines are having troubles as well." He gave her a knowing look that suggested she was in on a secret.

"Two security guards have been watching us," Mali said, noticing they looked their way too often.

"Is it TIM security?" Jax asked, a look of concern in his eyes. "They've been following me around for the past few days. Ever since I met with your roomie. Do you know about that?"

She nodded. "Yes, Brix told me. It looks like the guys are station security." She leaned closer. "But if TIM's guys are likely to show up, I better get going. Thanks for the information, Jax. Stay safe."

At that, he shot a curious look her way. "Are you staying here? We could talk again."

She shook her head, stepping away from him. "Sorry, no. I'll be leaving soon. Don't tell anyone you saw me."

Stepping away from the shadows, she turned left, away from the security guys, and forced herself not to run or hurry at a suspicious pace. Despite what she considered her normal-looking retreat, she felt eyes on her in that way you somehow know when someone is watching you. She fought to keep her steps even, not showing any panic, until she heard footsteps speeding up behind her.

Mali ran, heading for the lift, then diverted to the stairs as her pursuers responded. She could hear their footsteps closing behind her. Without doors, the stairs were always accessible, and she took them in a full run, heading down them as quickly as possible, jumping two at a time as she went.

She outpaced her pursuers, reached the bottom ahead of them, already planning where she might go to hide until they gave up looking for her. This level housed the film theater; she could dash in there. She raced out of the stairwell and straight into another pair of security guards who waited for her.

Well, crap. The sec guys above called for reinforcements.

Mali tried to twist away, but they were on her before she had time enough to escape. One grabbed her and swung her around to face him. At the same time, the other yanked her arms behind her and force-bound her wrists.

"What are you running from, girl?" the one facing her asked, a sneer on his face.

"Let me go." She put on a show of righteousness.

"You have no reason to bother me. I didn't do anything."

"Then why did you run?" One of the other guards asked as he came up.

Four to one. Not good odds. *Think*, Mali told herself. "I heard these two behind me. I didn't know what they intended, so I ran. Just 'cause you guys wear a uniform doesn't mean you couldn't be up to no good."

"Pretty cynical view," the first guard replied, a faked hurt expression on his face. "You don't trust the station security?"

"Not when they don't identify themselves or approach me with a little respect." She glared at him. "Not one of you did that much. So how do I know you're legit?"

"Fair enough," the guard said and whipped out his ID card. She glanced at it. "Officer Burroughs. It looks legit," she conceded.

"I've shown you mine; now show me yours," he said, putting the badge away.

Well, damn. She couldn't do that. "I don't have it with me. I left it in my room."

"Oh-kay, let's start with your name," Burroughs asked as the other two sec guys turned and headed back to their rounds, apparent problem handled.

"Dorothy Gale," she answered. Why not? It felt like she'd gone over the rainbow, and these jerks wouldn't know any different.

He punched the name into his tablet, waited a few seconds, read, then lifted his eyes. "Want to try again?"

"What?"

"You don't seem to be in the station database, Ms. Gale. Do you have a different name?"

"No. I'm not a stationer. I came in on a ship this morning from Titan." She prayed this bluff would work.

"Would that have been the Titan Express or the Grand Mercy?"

Thinking quickly of her cover story and which ship would serve the purpose, she said, "Grand Mercy."

With a nod, he keyed the information into his tablet.

"You won't find me on the roster. I stowed away on it. Didn't have the money for the fare, but I had to travel here." She dropped her eyes as she confessed, hoping they would buy her story.

"So, you're here illegally, didn't pay for the ride in, and you say you've done nothing wrong. Is that correct?"

She nodded. "I had to come to the station to board a moon-colony shuttle. My mother is seriously ill, and I need to see to her."

Burroughs gave his partner a look that even she could see said *bullshit*. "Let's take her to the office, so we can sort this out."

Shoulders drooping, Mali didn't fight as one man on each side grasped her arms, and they led her to the station security office. Once inside, Burroughs removed her sunglasses and looked into her eyes. "Let's see if our facial recognition can identify you coming onto the station." As he reached to push her hair back from her forehead, the wig slipped.

Arching an eyebrow, he lifted the whole hairpiece off her head. With her own hair held back by a net, he saw a clear view of her face. "And in disguise," he commented as he held up an imaging gun and scanned her features.

Mali knew she couldn't bluff anymore. The imager would scan her id chip and search for her in the station recordings.

A moment later, Burroughs confirmed her assessment. "Well, it appears you haven't been truthful. Mali Harper, a former Station Information Employee, considered missing after disappearing about a month ago. Obviously, not missing. What have you been doing, Ms. Harper?"

"Nothing illegal," she protested. "Not even coming on the transports illegally. I was here all along, just not communicating with people."

"This story is changing rapidly. It should be fascinating," he said, his gray eyes flashing in amusement. "Have a seat, and let's talk."

Dropping to the offered chair, Mali tried to spin the best story she could. "I was having some emotional problems and took a few days of leave from my job. Depression set in. I spiraled down, not wanting to see people or do anything, so I locked myself in my apartment and didn't respond to anyone. Two days ago, I came out of it and wanted to meet with one of my co-workers—the man in the coffee shop. I didn't want anyone else to see me. He told me I'd lost my job."

"Right," Burroughs said. "Why do I think that's not what really happened?"

She shrugged. "I'm telling you the truth. I had wild fantasies about traveling to another place and doing crazy things. So, of course, I was retreating from the world."

"Were you doing halucinators?" Burrough's partner asked. The drugs weren't illegal, just not readily available. But people had ways of getting them, and that wasn't unlawful either. So, she offered a weak smile and nodded.

"That makes as much sense as anything you've told us," Burroughs said. "Let's put her in the crib for now. I'm going to contact Station Information to see what they know."

Mali's heart jumped, pumping hard. Her story wouldn't hold long, except TIM might verify her employment. She needed to let Andover know they had apprehended her. Gaia's spit, he'd give her a bad time about this. She could time walk out of the crib, as they called it, but he had to know she'd done it. Once she was alone, she'd use her implant to send a message to him.

She'd left her tablet in their room, only bringing a station credit *chipit* and her pocket watch with her. Her hopes sank to the bottom of her stomach as they searched her, found her items, then put the contents in a bag, which they placed in a locker outside the door leading to the cell.

As they shoved her inside, she heard a little ping in her head as the communication implant went offline. The cell had a signal blocker, so she couldn't use her node to contact Andover. At least, they removed the restraints.

With barely room to lie down on the cot against the back wall, Mali curled up and closed her eyes. She tried to plan, looking for a way she could get out of this mess. If she could just contact her grandfather, he'd be able to do something. When she got down to it, her only option would be to attempt a time jump back to York, but she didn't feel confident enough to handle it. Her jumps had been so erratic, she feared she would make matters worse by trying again.

Although worried, the lack of sleep since early morning in distant London caught her, and she drifted off. In her dreams, she fought to find a way out. She imagined the time threads, looking at them but not seeing them clearly. They seemed different colored, each of the alternate universes showing with a new color. The oldest one, the original in the gold she was used to seeing, but the next older one looked green, while the most recent looked red. She saw the distance she had traveled on each line, so the gold was the longest, bringing her back to her present time. But it looked muddled at the end, as if all the colors had blended together. What could that mean?

Her eyes popped open, not because of a revelation,

but because she heard voices in the outer office talking loudly. A man's voice sounded angry; his words were incoherent to her until he raised his voice a little more.

"I want to see her now," he insisted. At first, she thought it might be her grandfather but realized it didn't sound like him or Jax. Who else knew she was here?

The door open and Burroughs stepped through, standing aside to allow a short, stocky man to enter as she sat up. Her hopes sank, her heart beating faster as she recognized the insignia on the man's shirt. TIM. He was security from TIM. Station sec notified them, and he'd come down to investigate. Well, Gaia's spit. This just got worse.

"Open the door," the man ordered as he pulled out a taser set to ready in case she caused any trouble.

Burroughs opened the cell with an angry jerk, annoyance at being ordered around by TIM security obvious in his scowl of disapproval. The jerk marched right up to her, held up a scanner, noting the results. "It's her," he muttered, motioning to two more men behind him. "Bring her up." He spun around to talk to Burroughs, demanding her belongings as he did.

As the men each grabbed one of Mali's arms, she dug her heels in, knees folding down like a child, forcing them to half-carry her from the room while she objected loudly. "Who the hell are you? What gives you the right to do this?"

"Shut up," the man growled as he turned to look at her. "You're not in a position to argue, Harper, and we have some questions for you to answer. Cooperate or make it worse. It's up to you." The annoyed glower on his face advised her she would be wise to cooperate.

The men hauled her upstairs, indifferent to how much she struggled or if they were hurting her. They dragged her half the way as she repeatedly tried to resist.

She positioned herself to apply any martial arts moves she knew, tricks that had gotten her out of difficult situations on Earth. But these guys knew the same techniques and didn't allow her the opportunity to do anything.

On the third floor, a few people saw them pull her to the TIM office, but they averted their eyes, not wanting to get involved in anything that wasn't their business. Once inside the Information Center lobby, they shoved her to the door on the right of the receptionist. The woman rose to her feet and stared wide-eyed as they pulled her toward it.

"Harper, Mali," the station computer confirmed as soon as they got within sensor range. "Security officer Shaun Levin and Security Officer Frank Wentz," it stated as they went through the door. Behind her, she heard the computer name the third man as Kelton Blackman. While Mali knew the name, she'd never met the head of TIM's security until now.

CHAPTER 23

Space Station 2238

FEAR MADE MALI'S BODY FEEL weak as she considered how much trouble they could cause. Short of a time walk which would reveal everything to them, she had no way out. They took her to a similar cell in their security office and pushed her in.

"Welcome back, Harper," Blackman said with nothing pleasant in his voice. "It seems we can charge you with several offenses from the minor ones that the station security has on you to the abandonment of your job on a time mission. Those would include failure to follow your team leader's orders, contributing to the death of Ross Bonde and injury of Brayden Coleman, and possibly to willfully altering the timeline that has caused great damage to this unit."

"No," she blurted out. "I didn't do that. I tried to help my team as much as I could."

"We'll see. Sit while I process you, then we'll discuss it." He motioned to the other two to lock her in. For a moment, she considered trying to rush them to fight her way out, but the taser remained in Blackman's hand, ready to use.

Reluctantly, Mali sat, aware that she'd gotten used to the cozier seating of the cushioned chairs and the wooden kitchen chairs that were not prevalent on this space globe. Molded plastic formed everything here, easy to clean and sanitize, but not nearly as comfortable. Not that they wanted anyone to feel at ease in the holding cells.

These thoughts didn't take her mind off the situation. As she puzzled through the changes, she considered it curious that people recalled things that occurred up to four weeks ago. Dianna had commented about not seeing Andover for several years. If an event changed the timeline that much, they would have no memory of the other events unless they happened in the alternative version as well. Yet, Blackman's comments led her to believe that they were aware of her mission and everything that went wrong.

On the other hand, they were TIM, and they had the history volumes stored. What if they had copied them somewhere for a backup, and they retained an original copy of the unchanged records? She had the ones she had downloaded on her tablet, and they hadn't changed. So, maybe TIM's agents knew what took place before in the same way.

Blackman returned with one guard–the man the computer had identified as Shaun Levin—who carried the few possessions she'd had with her. Most notably, he held the pocket watch in his hand, chain wrapped around his fingers. She fought the urge to tell him not to fiddle with it, but she didn't want to call attention to it. Relief washed through her when he took the timepiece and stuck it back in the bag along with her chipit. He set it on a small table just outside the cell.

Sitting backward on the chair before her so he could rest his arms on the frame, Blackman faced her with a stern look on his pudgy face. It would be almost comical if she weren't in such trouble. "Now, Harper, why don't you tell me your side of the story?"

She ran her tongue over her lower lip nervously, trying to determine what he wanted to hear. "About the mission and what happened there?"

"That's a start."

She began relating the complete tale from the moment they arrived in the clearing outside London. She avoided any detail about ignoring some of Bonde's rules, only saying they had disagreed a few times but were getting along well when they arrived in York. "I did everything possible to assist Bonde and Coleman. They didn't train me to be on an adjustment team when Edmonson assigned me to it, so I felt I needed to show them I could do the job." She coughed and asked for water.

Blackman nodded, then Levin brought her a cup. Mali hadn't realized how dehydrated she'd gotten in the past few hours until she had talked for nearly thirty minutes straight. Her throat felt dry and scratchy, and she could hear the hoarseness in her voice.

"So, is that your story? Not quite the same one that Coleman told when he returned. Although you admit you involved a local in your activities. According to Coleman, you brought the man back to the TU when you returned. What about your disappearance? Explain that."

Her eyes narrowed. "In the first place, I did not bring Doyle back. He followed me, and I didn't know it until he showed up. My mistake in getting acquainted with someone, but I certainly didn't plan to show him the TU."

"Nonetheless, you did, and he saw the unit, becoming aware of the time travel aspect. Then Coleman stated you both disappeared in 'a haze of golden light,' to quote him. What happened?"

She shrugged. "I can't tell you."

"Can't or won't?"

"Can't, because I have no idea what happened," she lied. She was not about to tell him her grandfather set the pocket watch to take her to Glasgow, and she accidentally activated it. Not with the timepiece sitting on the table. She didn't want them to know Andover Morrison still lived and could time walk.

"So, you're suggesting that you and this local magically disappeared from the clearing?"

She nodded. "I can't say how it occurred or why."

"Then what transpired? Where did you end up?"

"In another town and a different decade."

"Be more specific. Where and when? Did you actually time jump without a TU?"

"It appears that way. I can't tell you any more about that 'cause I have no explanation. We just transported to a place called Glenbrook near the Scottish border in 1765." She figured Blackman didn't know enough about Earth's towns to know if she was telling the truth.

"Right... How did you get back to the station? Did you somehow hitch a ride on a TU? Oh, wait. No more units were on Earth, were there?"

Uh-oh, here's where this is going to get complicated. My fabrications will bounce higher than a ball on the moon. But I can't tell them the truth. She shrugged. "Yesterday, I woke up in my residence on this station. I can't explain it."

He snorted at her answer. "You expect me to believe that?"

"Believe what you want, but that's what happened." She shifted her weight in the uncomfortable chair. "I have no other explanation."

"Oh, for... How could that be?"

"I haven't a clue."

"Try." Blackman lifted his body enough to shove his chair closer to her. "I want to hear at least a hypothesis."

"Well, Gaia loves me, and she's a powerful goddess. Maybe she took pity on me and transported me home. Or, more likely, we can't exist in the past, so the timeline brings us back to the present. I don't know!" she said, adding indignation to her bluff.

With a scrape of the chair's legs, Blackman was out of it and slapped her hard enough to knock her onto the floor. Gasping in shock, Mali crawled to her knees and pressed a hand against her throbbing face. Lances of pain pulsed through her cheekbone, making her dizzy. Blackman stood over her, hands clenched at his sides, as tense as a tightly drawn elastic band ready to snap. She glared up at him, not attempting to get to her feet.

Forcing her mouth to move, she mumbled, "Hitting me will not change my answer. I. Don't. Know. If you think things have altered for you, then you have no idea what the time shift has done to me."

Her words did not move him as he let go with a kick to her ribs that sent her flying again. Mali slammed against the curved station wall, jarring her body from spine to knees with the impact. She hurt as badly as she had when she'd hit the tree a mere two weeks earlier in her actual time. Barely able to budge, she slowly tried to shift her legs, fearing that she had spinal damage. One moved a little, then the other. At least, she could do that much, but it hurt as she struggled to sit up.

"Tell me the truth, girl!" Blackman's face twisted with an angry scowl. "This will only get worse. What happened when you disappeared? How did you return here?"

Cowering against the wall, Mali repeated exactly what she'd said before. Her voice broke with pain as she spoke, the words slurring a little as she fought back the tears. She refused to cry in front of these men. She noticed Levin stood just outside the cell door near the table, keeping watch on her things and looking away when Blackman got rough.

Now, he stepped forward as Blackman's eyes narrowed and darkened, then Levin said, "Maybe she needs a little time to think, boss. If you kill her, we won't get any more answers."

Kill? Would they go that far? Mali felt sick inside, like she would throw up. She struggled for the strength to tear into Blackman. If she had made her move earlier, she might have taken him, but with Levin there, she wouldn't have a chance. Her pocket watch was on the table, so close. If she could get enough energy, would she be able to reach and activate it before one of them caught her?

Even if she told them the truth, she doubted they would believe her. Unless they knew people could move through time without a time machine.

Blackman stepped toward her, and she cringed against the corner, tucking her legs in. Then he stood down as he considered Levin's words. "You're right, Levin. I need a short break. Watch her. Get her back in the chair. We'll resume when I come back."

As Blackman exited, Levin gazed down at her, and their eyes met a moment.

Did she detect sympathy? Maybe.

"Listen, girl, you'd better tell him something better than you have. That story is too fantastical. You Gaia worshippers like to believe in fairytales, but we all know they aren't true. Your so-called goddess can't do anything to help you 'cause she doesn't exist." His voice wasn't mean, but it didn't sound friendly either.

"Maybe not, but if more had worshipped her, maybe the Earth wouldn't have been messed up." Not that she was a follower. She just liked the expletives associated with the goddess. She took a careful breath, finding it easier to breathe as the initial pain subsided. She was bruised but not broken.

Levin sneered, then reached down, grabbed Mali's arms, and pulled her up to her feet, facing him. Gathering her strength, Mali jerked back with her shoulders, yanked him toward her, and used her forehead as a battering ram, smacking into his head. Shocked, Levin released her and staggered back. Free, Mali stumbled to grab the pocket watch, snatching it off the table and twisting the winder counterclockwise. Her fingers fumbled, and the timepiece fell, sliding under the table.

Mali knelt to grab it as Levin spun toward her

"You little bitch!" Levin's arms locked around her shoulders, prepared to drag her back into the cell.

The watch was just out of reach of her fingers, but a shimmering thread appeared before her eyes. Desperate, she reached for it.

CHAPTER 24

York England 1768

A LOUD THUNK, FOLLOWED BY thudding sounds, caught Brix's attention as she passed by Mali's room. She turned back to it. Were Mali and Andover back already? She'd thought they'd planned to return in the morning. She hesitated a few moments, uncertain if she should knock. Then an angry man's voice shouted, "What the hell did you do?"

She twisted the door handle and charged through the door. A guy, dressed in a security uniform, pressed one arm across Mali's throat, holding her to him while his free hand tried to grip her hands, which were grabbing at the restraining arm. She twisted in his hold, trying to wiggle free before he choked her.

Without hesitation, Brix charged across the room, leaped onto the guy's back, hands gripping his shoulder, and wrapped her legs around his middle. He staggered as her weight threw his balance off, but he didn't release Mali. Letting go with one hand, Brix fisted it and pummeled the side of his head over and over to draw his attention away from Mali.

The tactic worked, and his grip loosened. Mali slid

down enough to allow her to shift her hands under his hold, shoving his arm away and twisting free. She stumbled forward, and her jerky steps took her to the edge of the bed, where she grabbed the nearby chamber pot. Lifting it in both hands, she turned and stomped back to the man, then she crashed the crock into his head with a hard swing. As it thudded into him, last evening's contents sloshed into his face, and he staggered back from the impact.

"Fuck!" he yelled as the cold urine hit his eyes. He lifted his hands to his face to wipe at them.

At the same time, Brix released her hold on him and dropped to the floor like a panther, eyes scanning the room for a weapon. Grabbing a large vase, she didn't even bother to dump the flowers before she grabbed the neck end and swung it at him like a baseball bat. With a loud thump and the sound of shattering china, it broke against his head, and the man crashed to the ground, falling like a load of meteor rocks.

"Is he unconscious?" Brix shouted, eyes scanning for anything else she could use to hit him again.

Mali kneeled to check. "Looks like it. Thanks, Brix."

As Brix handed Mali an ornate figurine from the desk, she looked at her disheveled clothes and cut and bruised face and said, "You look like you've been battered. Use that if he wakes up before I find something to tie him with."

"Grab the curtain ties," Mali advised, taking the statue and hefting it in both hands. She kept her eyes on the man as Brix attacked the curtains to undo the tie-backs.

Although a little on the fancy side, the cords would be more than enough to restrain the intruder. Brix kneeled by him, grabbed his arms, pulled them behind him, and wrapped one tie-back around his wrists, tying it with a double set of knots. Next, she moved to his ankles and secured them the same way. He wasn't getting out of there easily.

"What happened to you?" Brix asked as she worked.

"Wrong place at the wrong time," Mali said shortly, catching her breath. "This guy is TIM security. He and his boss wanted to know how I got back to the station. You know I couldn't tell him."

Mali sat down on the floor, her back braced against the bed, and closed her eyes as she winced in pain. "The other guy roughed me up when he didn't like my answers. Actually, this one accidentally gave me the opening to get to my pocket watch and get out of there. Unfortunately, he grabbed me before I completed the turn, and I dropped it. So, I used a thread, and he came along for the ride. I'm surprised I'm actually back here. I expected the jump to skew."

"How badly are you hurt?" Brix asked. She saw blood on Mali's face, a cut lip, and she looked like she was in pain.

"Not too bad. At least, I don't think so. I can still move even though it hurts. I hit my back pretty hard against the station wall when Burroughs, that's the other guard, kicked me into it. So, maybe bruised or even cracked vertebrae... a couple of pulled muscles."

Eyes showing her concern, Brix said, "I'm going to get Bray."

"You do that," Mali said quietly as she lowered her head against her hands and closed her eyes.

Running down the hallway, Brix knocked on Bray's door and waited impatiently for him to answer. She looked up as he opened it. Her eyes scanned across his bare chest, then dropped to see he'd thrown on a pair of trousers, the top button still undone.

"What's happened?" Bray asked.

"Mali's back, but she had a problem on the station. Come with me to her room."

"What kind of problem?" he asked as he stepped back, grabbed a shirt, then followed her down the hall.

"You'll see." She hurried ahead of him, threw open the entry, and ushered him inside.

Bray took a few steps in and halted. "Who's he?"

Mali had managed to climb onto the bed and sit against the pillows while Brix was gone. She turned her head toward them. "Name's Shaun Levin. A TIM security guard. He hitched a ride back with me."

Brix stepped past him to go to the washbasin in the water closet. Thankful Harper had his house plumbed, she grabbed a washcloth, wet it, and then came back to hand it to Mali. "Wipe your face. You've got blood on it."

Without question, Mali took the cloth and began wiping from her eyes to her mouth, turning the fabric to a dirty red color as she got the worst of it off her. "Have you seen him before?"

Bray stared at the guy, shook his head, and hurried to help as Brix began to lift him up.

"Let's prop him against the wall," she instructed, and Bray helped her pull him over. Levin's limp body slouched down as soon as they released him, but at least he wasn't lying in the middle of the floor. Brix turned to Mali. "Now, tell us everything."

"Right. I have a few questions for you as well, Brayden. What did you tell the debriefing team at TIM when you returned alone?"

He cast a curious gaze at her, his eyes blinking with uncertainty. "I told them what happened, Mali. All the details. Most of it was already in the record on the TU. All the reports Bonde had made during the mission. I just filled in the parts after he died and when you disappeared from the clearing."

"You made it sound like I was a traitor," Mali hissed, her anger surfacing in an angry scowl at him. "Like I was uncooperative and a liability on the mission."

"I did not," he argued. "I said you were stubborn and hardheaded, but I never accused you of not doing your job. I was angry, Mali. Injured and angry and confused by what happened. But I didn't indicate at any time that you weren't committed to the mission."

"Well, that's certainly not the way they saw it."

"Look, guys," Brix interrupted. "Arguing about this isn't helping anything. What is the situation on the station now, Mali? Where's Andover?"

Her face scrunched into near tears. "He's still there. I didn't tell them anything about him, but I couldn't get a message to him about getting arrested."

"Start at the beginning, Mali. Tell us everything that happened."

She wiped her face again and asked Brix to get her a glass of water. She took deep breaths, visibly calming herself. After a couple of sips, she talked, telling them about everything from when they'd arrived, what they'd done and learned.

"Like I said, hardheaded," Bray muttered, shaking his head. "Always doing what you're told not to do. Did you at least learn anything else from Jax?"

Rubbing her jaw where it was still sore, Mali let the little dig go. "A bit, mostly to do with the situation at TIM. He told me the computers were wiped of all the time-thread information, even the backups. They can't restore them, so the threads aren't being drawn to the computers anymore. Except he said the monitor room holo-display is still showing all the lines with no variations. Why would it do that if the information wasn't still there somewhere?"

Tapping his fingers on the dressing table, Bray's

brow creased as he thought. "I believe the lines are static, computer-generated whether the timeline is feeding through it or not. If nothing is wavering, then it isn't actively reading them."

"You're probably right. So, who could have wiped all the computers? Who would know where all the files were and have access to do it?" Mali asked.

"The directors might," he answered. "The access is coded into the entry system, so they'd need an iris id check to get into the room where they're located. Once someone has access, three passcodes are required to change anything on the computers. Only someone with access to all three codes as well as iris id can do it. Not many people have that."

"Wouldn't the central computer have the record of which iris id entered the room?"

"Not if it was wiped." Bray ran a hand through his hair, and his shirt slid open wider across his bare chest. Brix's lips twitched as she appreciated the view.

A groan from their guest brought their attention back to Levin, who was slowly coming around after the head-bashing. He wrinkled his nose and squinted his eyes, disgust on his face. No doubt the urine still bothered him. Mali could almost smell it, even sitting several feet from him on the bed.

"Welcome back, Levin," she said. "That is your name, right?"

His eyes lifted to hers as he gritted his teeth and glared. "Where am I? What did you do?"

"Uh-oh, you sound grumpy, mister," she admonished. "I'd like you to meet my friends. This is Brix, my roommate, and this guy is Brayden Coleman. Have you guys met before?" She turned her eyes to Bray.

"Nope. He doesn't look familiar," Bray answered after a brief glance. "Not one of the people I talked to in debrief."

"Never met him," Levin spat out. "Where am I? Is this some weird holo-room on the station?"

"No, no. Nothing like that. You're in a house in York, England, in 1767. We've time traveled. The bad news is– we don't have a way to return you to the station, so you're pretty much at our mercy here."

"You're lying." He may have said the words, but Levin's eyes darted all around the room, pausing at the window where blue skies and green trees showed in the sunlight, and the shock on his face said he believed her.

"Who do you work for?" Brayden asked, rising and coming closer to the bound man.

"I'm a security officer, and that's all any of you need to know," he growled out. Anger oozing, he sat up straight against the wall, lips clamped in a tight line.

"Not exactly true," Bray said. "We need to know more than that. So, you work for TIM security, according to Mali. The other guy— What was his name, Mali?"

"Blackman. I didn't hear the first name."

"Right. Blackman. So, he's your boss?" Bray pursued. "Who does he work for?"

When Levin refused to answer, Bray hauled off and kicked him in the gut, looking satisfied as the man choked out a gasp of pain and doubled over. "What's to be gained by not talking? You're not getting back to the station. Your whole future will be here on Earth, and we're the ones who will determine your circumstances, so you might want to be a little more cooperative."

Levin struggled to work his way back to a sitting position, then his eyes roamed from Bray to Mali, then to Brix. "You're serious?"

"Absolutely. We're all exiled from the future now," Bray replied in a reasonable tone. "TIM had me on a watch list, Brix was marked as trouble, and apparently,

Mali's appearance back on the station was considered hostile. Why is that?"

Levin shrugged. "I don't know. I follow orders is all."

"Who's giving the orders? Not Blackman, right? Someone higher up?" Bray stepped back, turned in a circle as if he was considering something, then swung back around, bending his knees deeply, and came in with a hard right to Levin's chin.

The man's head snapped back, banging against the wall.

Mali cringed as it hit. "Don't knock him out again, Bray."

"All he has to do is answer." Bray stepped back, returning to the chair at the dressing table.

Levin shook his head to clear it, then spat on the floor.

"Tsk. Mrs. Renfrow won't like that," Brix said, speaking for the first time. "Listen to us. We don't want to hurt you, although you guys did a pretty nasty job on Mali. But we will if you don't answer our questions. But as Bray said, it can be worse than us simply turning you loose in a safe place in England. If you don't cooperate, we can dump you in a terrible place where you likely won't live more than a few days before something kills you. Is that what you want?"

"Take me back to the space station, and I'll tell you what you want to know," he said in a rush as his eyes narrowed. "That's the deal."

"Apparently, you didn't understand," Mali said sweetly. "We don't have a TU to take you back. None of us can go back to the station, so you're stuck here. Now, what's it going to be? Do you want the chance of a happy life in the past or a miserable one?"

Levin's head dropped to his chest, and he drew in a deep breath as he considered her words for at least a minute.

Mali gazed out the window, and Brix could guess her thoughts. What would they do with him if he didn't cooperate? She didn't doubt Brayden and Mali could carry out their threat.

Finally, he spoke. "I work for the executive board. Private security. They wanted me to work with Blackman when they found out Mali Harper might be on the station."

"That wasn't so hard, was it?" Brix said. She crossed her arms and leaned back against the door, hoping Renfrow wasn't going to make an appearance at any time. She would be up to start on breakfast soon, and they didn't have an explanation for Mali's missing grandfather. They sure didn't need for her to find this man in Mali's bedroom.

"Why are they hunting her?" Bray asked. "What even tipped them that she was on the station?"

"Someone called in anonymously, so station security was alerted. When we heard they'd found her, TIM responded. Our computers had been trashed, and she's the most likely suspect."

"Me?!" Mali's voice shot to a new high.

"Who else would it be?" Levin glared at her. "You were clearly on the station. I don't know how you got back to it without the TU, but you had means, motive, and opportunity."

"Well, you're terribly mistaken," she growled back. "How I got there is none of your concern, but I will tell you I wasn't there more than twenty-four hours. I sure as hellfire didn't have an opportunity to even remotely touch the computers in TIM. My guess is you should have been looking at someone within the company."

"Says you!" He strained against his restraints in his fury.

"Enough!" Bray interrupted. "We need information, Levin, and I hope you have it." He slammed his fist into his palm to emphasize what he might do if Levin didn't talk. "Start with when these computers failed. When they apparently were sabotaged."

Levin's jaw twitched as his gaze locked on Bray. Then he ground out a reluctant reply. "I don't know the exact date. It was about four weeks ago when Blackman involved me in the problem. He told me the TU's were having problems. They only had four left of the original six the primary designers had built. They'd hired an expert to look at the designs schematics and either repair or rebuild the units."

"What happened to the TU's?" Mali asked. She knew her grandfather had stolen one, but what about the other three?

"As I understand it, TU-Two had developed problems on the return from an expedition and malfunctioned when trying to load any new destination threads into it."

"That would have been the research unit sent out a couple of days before ours," Bray said.

"TU-One had already failed and was locked in its storage area. I don't know what was wrong with it. Then TU-Five had disappeared when it went back on a mission. TU-Three was Bonde's unit; you know what happened to that one."

"It only needed new solar panels." Bray was on his feet again. "It should have been repaired and ready to go again within a day or two."

"Not from what I was told," Levin shot back. "The computers are screwed up in it. They figured either you or Harper had something to do with it."

Bray shook his head. "Guilty until proven innocent, I guess. What a twisted mess."

"What about the main computers?" Mali asked,

ignoring Bray's outburst.

"According to Blackman, they went down unexpectedly. When they came back up about forty minutes later, the whole timeline unit appeared broken, not drawing threads into it anymore. They had to reboot it a couple of times before it resumed pulling the threads, and the monitoring unit started functioning normally."

"If it's working as it should, then what's the problem?" Brix asked.

Levin bit his lip, not eager to tell them. Bray took a few steps closer, ready to persuade him. "The main computers no longer have any contact with the thread program." He paused, sucked his lower lip, then resumed. His words came out slowly, with reluctance. "Or any records of the schematics or anything to do with capturing the time threads. Apparently, there never had been much on how the computers attracted and contained the threads in the unit. But what little they stored had been erased."

Shocked, no one spoke for a few moments as the full extent of the damage set in. Brix thought about it. Mali had said she suspected Dianna's group had hijacked the timeline during the shutdown, transferring or duplicating the active lines to their monitoring center. It made sense if they were tracking the changes and preventing the actual monitoring unit from seeing them. But to actually get into TIM's secure area and wipe the computer's data and the backup? Did Dianna have access to the main computers?

"Who could do that?" Brix asked after the long silence.

"We assumed one of you," Shaun replied, his gaze going from Bray to Mali.

"Not us," Bray answered. "We don't have the expertise to do it, nor the access." He shot Mali a questioning look.

She shook her head slightly, but her eyes narrowed, and she asked, "Where is Varsi right now?"

"I haven't seen him since just after dinner. I presume he's in his room," Brix answered.

"Go get him."

CHAPTER 25

York England 1768

BOUNDING DOWN THE STAIRS TWO at a time, Brix jumped the last three, almost slipping before she dashed to the dining room. She'd taken a few moments to check Varsi's room before she'd headed downstairs and hadn't gotten a response. While she wasn't positive, she guessed Mali suspected his involvement in the computer sabotage. If he'd left them during the night, it would pretty well point to him dropping the tip to TIM about Mali being on the station. And if Varsi had gone, how would they be able to get Andover Harper back?

As she turned the corner into the dining room, she caught her breath and slowed to a walk. She exhaled when she saw Varsi seated at the table, having an early breakfast, while Mrs. Renfrow bustled about the table to set it up for the rest of the house.

"Good morning, Ms. Brixton." Varsi looked up from his plate.

"Ah, one other is up now. Will the rest be down shortly?" Renfrow asked, glancing Brix's way as she placed the utensils next to a plate.

"It will be a few minutes yet, Mrs. Renfrow. We have

a minor problem upstairs, and we could use Mr. Varsi's help. Would you mind, sir?"

Varsi blinked, then wiped his mouth. "Of course. What has happened?"

"I'll explain on the way," she said and turned back toward the stairs.

He joined her a few moments later, catching up quickly.

"Mali and her grandfather time jumped to the space station last night so they could try to find out what Dianna and her crew have been doing. Mali returned about forty minutes ago, but she's not alone. One of the TIM security guards was hanging onto her when she jumped."

Alarm showed on Varsi's face as his eyes grew bigger and his mouth dropped open. "What about Harper? Where is he?"

"Not back yet. We'll tell you everything when we get to Mali's room." Brix pressed ahead.

As she opened the door, Mali looked up from the bed where she'd plopped down to wait. A look of relief crossed her face when she saw Varsi behind Brix, and she motioned to Levin. "We have a minor problem."

Varsi stood just inside the door, hands on his hips as he surveyed the room. "It appears you do. Explain, please."

Mali recapped everything which had happened on the station from the time they captured her until she arrived back in her room. Then she and Bray told him what they'd found out about the computer sabotage at TIM.

Brix turned to Varsi, eyes locked on his. "It happened within four weeks of the date Bray and I left the station, but the changes look more significant than just this sabotage. Were you involved in any way?"

Varsi stared at her for a moment before shaking his head. "No. Nothing I've done would impact the station." He turned to Mali. "Where is your grandfather?"

"I don't know. I left him asleep at the Traveler's Center when I went to meet a contact."

"So, he's stuck on the station," Varsi concluded. "We need to get him back as soon as possible." He shot a dark stare at Levin. "Has TIM arrested him?"

Still tied up with limited movement, Levin shifted his weight from one side to the other. "I don't know who you're talking about. All I know is what I've told them already." He tilted his head toward Mali and Bray, and his voice rose in volume as he spoke. "No one said anything about another person. You're all endangering the future with this meddling around in the past. I hope TIM catches all of you and convicts you for this act of treason."

"Shut him up," Varsi ordered, his gaze directed at Bray.

In response, Bray found a scarf lying on the dressing table, twisted it into a roll, and used it to gag their visitor.

Ignoring the not-so-gentle way Bray performed his task, Mali looked at Varsi. "If it wasn't you, who else could do it? The security on the computer is high level."

"Indeed, it is," Varsi agreed. "Three levels of authority are needed to open the room, and the computer itself requires three different passwords to access plus a confirmed voice identification. Only five people on the station have access to the room; all are on the board of directors. Three different people hold the passwords, and the voice protocol is only keyed for two people. One is the security chief, and the other is–or at least was–your grandfather."

"Grandfather is one of the access people?"

"I imagine it has most likely changed in the years since we went missing, but it's also possible no one bothered to change it. But I'm sure it wouldn't be Andy. He would never do it. The entire timeline integration with the time units was his mother's work."

"Whoever did, it took at least seven people," Brix noted. "Seven people working together willingly. Or did someone force them? Have any other employees of TIM vanished with no one knowing what happened? If not, then all could be willing participants."

Sputtering through his gag, Levin shook his head and made an exaggerated shrug with his shoulders.

"It looks like Levin doesn't know anything about disappearances," Mali said. "So, what do we do now?"

Varsi rubbed the back of his neck while he considered the question. He tilted his head toward Levin. "What are you going to do with him?"

"We thought we'd leave him in Scotland with enough money to give him time to find work. I'm sure someone would hire on a hard worker even though he's had no experience in this world." Mali's grin looked wicked.

Varsi nodded. "Very well, then. For now, let's leave him here, but make sure he can't get free, Coleman. Then, let's go down to breakfast before Renfrow comes looking for us. We'll need to invent an excuse for Andy."

"We can tell her he had an early appointment and left a couple of hours ago," Mali said, watching as Bray checked to make sure Levin was secure.

Brix paused a moment to glance at their hostage, then followed the others downstairs to breakfast.

§ § §

Mali drew another line on a sheet of paper she'd

found in her grandfather's office. She labeled it *Alt2*. Above it, she had marked two other lines as *Orig* and *Alt1*. Now she added one more and wrote *Alt3*.

Brix sat next to her, leaning her elbow on the desk, her hand propping her chin up as she watched Mali build her timelines. Confused, she tried to figure out which one she was on. Across from her, Rashid worked on his own version of the times lines, squinting his eyes occasionally, presumably to picture the lines in his mind.

"Okay," she murmured. "The first is my original timeline. It stretches from the station to 1763, the earliest date in this century I've visited. Doyle and I jumped into London in 1898 by accident. But I now believe it was on an alternate timeline. Varsi, were you in 1898 on an alternate line or the main timeline?"

He glanced up. "I wasn't in 1898."

Mali's head came up, her brow wrinkling in confusion. "But I saw you there. I almost followed your time jump."

Varsi stared at her and said nothing for a few moments as he thought. "Maybe I haven't done it yet."

"How would that work?" Brix asked.

"We're functioning out of time and in alternate universes," he replied. "Since Mali jumped ahead, she may have encountered something which will come in between the time where I am now and where she jumped. But I haven't done it yet."

"You were checking on power plants along—"

"Don't tell me. I don't want to know any details. It might influence what my original thought was in doing it." Varsi set his pen down and got to his feet, pacing in front of his seat as he thought.

"How do we know which timeline we're on?" Mali asked. "Is this one the original or an alternate?"

He halted. "Let's check."

"How?" Mali didn't understand that. How could she check to see which line she was on? All she saw when she envisioned the lines were the lines themselves, barely able to discern the years on them and then only if she concentrated on it. She landed on a specific date, mainly by visualizing the actual figures in her mind.

"When you see the lines, picture your location and see which line it shows on. You'll see a bump or a dot on the line representing your current location. Like everything else in connecting to the time threads, you need to ask for what you want and allow your mind to see it."

Rashid's explanation sounded simple, just as Grandfather's often did, but executing the advice was another issue. Nonetheless, she closed her eyes and focused on the time threads within her. She pulled them up, one by one–the original and the three alternates. *Where am I? Which line?* She asked the questions over and over, not seeing anything even suggesting a bump. She squinted her eyes enough to see Rashid standing still with his eyes half-closed, focusing on his own timelines.

"Got it," he said. "We're on an alternate line. One I've been to a few times."

Mali blinked, and for just a moment, she glimpsed a red dot on one of the shorter lines. Was it her indicator? "I think I saw mine. An alternate as well."

"I don't get it," Brix said. While she still sat at the desk, she'd straightened up. "I only saw the one line."

"You also time walk?" Rashid asked as his head whipped toward her.

"You're being generous," Brix answered. "Bray and I used one of Mali's watches to get us to Andover's house. I presume it would have been on the original timeline. Then, he set up another transport to bring us here. I figured it was the same thread."

"No, I don't believe so. Both Mali and I are on alternates, so I'm guessing Andy sent you to the alternate line where he knew this was happening. But you say you can see one thread, is that right?"

"Yes. Harper says I have the gene, but I've only done it once."

"Interesting." Rashid regarded her with the look of a man studying a new bug. He stepped closer, his dominant hand rubbing his chin.

"So, when you and your grandfather went to the station, was it in this alternate universe?" Bray asked. He sat near the bookcase in a comfortable armchair, but he sat up straight as he spoke to Mali.

"I don't know. It might have been. It looked the same as the one you and Brix described, but it also seemed off. Could it have been yet another one? I see three alternate lines now, but I think I've accounted for all of them. My original, the jump to 1898, then the one to Austria, and on to York. But I took Doyle back to his time. Does this mean I put him in an alternate timeline rather than the main one?"

"If you picked the longest line, then he is on the original," Rashid answered. "But when you returned, you must have—"

"I used my pocket watch. Grandfather set it to bring me back here, so he knows we're on an alternate line." Mali's shoulders slumped as she realized he'd known he was sending her to the alternate one. But she had chosen the original thread when they'd left the house in Scotland, hadn't she?

"Of course," Rashid agreed. "We had been working on this project together and agreed to start it on an alternate line rather than the main one until we saw how it panned out."

"So, you haven't been to the future to see the result of this yet?" Mali walked around the desk to sit on the edge as she talked.

Brow furrowed, Rashid paced to the bookcase and back. "Not yet. But I don't think this alone would result in the changes on the station. Something entirely different has happened there. I'm guessing it's unrelated to what we've done."

"Maybe. It seems to be more of a revolution, but it still means people who had the codes sabotaged the computers. Who might do it?" Mali stared at her feet, trying to make sense of everything she'd learned.

"It comes down to whoever has the codes now." Rashid waved the question off. "But who is going to accuse the board? They'd probably deny it, anyway."

"Could someone have a back entrance to the computer?" Brix asked.

Mali turned toward her. "What do you mean?"

"Well, in the past, a programmer would often leave a way to get into the computer through a so-called back door, one only they would have the codes to access. They considered it an emergency entrance, I guess, in case something went wrong."

Mali looked back to Rashid. "Who might have that kind of code for the TIM computers? Who programmed it?"

Varsi chucked. "Only one person I can think of... Adelle Morrison."

"What? My great-grandmother? But she's been dead for at least two decades and hadn't worked for TIM for longer than that." Mali rolled her eyes as if to dismiss the whole idea.

"That may be the case, but she was the main programmer of the system when it was set up. She would be the most likely person."

"Could she have given the codes to someone?" Bray asked. "For instance, her son?"

Varsi shrugged. "If Andy has them, he's never said anything about it. I doubt she passed them to anyone."

After a glance at the clock on the shelf, Mali said, "It's almost ten, and Grandfather hasn't returned yet. I'm afraid security has found him, and he's in one of their cells. If he'd used his programmed timepiece, he would have arrived by seven this morning. So, he hasn't activated it or walked back himself. We need to find him."

"You may be right," Varsi agreed. "But I should be the one to go to the station. You're already in trouble there, and both of those two...," He paused to wave at Bray and Brix. "... are already on their watch list as well. Since I am considered dead, they won't be looking for me."

"No, I need to go with you," Mali insisted. She stood to face him.

"I don't think so. You look bruised and move stiffly. Let's wait until noon to see if Andy is just running late. Since he's capable of returning without any aids, he should be back by then."

Mail frowned, her lips tightening. She didn't like the idea of Varsi going alone, and she wanted to retrieve her watch. She didn't want it lying around for anyone to accidentally activate.

"While we're waiting, let's talk about my plan for eliminating Hitler in the twentieth century. Since you stopped me from killing him as a fetus, I need to take–"

"Wait. I thought you hadn't been to that future yet," Mali said.

"I said I hadn't been to 1878, but to the year of Hitler's birth? Yes, we met there."

"Was this on this same timeline?"

Varsi smiled, a close-mouthed, sly-looking smirk. "Yes."

"So, you have already checked out the future of this particular event." Mali accused.

"I went to 1889, but not earlier. That year is on this thread, which branched off when your team came back to reset our changes."

That did it! She *knew* Rashid hadn't been telling her everything. But if he wasn't in London, then going to Austria had jumped another dimension. How was this happening? It couldn't have been anything she did. She barely made the jumps, let alone leaping into one she knew nothing about.

"How are you manipulating my time jumps?"

He blinked, giving her a hard look. "I told you before. I am not altering your jumps, let alone knowing how to interfere with them."

"Then how is it happening?" *Someone* had to be controlling it. Mali slammed her hand on the desktop in frustration.

Brix jumped at the sudden action, stepping back. "Hey, don't get so tense about it, Mali. There's an explanation, I'm sure. You just haven't found it yet."

"Like you would know." Mali growled her answer, then instantly felt bad about it. "Sorry, Brix. I'm just on edge with all this stuff happening."

"Yeah, we get it," Bray said. He turned his eyes to Varsi. "You were going to tell us about your plan for dealing with Hitler. While you're at it, give us an idea of what you hope to accomplish."

As Varsi began repeating the spiel he'd presented to her and Doyle, Mali tuned him out, sat back down, and focused on her timelines, adding dates and jumps. Somehow, she had to make sense of this and why she wasn't controlling her own jumps. She'd really thought she'd picked up on Varsi's jump from London, and it had somehow guided her to Austria. Now she had no idea.

As the clock struck noon with a series of bell-like chimes, Mali lifted her head and gazed at Varsi, who talked quietly with Bray and Jinx. "I'm going to check the house to see if my grandfather is back."

Varsi raised his head and nodded. "It seems doubtful. He would have looked for you if he were."

She agreed with that, but a quick look through the house would confirm it. She was sure he remained on the station, either arrested or still hiding out because he couldn't find her. The only thing holding him there was the uncertainty of her fate.

Within ten minutes, she'd confirmed he hadn't returned and evaded alarming Renfrow. "We need to jump to the station," she announced as she came through the door.

Varsi straightened his shoulders and rose to his feet. Mali slipped up beside him, putting her hand on his shoulder. He shifted his gaze to her hand, then her face. "You shouldn't come."

She shook her head. "I need to find my grandfather. If they have him, he'll be in the TIM holding cells, and I know where there are. I'm going."

"Be careful," Brix said. "Don't take unnecessary risks."

CHAPTER 26

Space Station 2238

WHEN THE WORLD SOLIDIFIED AROUND them, Mali gaped at her surroundings. They stood in a vast, mostly empty space with only a dozen or so racks against one wall and a heavy metal door directly across from them. She released her grip on Varsi's shoulder while her eyes focused on the protruding transparent box set on the curve of the outside wall. In it, thirty or forty golden strands ran through, pulsing and glowing with energy. Not anywhere close to the thick cables that usually ran through the boxes when a mission launched.

"You brought us to a TU bay." Her voice squeaked with sudden anxiety. She hadn't expected to be in the heart of TIM when they were trying to avoid drawing attention to themselves.

"I believe it's a safe location." Varsi strode toward the door, oblivious to any surveillance cameras or other security devices in the area.

"Isn't it watched?" Mali asked, scurrying to catch up with his long stride.

"Not this one." He stopped at the exit, leaning against it with his ear pressed to the metal. "This was our unit's bay. Since it wasn't replaced and isn't expected to return, they haven't monitored it for years. I doubt the cameras and recorders are even online."

"Oh. Can we get out of here?" She squeezed against the wall next to him, trying to make herself unseen, even if Varsi believed they weren't observed. Once the place was shut down, did TIM write it off, not expecting anyone would enter?

"Of course. It's not locked from the inside."

She felt stupid. Naturally, it wasn't. Only an adjustment team would come from within the sealed TU bay.

Lifting his head, Varsi opened the exit between the bay and the prep room area beyond. Mali peeked over his shoulder, seeing a setup almost the same as the one she had used with her team about three weeks ago in her own time.

She noticed Varsi's eyes darted around the space before he motioned her in. "This should be safe. No missions are being activated now, and it's a secure zone." He pointed to two corners where small round blobs extruded. "The cameras aren't active."

The computers caught Mali's attention, and she headed for the first one, logging on with the general monitor passcode. While she wasn't sure it would still work, it seemed to allow access to the central computer. When it asked for her id, she used Edmunds' code. She had watched him key it in once, and with her memory, never forgot it.

Meanwhile, Varsi had accessed the security reports. "I'll see if there is any mention of Andy while you find out as much information as possible."

"Working on it." She had the history storage up and plugged her tablet into it, hoping she had enough space for the last five centuries of updates. She'd gotten part of it on her previous visit, but the TIM storage would have more detail. While it transferred, she pulled up a schematic of the space. She knew where the cells were, but she wanted to find an internal route rather than going through the lobby.

She glanced up at the station chronograph, 20:28 hours displayed. It meant almost everyone was gone for the day. The only people on shift would be the monitors and a few guards. She located a path to the cells from inside the hallway, then she checked on her download. Only a few more seconds until it finished.

"See anything, Varsi?"

"Yes. I have a good idea where they're keeping him. Let's go. But first—"

He turned, crossed to the entry to the third TU unit, and entered a series of numbers. When the green light flashed and triggered the unlock, he snickered. "They didn't even change the entry code." He stepped inside to look at the time unit Bray had brought back.

Mali reluctantly followed him, wondering why the delay. Her eyes fell on the damaged unit, and her heart jolted, beating harder. Was this really their time unit? It looked far worse here than when she'd last seen it. The landing legs had been damaged, and she noticed a few nasty dents in it. But the solar panels were a mess. They'd been badly torn in the final few hops. Seeing them through more knowledgeable eyes, she wondered if someone had sabotaged their unit before they even left on their mission.

"Did Coleman hit a tree?" Rashid asked as he ran a hand over a dent.

"Not on our trip, although we did land in a garden planter," Mali answered, wondering if the incident accounted for the bent leg at the rear. "Why haven't they repaired it?"

"Good question. The damage isn't too bad. I'm

guessing they don't have the funds to repair them. This isn't an interface-with-the-computer problem, just simple fixes."

"What about the travel excursion computers, like the company Brix works for? Are their computers still working?" Mali asked. While she hadn't known her roommate worked for a time-travel company until recently, she knew three companies operated from the Alpha station with limited licenses.

"Since they tap into TIM's thread-summoning technology, I would say they can't work either." Varsi straightened and stepped away from the TU, gazing toward the mangled solar panel, and pointed. "What happened there?"

"Not sure. I think we might have tangled with some tree branches when we faded into the era on arrival." Mali thought it appeared more damaged than it had in York, then shifted her attention to the transparent thread box and frowned. "Why aren't any threads running through this?"

Varsi turned his head, barely glancing at it. "The time unit's out of order, so no threads would be drawn to the display. Anyway, without the computer to signal them, they aren't attracted to it."

"A few were in the other bay."

"Probably strays then. Sometimes they flow through the case, but not the way they do when they're summoned." He shrugged, then pivoted toward the door. "Let's go find your grandfather."

The computer summoned the threads? How did it work? Mali's list of questions continued to grow. So many things she never learned in her classes or in the basics of her job.

Mali took a final look. Painful to recall how excited she'd been to be on this adjustment team and looked forward to the adventure. Now, with Bonde dead, Doyle a bittersweet memory, and the future changed, she wished it had never happened. She followed Varsi out of the bay, through the ready room, and into the hallway.

The turn to the right led to the monitoring center and the front entrance to the business. To the left were more meeting spaces, the medics' office, and access to the security office, or so the schematics showed. It would also be the direction least likely to have any traffic at this time of night. They went left.

They passed the expected doors and came to the end of the hallway. No sign marked the entry in the center, but an electronic reader protruded from the wall on the right side. Varsi attempted to push it open. Not unexpectedly, it failed to move; the lock holding it in place. Varsi caught her hand and whispered, "Hold tight. We're going through it."

She thought she must have heard him wrong and frowned, trying to puzzle out what he meant. Going *through* it?

Before she could say anything, she felt her body slip out of sync with the time, and Varsi stepped forward, literally pulling her through with him.

What the hellfire was that? She lost the weightless feeling when her feet felt more solid on the floor beyond the entry. Already, Varsi checked to make sure no one saw them enter and pulled her to the side of the hallway on the same side as the lone camera watching the entry. Crouching down and motioning for Mali to do the same, they scurried like mice along the hall. In the dim lighting, they had a chance of getting in without being detected.

They came to another secured door where the holding cells should be. Varsi pressed up against it. He pressed a finger to his ear, then listened intently. Embedded hearing amplifier, Mali guessed, leaning next to him, with her face turned the opposite direction. If anyone approached , she wanted to see them before they saw Varsi and her.

She strained to hear anything from the other side, but all she could pick up were the muffled sounds and indecipherable voices. Varsi, on the other hand, seemed to listen intently. He whispered, "It sounds like Andy is in this area. I hear his voice, and someone's shouting at him to talk."

Her stomach lurched, felt as if it hit her heart, then settled again. Grandfather was in there—alive, so good news there. He could time walk, although he hadn't. Why not?

"He's worried about you," Rashid whispered, as if he'd read her mind. "He doesn't know where you are or that you've returned, so he's waiting to make his move."

"Then somehow, we need to let him know I'm all right." She leaned against the wall and thought. How could they manage it? "What about doing your little trick again and taking us into his cell?"

"You can't be serious?" His eyes narrowed, and he frowned at the suggestion. "That would just put us in the middle of it, and we don't have a clue how many are there. Besides, it's trickier to do it when the cell may be several feet from where we are. Whoops... One of them just mentioned your name. He asked where you were."

Varsi jerked away as if he'd been stricken. "Andy didn't answer, and it sounded like someone just hit him pretty hard. We have to get him out."

So, they want me? Mali grabbed Varsi's hand and pulled him away. "I have an idea. Let's go back to an empty room."

He nodded, and they crouched again, making their way up the hallway. At the second office, Varsi stopped and tried the door. It opened easily, and he smirked.

"This one."

Once inside, he shut it and turned the lock. Then Mali turned to him. "I think I have a way to let grandfather know I'm here. While security held me, they blocked the signals from any embedded com sets in the holding areas, so my direct link won't work, but I think I can connect to Blackman's remote cell." She pulled her tablet out and searched the downloaded TIM directory for the chief's name.

"Found it and calling," she said smugly. "If Blackman is close to Grandfather, and I might entice him enough to say my name, then he might overhear and react, then time–" She cut off when the security chief answered.

"I hear you're looking for me," she said without preamble.

"What? Who is this?" Blackman asked, surprise evident in his sharp tone.

"You can guess who I am. I had the displeasure of visiting with you a short time ago. Let's make a deal."

"You—you can't be. Harper? How did you--?" He stopped, and silence filled the gap.

"Aren't you interested in the deal I'm offering for my grandfather?" Mali prodded.

"I might be if I didn't figure you're up to something."

"Of course I am. Aren't you a little curious?"

She could hear him, his voice muffled, telling his men to find her and using her name loud enough for Andover to hear.

"Mali? Is that her?" Harper called out with enough force to be heard on the connection. "Run, girl, go!"

"Find her now!" Blackman shouted before he cut off the call.

As he dropped to the floor in the office, Varsi motioned to her to duck down. Mali clutched her tablet as she crouched beside him.

Varsi whispered, "If we stay low, his agents won't see us. And I locked the door, so they'll probably pass us by and search the TIM section, beginning with this area. Since you asked about your grandfather, they–"

"—realize I know they have him. That was the idea." Mali searched her tablet for a tie-in to the holding cell camera. She wanted to confirm Andover had time-walked when he'd learned her status. Besides, she hoped to find her pocket watch and retrieve it.

A scuffle outside interrupted her, and a gruff-sounding man said, "I left this door unlocked. I'll bet she's in there. Give me a minute to fetch the key."

"Well, Gaia's spit," Mali murmured. "Looks like—"

Abruptly, Varsi grasped her arm and pulled her into the golden mist surrounding him. Clearly, he could access the threads quicker than she could.

"No!" she gasped. "We don't know if Grandfather walked or not!"

CHAPTER 27

Space Station 2238

ALTHOUGH SHE EXPECTED TO BE IN the house in York, Mali gasped when she and Varsi arrived in the same TU hanger they'd come into earlier. "I thought you were taking us back," she said as she stepped away from him.

"You didn't want to go, so I brought us here. What's the problem?" He shook off the energy of the short jump and walked to the preparation room door, then leaned against it, listening.

"I didn't want to leave until we knew for certain that my grandfather walked. And I need to get my watch back. It's set to return me to the house. What if someone uses it?"

Varsi turned his head to peer at her. "First, the person has to be able to use the threads. If they don't have the ability to time walk, the watch won't do anything. They won't even see the threads. If they do, then it would deliver them to the house on the set day and time, where we would all be able to greet them since we were all there at that exact time. Since it didn't happen, no one used the watch."

"Oh, I didn't think it through." She should have considered that. The watch would only bring the user to a specific location and time, so once the time passed for them and no one arrived, the moment was gone, no matter how far ahead in the future the watch was activated. "I still want it back. It's important to me." She strode across to him. "Is it safe to go through?"

He nodded. "It quiet on the other side. Do you have a plan?"

"Well, everyone is looking for me, so the watch is probably still in the holding cells area of the office with only minimal, if any, guards there. I imagine they've put it on a shelf there. It's only been a few hours since Levin and I disappeared from the cell. So, if I can get into the office unseen, I can grab the watch and return to York."

"How will you get in?"

"Umm, I hoped you might help me out and take me there?" She put on a hopeful smile.

He stared at her, eyes intent and his lips a stubborn, hard line. "All right. I'll do a quick drop, which means I'll take us in, then I'll immediately depart. I'll go back to York two hours after we departed. You try for the same time if you can. Since you didn't pop in at the appointed time, you never used the fixed timepiece."

Mali blinked, followed his logic, and nodded. If she were to return, she'd have to use her own time travel skills again. She'd done it before. Could she do it again?

Varsi touched her arm again, and the haze of the jump hovered over her. A moment later, she stood in the security office with the holding cells across from her. For just a breath, Varsi was with her, then he vanished so quickly he would be little more than a blip on the security tapes while she was in plain sight. Mali turned to look at the shelf on the right wall where they'd put her sparse belongings and searched for the pocket watch.

When she didn't see it, a rush of panic swept through her. What if someone had taken it already?

She bent to look under the table where it had slid when she dropped it. She didn't see it, but as she scanned the area, she saw a pair of tan-clad legs step next to the table. She rose up to face Blackman.

"Are you looking for something?" The watch dangled from his fingers.

"That's mine, and I want it back." She growled the words through her clenched teeth.

His head swayed from side to side slowly. "I think you have a lot of questions to answer, Ms. Harper. Let's start with what happened to Andover Harper and how was he back on the station? He was presumed dead."

"If he didn't tell you, I certainly can't." She edged toward the end of the table. Could she rush him for the watch? If she moved fast, she might catch him off guard.

"Let's try this; how did you get out of here, and where's Levin?"

She grinned. "That's certainly a good question. But not one I will answer."

She took her shot, vaulting onto the table and sliding across it, booted feet out in front of her. She slammed into Blackman before he fully grasped what she was doing, and he fell backward, sprawling on the floor. The watch slipped free of his fingers, and Mali rolled off him, her hand flying out to grab it. In another second, Blackman shoved against her, flipping her off him. She landed on her back and pulled her legs to her chest to protect herself. It also set her up to kick the security man in the gut as soon as he tried to throw himself on her. Instead, his hand went for the taser pistol.

"Oh, no, you don't," Mali shouted. She brought her legs forward and sprang to her feet, plowing into Blackman with her left elbow and knocking his hand away from the weapon. She leaped back as he made a grab for her, took a moment or two to focus on the threads in her mind, then chose one. The room faded, and the unbalanced sensation took over.

In what felt like only a moment, Mali found her footing in Andover's office. She gazed around to look for her grandfather but only saw Varsi standing by the wet bar. Then she shot a glance at the clock. Two hours had passed since they'd jumped to the station. She guessed that Brix and Coleman had either gone to their rooms or were in the drawing-room. If her grandfather had made it back, he would likely be in his bedroom since he wasn't here.

"Did he jump?" she asked as if Varsi might magically know. *Andover had to be back, had to have gotten away from the station safely.*

They wouldn't be able to go back. Security on the station would be on high alert. Blackman had seen her vanish. Every frame of surveillance would be examined. They would figure out she had time walked, traveled without the benefit of a TU.

"I don't know." Varsi stepped away from her, shaking his head. "I hope." He didn't look confident as he ran a hand through his shaggy hair to push it back from his face.

For a moment, Mali's eyes lingered on him, caught by his handsome features and intense dark eyes in a strong-jawed face. He could be charming, she knew, but under that pleasing veneer, he was ruthless in his ambition to rewrite history. She had to maintain her edge around him, or it would be easy to succumb to his intelligence and wit. Yet, the best way to thwart his efforts, short of killing the man, would be to stay by his side. Could she do that?

Turning away, she shut down those thoughts and

swung into action, hurrying out the door and almost running to the stairs. She dashed up them, barely pausing when she hit the second landing, and raced down the hall to Andover's suite. She knocked once before she threw the door open and stepped inside.

"Grandfather?" she gasped, her heart pounding with anxiety. He wasn't here. The room was empty.

Then Andover's head popped over the top of the dressing screen at the back of the room. Bruises colored his right cheek and eye where one of the security men had struck him. His lower lip still dripped blood from a cut.

"Mali, thank goodness. Wait a moment."

She exhaled in relief, tears forming at the edges of her eyes. She'd feared he hadn't been able to jump. If he hadn't made it, what would she have done? She was adrift in time, and Grandfather was her anchor. She dropped onto his bed to wait, fatigue catching up after the adrenaline rush at the station.

Feeling dependent on anyone was new for her. Ever since she was nine, she'd been pretty self-reliant for her own needs and emotional support. The station foster care provided food, clothing, and education, but it sorely lacked anything else. No one cared about anyone's feelings, and the absolute cruelty of other kids had firmed up her outer shell. She'd flaunted her superior memory and self-reliance as a defense throughout all those years and into college.

Now she felt vulnerable, stranded in the past with no idea how to survive if she couldn't get back to her own time. Her grandfather provided psychological security for her, yet he'd abandoned her when she needed him after her parents died. If she'd lost him now, she wasn't sure what her next step might be. Find him in the past again and stay with him? But if time was branching, how many times might he disappear?

No, she needed to steel herself to survive without anyone's help in whatever era she was in. It meant acquiring jewelry or other saleable assets to provide money for her purposes. If she joined forces with Varsi, he could help her gain a certain amount of wealth while she tried to curtail his plans. Distasteful as partnering with him sounded, the move would benefit her in several ways. She might yet manage to undo the major damage to the future.

At least, the proof of their existence in the past meant they hadn't been eliminated from the future. Or did it? If a person could still exist in the past, even if the future was drastically changed and the traveler was never born, remained an unanswered question among the physicists. But if the time split and alternate universes were created, the traveler would still exist in the unchanged timeline. Following the logic, if the timeline you were created in remained as it was, you were alive no matter which universe you visited.

Andover stepped from behind the screen, dressed in trousers and an undershirt revealing more bruises on his arms. He pulled on his dress shirt as he turned to her. "Tell me what happened after you left before I woke on the station."

Mali's mouth tightened in an angry line at the sight of the damage. "I'm sorry, Grandfather. Those security people are *sarcasin* scum. They have no authority to treat anyone the way they did. I didn't expect any of this to happen."

"I know, Mali. But you went off without leaving word. So, tell me what happened. I can see you've been bruised as well."

She nodded, swallowed hard. "I thought I could learn more if I talked to Jax, so I put on my disguise and went to the café he goes to every morning." She began telling him everything that happened and how she and Varsi jumped back to let him know she was free. "I worried you wouldn't be able to time walk from the cell."

Harper's look hadn't softened during the recital, and he nodded solemnly now. "Thank you for coming back and alerting me to your freedom. Not knowing was the only thing keeping me from shifting out of there. Being a government operation, TIM has always acted as if they were above any laws and restrictions. I believe they are beginning to learn that's not the case. By the way, you malign the *sarcasin* by comparing them to the security at TIM." He cracked a smile then.

Chastised, she agreed she might have been rude in equating the irritating dust mites of the Martian desert with the station scum.

"Where is Rashid now?"

Mali glanced at the door, surprised the man hadn't followed her to Harper's room. "Maybe he's still in your office, or else he might be in my room. We have a hostage of our own." She hadn't elaborated about her stowaway when she'd told her story.

Andover's eyebrows lifted in surprise. She explained as she led him to her room.

Inside, she found Brix and Coleman chatting with Varsi while their guest glowered from the floor where he'd been stuffed along the back wall. Still trussed up like a wild beast, Levin could barely do more than shift from hip to hip.

"Did you learn anything more from Levin?" While she was curious about what her friends were talking about with Varsi, she was more interested in what they might have learned from the security man.

"We haven't talked to him since you guys left." Brix jumped to her feet from the chair she'd pulled over near the bed and looked their way. "It's good to see you safely back, Mr. Harper." Stepping away, she motioned to him to take her chair and settled on the floor between the other two men.

Andover acknowledged the offer with a nod, then moved a bit stiffly to the chair. He shifted it to an angle to see the others and Levin, then sat, closing his eyes briefly. While Mali's grandfather was a robust, almost sixty-year-old, he clearly felt the pain of his recent ordeal.

Mali certainly still felt sore from her own encounter, so she could sympathize. Overall, the past two weeks, real time, of her life had been a little rough on her body.

Instead of sitting, she strolled to Levin and yanked the cloth from his mouth so he could talk. He sputtered, trying to spit words at her, but nothing came out.

"I think he needs some water," Brix said. "I'll fetch a glass."

"The station is in disarray," Mali said. "The TU's aren't being repaired, and we heard rumors of other failures in the computer systems. It seems the whole directors' board may be suspect. What do you know about it?"

Eyes wide and concerned, Levin shook his head, managed a dry cough, and muttered a hoarse-sounding response. "No info on it. Just security."

"You're trying to tell us you haven't heard anything about what's happening? I don't believe you. Listen, sec guy, if you want to land in a favorable location on this planet, you'd better do better."

Coming back in the door, Brix crossed the room with a glass in her hand. "Water. This will help." She held the drink to his mouth, allowing Levin to sip a little at a time until he turned his head away and started to talk.

"I overheard a couple of things. Not much made any

sense. I know they said they had financial issues, funding problems from the government. I don't have any details. I'm just security. I even tried to be a little nice to you," Levin complained. He cast a glare at Mali, then ducked his head.

She almost felt sorry for him. Like Mali and her friends, Levin found himself stranded on a world as alien to him as being on a Martian moon. Not sorry enough to let him off the hook. She motioned to her grandfather. "Do you have any questions for him?"

Rising, Andover moseyed over, crossed his arms over his chest, and ran his eyes over Levin. "A few. Who is your actual boss? Blackman? Or someone higher up?"

Levin shifted uncomfortably, turning his head away from Andover's gaze. "I report to Blackman."

"That doesn't answer the question. Who's running the show?"

"I don't know. I just follow Blackman's orders."

Andover persisted, pressing for a more concrete answer. "Is it Kassidy? Have you heard the name or passed any information along to him?"

A split second of surprise showed in Levin's eyes before he shut down his reaction. "Never heard of him."

"There's no point in protecting any of them," Mali told him with a smirk as she studied her fingernails as if she might use them to scratch his eyes out. "You won't see them again... ever."

"You could take me back," Levin argued as he turned his gaze to Andover. "You went to the station. She went there. You have some way of doing it, so if you want to make a trade, let's talk. I'll tell you what you want to know, and you return me to the station in my own time."

Andover chuckled as he turned away and returned to the chair Brix had offered. "I thought you said you didn't know anything. Now you think you have enough information to bargain with me. The only deal you can get is where on this planet you'll end up living the rest of your life."

Alarmed, Levin jerked forward, trying to break free of his restraints. "You can't do that to me!"

"Oh, yes, we can," Andover answered. "I'm done talking to him, Mali. Where do you want to exile him?"

"We were thinking Scotland," Bray said. "Way to the north or maybe on one of the islands."

Andover ran a hand over his chin in thought. "I don't know. I rather like the Scots and wouldn't want to give them a troublemaker. But an island off the coast might work. You'd have to deliver him there, though. The train goes through to Edinburgh, then you take an auto or a wagon to John O'Groats, and finally, a boat across to Egilsay."

"By Mithras, man," Levin objected. "Don't strand me in a place where I can't survive. Just kill me now. I was only doing my job and didn't hurt the girl. That was all on Blackman."

"Let me have some time with the man." Andover's eyebrow went up, and he motioned them from the room. "Maybe we can make a bargain after all."

Mali hesitated, not wanting to leave her grandfather alone with Levin, but he seemed to have the situation under control. Rashid hadn't spoken at all, but now he rose to leave the room, motioning for Bray and Brix to follow him. Interest piqued, Mali gave Andover a brief nod and followed them out. Whatever information her grandfather was after appeared to be a private matter. But Rashid was up to something with the others, and she wanted to know what.

They went downstairs to the parlor, pausing to ask Renfrow to bring tea and letting her know Andover had returned and would probably be down a little later.

"He had a little altercation with someone at the factory, and they got into a fight," Mali warned her. "He's a bit banged up, but he's fine."

The housekeeper's look suggested she didn't believe her story. When she gazed pointedly at Mali, her eyes took in the bruises on her face as well. Mali knew she suspected more had happened, but Renfrow dipped her head in acknowledgment and went off to prepare the refreshments.

Mali slid into a seat facing the sofa and coffee table where Bray and Brix settled while Varsi took the other chair and angled it to them. He cast a questioning eye at her. She interpreted it as asking why she'd come with them.

"Making plans, are we?" she asked.

"We are," Varsi replied. "Are you interested in being part of it?"

"Depends on what it is." Mali still wasn't sure how much she wanted to get involved in his plans. But he seemed to have Bray and Brix on the hook for something.

Varsi smiled, a surprisingly inviting look on his face. Most of the time, he'd been stern or scowling at her. "We have pretty much determined the plan for Coleman and Ms. Brixton, who are agreeing to help with the next phase of my plan to avert World War Two."

Startled, Mali's gaze darted to Brix, who shifted uncomfortably, then lifted an eyebrow. She nodded before dropping her eyes to avoid the accusation in Mali's glower.

"Really?" Mali's stare shifted. "You too, Brayden?"

He didn't seem intimidated at all and met her eyes with confidence. "Yep. It seems like a good plan and worth the try. After all, it's an experiment on an alternate line, and it won't affect the mainline, so why not see if we can save the planet?"

Mali's mouth quirked into a crooked line. "Well, Gaia's spit. That's really counter to your adjuster training, isn't it?"

"Come on, Mali. You're seeing the planet as it should have been rather than being obliterated by humanity in about five hundred years. If there is a way to save it without destroying future space expansion, then I think it's worth a try."

"Even if you have to kill someone?"

Coleman's shoulders slumped a bit as his face grew grave, and a touch of sadness lowered his lips. "You never had adjuster training. Terminating someone was always a possibility of the job. If you have to stop someone, you use whatever means necessary. Did you think Bonde took the action he did for the first time? No, he was ready to kill or be killed to reverse the damage to the timeline. Too bad he gave his life for something that didn't even affect our timeline."

Mali shuddered. She hadn't realized the job could entail murder. Yet, Bonde had come to it armed and with explosives.

Varsi directed his attention toward her, steepling his fingers as he spoke. "What about you, Mali? What are your plans now? Are you going to chase after all of us and try to stop my plans?"

The gaze she shot in his direction could have sent a bolt of lightning into his head. Was he deliberately trying to agitate her? "You tried to talk me into joining you the last time we met, which was actually in the future. I didn't consider it then, but maybe I was wrong. Maybe the best way to keep tabs is to join you. That way, I can try to minimize the actions I think will cause the most damage to the future."

He laughed, a loud, boisterous sound seeming

utterly out of character for him. She didn't know he had it in him. After a gasp for air, he resumed his more contained demeanor. "So, by joining me, what do you expect?"

"To be by your side all the way. Where you go, I go."

After a moment of surprise, he caught his breath to speak. But his response died before he had a chance as Mrs. Renfrow brought the tea and a tray of afternoon sandwiches. Smiling, Mali admitted to a fondness for this English ritual. It tended to cool tempers and provided some relaxing moments while nourishing the body in the afternoon. Wherever she ended up in time, she planned to continue the practice.

As they all reached for a sandwich, Varsi appeared to be considering her words before he responded. He sat back, crossing a leg over his knee as he chewed a salmon biscuit and sipped his tea. When he finished, he turned his eyes to her, studying her like some new exotic creature. "Very well, Ms. Harper... Mali. I accept your offer. You will be my assistant in my work. If you can convince me something I want to do won't work or will be disastrous, I might change it. But I expect you to work with me if you're going to tag along."

Mali caught her breath, replayed every word exactly as he'd said it, and considered any non-obvious implications. He would allow her to argue any changes, but he wouldn't guarantee he wouldn't proceed even if her case was valid. But it would still put her in a position to change the outcome. She breathed out. "I agree. Where are we going first?" Her eyes darted to Brix and then to Bray with excitement shining in them.

"I haven't quite narrowed down *my* next step," Varsi replied. He reached to refill his tea. "I have a couple of spots in mind I wish to investigate more, but Ms. Brixton and Mr. Coleman will be off in the morning on their assignment. It should prove interesting."

Mali's stomach lurched as she realized Brix and Bray were going off on their own. She turned her gaze back to them, her mouth suddenly dry. "Where?"

"Germany in 1934," Varsi replied.

CHAPTER 28

York England 1768

LATE AFTERNOON SUN PEEKED THROUGH the clouds as Brix strolled in the garden behind Andover's house. Pink roses bloomed, scenting the air with their delicate fragrance as a gentle breeze distributed it directly to her. She'd gone to the arbor on Alpha One many times and wandered through the paths filled with shrubs and flowers. The roses there never smelled as sweet as the ones in this little garden.

Although a vast space architectural achievement, a good portion of their biosphere was dedicated to growing food. Until settlers established the moon colonies, the garden had supplied most of the food for the residents and the colonists and still added to their supplies. The station claimed their domed park was as large as the Royal Botanic Gardens at Kew, but she wondered about it. Perhaps she would visit Kew one day to see for herself.

She paused to caress a rosebud in her fingers, savoring the delicate feel of the about-to-open petals. It seemed magical, dreamlike. She still had a hard time reconciling her future to living in the past. At the same time, there was so much to see and do on this world that she could never be bored. She didn't see it as a prison or a trap. It was a tremendous opportunity that she couldn't have imagined. She'd thought a trip to Mars or the Moon would be a high adventure, but this world was amazing. The home planet. The source of life for everyone now populating the solar system. In its own way, it humbled her. Maybe Varsi was right, and they needed to do whatever they could to save it.

She heard the click of the house's back door opening, followed by the crunch of footsteps on the path growing louder as they approached her. She turned to face Mali, smiling at her friend. Even though they hadn't seemed close throughout the school years or even during their time as roommates, she felt connected to her. Maybe because they had a shared history, a time walker heritage, and now exile in the past.

Mali greeted her with a bit of a hand wave and a small smile. She didn't look happy. "Mrs. Renfrow told me you'd be here. It's a lovely garden, isn't it?"

Brix nodded. "Yes. It's relaxing to spend a little time out here, enjoying the scents, the fresh breeze, and the whole feel of a real world rather than the space station. We never knew what we were missing, did we?"

"No, we didn't. I'd never even left the station prior to this trip, so it was a totally novel experience. Didn't you even take one of the trips to Earth your company offered?"

Laughing, Brix shook her head. "No, I went on a couple to the moon and one to Mars. They were fun and interesting. But I hadn't signed up to do any past adventures on Earth. It sounded too dangerous to me. So much ruin and destruction. We could only go up to one hundred years, you know. It wouldn't have been *this* planet Earth."

"You're right. Have you fallen under the spell of the planet, Brix?"

She laughed, turning toward a bench set up near a pond in the yard. In a tree near them, a bird chirped several times before flying to a higher branch. Brix watched the brightly colored avian with amusement. "Any idea what species of bird that is?"

Mali peered at the blue bird with a copper breast. "None. I had no idea so many varieties of wildlife existed in the world. I didn't study much about the wildlife here."

Brix sat and waited for Mali to join her. Folding her hands in her lap, she leaned forward and turned her gaze to the dirt path, where a small bug scurried along. All kinds of life filled the garden, each contributing something. So much to learn about this world. Glancing back at Mali, she noticed her eyes had dropped to the ground also, but she wasn't saying what was on her mind.

"You're not happy with Bray and me deciding to join forces with Varsi," Brix stated. She waited for Mali to meet her eyes. "It's not abandonment, Mali. But Bray and I feel the best way to control the change is to be in the middle of it. Is killing Hitler the right thing to do? Maybe or maybe not. We feel that getting some perspective by being in it is the way to decide. We're not going to betray the future if that's what you think."

"I'm not sure what I think," Mali answered. "It was a surprise. It did feel like you'd gone to the other side. That you would be aiding Varsi in his plans."

"It could seem that way," she admitted. "What about

you? Suddenly, you're teaming up with Varsi. Side by side, as it were. What's with that?"

Mali's shoulders relaxed as she chuckled. "Same approach as you, I suppose. It occurred to me that the best way to thwart Varsi was to be right at his side whenever he tried to do anything. I hope I'm not making a mistake."

"How so?"

Mali folded her hands and rubbed at her thumbnail with her opposite thumb, a nervous habit she'd never been able to kick. "Rashid is a very persuasive man. He makes everything sound reasonable and right, even if it will make a possibly devastating ripple to the timeline. I hope I have enough wit and willpower to stand firm against him when it's needed."

Brix smiled and laid a reassuring hand on top of hers. "I know you will. You're not a pushover for anyone. Never have been. Trust your instincts, just as I will trust mine."

Mali looked at her, eyes seeming to search hers for something—reassurance or sincerity, maybe. "What about Bray? Will you trust his as well?"

"We won't agree on everything, I'm sure. But I will stay strong in my own convictions even if he disagrees, so long as I am sure that my path is the correct one. Then it will be up to me to convince Varsi alone. We're pretty much in the same position, aren't we?"

"It seems that way. But the time could come when we might disagree with each other."

"Of course. Then we cross that gap when we come to it."

Mali opened her hands, caught Brix's, and squeezed them firmly. "When are you two leaving?"

"Tomorrow morning... early. "

"Are you going to do the time hop?"

Brix laughed. "No, not yet. I need to practice more before I attempt it. I'm barely able to touch those mental lines yet. Varsi is taking us to our starting point. We'll work there until he joins us."

"What if you need an emergency exit?" Mali asked, concern shadowing her eyes.

"Your grandfather is setting two exit jumps for us. One will be in the watch I brought here, and the other is a gadget with a winder. We'll have a way out, even if we get separated."

Mali visibly relaxed. "That's good. I wish you luck with it. I expect we'll catch up with each other later on. If Varsi's going after Hitler again, I'm pretty sure our paths will cross."

Mrs. Renfrow's voice cut into their conversation as she called them to dinner.

"I expect we will," Brix answered as she swept to her feet a moment ahead of Mali, and they strolled back to the house.

After dinner, Mali and her grandfather sat in his office, enjoying an after-dinner brandy. Her grandfather explained it was cognac from France while he poured a small amount of amber fluid into a large glass and told her to inhale its fragrance before drinking any. "Take a small sip and savor the flavor of the cognac before you swallow it."

She did as he instructed, detecting the sweet fruit scent, then taking a little of the liquid in her mouth and holding it as it warmed her mouth. The liquor rolled over her tongue, setting her taste buds ablaze with the piquancy of the drink. Then she swallowed, choking as it flowed down her throat. A heated sensation blazed a path down to her stomach, courtesy of the alcohol. She coughed a few times before she managed to speak. "On my, sweet Gaia, that is potent."

"It takes a little getting used to," Andover admitted. "Especially when you're not a drinker. But you should acquaint yourself with some beverages from this era. Oh, and you should also lose that expression. Gaia isn't worshipped much in this era."

"I knew that," she squeaked out, chagrinned at the reminder. "It's a hard one to break." Of course, he was correct. She'd been using it without thinking. What was the proper one for now? Dear lord or my god—something like that.

"Have you become Gaian?" Andover asked.

"No. I started using it to annoy people who were so judgmental about the nature-inspired religion. I don't think it hurts to remind them we are all part of biological life."

Her grandfather chuckled. "Good point. Look how desperate we are in the future to try to recreate it and grow enough to survive."

With hesitation, she ventured another tiny sip of the alcoholic drink, prepared now for the effect it would have. As her grandfather gave her an approving look, she relaxed a little and held the glass in her hand, wishing for a glass of water to wash it down.

"I've wanted to ask you something. When we were on the station and about to be discovered, Rashid did a partial time shift that moved us to safety. What exactly did he do and how?"

"Ah, it's a phase shift like we can do with the time units. It takes the unit out of its position on the planet to a different frequency adjacent to the one it's occupying. To anyone passing by it, it's not there."

Mali frowned and recalled the moment. "But we went through the door. Does that mean you can move through objects by using it?"

"If you have the skill or a phase shifter, you can do it."

"And Varsi has this skill?" Mali's shock showed on her face. With that kind of power, he could get to anybody he wanted to kill.

"Actually, he has a phase shifter, a small transmitter like the one on the TUs. It has limited power, but enough that he could get the two of you through the door."

"That gives him a definite edge at getting to people he wants to eliminate."

"Maybe," Andover replied. "It has its limitations as well. For one, it uses a lot of its stored energy to move and needs to be recharged before it can be used a second time." He poured another splash into his brandy glass, then asked, "So, what have you discovered from our visit to the station, Mals?" he asked as he leaned back in his chair.

She'd been scanning through the information she'd retrieved from TIM's computers and was still trying to piece all the bits of it together to form a clear picture in her mind. "Not as much as I'd like. I saw where the course toward the Third World War changed when the Chikopan leader was assassinated by his second in command. That action moved up the second in charge of the country and allowed him to negotiate peace with the Euro Coalition. From that point, history grew rosier except for the Earth growing hotter. Do we know which timeline this was on?

Andover nodded, sipped, then cleared his throat. "I checked my lines to be certain, but I'm 98 percent sure we were on this timeline, which is the second one. What effect did our changes that slipped through have on the future?"

"Apart from the political change, what I could determine was that the Earth's warming slowed and pollution throughout the 20th and 21st centuries was reduced tremendously. Despite that, the natural cycle of the Earth still moved to hotter temperatures, but it wasn't damaged."

"If that's right, then the Earth now would continue to support life if it adapted to the more gradual change."

"Correct. Plants, animals, and people—all were beginning to adapt to the warmer temperatures. Melting ice caps played havoc with the coastlines, though, so there was less land for people to live. Interestingly, some of the places that had been deserts are now getting more rain."

"Did Rashid stop the second World War?" Andover asked.

"Not in the information I have, but I haven't read all the details. It seems just altering the fuel source for most vehicles worked to reduce the pollution."

She ventured another sip of the brandy and suffered the same reaction. She didn't think she'd ever get used to it. "Is there water?" she choked out as the smokey fire rolled down her esophagus.

Andover rose and padded to the sideboard, where a pitcher sat along with glasses. He poured some, then brought it to her.

Taking the glass, Mali gulped it down, washing the taste and the lingering alcohol burn from her throat. "I think I'll stick with cider," she said, her voice sounding hoarse.

Chuckling, Andover sat on the side of the desk and squinted his eyes, taking on a distant look. She guessed he was reviewing his inner time threads. A scowl of frustration twisted his mouth, then he growled under his breath. "I can't see them."

"What? The threads?"

"No, I see the threads, but I can't look at the future

on any except the one we went to. That one had to be the main one since it was the only one I could access, but we weren't making changes to it except for the steamers and a few patents."

"Why can't you see the others for the same time? How have we been able to jump to alternate timelines in the future?" Mali's confusion reflected on her face as she frowned.

Snapping out of his almost trance of viewing the threads, Andover turned his gaze to Mali. "I think it's because we can only extend fifty years into the future from our departure time. For me, it was 2221."

"So, you can only go forward another 50 years to 2271," Mali clarified.

Nodding, he stood and returned to the chair behind his desk. "That's it. Unless I can connect with someone from the future, which would extend my view to their future date. That's how your great-grandmother took us this far in the past."

"Wait. No one's been able to take the line farther back than your mother took it?"

He grinned. "It was one of her talents, special gifts, that she could connect the timelines to her main one. The timelines summoned to TIM's computers are all hers; Adelle linked every one of them. She was a genius."

"And she never showed you how to do it?"

He sighed as he turned his gaze to the bookcase. "No. She never wrote about how she did any of this. She left instructions and diagrams on how to build new time unit elements and the technology needed to attract threads to the computers. But she said nothing about how she connected her strands to other people's. In fact, she never let anyone know she could travel without a time unit. Initially, she constructed a dummy model that she claimed took her back in time. As far as TIM knew, the computers were controlling it."

He laughed. "Right now, on the station, someone on the TIM board probably thinks we have designed a hand-held time unit."

As she considered this, Mali took to her feet and paced the room, going to the bookcase, then back to the sideboard on the other side. Thoughts raced through her mind about everything that had happened on the space station that caused problems for TIM. Who would have access to the computers and know how to use them? Would it be possible?

"What if...?" Mali asked as she halted next to Andover and leaned her hands on his desk. "What if great-grandmother is the one who removed the information from the computers? What if she sabotaged the time units?"

Andover gazed at her as if she'd proposed the moon was made of glowing algae. "Impossible. She's been dead most of your lifetime, Mali."

"Dead in our time, but alive in the past," she answers. "Do you know where and when she was at some point in the past where we might find her now?"

Thinking it over, he said, "I might know a place, but I don't know that I want to take you there."

Mali's lips tilted into a sad look. "I would like to talk with her. She knows more than everyone about all this."

Andover hesitated, then with a distant look in his eyes, said, "Paris, April 24, 2083. That's where she met your great-grandfather on a 'fun' time walk she made back when she was developing the complete process of attracting and containing the timeline. They were both scientists, but he was from that period."

"Did he move to the future to be with you and her?"

He sucked in his breath and looked her straight in the eyes. "No. He never came forward. When I was a child, my mother sometimes took me to a park in Paris where he met up with us, and we would go to dinner. I didn't understand it for a long time. I knew we lived on the station, but my father's work was on Earth. Until later, I didn't realize it was in a different time."

"So, you weren't very close." She assumed that based more on his expression than his words.

"No. Not close."

"Can you take us there?" Mali asks.

"Maybe," he answered. "But what are you thinking, granddaughter? It's risky to meet either of them and risk changing *our* future. Besides, I doubt Adelle would want to destroy what she created."

"Are you confident of that? Maybe she has seen what's happened with the timelines splitting and how it's skewing the future.

"Mali, she's been deceased for the past eleven years in station time. She wouldn't even know if things changed in the future."

"We can see it. We can go back from here. Maybe she did, and we wouldn't know it until the date she did it, and something happened." She thumped her hand on the desk. "It's possible. Will you take me there?"

Andover's eyes shifted to a darker color, hinting at annoyance. "Let me think about it. Aren't you heading off with Rashid soon? Isn't that mission enough to occupy your thoughts for now?"

She stepped back, surprised by the rebuff. What was between him and his mother that he didn't want her to meet Adelle? Or was he afraid of what she might learn from her great-grandmother? Whatever it was, she knew enough to back down. For now.

"You're right. Goodnight, grandfather." She pivoted away and marched to the door. Her hand paused on the knob, waiting for a word from Andover. When none came, she turned it and stepped through, then headed for her bedroom.

Andover was right. She should focus on her upcoming partnership with Varsi. She would have her hands full, keeping him in check. In fact, she'd like to get her hands on that phase unit.

But the conversation about Adelle Morrison would resume another day. In her heart, she felt her great-grandmother had something to do with what was happening.

End Book Two

Continued in Book Three

From the Author:
Thank you for reading. If you've enjoyed this novel, please leave a review with your honest opinion. Reviews are the lifeblood of an author as it's the best way to connect with other readers. Your review would mean a great deal to me.

ABOUT THE AUTHOR

 A sometimes musician, sporadic artist, occasional poet, and obsessed writer, Lillian Wolfe has spent most of her life concocting stories. From fan fiction to short stories, novels, training manuals, newsletters, and other documentation, she has constantly been putting words on paper or a computer screen. She is, in fact, extremely grateful for the invention of the computer because using a manual typewriter is tedious. While she loves all types of fiction, her favorites are fantasy and mystery novels.

Lillian shares her home in northern Nevada with her best friend for the past thirty-odd years and three feisty felines. She is a member of the High Sierra Writers and the Fiction Writers Group.

You can contact Lillian through her web site:
http://www.lillianwolfe.me/
and/or at her Facebook Page:
https://www.facebook.com/LilliansLoft

FUNERAL SINGER SERIES

By Lillian I Wolfe

Music is a passion for Gillian Foster, a struggling musician with dreams of success. When an accident bestows a paranormal talent, her whole life takes an unexpected turn. Getting gigs as a funeral singer, she finds her conscious-self transported to an interim cemetery where she can speak to the recently departed *while she is singing*. Inexplicably, she is bound to help the spirit to complete any unfinished business.

But more than departed spirits haunt the transitional plane, and they pose a threat to not only the souls in transit, but those still living as well. And they've identified Gillian as a danger. She's one soul against hundreds, and she needs help.

Can she find others like her and rally enough to stop the spread of evil that can take everyone she loves?

The *Funeral Singer* series of five books explores the overall theme as each thriller takes Gillian deeper into danger as she tries to help the departed souls cross to safety on the next plane.

Enjoy these other novels … *from Pynhavyn Press*

By Lillian I. Wolfe
O'Ceagan Saga (Sci-Fi Fantasy)
O'Ceagan's Legacy
In Strange Waters
Outer Rim (coming in 2022)

Time Threads (Sci Fi Fantasy/Time Travel)
Time Walker
Splintered Time

By M.L. Weatherington
The Franklin Logs (Police Mystery)
For Eleven Million Reasons
idewiped!
The Gentle Giant Returns
Sometimes Love's Just Murder

By Riona Kelly
(Romantic Suspense)
Bitter Vintage
Echoes of the Past
Signature of a Soul
The Cat Whisper (coming in 2022)
Tainted Truffles (coming in 2022)

By Angelina Fasano
Les Loups-Garous (YA/Urban Fantasy)
Alpha's Song
Beta Rising